WHY EVERYONE IS RAVING ABOUT

The Next Big Thing

"Reality TV meets actual REALITY! Take a bunch of women struggling with weight, body image, and relationship problems and lock them in a house with a gym, a trainer, a pantry full of treats and nothing but time, and what you get is a perfect combination of catfights and self-discovery. In *The Next Big Thing*, Johanna Edwards asks us to wonder what life on such a reality show would be like, and through the eyes of her feisty heroine Kat Larson, we get a pretty good idea of the ups and downs. But more important, we get a very clear picture of the diversity and humanity of women who are dealing with their own feelings about their weight issues, as well as society's hang-ups. Kat is as flawed as any of us, and on her journey discovers that her flaws actually have little to do with her size and more to do with her attitude. Funny, but also honest with some real power, *The Next Big Thing* is a very entertaining read that also makes you think. Great fun!"

—Stacey Ballis, author of *Inappropriate Men*

"A deliciously dishy tale of life behind the scenes of reality television. Peeking into the lives of contestants on *From Fat to Fabulous*, Johanna Edwards has created a cast of characters who keep you rooting for them from start to finish (as well as a few you'd like to strangle!). Protagonist Kat Larson is a sympathetic and complex plus-size gal who gives readers a real feel for what it's like to be an overweight woman in America. While poignant and touching, Kat's plight keeps readers laughing throughout this delightful tale."

—Jennifer Coburn, author of *The Wife of Reilly*

The Next Big Thing

Johanna Edwards

BERKLEY BOOKS, NEW YORK

THE BERKLEY PUBLISHING GROUP
Published by the Penguin Group
Penguin Group (USA) Inc.
375 Hudson Street, New York, New York 10014, USA
Penguin Group (Canada), 10 Alcorn Avenue, Toronto, Ontario M4V 3B2, Canada
(a division of Pearson Penguin Canada Inc.)
Penguin Books Ltd., 80 Strand, London WC2R 0RL, England
Penguin Group Ireland, 25 St. Stephen's Green, Dublin 2, Ireland (a division of Penguin Books Ltd.)
Penguin Group (Australia), 250 Camberwell Road, Camberwell, Victoria 3124, Australia
(a division of Pearson Australia Group Pty. Ltd.)
Penguin Books India Pvt. Ltd., 11 Community Centre, Panchsheel Park, New Delhi – 110 017, India
Penguin Group (NZ), Cnr. Airborne and Rosedale Roads, Albany, Auckland 1310, New Zealand
(a division of Pearson New Zealand Ltd.)
Penguin Books (South Africa) (Pty.) Ltd., 24 Sturdee Avenue, Rosebank, Johannesburg 2196,
South Africa

Penguin Books Ltd., Registered Offices: 80 Strand, London WC2R 0RL, England

This book is an original publication of The Berkley Publishing Group.

This is a work of fiction. Names, characters, places, and incidents either are the product of the author's imagination or are used fictitiously, and any resemblance to actual persons, living or dead, business establishments, events, or locales is entirely coincidental.

PRINTING HISTORY
Berkley trade paperback edition / March 2005

Library of Congress Cataloging-in-Publication Data

Edwards, Johanna.
    The next big thing / Johanna Edwards.
        p. CM.
    ISBN 0-425-20028-0
    1. Reality television programs—Fiction.   2. Overweight women—Fiction.   3. Weight loss—
Fiction.   4. Body image—Fiction.   5. Internet—Fiction.   I. Title.

PS3605.D886N49   2005
813'.6—dc22

                                                                          2004057003

PRINTED IN THE UNITED STATES OF AMERICA

10   9   8   7   6

For Mom and Dad
(Because, really, isn't everything?)

And for Selena

Acknowledgments

Many, many thanks go out to the two women who made this all possible: My fabulous agent, Jenny Bent, and my amazing and gifted editor, Allison McCabe. Working with them has been an absolute dream come true. I don't know how I got so lucky. Thanks also to everyone at Berkley for giving my novel a happy home.

To my mother, Paula Edwards, who believed in this book from day one and who has always been my strongest supporter. To my father, Les Edwards, for showing me the world and for teaching me the value of a strong work ethic. I owe so much to my sister, Selena Edwards, who was a faithful proofreader and frequent sounding board.

To James Abbott, who was the inspiration for all of Nick's dialogue (and none of his personality). Thanks for so many things: for showing me around England for six months, for reading my roughest drafts, and for coaching me on the often-puzzling (and always amusing) idiosyncrasies of British culture.

To Chris Carwile, for sharing the dream ("It's just a chapter a week!") and for being a terrific buddy and writing pal.

I am grateful to Candy Justice at the University of Memphis, who was a wonderful writing coach and who gave me my "big break." To Chris Allen, my very first creative writing teacher at Colonial Jr. High—your class meant the world to me.

Thanks also go out to Dr. Cynthia Hopson, Velda Nix, Teresa Johnson, Alan Turner, Penny and John Abbott, Anastasia Nix, Paul Turner, Stephen Usery, Susanne Enos, and Christy Wheeler.

And last, but certainly not least, thanks to my coworkers at WYPL-FM and the Memphis Public Library. I couldn't have done it without you!

The Next Big Thing

Prologue

All my life I'd been waiting for things: calls that never came, guys who never showed, invitations that got "lost in the mail." But mostly, I'd been waiting to be thin. I wanted a thin body so badly I could visualize it, like a beacon in the distance. I spent a lot of time preparing for my "thin life."

I even bought clothes for it.

I have a box filled with supplies—my skinny box—lodged in the back of my closet.

Before the show, I'd never told anyone about it, not even Donna, my closest friend. Every fat girl has her skinny outfit, the one she pictures herself wearing when she miraculously drops seventy pounds overnight. The dress she imagines all her friends and ex-boyfriends swooning over. I was walking through the Oak Court Mall when I spied it: my dream dress. It was made of black velvet and was absolutely jaw-droppingly gorgeous. My eyes locked on the mannequin wearing it, and something inside me came to life.

The mannequin was thin—but not as thin as they generally

are—and in addition to the velvet dress she had on a pair of knee-high black leather boots. Everything about the image overwhelmed me.

This mannequin was *me*—the me I would become.

My mind flashed forward, spiraling past a summer of strict dieting and hard-core exercise, and I could see myself wearing that gorgeous dress with the knee-high boots. People would stand with their mouths agape, watching in awe as I passed by. My hips, my slim little hips, would swivel seductively from side to side.

No more size eighteen.

Who the hell is that? they'd wonder. *She must be from New York or maybe somewhere on the West Coast. No one that cool lives in Memphis, Tennessee.*

I usually don't shop in skinny stores; I don't like the stares I get from salesgirls. *What is she doing here? We don't have clothes in her size.* I could feel their eyes on me the second I walked in. I was pushing two hundred pounds at the time, and I knew this particular store didn't carry anything larger than a size fourteen; I didn't care. I was feeling invincible, spurred on by the vision of Kat Larson, thin person. I walked in, head held high. I wasn't worried about checking to see whether or not I could squeeze into an XL.

Today I was buying mediums.

I spent more than two hours gathering clothes left and right, snatching up anything and everything that caught my eye. A leather skirt, a tight gray turtleneck, a plaid jumper, a deep-red button-down shirt with black cuffs. No one spoke to me the entire time. No one asked how I was doing, or whether I was having a good day. None of the sales reps offered to help. I knew they thought I was strange, but I felt like a genius. I had found the secret recipe to weight-loss success! Wasn't it all about motivation? And nothing would motivate me more than a closet full of expensive, thin-person clothes. I would look at them every morning and they would remind me of who I wanted to become.

Who I *would* become.

In the end, I bought nine things, including the spellbinding black velvet minidress and the knee-high boots. The salesgirl—a snazzy redhead hell-bent on ignoring me—folded and wrapped my purchases in tissue paper, then placed them gingerly in a large white and purple bag that I held like a trophy as I made my way out of the mall.

I did not get slim that summer, and I never wore those clothes.

They sit in my closet to this day, still in the tissue paper, and horribly out of date.

1

Put the "Real" Back
into Reality TV

No matter where you work, dragging yourself out of bed into the office after a weekend is never pleasant. But at Hood & Geddlefinger Public Relations, Mondays are especially brutal and Richard Geddlefinger is the man to thank for it. He doesn't believe in easing into the workweek. "Nobody ever got anywhere in life by taking it easy," he's fond of saying. "Monday sets the tone for the whole week." So he holds an hour-long mandatory staff meeting every Monday at 8 A.M. sharp to "kick things off right." His words, not mine.

I'm not a morning person by nature. Unless I have some profoundly exciting reason to be out of bed at the crack of dawn—like, say, a date with Colin Farrell—it usually takes several hours and about a gallon of coffee before I fully wake up.

That particular Monday, the day I first learned about the show, was worse than usual. I hadn't received my nightly e-mail from my Internet boyfriend, Nick, and I'd stayed up late trying to catch him online before he left for work. London is six hours ahead of Memphis, and I knew Nick got online promptly at 7:30 A.M. (I knew because I'd waited up for him on more than one occasion.)

When he hadn't signed on by 1:30 A.M. Memphis time, I panicked. Nick and I had a routine, and we never varied from it. In the three months we'd known each other, Nick and I had spoken on the phone at least once a week and he'd e-mailed every single day without fail, even if it was just a short note telling me he was too busy to write.

His e-mails mean everything to me. I print them out and whenever I get bored, or sad, or lonely, I read them. It's strange how someone so far away can have such an impact on my life. Like the day, so many weeks ago, when Nick finally told me that he loved me. I carry a tattered copy of that e-mail in my purse.

Dear Kat,

It's nearly 3 A.M. and I should be sleeping, but I'm not. Instead I'm lying here, thinking about you. The things you say, the way you laugh. I memorize everything so I can play it over in my mind. Maybe this is what it means to fall in love. It's as though all the other girls I've been with were a trial run. As though this is what I've been preparing for all my life.

I love you,
Nick

Nick is never shy with his emotions and he's always prompt. So when I didn't hear from him, I freaked. What if something bad had happened? I debated calling, but it was still early in our relationship; I wanted to keep psycho possessive girlfriend behavior to a minimum. After hours of obsessing, I wound up typing him a quick e-mail: *Hey baby, hope all is well. I missed hearing from you tonight. Love, Kat.*

So that Monday I woke up later than I'd intended, and had just enough time to grab a quick shower and visit the drive-thru Starbucks before coming into the office. I burst through the door at 8:04 A.M., making it into the conference room just as Richard called the meeting to order.

"Sorry," I said breathlessly, squeezing my chair around the crowded table. I set down my Venti house blend and cracked open my notebook. I glanced around and realized my best friend and coworker, Donna Bartosch, hadn't arrived yet either. This surprised me; Donna had recently been issued an official warning from Human Resources, informing her she was being closely watched for "excessive tardiness."

"As I was saying before *Kat* got here." Richard shot me a brief look and then continued talking, "I lined up several prospective clients over the weekend. I may have bitten off more than we can chew, and I'm going to ask all of you to put in a bit of overtime, but I think you'll find it's worth it. We're talking big names, people. If we can land these clients, it's going to take Hood and Geddlefinger to a whole new level."

All around the conference table people cringed, including me. We'd been down this road before. The last time Richard said "a bit of overtime" I wound up working nearly seventy hours a week for a month.

"Great work, Mr. G.," Cindy Vander, a sprightly blonde who worked my last nerve, responded. "I'm sure I speak for everyone in the room when I say we will do whatever it takes to make these deals happen."

I groaned inwardly. It figured that she would say that. Cindy couldn't resist an opportunity to suck up to the boss.

"Good, I knew I could count on all of you." Richard beamed. "I'm going to need to meet with each department and with certain people individually." He reached down and picked up a piece of paper, scanning through a list of names.

It seemed all we ever did at Hood & Geddlefinger was meet. We even had meetings to plan meetings. It was a wonder we got any work done at all.

"After we adjourn, I want to talk with the researchers and fact checkers," Richard said. "Kat, Donna, and William." He paused, looking around the room. "Where is Donna?" He said this to everyone, but I knew the question was directed at me. It was common knowledge that Donna and I were best friends.

I thought fast. "She's probably having car trouble," I covered. "Her beat-up old Nissan's on its last leg."

"That's a poor excuse," Richard griped. "If your car doesn't run, get a new one."

"Well, you know, maybe if Donna earned a little more money," I said in an *I'm-joking-but-I'm-really-serious* tone. It was true. We made peanuts at H&G. A few people around the conference table giggled politely.

"I'd be happy to take notes for her if you'd like," Cindy the kiss-ass volunteered.

"That's not necessary." Donna came breezing through the door as if on cue. Her face was flushed red and her shoulder-length blonde hair was still damp. Her earrings didn't match, she had a copy of *USA Today* tucked under her arm, and I noticed offhandedly that she wasn't wearing any makeup. Not that she needed it. Donna's skin is flawless. If it wasn't for her wicked sense of humor and never-ending generosity, I'd probably hate her size-four guts. Donna pushed a chair over to the conference table and plunked down next to me.

"I suppose you have a good excuse," Richard said flatly.

"Actually, sir, I do," Donna said. "In the local paper this morning, did you read about the house fire in Bartlett?"

"I read the paper, Donna." Richard held up a hand. "Don't try to claim that was *your* house, Bartosch. I know you live down-town."

"It was my boyfriend Chip's place. He lost everything he owned," she said, sounding righteously aggrieved. "He had to sleep at my apartment last night, and this morning he woke up crying. *Crying*," she said again for emphasis. "By the time he pulled himself together, I was running behind."

I eyed her curiously. If I wasn't mistaken, Chip lived in an apartment.

Richard cleared his throat. "I'm sorry to hear about that," he said, turning his attention to his laptop. "I've prepared a brief PowerPoint presentation detailing some of what we'll need to do to get started."

I took a quick survey of the room. Richard was busy fiddling with his computer, and everybody was waiting for him to begin. I saw eyes fixed on the floor, the walls, the ceiling. No one was looking at me. I hastily scrawled a message in my notebook and passed it to Donna. *So what's the real story?* I wrote, thinking she had a lot of balls lying about a thing like that. I'd never have the nerve.

Donna slid my notebook back, along with the Life section of her *USA Today*. "You should think about it," she whispered in my ear. "It sounds kind of fun."

I looked down at the paper and discovered she'd drawn a big arrow pointing toward one of the stories. As discreetly as possible, I unfolded the newspaper on my lap and started reading.

REALITY SHOW AIMS TO BE THE NEXT BIG THING
by Mark Tibulini, Staff Writer

If Zaidee Panola has her way, the days of skinny *Survivor* and bikini-clad *Big Brother* contestants will soon be a thing of the past.

Panola, executive producer of the upcoming reality show *From Fat to Fabulous,* thinks America is ready for a little more fat in its television diet.

"We're going to put the 'real' back into reality TV," said Panola, speaking via phone from her office in Los Angeles. "In its earliest days, the genre was a bit more open [to different body types]. Now, every single reality show, from MTV's *The Real World* to ABC's *The Bachelor,* is overrun with people who could easily pass for models. Sure, models make nice eye candy, but when was the last time you saw someone who looked like that in real life?"

The concept of *From Fat to Fabulous* is simple: A group of young women, all size 16 or larger, will battle the bulge—and each other—for 15 weeks on national television. Holed up in a Hollywood Hills mansion, they'll be given access to the best weight-loss tools money can buy: a spacious home gym, an on-call nutritionist, a personal trainer, and a weight counselor. The house also contains a large fridge full of healthy snacks—and an even larger pantry crammed with junk food.

"We call it the Tomb of Temptation," Panola said, laughing. "Our primary goal is to help these girls win their personal war with weight, but we're not going to force them into deprivation. The so-called 'bad foods' will be there in the house, but we'll do everything we can to persuade the girls not to touch them."

However, should a contestant be tempted to cheat, Panola and crew won't hesitate to document it.

"If someone sneaks downstairs to eat a brownie at 2 a.m., you'd better believe we'll be there," she said.

The end of every episode will feature a weigh-in, the results of which could be worth thousands of dollars.

"Each girl has her own personal bank, and we add or subtract money according to what the scale says," Panola revealed. "If she's down two pounds or more, then we add $10,000. But if her weight has increased by two pounds or more, then we subtract $20,000."

Staying the same weight as the week before or having an increase or decrease of less than two pounds will result in no change to the bank. Additionally, the contestants can earn extra dough by logging hours in the gym. At the end of the game, whoever has earned the largest bank wins the cash. Panola said designing the reward system proved extremely difficult. Several alternatives were considered, including awarding a pre-set amount of money to the girl who lost the most weight overall. The system they wound up choosing was designed under the guidance of several medical experts.

"Since the show is about weight loss, at first we thought it made sense to give the money to the girl who'd shed the most pounds. But everybody loses weight differently," Panola said, "and it wouldn't be fair to reward someone based solely on the fact that her body responds the quickest to diet and exercise."

Lest viewers think the whole routine could grow old, Panola hints that a few twists are in store.

"We do have some stuff up our sleeves, yes," Panola said. "I can't tell you much, but I will say this: The girls are going to have other opportunities to earn money, aside from the weigh-ins. They'll be able to perform special tasks and compete in some very unusual competitions." Ultimately, the show is about testing one's motivation.

"We're giving them the best incentive in the world to lose the weight," Panola said. "If they can't do it in this kind of a situation, they probably can't do it period."

A sidebar next to the article gave the show's website and listed the instructions for applying. "Submit application form (available online) and a two-minute video telling us why you'd like to be a part of the show. All materials must be received (read: received, not postmarked) by Friday, April twenty-sixth." *This upcoming Friday.*

"So, what do you think?" Donna whispered as soon as I'd finished reading.

I didn't respond at first. I was still digesting everything. The last sentence of the article—*We're giving them the best incentive in the world to lose the weight*—really struck a chord in me.

From the age of ten, my life has been about diets. All through middle school I ate nothing but Healthy Choice and Lean Cuisine. In high school I moved on to Jenny Craig, then got inventive and crafted my own weight-loss methods. There was the "Chew and Spit," which involved chomping on things like barbecue potato chips while leaning over the toilet. After chewing the food into pure mush, I chucked it straight out of my mouth into the toilet, savoring the taste while discarding the calories. If I didn't have a major aversion—bordering on a phobia—of throwing up, I'd have likely made the jump to bulimia.

Then there was the "Nothing But Five Fat-Free Yoplait Yogurts Every Day" plan. I lost forty pounds in less than three months, but I also lost huge clumps of my hair. By the time I graduated college I could name the number of Weight Watchers points in any fast-food item. I'd gone through stints eating both low-fat and low-carb. I'd also tried LA Weight Loss, Sugar Busters, and hypnosis. Most recently The South Beach Diet. All of these worked for a little while. But you can only down so many Subway sandwiches before the sight of a Veggie Delite starts to makes you gag.

Incentive.

Maybe that is the secret ingredient I've been missing all this time.

And what could be a better incentive than being paid ten thousand dollars every week to lose weight? When I began talking to Nick online, I had hoped he'd be the perfect motivation. Nick Appleby works as the fashion editor for *Status,* a sophisticated men's magazine in London. We met in a chat room. I know, I know, insert groan here. It embarrasses me how we met, and I have carefully avoided telling people the truth. Instead I say we got together while I was visiting my parents in Denver. "He was there on holiday with friends," I lie. "We met at a ski lodge. It was love at first sight. It was devastating when I had to return to Memphis and he had to return to England, but our love is strong enough to survive the long distance." It's pure bullshit, but most people buy it.

Only Donna knows the truth, the whole truth, and nothing but the truth.

"It's not like you're one of those dorks who only has Internet friends," Donna said when I told her. "You were bored and looking to have some fun. You couldn't have predicted you'd meet a guy who would sweep you off your feet."

It was a massive understatement. I'd never known anyone from England before and our e-mails were so great, so *connected*. Nick painted a magical picture of London, and often promised to fly me over for a visit. Money wasn't a concern for him; his journalism job was low-paying, but his family was loaded. "You'll love it here," he wrote. "We can stroll hand-in-hand along the bank of the Thames, visit Oxford Street, eat Indian food. London's a multicultural city, which I absolutely adore. We have the biggest Indian population outside of Asia. I can't wait for you to learn all about Britain."

It was a wonderful fantasy, but I had no idea how to make it a reality. I didn't plan to meet Nick in person, at least not for a very long time. Even though I trusted that we'd one day live happily ever after together, I hadn't been perfectly honest with Nick. To put it bluntly, I first blew it when I told him I had a flat stomach. It was, without a doubt, the dumbest mistake I have ever made in a relationship. The thing is, Nick alluded to the fact that he wanted a woman who could "comfortably fit into a size four, though I can handle a size six." We had exchanged blurry scans of ourselves. His showed him to be tall and handsome, with jet-black hair and dark eyes. Mine showed me to be thin, a feat I'd accomplished by taking a picture of myself snapped eight years earlier when I was at 174 pounds, my lowest weight ever—and doctoring it in Photoshop.

Nick wrote back that I was pretty, and he was happy I had a flat stomach. He went on to say he thought a size eight was "really pushing it" and a size ten was "way too fat for my tastes. I make a lot of public appearances for *Status,* so these things have to be considered."

I didn't have the heart to tell Nick I wore a size eighteen. Instead I told myself, *Finally, just what I need to kick start my weight-loss dream.* I knew I either had to lose the pounds or I'd lose Nick. Sooner or later, he'd demand a meeting. Yet even with that horror hanging over me, I hadn't made any headway.

Maybe a monetary incentive was exactly what I needed.

"So?" Donna prodded, growing impatient.

If anyone other than Donna had handed me that article I'd have rolled it into a ball and shoved it up their ass. But I knew her intentions were good.

I thought about the downside. For starters, I'd have to reveal my *real* weight on national television. I don't reveal my weight to my closest friends and family, not without knocking thirty pounds off. How would I do it on TV?

I rationalized. *True, all of America will see how fat I am, but then they'll also see how hard I work to fix it.* I often think the general public believes people my size do nothing but sit around and eat cake and bacon (not at the same time). This would be a great opportunity to prove this isn't true.

I picked up my notebook and wrote, *You think it's worth a shot?* Then passed it back to Donna.

Absolutely! Imagine if you won all that money? What would you even do with it?

That was easy. I was grinning at the thought. *Quit my job and move to England. Marry Nick. Then launch a career as a—*

"Excuse me, Kat."

Instinctively, I dropped my pen.

"You want to share that with the rest of the group? If it's so fascinating, I think we all ought to know."

Richard had stopped his presentation and was staring straight at me. Around the room a few people snickered. My ears started burning and my face felt prickly with heat. It was like being in grade school, getting caught passing notes by the teacher.

"I'm sorry, Richard," I said, quickly putting the notebook away. "I was filling Donna in on what she missed."

I hoped he would buy it, but he didn't.

"I'm paying you to work, not pass notes, kiddo," he said, pausing before pulling up a new PowerPoint screen. For some inane reason, Richard has taken to calling me "kiddo." Never mind the fact that I'm twenty-seven. "Now, if you wouldn't mind paying attention, I think we'd all appreciate it."

I breathed a sigh of relief. It had been embarrassing, but at least he hadn't grabbed my notebook and read what I'd written. After such a close call I tried to pay attention. But I was already planning my post–reality show life.

I was going to be a star.

A rich, beautiful, *thin* star.

2

The Lane Bryant Dance

The deadline for *From Fat to Fabulous* was in less than four days. If I wanted to audition for the show, I'd have to act fast.

The first order of business was to buy something new to wear for my audition video, a nightmare I tackled after work on Tuesday. When you're fat, buying a new outfit isn't a casual affair. You can't simply drop by the mall and scope out the latest fashions. You need a well-thought-out plan. It's the only way to avoid disappointment, overspending, or worse yet, mortal embarrassment.

The one thing every big girl knows about clothes shopping is that you've got to have a partner. Even though Donna is my best friend, I never even entertained the thought of taking her along. I'm not stupid. There is only one person I trust in a shopping situation: Cara Magley, my old college roommate. Cara and I see each other about four times a year, almost always when one of us requires something new to wear.

Cara is a size twenty.

Even most big guys simply do not get what we plus-sized gals go through to find a decent outfit. While a size eighteen girl is hard-pressed to find even one piece of clothing that fits her in Gap, a similarly sized man will have no problem whatsoever. Retail clothing stores rarely carry above a size XL in women's outfits but they stock 2XL and bigger for men. Gap even has a 3XL for those guys who "need extra room." Why provide stuff for plus-sized men but forget about women altogether? Aren't we viable consumers? And everyone knows men's clothing sizes are cut much more generously to begin with.

When I phoned Cara and explained about the reality show she was jazzed for me. We made plans to meet after work; she didn't ask what store I wanted to go to. She didn't have to. There was pretty much only one place in all of Memphis that carried what I was looking for.

"I can't wait—an evening at our favorite store!" Cara rubbed her hands together in mock anticipation as we entered the mall.

"More like fifteen minutes." I snorted. "That's all the time it takes to go through their stock."

"Ah, come on, Kat. Lane Bryant's not so bad," she said.

"True." I nodded. "I just wish they didn't put all the best stuff by the front door."

The marketing geniuses at LB, in an attempt to attract more customers, always place the most striking items right in the store-front windows. The trouble is, no one wants to be *seen* shopping there. You never know who might walk by and catch a glimpse of you browsing in "the fat girl's store." And it isn't just the fear of seeing someone you know. I had an upsetting incident once, when a group of frat guys paraded past Lane Bryant yelling "Sooooey!" as though calling a pig. I've heard of overweight girls who are so paranoid about things like that happening to them that they shop exclusively on Lane Bryant's website.

And thus, to combat any potential problems, Cara and I have devised and perfected "The Lane Bryant Dance."

Since I was the one shopping today, and she was assisting, Cara guarded the door. "Make it quick," she instructed, positioning herself behind a rack of clothes just to the left of the entrance. I watched her pretend to rummage through a bunch of dresses, while keeping a firm eye outside. She was poised and ready to give a signal should trouble arise.

"All right," I said, "here goes nothing!"

I shot through the store like a marathon runner, snatching clothes off the racks as fast as humanly possible. It took me all of twelve minutes to locate and try on a deep purple button-down shirt and a pair of nice black slacks. After snagging an acceptable outfit, I made a mad dash toward the cash registers. I was grateful to have found something that would fit without emphasizing my butt, thighs, or any other unflattering body part.

The salesgirl rang up my purchases and placed them in a giant navy blue bag with LANE BRYANT printed across the front, back, and both sides. Before we'd even made it out of the store, Cara reached into her purse and retrieved a folded Gap bag.

We quickly transferred my purchases.

"I've got an *exquisite* treat in store," Cara said, as we made our way out to the parking lot, tossing the offending Lane Bryant bag into the first trash can we found. "Remember that quadruple extra large T-shirt we both swooned over at Wal-Mart last year, the green one with the giant rooster on the front?"

"I think you mean *puked* over, not swooned."

"I recall you tried it on and discovered what a great fit it was, how it hung down to your knees and pouched out like maternity wear. Well, today is your lucky day, 'cause you're finally going to get your hands on that treasured piece." She winked. "And to show you what a great friend I am, I'm buying."

I burst out laughing. "You brat!" I said, even though, secretly, I kind of wished she *would* buy me something. It's not that I'm greedy, but Cara's parents are exceptionally wealthy.

"Come on. You know you're dying to wear the rooster for your audition. It would really knock their socks off," she promised.

"That's putting it mildly."

We drove over to Wal-Mart, where we discovered the plus-sized clothing choices had slightly improved. The rooster T-shirt was nowhere to be found, but I did buy a nice brown top, a blue button-down, and a halfway decent pair of flared jeans. Having already spent close to a hundred and fifty dollars I decided to call it a day.

Just as we neared the exit Cara stopped. "Kat, look!" She grabbed a light blue shirt with a picture of a big yellow pitcher sewn onto the front. A kaleidoscope of pastel flowers sprouted up from the center. "What do you think?" she asked, holding it up to her chest. "Is this perfect for a night out or what?"

I smirked, grabbing the shirt from her hands and steering her out of the store. "I think we've had enough fun for one day."

"You know," Cara mused, "the fashion industry must think bigger women have heinous taste."

"If I get on *From Fat to Fabulous* you'd better believe I'm going to tell America how sucky the plus-sized clothing industry is," I said, opening the car door. I started up the engine and headed out toward Union Avenue. "After I'm finished, I'll bet stores like Victoria's Secret"—we both groaned at the mention of the lingerie chain—"will start carrying our sizes."

"Don't bet on it. You're not a miracle worker," Cara said.

"Hey!" I exclaimed as a thought hit me. "Why don't you try out, too? It'd be a riot if both of us got on."

Cara winced. "No," she said, looking down at her lap. "I couldn't deal with it. It'd be like announcing to everybody in the country that I have a weight problem. Plus, my parents would *kill* me. And while we're on the topic I have to be honest with you." She paused, searching for the right words. "Are you *sure* you want to do this, Kat?"

"The more I think about it, the more excited I get," I told her. It was true. "If I get on, I can be a good role model," I suggested, "for fat women everywhere."

Cara considered this for a moment. "Yeah, *if* you get on— that's a big if. Don't count your chickens before they hatch." Her tone shifted and she gave me a sad look, one that belied many years of big-girl heartache. "When you start counting on something, that's when you get disappointed."

* * *

"They want to know if I have difficulty reaching orgasm."

"What! *Who* wants to know?" Donna demanded. She was practically shouting into the phone.

"The casting people with *From Fat to Fabulous*. I'm filling out the application as we speak."

It was Wednesday night and I had just downloaded the massive PDF file from their website. And I do mean massive. All things included, it spanned thirty-three pages.

"That's nuts," she said, lowering her voice. "Why do they need to know about your orgasms?"

"You've got me. But the entire application is like that. I figured the questions would be personal—we are talking about weight after all—but I had no idea they'd be this bad."

"Sounds intrusive."

"It's an interrogation, that's what it is," I told her. "By the way, I do have some good news. Nick finally wrote me back."

It was more than good news. Words couldn't describe how deeply relieved I felt. I'd spent the past three days in a state of total anxiety over why he'd been out of touch.

"Did he say why he's been MIA?"

I groaned. "That's actually why I'm calling. He told me he was too busy with work to write. What do you think that means?"

"Well . . ."

"Come on, Donna, give it to me straight. I can take it."

She hesitated. "It's tough to say. He could be telling the truth. From what you've told me, his job sounds pretty intense. He probably keeps pretty busy going to all those fashion shows, all that manly stuff he does." She burst into giggles.

I knew what she was hinting at.

"Nick's not gay," I said defensively.

"I know, you've told me he's not. But you've got to admit, his job . . ."

I knew I shouldn't get angry, but I was. "Did you forget what I told you? *Sexually* . . ." I emphasized, letting my voice trail off.

"Yeah, yeah, Nick's into giving oral sex. Trust me, I didn't forget," she said. "You mention it every five minutes—you're awfully proud of that, aren't you?"

"I am, actually," I said sheepishly.

It seemed an important conquest. It wasn't often that I "got some," and I was pretty excited about the prospect. The guys I'd been with in the past subscribed to the wham-bam-thank-you-ma'am sexual philosophy. It would be nice to be with a man who was concerned about my pleasure for a change. "Well, I'd better go," I told her. "I just wanted to update you on everything. Now, I've got to get this finished before I go to bed."

"Have fun."

I got to work as soon as we hung up. The first couple of questions were a breeze.

Name: *Katrina Lynne Larson*

Age: *27*

Height: *5'6"*

Weight: *227* (Painful as it was, I put down my real weight without bothering to knock off the usual thirty pounds.)

List all previous boyfriends:
That was easy enough. There were only three: *Bryce, Josh, and Nathan.* I thought briefly of including Nick, but opted against it. There was no telling how many people might ultimately see my application. And we hadn't actually met, so I reasoned it was okay to leave him off.

The next question asked for my favorite book. I thought about this one for a minute. My real favorite book is *To the Nines,* by Janet Evanovich, but I couldn't very well write that down. I needed something literary, something that would show the producers I was intelligent. I racked my brain, trying to remember the last important novel I'd read. After much deliberation, I settled on *The Great Gatsby.* It was one of the few books I'd been required to study in a college English lit course that really held my interest.

I kept on for a while, jotting down everything from my favorite movie (*Pretty Woman*) to my favorite type of ice cream (chocolate chocolate chip). I told them I was an Aquarius, that I loved roller coasters, and that my secret dream was to be a novelist.

Then things got uncomfortable.

How long have you had a weight problem? *Since age ten.*

Have you ever been given a cruel nickname because of your weight? If so, what was it, when was it given to you, and by whom? *I've been called Fat Kat, Kat Lardson, Kat Largeson.* **When?** *Grades five through twelve.* **By whom?** *There's too many people to list.*

Is anyone else in your family overweight? *Nope, I'm a lone wolf.*

Are you jealous of skinny people? *Every minute of the day.*

If you could change one feature on your body, what would it be? *My hips. I'm as pear-shaped as they come: 38-34-46. If you stretched my hips out, they'd be almost four feet tall!*

Predictably, the questions about weight spanned several pages. Then the unpredictable stuff began. In addition to asking whether I came during intercourse, the people at *From Fat to Fabulous* wanted, inexplicably, to know every sordid detail of my sex life. This wouldn't have been so bad if I actually had anything to tell. The sad truth of it was, I hadn't slept with anyone in fourteen months, ever since breaking up with my last boyfriend, Josh.

Or, if you want to get technical about it, being dumped by Josh.

I answered them to the best of my ability.

At what age did you lose your virginity? *19*

Describe your first sexual experience: *Describe it? It happened so fast I can barely remember it! Suffice to say, it was NOT good.*

How many sexual partners have you had? *3*

Have you ever had a one-night stand? *No, I'm too scared of diseases.*

Have you ever engaged in sexual activities with another woman? *That would be a great big NO.*

When was the last time you masturbated? *I plead the fifth!*

By the time I was finished, the show's producers knew me better than my dearest friends. They knew I stole a bottle of nail polish when I was seven, two of my three boyfriends cheated on me, I never attended the prom because I couldn't find a dress that fit, the only medication I took was Ortho Tri-Cyclen, and I'd tried pot a few times in college but that, otherwise, I'd always steered clear of drugs.

I debated the last question—what would my autobiography be titled—for almost fifteen minutes before putting down, *Height/Weight Disportionate*. I was especially proud of that answer. It seemed pretty clever; when I finally launched my writing career, they wouldn't have to hire someone to market my book. I could easily take that on myself.

By far, the hardest part of the entire application was the essay. We were supposed to write three to five hundred words, finishing the sentence "When I'm thin . . ." It was deceptively difficult.

I had already spent so much time listing things that I longed to do when I lost weight: sky-diving, wearing a bikini on the beach, going on a blind date, shopping for lingerie. In fact, question number twenty-nine had asked: *What would you do if you could snap your fingers and become a size six?*

I thought about that essay for hours. I got up and fed my fish, flipped on the TV and watched Letterman, visited a few web-sites. I was stalling, I knew, but I was also stumped. Finally I decided it was better to put something down and not worry about how it was received. I picked up my pen and wrote:

When I'm thin I want to be a tall skinny blonde.

This is probably because I'm a short fat brunette.

Although, for a while, I longed to be Kate Winslet, when *Titanic* was all the rage. She was so pale (like me) and lithe-some, even though she wasn't all that tall or thin. I mean, she was certainly thin enough, but by Hollywood's standards she was big.

Of course, we all know how messed up Hollywood's idea of women is.

Turn on any TV or go to any movie and there it will be, staring you in the face, like one giant advertisement for anorexia. Magazines are atrocious on our self-esteem, and books aren't much better. Any way you slice it, fat people are the butt of every joke. The scary part is how readily we accept it. Fat people are easy to pick on. What can we say? We can't deny we're overweight. It's written all over our bodies.

But what I want to know is, how fat is fat?

Howard Stern slams girls who weigh 105 pounds but have a tiny bit of cellulite, and everyone tunes in to egg him on. Pencil-thin actresses like Gwyneth Paltrow and Courteney Cox slap on fat suits and America howls with laughter. Am I the only one who finds this offensive? I know a lot of tubby guys who just adored *Shallow Hal.* I couldn't even bring myself to watch it. The trailers made me feel violated and sick. Gwyneth Paltrow has no clue what it's like to be an overweight woman. For her to claim otherwise is a gigantic slap in the face. And Monica's fat phase on *Friends* is a bad joke. A before and after picture would never look like that! I could starve myself every day for the next fifty years and I wouldn't be as slender as Courteney Cox. My right arm undoubtedly weighs more than her entire body. Which is why I think it would be funny, in an ironic way, if I end up a TV star. Big old me, next to all those little actresses.

Okay, so I'd be a reality TV star. But that's close enough for me!

Finishing the essay seemed to clear a mental block; I breezed through the rest of the application. Even the other free-form section—a blank space on the last page that encouraged us to "tell the producers something you'd like them to know" came easily. Inspired by Letterman, I drafted a Top Ten list of the annoying things people tell fat girls.

1. *You have such a pretty face.*
2. *There's this great new diet you should try.*
3. *Being overweight must suck.*
4. *Have you ever heard of exercise?*
5. *Fat people are really unhealthy.*
6. *It's okay for someone like me to eat fatty foods because*

I'm so thin. It's too bad you have to watch what you eat.
7. *I've heard great things about gastric bypass surgery.*
8. *So-and-so lost fifty pounds practically overnight with Tae Bo-Slimfast-Atkins-Jenny Craig-Weight Watchers-Hollywood Diet.*
9. *Skip dessert.*
10. *Just eat less and exercise more.*

I was proud of myself for being so honest. When all was said and done, I'd only lied about one thing; I omitted any mention of Nick. I felt a momentary pang of guilt, but knew that it was for the best. When it came time to divulge my current relationship status, I checked the box marked "single," and moved on without a second thought.

3

Nobody Gets on a Reality TV Show by Acting Natural

"From the looks of this, Kat, you haven't made any progress at all. And frankly, I'm surprised. It's completely out of character for you to blow off an assignment."

My job at Hood & Geddlefinger consists of one thing: researching prospective clients—individuals as well as corporations—and then preparing a dossier of information about them. It involves combing through tedious company reports, news clippings, and Internet resources. After Monday's meeting, which I fantasized through, Richard gave the research team a list of seven businesses. He requested info packets on all of them by Wednesday afternoon. William and Donna each took two companies, and I took three. To an outsider, it may sound like I got the short end of the stick, but the opposite was true. Preparing a dossier on my three small companies would have required very little effort on my part.

I say "would have," because I never did it.

I worked on my *From Fat to Fabulous* application instead.

Suddenly, it was Thursday morning, and I was seated in Richard Geddlefinger's office. He had accosted me the second I walked through the door and dragged me off for a one-on-one meeting. I don't like Richard's office. It's a striking mix of highbrow and white trash. Between the rigid green and brown furnishings, the tan walls with their stucco finish, and the swimsuit model calendar, it feels like a gentleman's study run amok. All that's missing is a painting of dogs playing poker. But what really bugs me are his chairs. I can't fit into them. The sides cut into my thighs, scrunching my legs together like two giant sausages. Sitting there, I felt enormous.

"Richard, I've tried my best. Really, I have." I fidgeted, trying to make myself comfortable, while feebly defending my lack of productivity. "I went to the websites—their servers were down. I searched *The Commercial Appeal* for articles and turned up nothing. I left messages at every company and no one called me back. I'm not sure what else you want me to do."

Even to my ears, the excuses sounded ridiculous.

Richard fixed me with a pointed gaze. "How many times did you try to call?"

"Once, maybe twice—I tried everyone at least twice," I quickly amended.

"You called twice!" he exclaimed. "Come on, kiddo, you know you can't leave one message and then throw in the towel. You call, you fax, you e-mail!"

I shifted awkwardly in my seat. "I'll do better, I promise."

"Do better by the end of today. I want that info before you leave."

"I don't know if I can do that. I'm leaving early today. I've got three hours of comp time left over from last week, remember?"

Richard raised his eyebrows. "Not anymore." Seeing the look of shock on my face he added, "I'll let you go early tomorrow. You can get a jump start on the weekend."

Under any other circumstances I would have been thrilled. Richard rarely lets anyone out early on a Friday. But I had been counting on leaving early today so I could film my audition video and get it to FedEx in time to make the cutoff for overnight delivery.

"That's no good," I said miserably. "I really can't stay late today, Richard. I . . . I have a dentist appointment this afternoon?" I tried.

He snorted. "You sound like Donna. Now, seriously, I need that information by the end of today. Got it?" He waved me away, and I headed off down the hall.

Donna knew something was wrong as soon as she saw me.

"Oh, shit, Kat, what did Richard say?" she asked, nervously, as I made my way to my cubicle. "He didn't fire you, did he?"

I sighed. "No, but he said I've got to finish those three dossiers before I leave today." I sat down at my desk, burying my head in my hands.

Donna leaned over and patted me on the shoulder. "Maybe it won't take as long as you think. How far into it are you?"

"Donna, I haven't even started."

I looked up just in time to see her eyes bulge. I had hoped she'd cheer me up with a well-timed wisecrack. But she looked alarmed. "What do you mean, you haven't started? What on *earth* have you been doing since Monday?"

"Daydreaming." I gave her a crooked smile. "About the show, about Nick. Shopping for my audition video. Filling out the application. Now I'm royally screwed. I'm going to miss the deadline!"

"Maybe, maybe not. I'll tell you what, give me half your to-do list, and I'll see if I can help you out."

She couldn't be serious. "What about all of *your* work?" I asked. "Don't you need to get that done first?"

"I got it finished yesterday. Richard's already okayed most of it." Seeing my reluctant expression, she added, "I don't mind helping you out. Just promise me one thing, okay?"

"Sure, anything."

"Don't forget me when you're rich and famous!"

* * *

With Donna's help, I made it out of the office by 3:15 P.M. I got home in record time, walking in the door as the clock struck 3:30. That gave me several hours to film something that could only be two minutes in length, max. Once I got the tape made, my application could be signed, sealed, and delivered. Simple.

I ran into trouble right away.

I only had two minutes to impress *From Fat to Fabulous*'s producers, so it was crucial to make every second count. I needed a killer opening line to hook them. I picked up my spiral notebook and scrawled, *Are you ready to let the Kat out of the bag? Pick me and I'll show you the true definition of Kat Scratch Fever!*

I quickly crossed it out. It was beyond cheesy, even for a reality show.

Hello! I'm Kat Larson. Welcome to my new and improved thinner life!

Too upbeat. Besides, I didn't *have* a new and improved thinner life yet. That's why I needed to go on the show.

I'm Kat, and I am desperate. I can't live one more day as a fat person.

Too depressing. They'd think I have suicidal tendencies.

I went on like this for almost thirty minutes before the phone rang. Grateful for the interruption, I dashed into the living room and picked up the cordless, glancing down at the Caller ID.

It was Nick.

"Hi," I said, trying to sound nonchalant. I didn't want to slip up and tell him about the video. I wasn't planning on *ever* telling him about the reality show.

"I didn't expect you to answer," he said, taken aback.

"Why'd you call, then?" A reasonable question.

"I felt bad. I haven't been available much lately. I wanted to leave you a sweet little message. Tell you how much I miss you and all," he said.

"Aw, that is *sweet*." I glanced at the clock. It was 4:03 P.M. Time was running short, but I figured I could spare five minutes. "How are things going at *Status*?"

"State-us," he corrected. "You Americans never pronounce anything right."

I knew something was wrong. It wasn't like him to get snippy. "Are they keeping you very busy?"

"Not anymore," he told me, sighing. "They shorted my section for next month. In fact, it was really quite absurd. I lost four pages, which means I'm going to have to toss out a number of articles."

"Why'd they do that?" I asked.

"Some twat in entertainment landed a last-minute interview with that prat Johnny Depp. Apparently, Johnny is more important than the new Gucci line. What a load of cack!"

I'd take Johnny Depp over Gucci any day, but I didn't tell him that.

"A load of cack," I repeated, smiling. I love Britspeak. "What does that mean?"

"Oh, go on, guess. It's not that difficult."

I couldn't tell if he was being sarcastic or not.

"It means a load of shit. You say it when something is out of order."

"Like an elevator? Or a lift, as you Brits would call it," I teased.

"Oh, dear, are we going to do this all night? 'Cause I can think of many other things I'd rather talk about . . ." His voice grew soft.

I looked at my watch. Five minutes had passed already. . . . Oh well, I reasoned, I could spare five more.

"I've been thinking about you lots today," Nick said shyly. "I imagine the things we'll do together . . . sipping brandy by the fireplace, long conversations over coffee. I've never met someone I can talk to like this before."

I smiled. "I know. Me too." It was the truth. Despite the great distance between us, I was closer to Nick than almost anyone. He didn't hoard his emotions the way most men did. He was so honest, genuine. And he was passionate about everything—from movies to politics to art to culture. I felt I could learn so much from him.

"It's such torture being without you, Kat. These past few days I've done nothing but think of you. I kept hoping you'd fly over and surprise me. That's a hint, by the way."

Fat chance of that happening. "I'd love to, Nick, but you know I can't afford it."

"I just imagined you walking in through the front door of my flat, how beautiful you'd look . . ."

I blushed. I wasn't sure what to say.

"I'm being serious. Or perhaps I could fly out to Memphis. I'm off deadline right now and I could stand to get away. Say yes, Kat, and I'll be on the first plane out."

I sat dumbfounded, staring at the phone. *Why the sudden urgency to meet?* "What's the rush?" I asked, trying to keep my tone even. I was praying my voice didn't give away how frightened I was.

Nick sighed. "I've been feeling really down lately. It's hard wanting someone and having them over four thousand miles away. It does your head in." I was silent for a minute, then Nick added, "I've got a better idea, Kat. Let me buy you a ticket to London. Can you get a week off work? Or how about coming over for a long weekend? Think about how it would feel. Wrapping ourselves in each other's arms. Spending the night together. Making love for the first time . . ."

There was no way he'd want to make love to all 227 pounds of me. "I wish I could Nick, but it's just not possible."

Silence.

"Nick?"

"I need to go, Kat. I've got stuff to do, things to think about."

I had never heard him sound so abrupt. I felt a stabbing pain right in the center of my chest. "You're not thinking of breaking up with me, are you?" I whispered. The clock was nearing 4:45 P.M. but suddenly the audition didn't seem so important.

"No, no, nothing like that. I just need some space." His tone softened, and I felt my whole body expand in a sigh. "Like I said, I'm just stressed. Think about the date you want to meet. I'll call you in a few days."

"I love you, honey."

He paused for an agonizing minute and then said, "I love you, too."

We hung up, I took a deep breath, and then went straight to work on my video. I needed my new and improved thinner life NOW. I threw off my work clothes, changing into the purple button-down shirt and black pants from Lane Bryant. I set the camera up on my bureau and started recording. Since I hadn't figured out what I wanted to say, I'd have to wing it. *Be yourself,* it had said on the *From Fat to Fabulous* website. A noble piece of advice, but I wasn't stupid.

Nobody gets on a reality TV show by acting natural.

I botched the first two takes; I had the camera set too low and wound up filming my boobs. Annoyed, I stuck a phone book under the camera's base and tried again. I waited until the tape finished rewinding and then hit Record. Smoothing out my shirt I walked over and began talking. "Hi!" I shouted, smiling brightly. "I'm Kat Larson, and I'm gonna be *the* new It Girl of reality TV!" I would take an upbeat approach. It was doubtful the producers wanted some boring girl who sat on a couch all day staring at her hands. I rambled on about the trials and tribulations of plus-sized clothing, the pain of growing up a size eighteen in a size-two world, and the endless search for a guy who wasn't scared off by the stigma of dating a "fat chick." Since I didn't have access to any editing equipment, I needed to film straight through in one take with no flubs, no stumbling over words, no losing my train of thought. And I couldn't run over my allotted time. A good closer is just as important as a good opener, and I had to make sure to leave myself enough space to finish properly. I didn't want to just trail off.

So I rewound the tape, and started over again.

I timed myself, and discovered that my exit—a showy cartwheel out of the room—took around ten seconds to complete, from start to finish. That left me a minute and fifty seconds to get everything in.

Which isn't very long.

Finding something to keep time presented a problem. I placed my alarm clock on the floor in front of me. I couldn't set it to go off in two-minute intervals, for obvious reasons, but I figured I could keep one eye trained on it. Unfortunately, when I watched the playback of my next run-through I could plainly see my eyes kept drifting down. I looked like I was struggling to stay awake. Definitely not a good sign.

I didn't want them to think I had narcolepsy.

I realized I could set the alarm on my cell phone to vibrate, so I did, and then I stuck it in the back pocket of my pants. It was the best I could do. The thing was it would come crashing to the floor as soon as I launched into my cartwheel. I fiddled around for a few minutes but couldn't secure it, and it was already creeping up on 5:30, so I decided not to worry about it. If my phone got broken, at least it would be for a good cause.

After several more botched attempts I finally nailed a take.

I sounded smart, funny, and interesting. I didn't screw up any of my words, and I never lost my train of thought. Unfortunately, I lost my balance midway through the cartwheel and landed in a heap on the floor, ruining the whole thing. "Who am I kidding?" I mumbled out loud, feeling my mood fall. "I am turning into a big fat joke of a person." A feeling of defeat was sinking in. There was no way in hell I'd get on TV, no matter how good my audition video was. It didn't matter what the *USA Today* article said— the producers were sure to cast only beautiful people.

They'd do a show about some "fat" chicks who weighed in the neighborhood of 150 pounds and hid their beauty behind bad hairdos, ridiculously thick glasses, and muumuus. The first episode would show lots of shots of these pseudo fat girls crying their eyes out, sitting around a table and stuffing their faces with lasagna and cheesecake. By the end of the series, they'd all drop forty pounds and start dressing better. The finale would feature them falling in love with a group of Brad Pitt clones, while claiming they "always take the stairs now, and that makes all the difference." It would be the worst, most stereotypical show on television. I should have known it all along. No one wants to make a show about a semi-confident girl who weighs more than 200 pounds.

I let out a deep sigh.

Then couldn't help giving it one last try. I positioned the camera and hit Record.

"Hi, I'm Kat Larson," I began, "and I know firsthand what it's like to be young and fat in America. . . ."

4

Duds Not Studs

"So what are you going to do about Nick?" Donna asked. It was late Wednesday night and we were sitting in a booth at On the Border, downing drinks and waiting for our food to arrive.

"He said he wanted some time to think things over, so that's what I'm going to give him . . . lots and lots of time. No e-mails, nothing. Total silent treatment." I made a face.

Donna laughed, then eyed me quizzically. "You've already given him almost a week of alone time. I don't know if it's such a good idea to wait for him to call."

"Excuse me for interrupting, but I couldn't help myself. You have the most incredible laugh. It's like music."

It was the worst pickup line I had heard in a long time. The guy delivering it was decked out in an expensive suit, yet his hair was tied in a frizzy ponytail. I got the feeling he was an artist who hadn't yet come to terms with his corporate self. He wasn't Donna's type, but she seemed taken nonetheless, and flashed him a big grin.

"Thanks for the compliment," she said. "You're sweet."

"I'm Jon," he said, extending his hand. "What's your name?" He hadn't so much as given me a second look.

Donna introduced herself and invited Jon to sit down. He grabbed a free chair from a neighboring table and pulled it to the edge of our booth. "I won't keep you long, I promise. I'll let you get back to your friend."

Your friend! I was indignant. He couldn't bother to ask my name?

"Like I said, I simply had to meet the woman with such a hypnotic laugh." He smiled cockily, leaning over the table until his face was only a few inches away from Donna's. "I was walking toward the door when I passed by your table. Your laughter literally stopped me in my tracks."

I rolled my eyes so violently I thought they might get wedged into the back of my head. Donna is blessed with stunning features—an elegant face, shiny blond hair, flawless skin—but there is nothing about her laugh that stands out. It isn't cute or lilting. It isn't even loud or annoying. It's just there.

Who did Jon think he was fooling? Pretty girls hear how pretty they are all the time; the best way to score points is to try a different angle.

"Well, I'm flattered I made such an impact," Donna said.

They kept on for a few minutes, flirting and exchanging small talk. I tuned most of it out, focusing instead on my drink. I was in a terrible mood to begin with; despite his promise to call, Nick had been avoiding me since our semi-fight nearly a week ago. Now my girls' night out was shaping into a first date for Donna. I felt like a bad joke, the proverbial third wheel. I tried to look on the bright side. Despite his corny pickup line, Jon wasn't turning out to be so bad. He was an architect and had attended the same college as Donna, graduating three years before she did. His passion was volunteering for Habitat for Humanity (or so he claimed) and he drove a Mercedes, which he casually worked into the conversation. It never ceases to amaze me how guys drop cars the way most people drop names.

"I'd love to take you out in my Benz."

"Sounds fun." Donna smiled.

I downed my sangria and ordered another. "Make it a double, no a triple," I joked to our waiter.

He studied me for a minute. "It's not a mixed drink," he informed me. "It's wine. It only comes one way."

"I know that," I said flatly. "I was kidding."

If Donna had cracked the joke, I bet the waiter would have laughed for days. I was fast approaching a new level of bitterness.

"Maybe after dinner you and I could go out dancing," Jon was saying. "I know a great little salsa club. They make the best margaritas in town."

I yawned loudly, reminding them of my presence.

"Oh, I don't think so." Donna gestured toward me. "Tonight is a girls' thing. I'm sorry."

He stood up and retrieved his wallet from his back pocket. "Here's my business card," Jon said, smiling. "Give me a call this week or drop me an e-mail. We'll set something up."

He grasped Donna's hand in a prolonged shake. "Enjoy your ladies' night," he said, backing away from the table. He kept moving backward—narrowly avoiding a collision with a busboy—until he'd reached the exit, as if he couldn't bear to take his eyes off of Donna. As for me, well, Jon had managed to make it through the entire exchange without ever directly acknowledging my presence.

This kind of thing has happened to me numerous times. I've had men hold the door for the girl in front of me, only to let it slam in my face. I've sat staring at the wall as guys introduce themselves to every girl at the table and then skip over me altogether.

"Sorry about that," Donna apologized, tucking Jon's business card into her wallet. She was positively beaming. "That was kind of weird, wasn't it?"

"Not really. It would be weird if it didn't happen to you all the time." I tried to keep my voice even, but it didn't work.

"What's wrong?" Donna asked. As if reading my mind, she added, "I didn't mean to make you feel left out."

"No biggie," I said, brushing it off. "So I noticed you didn't tell him you have a boyfriend."

"Nope." She flashed me a coy smile. "Sure didn't."

"Donna! You're not seriously thinking about cheating on Chip?"

She considered this. "I haven't made up my mind. Do you think I should?"

"Cheat? Hell no!"

"I've been doing some thinking. Maybe it's time to throw in the towel on old Chip. We've been together practically forever, and our relationship has lost a lot of its spark. He's not as much fun as he was when we first started dating."

I couldn't believe what I was hearing. "You guys haven't even been together six months!"

A waitress arrived at our table, her arms loaded down with food. "I've got a Sizzling Fajita Salad, no guac, no sour cream, no cheese."

I raised my hand. "That's me."

Her face registered surprise. She didn't say anything, but I could read her reaction. It said, *Fat girls only eat things deep fried in a vat of lard.* She set the dish down in front of me.

"Stacked Border Nachos?" she asked. Donna nodded. The waitress placed the plate in front of her. It was overflowing with chips, ground beef, and at least three kinds of cheese. "Enjoy. Your server will be around in a minute to check on you guys."

I wanted to smack that waitress. I wouldn't be caught dead eating something as fattening as Stacked Border Nachos in public. If they'd had a fruit plate, I'd have ordered it. She should get her facts straight: Big girls rarely pig out in public. We don't want to give the general population any more ammo than they already have. I chomped angrily on my salad and thought about how Jon had ignored me. Men were so predictable. Just once, I'd like to have a fantastic guy lavish attention on *me*.

Once I got skinny and fabulous, I would treat all people equally—the good, the bad, *and* the ugly. Even though I'd have the kind of body that would garner attention from male models, I would ignore them in favor of average-looking men. I wouldn't *date* any of these guys, of course. I'd be with Nick. But I could make them *feel* special, just by flirting.

Duds, not studs. That would be my motto.

"So back to Nick," Donna said, scooping up a chip and popping it into her mouth. "I hate to say this, but it might be best to call him and apologize."

"No way," I snapped between bites. "If he wants to talk, *he* can apologize to *me*."

"Kat . . ." Donna's voice trailed off. She twirled a chip around, stringing it with cheese.

"What?" I demanded.

"Look, do you want me to give this to you straight? No gay jokes, no sugarcoating."

"Of course."

"I'm serious, Kat. You can't get mad at me for saying this."

"I can take it," I lied.

"It's been over three months since you and Nick first started talking. And in this time you've sent him, what, one picture of yourself? He has no idea about your, you know, size." She averted her eyes from mine. "Nick's not a saint and, quite frankly, he'd be a fool to put all his eggs in one basket. I wouldn't be surprised if he's got someone else on the side." I started to interrupt, but she held up her hand to stop me. "You did tell me to give it to you straight, remember?"

I nodded miserably, grabbing a nacho off her plate. "Go on."

"Even if he doesn't have another girlfriend in England, which I think is unlikely, it's only a matter of time until he gets tired of your runarounds. You guys have already invested *way* too much time in a relationship that was—in all likelihood—doomed from the get-go. I bet Nick just wants to meet you so he can find out one way or the other."

I ate my salad in silence, glaring hard at Donna. She had basically said I was lucky to have someone like Nick interested in me and I should bend over backward to keep him.

As if reading my mind, Donna reached over and squeezed my forearm. "I'm sorry, Kat," she said softly. "I don't want to hurt your feelings. It's tough, 'cause I know how much you care about Nick. I don't want to see you lose him. Honest. Take my advice and call him as soon as you get home tonight. You'll see. I bet he'll be thrilled to hear from you."

"Even if I did call him, there's nothing I can say to make things better. He'll start in, offering to buy me a ticket to London . . . Don't you think it's best if I stall until I can think of something to say, some good excuse that will smooth things over?"

Donna bit her lower lip. "Opportunity," she said, "is fleeting.

If you wait too long, Nick may wind up being the one that got away."

It was a horrifying thought, but I knew she was right. "But what am I going to tell him when he wants to know why I can't come to London?"

"Tell him your mom's sick, tell him you totaled your car," she said. "Use the newspaper for inspiration, like I do—whatever it takes. But if you want to keep him, you've got to keep him interested."

I took a huge gulp of sangria and tossed her words around in my head. I was attempting to play hard-to-get, but what if it backfired? "I thought guys didn't like girls who were too available. You know, the thrill of the chase and all that."

Donna laughed. "Kat, you're an ocean away. I'd hardly call that available."

I was starting to come around. "Maybe I'll send him a quick e-mail when I get home. . . ."

"Call him, don't e-mail," Donna insisted, dipping her fork into my salad and trying a bite. "Ugh." She wrinkled her nose.

"England's six hours ahead of us, so I can't call him tonight— it'll be nearly four in the morning. I'll call him tomorrow, when I get home from H and G."

Donna nodded approvingly. "Guys like Nick don't stay on the market long. Do it the first chance you get."

* * *

The following night I rushed home from work, speeding through yellow lights and nearly sideswiping a mail truck on Union Avenue. Despite what Donna had said, I didn't believe Nick had another girlfriend in England. Not for a minute. But she was right about one thing—guys like him don't stay on the market for long. I pulled my car into the parking lot of my apartment, leapt out, and dashed up the stairs to my place. The phone was ringing when I got inside. I grabbed it off the receiver without bothering to check the Caller ID. It must be Nick!

"Hello," I said, gasping to catch my breath.

"Hi, this is Zaidee Panola calling with *From Fat to Fabulous*. I'm trying to reach Katrina Larson."

My jaw dropped. Zaidee Panola! I recognized the name from the *USA Today* story. I'd read the article so many times every detail of it had become emblazoned on my brain. *Be cool*, I coached myself, *just be cool*. "This is Kat," I said, trying my best to sound at ease.

"Hi, Kat, I'm glad I caught you. Is this a good time to talk?"

Hell, yeah, it's a good time to talk! I thought. "I'm free," I said in what I hoped was a casual voice.

"Good, because I'd like to go over a few things with you. First off, the assistant producers and I have reviewed your audition tape and we're interested in *possibly* having you on the show."

She put grave emphasis on the word *possibly*, as if to drive the point home that I was still one of many candidates.

"The audition process is fairly complex, but I'm happy to say you've survived our early eliminations. So congrats on that front. Now, what I need to do today is get you to expand on some of the things you touched on in your app and video."

I took a deep breath. I wished I'd had even the slightest bit of warning, some time to prepare. I hadn't expected them to call me for at least a month, and it hadn't even been a full week. "Fire away," I said. My heart was pounding hard and fast, and I could feel pools of sweat forming under my arms.

"Great! Make yourself comfy, Kat. This is going to take a few minutes."

I slumped against the couch and drew in a deep breath to steady my nerves.

Zaidee started off with a bang. "You've slept with only three men in your entire life. Do you feel your weight has played a role in that?"

I gulped. It was a tough question, and not something I felt comfortable discussing with a total stranger. I didn't want to answer outright, so I responded with, "My weight has played a role in everything I've ever done, so yes."

But she wouldn't let it drop that easily. "And how has it played a role in your sexual relationships, if you could be more specific? Do you have a hard time exposing your body to men? Are you shy about undressing in front of a lover?"

I struggled to keep my tone as upbeat as possible. I was starting to be plagued by a very real fear that I might cry. I figured as long as I kept joking I'd be okay. "Uh, yes and yes." I laughed. "When your hips are four feet tall, you kind of want to keep them covered."

"Right. I wanted to ask you about that. You made a comment in your app that your hips are almost four feet tall. I've got to admit I've never heard that one before. What's the story?"

I explained that my hips—which measured forty-six inches—would stand nearly four feet tall if stretched out.

"Clever. You've found a way to make light of a depressing situation. I applaud that," Zaidee remarked. "Now, can you tell me about your ex-boyfriends?"

It went on for quite a while. Our phone call was like a tennis match, with Zaidee throwing out questions and me batting them back. We discussed everything from my written application and virtually nothing from my videotape. In fact, she didn't even mention the video until the tail end of our thirty-minute conversation.

"I had a good feeling about you from the moment I saw your audition tape, and I've gotta say, Kat, you do not disappoint."

"Wow." I breathed, unsure of how to respond to her praise. "Thanks. I'm glad you liked it."

"Liked it? I *loved* it! The guys around the office haven't stopped talking about it."

"Oh, uh, great," I mumbled, thrown off.

"You've been very forthcoming, Kat, and that really helps us in this process, so thanks. Oh, and before you go, I've gotta get you to do one more thing for me. E-mail me two digital images of yourself, one head shot and one full body. They'll need to have been taken within the past six months, and be in jpeg format, three hundred dpi. Are you familiar with how to scan and upload pictures?"

I told her I was. My knowledge of Photoshop, after all, was what helped me doctor the photo I'd sent to Nick.

"I'd like those as soon as possible. As inventive as your idea of the 'talking breasts' video was, we have to see a more accurate picture of you before we can make any kind of decision."

"Talking breasts?" I repeated, horrified. *I erased that take, didn't I?*

"Sorry, didn't mean to offend you. That's just what the folks around the office dubbed your video. Kind of like how you get talking heads when you watch the news. But whatever you call it, I've gotta tell you, it was a creative approach."

I wasn't sure what to say.

5

So, As You Can See, I'm Majorly Screwed

"I've got a surprise for you."

These were the first words out of Nick's mouth when I called him the next day.

No "hello," no "I'm sorry we haven't spoken in a week."

"Okay." I breathed, bracing myself for the worst. "What is it?"

"I can't very well tell you! Then it wouldn't be much of a surprise, would it?"

"Come on, Nick, give me a little hint."

"Nice try, but no. This is too good to spoil."

"Okay. Then what have you been up to this past week?" I asked, shifting topics.

"Not a lot, really."

"Is work keeping you busy?" I ventured. The conversation was so awkward.

"No. Remember, I'm off deadline at the moment."

"Oh, right," I said, silently scolding myself. His editor had cut his section in favor of a Johnny Depp feature. How could I have forgotten? "How is the weather in the UK?"

"It's quite rainy at the moment, a typical English spring. And Memphis?"

"The heat's suffocating," I told him. "It hit ninety-two degrees yesterday, and the humidity was around sixty percent."

After our pleasantries about the weather I sat there, tongue-tied. There was so much I wanted to tell him, so much I longed to explain. "Nick . . ." I began, trailing off. "I've . . . um, really missed you."

"Me, too," he said, his voice softening. "It's been ages since we last talked."

"Well you wanted space, remember?" I said, feeling shy. "You said you wanted time to think."

He chuckled. "I'm foolish like that sometimes. I never know what I want."

"Does this mean you're not mad at me anymore?"

"Mad at you!" Nick exclaimed. "Kat, I was *never* mad at you. I was disappointed and hurt and confused that you didn't want to see me. But I wasn't angry."

I let out a deep breath I hadn't realized I'd been holding. "When you didn't call for a whole week I jumped to all sorts of horrible conclusions. I thought our relationship was doomed."

Nick sounded alarmed. "Why would you think a thing like that?"

"I don't know, I guess I was just worried. I expected you to call."

"I intended to ring you," he apologized. "But then Mum phoned and invited me to Salcombe in Devon. I was aching to get away from the city, so I went for a few days. I love it, the air's so much fresher in the country than in London. My family has a holiday home there—a converted eighteenth-century farmhouse."

I pictured a quaint little farmhouse on the coast of England. It reminded me of something straight out of a Regency romance novel. It was ironic, really, because I'd spent so much of my life reading romances. Now I was living one. "That sounds amazing. What did you do while you were out there?"

"We have twenty-two acres and riding stables, so I spent a good deal of time wandering the local area on horseback," Nick began.

I imagined him in jodhpurs and a riding jacket as he cruised along atop a mighty steed. Maybe one day we'd ride together, me sitting behind him, my arms clasped tightly around his waist.

I sank back against my bed. I could listen to his accent all night. It was so elegant and charming.

"It was a wonderful holiday. I'd love to show you someday. Devon's in the southwest of England, Kat."

"I've heard of it."

"Sorry, I didn't mean to be patronizing. But I know how you Americans are when it comes to geography," he teased. "If it's outside of the States you barely know it exists."

"Hey!" I protested. "My geography skills are pretty good, thank you very much."

"Are they now? Okay, think fast: what's the capital of Sweden?"

"Stockholm," I shot back.

"Very well." He sounded pleased. "But even if you'd gotten it wrong, I'd still be madly in love with you, Kat."

I felt giddy, like a teenager. I drew in a breath. "I love you, too."

"I feel so lucky to have met you," Nick said. "The way things are sometimes, I just get so lonely."

It was hard to believe. His life seemed so glamorous. "You have a lot going for you."

"Now," he said, "I have everything."

I blushed. "Yeah, me too. . . ."

We kept chattering on excitedly, flirting and catching up on everything we'd missed during the past week. Right as we were about to hang up the phone, Nick dropped his bombshell.

"In regard to the surprise I mentioned earlier. You'll need to make sure you're home between the hours of noon and four P.M. next Saturday. Is that going to be a problem?"

Yes, it sounded like a very *big* problem!

"Uh, I'll do my best," I said. "I may have to work, you know. Richard's got us doing tons of overtime because of these new clients."

"Kat, it's incredibly important that you be there. Try your best."

I assured him I would. We said good-bye and I immediately dialed Donna's number. "Is it okay if I crash at your place next Saturday?" I asked as soon as she'd picked up.

"Why? Is your apartment being fumigated or something?"

"Oh, I wish!" I hyperventilated. "I'd give anything to have my apartment overrun with termites, or roaches, or ants, or armadillos! Compared to this, that would be a picnic!"

"Armadillos? They'd eat the ants, wouldn't they?"

"I was trying to make a point!" I shrieked. "Can I stay with you or not?"

"Calm down, Kat, you're not making any sense."

"Nick's coming!" I thundered. "He's coming to Memphis a week from tomorrow! He's going to show up on my doorstep next Saturday."

"Oh my God!" Donna screeched. "How do you know?"

I quickly caught her up to speed. "So, as you can see, I'm majorly screwed."

"Maybe, maybe not," she said slowly. "I think you're jumping the gun. What if he just ordered you flowers or something?"

"No way. For a guy like Nick, flowers are no big deal. He wouldn't plan that a week in advance."

"Well, excuse me." Donna sounded irritated. "I didn't realize he was a flowers every day kind of guy."

I felt a brief pang of guilt for bragging. As far as I knew, Chip had never sent flowers. Not even on Donna's birthday.

"Kat, what good will sleeping at my place do? It's not like that's going to change anything."

"Nick will never look for me there." It was an ill-conceived plan, but it was the only thing I could come up with.

"So, what, you're going to let this poor guy travel thousands of miles and then leave him stranded outside your apartment?"

I closed my eyes. "Yes. No. I don't know!"

"Don't you think that's incredibly cruel?"

Cruel didn't even begin to describe it. "It kind of is, yes." Already, guilt was sinking in.

"You're going to have to meet him eventually, you know."

"Not before I get skinny," I said firmly. "I can't let him see me while I'm still"—I thought rapidly, trying to remember what I'd told her in the past—"almost two hundred pounds."

Donna didn't say anything, so I pressed on. "So can I stay or not? 'Cause if your answer's no, I'm booking a room at the Ramada."

Donna sighed. "Not necessary. I'll make up the couch."

* * *

The following Tuesday found me back in Richard's office. Only this time, it was under better circumstances. Instead of scolding me for not finishing my work on time, Richard was praising my efforts.

"You've been a real trooper, kiddo. Ever since our little talk I've noticed how you've buckled down and gotten your act together. I know I can count on you in a bind."

I smiled, to show I appreciated his compliments. "Thanks. That means a lot."

It was just past 9:15 A.M. when he gave me the news. I can be certain of the time, because I was watching the second hand on his Cindy Crawford wall clock when he said it. My mind had been drifting in and out of the conversation, *What will Nick do when he finds out I'm not home next Saturday,* when I heard something that snapped me to attention.

". . . this promotion."

There were two words Richard Geddlefinger rarely said: *raise* and *promotion.* I hoped one wouldn't come without the other.

"Are you serious, Richard?" I asked.

"As a heart attack."

"Wow. I'm so . . . surprised. Can you elaborate a little?" It was a last-ditch attempt to get him to repeat what he'd said while I wasn't paying attention. Fortunately, it worked.

"Well, nothing's official yet. I'd have to talk things over with my partner, Jake Hood, but I'd like you to start taking an active roll in our presentations. In fact, I've got a potential client coming in a week from Wednesday. Mercer and Sons Funeral Home. Are you familiar with them?"

I told him I was. "Only in passing reference, though, thank God."

He chuckled. "I want you to spend this next week getting even *more* familiar with them. Do some digging, compile some information." He smiled broadly. "And then next Wednesday, you and I will sit down and sell them on our company."

"Thanks, Richard!" I was glowing. Landing a slot on the presentation team would be a big step up for me. It wasn't my dream job, but *still.* "What do you want me to talk about?" I asked. "I'll need to prepare some sort of a speech, right?"

"Nah, that's not necessary. I find spontaneity works best in these situations. You don't want to sound too rehearsed."

We were interrupted by a knock at the door.

"Excuse me," Cindy Vander said, popping her head in. "I don't mean to be rude, but there's an urgent phone call for Kat. It's *long-distance.*" She raised her eyebrows.

I leapt up, nearly knocking the chair to the ground. It wasn't unusual for me to receive long-distance phone calls; I dealt with out-of-state clients all the time. But something in the tone of her voice made me think it had to be Nick.

"You're answering my phone now?" I demanded, scurrying toward the door.

She was the picture of innocence. "Oh, no. I happened to be walking by your desk when I heard it ringing. I knew you were in a meeting and I thought I'd make myself useful. So I took down a message."

"That's what voice mail is for," I groused, dashing down the hall to my cubicle. I grabbed the phone and took it off hold.

It was Zaidee Panola.

Funny how she always calls when I am expecting Nick.

"Hi," I said uneasily, caught off-guard that she had used my work number. "Sorry to keep you waiting."

"That's no problem; the girl who answered the phone was kind enough to track you down for me."

Uh-oh, I thought. *This doesn't sound good.* "You didn't tell her why you were calling, did you?"

"She did ask."

"And?" I held my breath.

"I told her it was personal. She was pretty persistent, but don't you worry. I stonewalled her."

I laughed. "Thanks."

"Anytime. You girls got some kind of office rivalry going on?"

"Something like that." I snorted. "Let's just say we're not on the best of terms."

"Gotcha. Anyway, the reason I'm calling. First off, thanks for your pictures, Kat. I appreciate your sending them so quickly. Now, I just have a few more questions to ask, and then we can move on to stage two of the process."

"A few more questions" wound up taking nearly half an hour to answer.

At first I tried to be discreet, flipping through a file of paperwork as we talked. At one point that tattletale Cindy Vander sidled up to my cubicle and I had to put Zaidee on hold for a few minutes. I didn't know if she bought my act or not. It's hard to pretend you're on a business call when you're discussing diet programs and plus-sized lingerie.

When Zaidee finally finished quizzing me, she thanked me for my time again.

"Okay, then, looks like I've got everything I need," she concluded. "I'm about to go into a meeting with the other producers. We've got to compare notes and after that I'll be calling you back before five o'clock with a firm decision, one way or another."

I gasped. "You mean you're going to decide right now if I'm on the show?" My shock was palpable.

"Not now, no." Zaidee laughed. "Calm down, honey. We're merely narrowing the field to twenty-five finalists to bring out to the Los Angeles try-out. Didn't you read the application packet?"

"I must have missed that part," I said lamely. "I was in a pretty big hurry when I filled it out." I wanted to kick myself as soon as the words left my mouth. I didn't want her to think *From Fat to Fabulous* wasn't important to me. "What I mean is, I didn't find out about the show until right before the deadline."

"Good deal. Talk to you in a bit, Kat."

"Okay, I'll wait for your call."

I didn't leave my desk the entire afternoon, not to use the bathroom, not to get a drink from the water cooler, not even to go to lunch with Donna.

Five o'clock came and went, and there was no word from Zaidee.

* * *

"Maybe she meant five o'clock Pacific time," Donna offered later that night as we drowned our sorrows over dinner at Buckley's. I was mourning shattered expectations, and Donna was mourning the loss of a relationship; she'd officially broken up with Chip earlier that afternoon. A delectable meal of pasta and red wine seemed in order. Fuck my perpetual diet. If I wasn't going to be on television, what did it matter anyway?

I shook my head. "I thought of that, too. But California is only two hours behind Memphis. I didn't get out of the office until after seven-thirty. If she'd called, I'd know."

"Maybe she assumed you'd gone home and tried your apartment," Donna suggested.

"Nope, nothing on the Caller ID. I checked." I took a big bite of Italian spinach.

"Oh." Donna gulped down her glass of wine, and poured herself a fresh one. It was her fifth in less than an hour. For someone who had initiated a breakup, she wasn't handling it very well. "You know how these Hollywood types are. Busy as hell! *From Fat to Fabulous* here you come!"

"*Shhh!* Keep your voice down!"

Donna shrugged in confusion. "What's up?"

"I'd kind of like to keep it quiet," I whispered, looking around the dimly lit restaurant. "You can never be too careful."

"Oh." Donna shook her head knowingly. "Legal reasons, right? You could get disqualified for talking about it." She stuffed a whole piece of garlic toast in her mouth.

"No, nothing like that. It's just," I paused, searching for the right words, "I guess I'm embarrassed about it, that's all. The title alone is kind of humiliating. I don't want people to know."

"It's going to be hard to keep secret once you're on national freakin' television," she snickered. Suddenly, her eyes got huge. "You know what you've gotta do, Kat? If you wanna get on the show, you gotta be proactive about it."

"Proactive," I repeated, through bites of ravioli.

"Don't sit back and let this Zula woman come to you."

"Zaidee," I corrected.

"Whatever. Show her you mean business. Let her know that Kat Larson wants a shot!"

When I didn't say anything, she continued, "Call her office first thing tomorrow, pester her a little. It'll prove how interested you are. That's exactly what my cousin did to get her internship at that Wall Street firm. She sent their office semiharassing faxes for weeks."

"Somehow I think this is a little bit different. Wall Street versus a cheesy reality show," I said, weighing the two options with my hands. "They're not exactly in the same league, if you catch my drift."

Donna chugged down more wine. "Yeah, if you ask me, the reality show is a hell of a lot more *interesting*. Who wants to work at the stock exchange?" She scrunched up her face.

"Well, anyway, I can't call. The application specifically said *not* to."

Donna dismissed this. "Don't listen to that BS. That's the message the Wall Street brokers spewed, and they didn't mean a word of it. Come on, I bet this will increase your chances big-time."

I wasn't so sure. For Donna maybe that kind of strategy might work. But I'm just not aggressive enough to pull it off. "It's a bad idea."

"What-*ever*, Kat. You'd be great! I could coach you on it."

I motioned again for her to keep it down. "I don't have Zaidee's office number," I lied.

"The Yahoo directory, baby. They've got every commercial listing in the country."

"That reminds me." I groaned, moving on to another sore subject. "Nick sent me an electronic greeting card today. The message read, 'Less than a week! The big surprise will soon be en route. Love always, Nicholas J. Appleby.' He signed his full name, which he never does. He says it reminds him of a Charles Dickens character. What do you make of that?"

"Charles Dickens!" Donna erupted in a fit of laughter. "*Dick-*ens," she said, emphasizing the first syllable. "Why don't we call Richard 'Dick'? *Dick* Geddlefinger. That sounds about right."

"Oh brother." I stared at her. "You're completely drunk. I can't believe I'm bothering to ask you for advice."

"No, no! I'm fine Kat, I'm perfectly fine."

I pulled the bottle of wine over toward my side of the table, tucking it safely out of Donna's reach. "Good thing I'm driving," I said.

Donna smiled. "I do."

"I do?" I repeated.

"I do think Nicholas J. Appleby sounds like something out of a Charles Dickens novel."

6

Some Ferocious Cockroaches

"My head is throbbing." Donna rubbed her temple for emphasis.

"Serves you right," I scolded. "You only drank a whole bottle of wine last night." I poured her a cup of coffee. "Drink this. It'll make you feel better."

She took the cup from my hands and staggered back to her desk, making a face at me as she went.

I trotted over to my cubicle and began compiling data on Mercer and Sons Funeral Home, but every time the phone rang, I jumped a mile. I was still hoping Zaidee would contact me. I tried to keep my calls short and simple, though twice I got stuck on the line; the first time talking to a client about a press release, the second time talking to my dad.

"Hello, Katrina!" he yelled, nearly blasting my ear off.

Ever since moving to Denver, my father has become a shouter over the telephone. The idea that I am still able to hear him loud and clear even though he is now a thousand miles away has never quite sunk in.

"How's my favorite daughter?" he boomed.

"I'm doing well, how are you and Mom?"

"Homesick," he griped. "Your mom can't stop talking about Memphis. Me, I just miss the barbecue."

"Well, Memphis misses you," I said, feeling like a first-class dork.

"Your mother was looking on the World Wide Web today," he said. My father is the only person I know who still calls it the World Wide Web. "And she found a cyber savers flight from Denver to Memphis. You know what cyber savers is, Katrina?"

"Yes, I do," I said, eyeing the clock. Zaidee could be trying to get through to me right this second. We have call waiting, but I don't trust it in a pinch.

"They do special deals where you can take a weekend trip for next to nothing. We can go round-trip for ninety-nine dollars on Northwest Airlines. Sound good?"

I blinked in surprise. "Dad, you've lost me."

I could hear my mother shouting in the background, taking him to task for not giving me the full details.

"Right, right," he said. "Your mom and I were thinking we'd like to take a weekend trip out to Memphis—Saturday to Tuesday. Are you free this weekend?"

It seemed a cruel irony that everyone was plotting to show up on my doorstep this Saturday.

I weighed my options. If I told him no, my mom would get on the phone and hit me with a major guilt trip. I am, after all, their only child. And they aren't getting any younger. All they want to do is come and visit me. Couldn't I spare three days out of my busy schedule?

But if, on the other hand, I said yes, they'd inevitably want to stay at my place. A mental image flashed through my mind: my dad, decked out in a pair of tacky boxer shorts with flounders on them, swinging open my front door and welcoming Nick inside. "Always nice to meet Katrina's boyfriend," he'd say, slapping him on the back. "You talk kinda funny. Where are you from? Connecticut?"

No, it couldn't happen.

"Gee, Dad, that sounds awesome, there's just one problem." I crossed my fingers behind my back, and prayed for forgiveness. "They're fumigating my apartment this weekend," I said, capitalizing on my conversation with Donna.

"Fumigating? What's the problem?"

"Roaches."

"Roaches!" I heard my mother scream. She had picked up the extension. "Kat, you've got to go to a hotel. You can't stay there while they spray those chemicals. I saw a special on *Dateline* the other day about a girl who *died* from staying home while her apartment was fumigated."

Oh, brother. Here it comes.

"Do you need money to rent a room?" she asked. "Because if you do, don't be ashamed to say so."

"No, Mom, it's fine. I'm going to be staying with Donna."

"And that's not going to inconvenience her?" she asked.

I sighed. "Of course not. Donna's cool with it."

Dad interjected, "Sorry to hear that. We can come another weekend."

I breathed a tremendous sigh of relief. "Thanks for understanding."

"Well, I'm very concerned here. How long have you had this roach problem?" my mom demanded.

"Uh, it's only been going on for about two days."

"Two days!" my dad exclaimed. "Those must be some

ferocious cockroaches if they've multiplied enough to fumigate after only two days."

"They're a special breed," I said, "or species. Or whatever bugs are called," I fumbled. I was a terrible liar.

"I've never heard of anything like that," Dad said.

"Uh, yeah, these roaches are pretty rare. Humongous and impossible to get rid of, unless you wipe them out in the earliest stages. . . ."

* * *

Around noon, Zaidee called.

She didn't mince words.

"I hope you don't have any important plans for this weekend, Kat," she said as soon as I answered. "Because you're coming to Los Angeles."

I was so shocked I actually dropped the phone.

"HOLY SHIT!" I shrieked, picking the receiver back up. My hand flew up to cover my mouth. "Excuse me, I'm not usually so vulgar."

"No problem. It's shocking, I know."

"*This* weekend," I repeated. "That's only three days from now!"

"Two, actually. You'll be leaving Friday evening, and returning on the red-eye late Sunday night. We've worked it out so most people won't have to miss work. At least, that's our tentative plan. It may change as we proceed."

I drew in a breath. "What time's my flight?"

"They haven't arranged it. I had to talk to you before I gave the go-ahead. You're able to make it, right?"

"Oh, yes! Absolutely. In fact," I said, grinning, "you couldn't have picked a better weekend if you'd tried."

Zaidee filled me in briefly on the details. Her office would overnight a package to my apartment with my plane ticket, hotel reservation, and taxi vouchers.

"You'll be all set. If for some reason you don't receive the package by tomorrow evening, call my assistant immediately." She proceeded to give me the contact information.

As soon as we hung up, I went racing over to Donna's desk.

I tried my best to sound casual, but Donna knew the moment she saw my face.

"The show called," she guessed, smiling.

"It looks like I won't need to hide out at your place this weekend," I said, pausing unnecessarily for effect. "I'm going to Los Angeles!"

I had a million things to do, and virtually no time to do them. The first and most vital step, even more important than packing, was to get things squared away with Nick. Fortunately, the conversation with my dad had inspired me. I called him on my cell phone during lunch. Expensive international surcharges be damned.

"Kat!" he exclaimed. "It's so good to hear your lovely voice. Are you ill?"

That was a strange reversal. One minute, my voice was lovely, the next I sounded sick. "No, why, do I sound congested?"

"Oh, goodness, no! I'm not accustomed to hearing from you in the middle of the day is all. I assumed you'd phoned in to work."

"I'm on my lunch break. What are you up to, baby?"

"I was having a Jen-A-Thon when you rang."

I had no idea what the hell a Jen-A-Thon was. It had to be some kind of bizarre British lingo. "What's a Jen-A-Thon?" I asked nervously. Part of me was afraid to find out. "You're not cheating on me with some girl named Jen, are you?"

"In a manner of speaking, yes."

"Oh my God . . . please tell me you're joking."

"Jennifer Garner," he explained. "The actress. I'm a big fan."

"I didn't realize she was famous in England."

"She is. Besides, I make it a point to know all the gorgeous actresses."

I hoped he didn't mean personally. Nick's job at *Status* afforded him the opportunity to hobnob with lots of celebrities.

"She's a goddess," he said.

He then talked about her "full, luscious lips" and her "slender legs that go on for miles" and her "toned, tight little bottom." Which pretty much sucked. Why do men feel the need to drone on about how "fine" other women are? Is it a misguided attempt to impress us? "She's not half bad," I mumbled. "Kind of gangly if you ask me." *Thank God Zaidee had finally called.*

I was more relieved than ever that I had applied for *From Fat to Fabulous*. It was a pretty smart move. When I got finished with the show I would be closer to the kind of woman Nick wanted. "I need to tell you something," I began. I wasn't sure how to break the news, so I came right out with it. "I'm not going to be in town when you—*your present* arrives Saturday." I struggled to make my voice sound pissed off rather than relieved.

"Why on earth not?" he asked, then his voice changed dramatically. "You're flying to London, aren't you!" he exclaimed. "Kat, that's brilliant."

He sounded so excited. It pained me to let him down.

"Um, no, that's not it. My dad called a few minutes ago and, well, he bought me a plane ticket to come out to Denver. They had this cyber savers deal on Northwest Airlines where you can fly round-trip for only ninety-nine dollars. I'm *so* incredibly sorry. He bought it as a surprise."

Nick's mood fell. "I don't suppose that leaves you much choice."

"I'm caught between a rock and a hard place."

"I see." Nick paused. "Can you get someone to come by your flat and meet the package when it gets there?"

"The *package* is still coming, even though I won't be here?"

"I posted it this morning, via FedEx. It's too late to get it back."

I wrinkled my brow in confusion. "My landlord can hold on to a package until I get back Monday," I said. *So it really is a package?*

"I don't trust this in some stranger's care. What I've sent you is quite valuable."

"It is?"

"Yes, and rather expensive. If you can't be there, well—I'd feel more comfortable if I knew you had someone there to meet it."

"Donna can do it!" I blurted out. Now I was dying to know what the surprise was. "I've got to get her to come by and feed my fish while I'm gone."

"Good-o," he said, sounding relieved. "Well, then, have a wonderful time, Kat. I'll speak to you when you get back."

"I love you, baby."

"I love you, too."

I placed the receiver back in its cradle and sank into my chair. My mind was spinning, and my heart was beating so fast I thought it might pound right out of my chest.

A surprise. Valuable. Expensive.

Slowly, everything was coming into focus.

Nick was going to propose to me!

I ran the length of our office searching for Donna. She was in the break room, sitting by herself, reading a fashion magazine and munching on a sandwich.

"Donna," I squealed, racing in the door.

She jumped. "Geez, Kat, can you keep it down?" she moaned. "Some of us had a rough night last night."

I ignored her. "Brace yourself," I said, taking the seat opposite from her. "I think Nick's going to ask me to marry him!"

"Huh?" She put down the peanut butter and jelly sandwich she was eating and stared at me through squinted eyes. She looked more bewildered than impressed.

"That surprise package that's arriving this Saturday? It's an engagement ring!" I blurted out.

Several people nearby turned to stare.

"Do you mind?" Donna asked a group of women seated near us. "We're trying to have a private conversation."

"A private conversation at the top of your lungs," one of the women retorted.

Donna shook her head in confusion. "Kat, you've lost me. I thought Nick *was* the surprise. What's this about a package?"

I quickly went over the details of our conversation. "So as you can plainly see, that's the only logical explanation," I concluded.

She took a long, purposeful drink of her orange juice before speaking. "You have officially lost your mind."

"No, I haven't. Just listen to the facts—"

"I've *heard* the facts. I still think you're nuts."

"But he said it was expensive," I protested.

"Lots of things are expensive, Kat. Almost any kind of jewelry is expensive. He probably bought you a pair of earrings, or maybe a watch."

My face fell. "Hey, just because you're in a bad mood over

breaking up with Chip doesn't mean you have to rain on my parade."

She rolled her eyes. "Don't you think you're getting a bit carried away? It's a pretty big jump from 'expensive present' to 'engagement ring.' And, anyway, only a moron would propose to someone they've *never even seen*!"

"My relationship with Nick isn't based on *looks*. Our love is stronger than that."

"Oh, please! If it's not based on looks then why don't you send him an accurate picture of yourself?"

"Whatever." I stood up from the table. "You're just jealous."

"Oh yeah, I'm *so* jealous," Donna said sarcastically. "I just can't stand that you have an Internet boyfriend who lives twenty thousand miles away. Grow up, Kat. I'm not jealous of your loser."

I couldn't believe what I was hearing. Donna had never spoken to me this way before. "Last week you were telling me what a catch he was. Now he's a loser?"

"Get over yourself, Kat, the world doesn't revolve around you."

My jaw dropped. I didn't want to dignify her statement with an answer. "I'll see you when I get back from California," I said, stalking out of the room. Nick's surprise would have to wait with my landlord until I got back on Monday. There was no way I'd ask Donna to pick it up. "Oh, and one more thing," I said indignantly, sticking my head back in through the door. "Learn a little something about geography. Great Britain is *four* thousand miles from here, not twenty."

Donna kept right on eating her lunch. She didn't even bother to glance up.

7

Fat Chance

I spent the plane ride from Memphis to Los Angeles fighting off airsickness—I've only flown twice in my life—and stressing out over where to find a taxi once we landed. My limited knowledge of the West Coast, which came mostly from magazines, movies, and TV shows, did not serve me well. I didn't sit next to Steven Spielberg on the plane, there was no limo driver awaiting my arrival, and I didn't run into Tom Cruise at baggage claim. I had expected glitz and glamour, celebrity sightings, and movie-star mansions.

What I got were crowded freeways and garbage-lined streets. To be fair about it, I didn't see much of the city.

From the time I arrived at LAX and right up until I departed, I was kept under virtual lock and key at the Brentwood Bel-Air Holiday Inn. There was nothing elaborate or fancy about the hotel—a tall, white cylindrical building located off the freeway, but I liked it. It sat cramped onto a small lot of land between a funky art-deco apartment complex and the Getty Center Museum, and you could see it for miles. I got to the hotel from the airport in a

Yellow Cab, paid for with a taxi voucher provided by *From Fat to Fabulous*. As it turned out, it was easy to find a cab.

All I had to do was follow signs that read TAXI.

I bypassed the front desk and checked in at the hospitality suite on the sixteenth floor, as it instructed in the packet Zaidee sent. My room reservation was under the show's name, and I needed to retrieve my key from a member of the production staff. By the time the elevator had reached the sixteenth floor, I was a ball of nerves, clutching my stomach and trying to keep my knees from buckling underneath me. My body doesn't respond well to stress—I shake, I sweat, I stammer, my stomach flips. I don't know if it's genetics, or if it's the by-product of growing up in a worrisome household. Either way, I blame my mother. "For God's sake, pull yourself together, Kat," I lectured myself. "You've made it this far. What could possibly go wrong?"

When the elevator reached the sixteenth floor, the doors parted to reveal a metallic easel with a sign that read FAT2FAB AUDITIONS in bold pink letters. A door to one of the rooms popped open and a heavyset black girl carrying a duffel bag made her way toward the elevator.

Yep, I was in the right place.

I pushed open the door and stepped inside.

A short, stocky man appeared at my shoulder. "You here for the auditions?"

I looked at him. I wanted to say, "No, I'm a 227-pound girl who just happened to wander up here with an armload of luggage." Diplomatically, I settled on, "Yes, I am."

"You can set your bags down here." He gestured to a spot near the door where a pile was already forming. "Check-in's over at that desk. They'll give you your room assignment."

I dropped my luggage and headed over to the desk. Directly

beside it was a large buffet table, loaded down with platters of cookies, bagels, and tiny sandwiches. Clearly they wanted to make sure we were good and fat before we went on TV.

The girl in front of me stepped aside to fill out some paperwork. The whole scene reminded me of college orientation, everyone milling around nervously, waiting to get their class schedules and dorm assignments.

"Next please!" called a pixie-haired blonde.

I moved up to the desk. "Hi, I'm Kat—"

"Give me your driver's license," she cut me off.

Startled, I fished in my purse for my wallet. She stared at me impatiently as I struggled to find it. I glanced behind me. There was no one else waiting to be served. I located my license and handed it over.

"I've gotta photocopy this," she said, jumping up and going over to a small Xerox machine sitting on top of a table. She returned a minute later and passed back my driver's license, along with a room keycard and a stack of paperwork the size of a textbook. "Sign and date this here, here, and here," she said, flipping the document open and singling out several pages. "When you're done, go through and initial the bottom of each page. Go get settled in your room and then bring the forms back up here as soon as you're done." She thrust the papers into my hands.

"But it's over fifty pages!" I gasped. "Do I need to read all of it?"

She let out a big breath, causing her bangs to stand up on her forehead. "I'd advise you to do so," she said, curtly. "Never sign anything without reading it first. There's a little business tip for you."

"Sorry. I didn't realize I'd have to do so much work before the audition started."

"The first part of this is a confidentiality agreement; the second part's a release form authorizing us to conduct a background check and a drug test."

"You're drug testing us?" I stood there with my mouth gaping.

"You'll be getting a full physical," she informed me. "It's all in your packet." She turned and busied herself neatening up the desk. I sensed the conversation was finished, and walked over to retrieve my suitcase.

My room was located on the fourth floor. There were two double beds in it. I pitched my stuff down on the bed closest to the window, anticipating a roommate would show up and claim the other one. No one did.

When I finally finished reading and initialing the lengthy document it was after 10 P.M. I took the elevator back upstairs and returned the paperwork. I was disappointed to find the abrupt blonde woman was still on desk-duty. I'd been hoping to meet someone a little friendlier, as I had a few questions about the casting process. Without so much as a "hello," she snatched the documents from my hand. She made me photocopies of the pages with my signature on them, and then gave me an itinerary of the following day's events.

They'd set out fresh sandwiches as well as chips and cake, so I snagged a plateful of food and headed back to my room. I pulled out the itinerary and studied it while I ate.

Audition Schedule—Saturday, May 11*
PLEASE REPORT PROMPTLY TO ALL SCHEDULED EVENTS!!!!
FAILURE TO BE ON TIME MAY RESULT IN
YOUR DISMISSAL FROM THE CASTING PROCESS. AS ALWAYS
PROMPTNESS IS A VIRTUE.

7:30 A.M.	*Continental breakfast in Meeting Room 1603*
8:00 A.M.	*Group A interview in Hospitality Suite*
9:30 A.M.	*Group B interview in Hospitality Suite*
11:00 A.M.	*Group C interview in Hospitality Suite*
12:30 P.M.	*Buffet-style lunch served in Meeting Room 1603*
1:30–6:30 P.M.	*Medical examinations and drug screening, location TBA*
7:00 P.M.	*Buffet-style dinner served in Meeting Room 1603*
8:00 P.M.	*Group D interview in Hospitality Suite*

*Contestants are advised, though not required, to remain on the hotel premises for the duration of the day. Please note that additional interviews may be scheduled during "off periods" of your schedule. Also note that immediately following your group interview you will be asked to complete a follow-up questionnaire, which may require a substantial time commitment.

Much to my horror, *Kat Larson—Group A* had been scrawled across the top of the page. It figured. I was the world's biggest night owl so, of course, I was scheduled for the early-bird interview.

I glanced at the clock on the nightstand. It was almost 11 P.M., 1 A.M. Memphis time. Donna would still be up. She never went to bed early on the weekends. I'd been feeling pangs of sadness about our fight. Other than cursory "hello's" we had barely spoken over the past few days. I'd vowed to give her the silent treatment until she apologized for insulting my relationship with Nick. But now, distance made our argument seem silly; definitely not something worth ruining a friendship over.

I picked up the phone.

"Hello?" she answered on the first ring.

"Hey, it's me. I didn't wake you, did I?"

"No, I was still up." She didn't say anything for a minute. "Kat?"

"The one and only," I joked.

"I thought you were going to Los Angeles today?"

"Three guesses where I'm calling from. The Sunshine State." She chuckled. "That's Florida. I think California is the Bear State."

"Bear?" I repeated, uncertain. I snapped my fingers. "The Golden State! That's it!"

We cracked up. Donna said, "It's nice to hear from you. I've been wondering how you were holding up. So, what's it like out there in the old Golden State?"

It was as if our fight had never happened. I caught her up to speed on everything, and she filled me in on her day. She'd met Jon, the guy from On the Border, for drinks after work.

"All he did was talk about his Mercedes and his 'healthy' investment portfolio," she complained. "Then, when the end of the date comes, he has the nerve to ask me if I want to pick up the tab! What the hell? Going dutch is one thing, but when a guy's rich, I'm sorry, he's paying."

We were having such a good time that before I knew it an hour had passed.

"You need me to go and feed your fish tomorrow?" Donna asked.

"No, Cara's taking care of it. But, there *is* something you could do for me if you're not too busy."

"I'll get Nick's package," she agreed, cutting in before I'd even asked. "Hmm . . . that didn't sound right. You know what I mean. Not his *package* package."

"Donna!"

"I'm tired. Anyway, you need to get a good night's sleep so you can be in top form for tomorrow."

I hung up the phone with the promise to call her the following evening and give her the scoop. Even though it was 2 A.M. Memphis time I wasn't the least bit tired. Anxiety had gotten the best of me, revving up my body to the point where sleep seemed unattainable. I settled into bed and flicked on the TV, channel surfing until I'd located a station showing *The Breakfast Club*. The film was halfway over, but I'd seen it enough times that it didn't matter. By the time I finally dozed off, the sun was already on the horizon. Still, when the alarm clock sounded at 7 A.M. the next morning I sprang out of bed with so much energy you'd think I'd had a full night's rest.

It's amazing how little sleep you can get by on in a crunch.

* * *

"So how do you think I should play this: Richard Hatch or *Joe Millionaire?*" asked an extremely heavy girl—probably in the neighborhood of four hundred pounds—with flowing brown hair that hung down to her waist. She was wearing a pretty yellow sundress, at least a couple of sizes too small. The neckline was so tight it pushed her enormous breasts up nearly to her chin.

It was 8 A.M. Saturday morning, and the six of us who made up Group A were milling around the hall of the sixteenth floor, waiting to go into the hospitality suite for our first interview.

"You're going to imitate that *Joe Millionaire* buffoon?" shrieked a short redhead. "You can't be serious. That guy has the personality of a lettuce leaf. He's as boring as watching paint dry!"

"I'm sure the *Joe Millionaire* people had hundreds of guys to choose from, and they picked *him*," the big girl said. "Obviously, he has some wonderful qualities. Don't you agree?" She motioned for me to join their conversation.

"Uh, yeah," I said, glancing back and forth between them. They were speaking a bizarre, alien language. In its earliest days, I'd loved *The Real World,* back before it was a bunch of wannabe actors engaging in threesomes. And while I faithfully watched the first season of *Survivor,* I honestly haven't followed a reality show since. "I'd love to help you out, but I never discuss world affairs before I've had my first cup of coffee," I said.

It was a half-assed attempt at a joke, but the heavy girl burst out laughing. "You are so right," she said. "My name's Regan, by the way, and this is Sarah." She gestured toward the redhead.

"I'm Kat," I supplied. "Regan," I repeated. "What a cool name. How's that spelled?"

"Thanks!" she beamed. "R-E-G-A-N. Here's the simple way to remember: it's spelled like our former president, but it rhymes with vegan."

"Ronald Reagan spelled his name with an A," I pointed out.

"So do I!" she bubbled. "Remember, R-E-G-*A*-N. It's a traditional Irish name. My parents emigrated here from County Mayo before I was born. Isn't that funny? A whole county named after a condiment."

I was sorry I'd asked.

Sarah gave me a sympathetic look. "She's told me this story at least twenty times."

"So, anyway." Regan giggled. "*Joe Millionaire* or Richard Hatch?"

Sarah looked her dead in the eyes. "I hate to break this to you, but they're both men."

Regan jutted out her lower lip. "So. That doesn't mean I can't model my performance after them."

"What performance are you talking about?" I asked.

"The audition!" Regan replied, with exasperation. Noting my confused expression, she added, "The one starting any minute now. Duh!" She playfully thumped me on the side of the head, hitting me hard.

I rubbed the spot where she'd knocked me. "And here I thought we were trying out for a *reality* show," I said, my voice dripping with sarcasm.

"Well, we are. But the real Regan isn't exciting enough. If I want to get on TV, I need to camp it up a little," she said.

"Regan wants to be America's next sweetheart," Sarah explained.

"Good luck with that one." I guffawed. What I really wanted to say was *fat chance,* though I knew from personal experience how cruel that would be. Most big girls would rather be called a bitch than be called fat. To the overweight, fat is the dirtiest word on the planet.

Regan and Sarah continued to debate the roster of reality show contestants, while I tried my best to tune them out. *Please, oh please, let the interviews start soon,* I prayed. At last the door swung open, and the huffy blonde from the night before poked her head out. "Okay guys, you can come on in."

I glanced down at my watch. It was past 8:20 A.M. They had a lot of nerve making us wait so long, after emphasizing how important it was that we show up for interviews on time. We charged into the hospitality suite, pushing and shoving like a herd of cattle. As I struggled to move through the door, Regan stepped on the heel of my shoe, causing me to stumble and nearly topple over. I shot her a dirty look. I couldn't believe how eager everyone was to get inside.

As soon as I saw the setup, I knew why.

The room had been completely rearranged from the night before. Gone were the desk and buffet tables. A huge white screen was set up against the back wall, and in front of it sat two rows of folding chairs. Wires lined nearly every inch of the floor, connecting with cameras, microphones, and a dozen of the most gigantic lights I had ever seen. An enormous camera sat propped up on a fancy-looking tripod and several guys were standing around shouldering various pieces of equipment.

Everyone went scrambling toward the chairs, dashing forward to find a seat in the front row. I had never seen a group of big girls move so fast.

"All right everyone, before you get too comfortable, I need you to come over here and get miked up," the blonde called, snapping her fingers and pointing toward a table.

We fought our way over to line up next to it. I found myself huddled near the back of the line, right behind Regan. I could hear a man's voice instructing girls how to clip the microphones onto their clothing and run the wire underneath their shirts. I stood up on my tiptoes, straining to see what was going on. It was no use; Regan was blocking my view. I made a mental note not to get stuck sitting behind her during the interview.

When my turn finally came—it felt like a year had passed by the time I reached the front of the line—a lanky guy with pockmarks handed me a wallet-sized black box. The top of the box had a long black cord with a small lapel microphone attached to it.

"Clip this on the back of your pants," he instructed gruffly. "Run this cord under your shirt and put this up here on your collar." He motioned to the tiny black microphone.

I fumbled with the box, trying to attach it to my belt.

"Turn around," he barked. I did, and with a quick movement, he snapped it into place. He handed me the wire. "Real quick, run this up top."

It annoyed me that he was being so impatient. He had allowed the other girls to take plenty of time getting hooked up. Regan, for instance, had required special assistance to get the microphone box attached to the back of her dress.

"Don't turn away from this when you talk," he instructed once I'd finished clipping on the microphone. "Won't pick up nothing if you do."

I pulled the back of my shirt over the microphone box self-consciously. This was beyond surreal. I felt like a news anchor. I couldn't wait to tell Donna all about it.

By the time I got finished, the only seats available were in the back row. It wasn't the ideal position, but I was relieved to see that none of the girls occupying the front seats were particularly large. I quickly skirted over and plopped down next to Sarah.

"Hi, everyone, and welcome to phase two in the casting search for *From Fat to Fabulous*. I'm Gigi Rucker, the assistant producer."

Gigi. So that was the evil blonde's name.

"I'd like to start out by saying, on behalf of everyone involved with the show, how much we appreciate your patience. The next few days are going to be intense, but I want you to all relax and have a fun time!"

"Easy for her to say," Sarah whispered. "She's not the one under the microscope."

I nodded. I was so uptight that "fun" was the last thing I had in mind.

"Before we go any further, I need to lay down a few ground

rules," Gigi continued. "This is very important so I'll need everyone's undivided attention."

I heard a few people groan in the front row, but Gigi silenced them with a stony glare. "We've gone over this before, but it bears repeating. I want to make sure you understand the importance of the confidentiality statements you signed last night." She picked up a copy from the table and waved it around as if to remind us. "There's a lot of jargon in here, but I'm going to hit the highlights. First point—and this is absolutely crucial—what goes on this weekend must be kept confidential."

Gigi paused, scanning the room. Slowly, her eyes locked in on each of us, as if trying to judge our reactions.

"You are *strictly* prohibited from discussing matters of the casting process with *anyone* outside these four walls. That means no going home and dishing to your best girlfriend. No e-mailing Mom to let her know the outcome. Family and friends are bound to ask how it went, and when they do, I want you to look them square in the face and say, 'Uh-uh, my lips are sealed.' Come on everybody, say it with me!"

She waved her arms around, motioning for us to join in. "Uh-uh, my lips are sealed!" Gigi repeated.

"Is this for real?" I mumbled, through gritted teeth.

Sarah threw me a bewildered look. "Sure looks like it," she mouthed.

"Come on, girls, I can't hear you!"

"My lips are sealed. My lips are sealed. My lips are sealed!" we chorused. I felt like a grade-A moron.

"Good job," Gigi said briskly. "It may seem silly, but there's a big risk involved in these kinds of projects. If word leaks to the press it could jeopardize months of hard work."

"So, then, is it not okay to talk to the news?" Regan asked. "Like, if my local paper wants to do a feature on me would that be okay?"

A few people teetered on the brink of laughter. I couldn't blame them; it was a pretty foolish thing to ask.

"I thought we were beyond these kinds of questions, but apparently not. Look on page three," Gigi instructed, not bothering to hide her annoyance. "You cannot talk to the media without express written permission from the producers of *From Fat to Fabulous*. If you start getting calls from news outlets—which, believe me, you will—do not allow yourself to be engaged in any conversation. Don't bother explaining your situation to them. If you give those vultures even the slightest response, they're going to run with it, take your words out of context. 'No comment' is your safest bet."

"I'm sorry," Regan murmured, "I didn't know."

Gigi nodded. "These are legal documents, guys, so I can't tell you how important it is that you follow our instructions. Failure to comply could result in, at best, your automatic removal from the show. At worst, you could find yourself saddled with a *very* pricey lawsuit."

I looked around the room. Up to this point, I had shared everything with Donna, filling her in bit by bit on the process. It would be next to impossible to suddenly shut her out!

"In order for the show to go off without a hitch, we have to ensure the utmost secrecy," Gigi explained. "Which brings me to point two. While it is perfectly fine for you all to socialize this weekend—in fact, we prefer it if you do—you'll need to keep certain personal details private. It's fine to discuss your likes and interests and your experiences with your weight." She paused, smiling brightly. I imagined Gigi felt pretty superior, being the lone thin girl in a room of fatsos. "Do not reveal your last name, no state of residence, or your occupation. No exchanging e-mails, phone numbers, or personal website addresses. Are we clear on that?"

We told her that we were. Several girls looked so petrified I imagined they might have already blown it.

"Good. If you break the rules, you're off the show. It's as simple as that."

I couldn't help wondering what the big deal was. What did it matter if I knew Regan's or Sarah's last names, or if they knew mine? What were the producers afraid might happen?

"Now, for the fun part. As you may know, we narrowed the applicant pool through a series of phone interviews," Gigi continued. "Some of you spoke with me, and some of you spoke with Zaidee Panola, our exec producer. Zaidee will be coming out here to talk with you . . ." Gigi glanced at her watch. "Any minute."

"I wonder if anyone told Zaidee that promptness is a virtue," Sarah whispered.

"Before she gets here, let me give you a little background on Zaidee."

I wasn't particularly interested in hearing Zaidee's life story. I was itching to get this interview out of the way.

"Zaidee is a very hands-on producer, she likes to be involved in every single aspect of the process. And I respect her immensely for that," Gigi said. "This is truly her baby. Without Zaidee, there would be no *From Fat to Fabulous*. She created it and she secured the funding that makes it possible for you lovely ladies to be here today."

"Good grief, what is this? A&E *Biography*?" Sarah hissed.

"Zaidee comes from a heavy writing background. In addition to authoring half a dozen movie-of-the-week scripts, Zaidee worked in daytime television as a screenwriter for fourteen years. Prior to executive producing *From Fat to Fabulous,* she worked on many popular soap operas, including *Days of Our Lives* and *All My Children*."

Someone in the front row gasped. "Does she know Erica Kane?"

"In a manner of speaking, yes," Gigi said, smiling.

"Does she ever mentor novice writers?" I called out. "You know, give them advice about their careers and stuff?"

"Zaidee has helped a number of—"

"What about Sami Brady?" the girl in the front interjected before Gigi could finish answering.

"Yeah, she knows Sami, too." Gigi smiled wryly.

Who cared about some stupid character from a soap opera? I was on the verge of getting a very important question answered! I opened my mouth to speak again when a slender, auburn-haired woman came bursting into the hospitality suite.

"Sorry I'm late, gals. Traffic was a beast. The freeway was clogged for miles."

Zaidee Panola.

I knew it right away. Even without the benefit of a formal introduction, it was impossible not to know who she was. She was dressed in a gorgeous black pantsuit, and carried an expensive-looking leather briefcase. I watched the way the crew submitted to her; one man appeared at her elbow with a bottled water while another pulled forward a chair in case she wanted to sit down.

"Thanks, boys," she said, before turning her attention to us. "You must be my lovely contestants! I'm Zaidee." She moved through the crowd shaking each of our hands. "Now, before we get started, do any of you have any questions you'd like to ask me?"

"Nice outfit," Sarah called. "Where did you get it?"

Zaidee grinned, flashing a mouth of perfect white teeth. "This old thing?" She twirled around. "It's a Ralph Lauren, from last year's collection. But, shhh, don't tell anybody."

We giggled. She had a real way of putting people at ease.

"All right, now that we've gotten all the vital fashion questions out of the way, what do you gals say we start with some interviews?" She flipped open her briefcase, retrieving a stack of folders. "Now I know we've dogged you to death with questions, but I have a couple more."

Someone groaned.

"I promise to go easy on you," Zaidee vowed. "This will be smooth sailing. Not painful at all . . ."

* * *

"I didn't expect it to be so . . . embarrassing!" I said when we were finished. Sarah and I had parted ways with Regan, who'd gone off to take a nap, and we were heading to the lobby for a drink.

Sarah shrugged. "It's the same stuff they asked on the application and over the phone. What's the difference?"

"I don't know," I told her, punching the elevator button for the lobby. "I guess it's worse in person."

"If you think that was bad, you should see what they ask you for *The Real World*." She shuddered. "My God, every other question is about sex."

I stared at her in surprise. "You tried out for *The Real World*?"

She nodded. "And *Survivor, Extreme Makeover, The Bachelor*. You name it, I've auditioned for it. Hell, I even tried out to be one of the suitors on *The Littlest Groom*! The only one I can't audition for is *American Idol*, and that's because I have no talent."

"But why?"

"I love reality TV," she said simply. "I'm completely addicted to it."

I leaned back against the elevator wall and thought this over. "Do they ever let big people on those shows?" I asked.

"Every once in a while they do. It's not often. I made the finals of *Survivor* and *The Real World*—I got flown out here to audition for both. But none of the other shows ever called me." She grinned. "That's why this is so exciting. Finally, I have a real chance to make the cast! Before, I was always hampered by my body, but this time it's going to work in my favor."

We reached the first floor and walked into the lobby. "So what do you think our chances are?" I asked, as we grabbed two diet Cokes from the drink machine and sat down on one of the couches.

"It's tough to say," Sarah mused. "Making it this far is a pretty big deal. I'd say it's fifty-fifty." She took a giant swig of her drink.

"Really?"

"Think about it. There are twenty-five of us here. They're probably going to pick between ten and fifteen for the show. Odds are, either me, you, or Regan will get picked."

At the mention of Regan's name I made a face. "What's with that girl?" I asked. "She seems kind of ditzy. Really immature."

"Ah, she's not bad," Sarah said. "She's only nineteen, what do you expect?"

I changed the subject. "What do you suppose the producers will base their decision on?"

"God, I couldn't even begin to tell you. If I had the secret formula, I'd have aced my auditions for *Survivor* and *The Real*

World." Her eyes misted over at the thought. "I was so close both times, that's what kills me."

I patted her on the shoulder. "Don't stress it. I bet you'll get *From Fat to Fabulous.* If you play up your previous experience they're bound to pick you."

Sarah shot straight up in her seat, shaking her head vehemently. "Uh-uh. That's the kiss of death. I'm going to play it *down,* if anything. I seriously considered lying on my application. But you can't be too careful. It would be my luck that one of the crew here would recognize me from a previous reality-show audition."

I eyed her quizzically. "Why is it such a big deal? I mean, I honestly can't see how it would hurt."

She tilted her head back and took another long drink from her diet Coke. "It turns the producers off, that's how. They wonder why all these other shows rejected me, like maybe there's a good reason I've never been selected before. Think of it like this: You wouldn't go in for a job interview at UPS and say, 'Federal Express didn't want me, Airborne Express didn't want me, but I'm hoping you guys will!' "

She had a point. "Why do you think they interviewed us in a group?" I asked, shifting subjects. "They're so hell-bent on secrecy I'm shocked they even allow us in the same room."

"It helps them see how we respond in social settings," Sarah informed me. "They don't want to get saddled with some giant wallflower. The individual stuff tonight and tomorrow, that's what I'm looking forward to. That's where you really get the chance to shine, to show them how hungry you are for it."

We both smirked. "No pun intended," she added.

8

A Walking Ad for Prozac

When Gigi informed me we'd be getting medical exams I had imagined a huge group of big girls in wispy paper gowns lined up against a wall. When the itinerary revealed the location hadn't yet been decided I imagined them parading us out into the hallway and examining us there.

Or taking us to the lobby.

So when one of the crew members of *From Fat to Fabulous* came through the dining room at lunchtime passing out information about the doctor's visits, it was all I could do to keep my food down.

"Can you believe they're forcing us to get a medical exam?" Regan asked nervously.

Regan, Sarah, and I had snagged seats close to the buffet table and were hurriedly scarfing down burgers, pizza, and fries. I nodded sympathetically. I could only imagine the flack a girl like Regan must get from doctors. The first thing I always hear from a doctor is, "We've got to do something about your weight."

The last thing I hear when I walk out of their office is, "Next time you're in I want to see less of you." The first time I saw that my internist, Dr. Irwin, had written *treating for obesity* on my medical chart I nearly cried. Okay, forget the nearly. I *did* cry. What he wrote shouldn't have shocked me—I know he was just doing his job—but it did. It's not that I don't know I'm fat. And, lest I ever forget, there are plenty of people—even total strangers—who are more than willing to remind me. I sure don't need to hear it from a doctor. And I especially don't need their empty promises.

Three different times, in fact, I have visited doctors who professed to know how to "treat" my weight problem. One prescribed pills, which, after reading the side effects (bowel incontinence), I decided not to take. I'd rather be 227 pounds than have to wear an adult diaper. Another doctor touted gastric bypass surgery. "There are some risks involved, including bleeding ulcerations and incessant vomiting," he told me. "But I can't overemphasize how rare those are. Overall, it is a very positive procedure. I've seen patients who couldn't walk because they were so large get their lives back."

"I walk just fine," I said. "But thanks, anyway."

But the worst was Dr. Irwin. He really had me psyched to get thin.

"We're going to knock this weight off you, Kat," he told me the first time we met. "And we're going to do it the right way, without surgery or dangerous medications."

He checked my thyroid, my blood sugar, my kidneys, my gallbladder, and a whole bunch of other things. His nurse took seven vials of blood from me. The spot on the crook of my elbow where she pricked me was a sickly green for days.

"If it's an underactive thyroid we'll have you sorted out in no time," Dr. Irwin assured me. "Thyroid medicine makes you lose weight like you wouldn't believe."

He sounded so assured that he'd figured out the problem, and was halfway to solving it. I was overjoyed. Finally, my prayers were being answered! I went around on cloud nine for days, anticipating the miracle thyroid medicine that was going to "sort me out."

The day the test results came in was devastating. Dr. Irwin found nothing, and believe me, he checked everything. Even weird stuff like my BUN/Creat ratio. But nope, all levels were normal. Usually, this would have been great news. But I took it like a death sentence. My easy fix had evaporated into thin air.

I kept on going to Dr. Irwin after that, but I never quite trusted him again.

Sarah interrupted my thoughts. "They do medical exams at all the reality-show auditions. The producers don't want to bring on anybody who's likely to get sick or hurt. That's a lawsuit waiting to happen." She popped a few French fries into her mouth. "I'm actually relieved about this one. At least I'm not the only overweight person."

We finished eating and got up from the table. We'd been divided into groups for our medical exams but, unfortunately, this time neither Sarah nor Regan was in the same one as me. I waved good-bye and went back to my room to freshen up.

My doctor's appointment was scheduled for 2:00 P.M., which gave me just enough time to shower and change. The medical exams were being held on the seventh floor. I had assumed they would take place in a suite or a meeting area, but the location turned out to be a regular double room like mine.

At least it wasn't the lobby.

The doctor, a young, smiling woman in a white coat that read *Dr. Sloane,* greeted me at the door. "Kat?" she asked tentatively.

I nodded and she held the door open and motioned me inside. A nurse stood by a table with various vials on it. Two other girls were perched nervously on one of the beds. A few minutes later, a third arrived.

"Now that we're all here, do any of you have questions about what we're going to be doing today?"

I raised my hand. "I have a lot of questions. Nobody has told me *anything.*"

She briefly detailed the procedure. "I'm going to do a routine physical. Listen to your heart, check your blood pressure, breathing capacity, and so on. We'll also take urine, blood, and a small hair sample from the base of your neck. Nothing invasive. Nothing to get too upset over. You girls look like you've been paid a visit by the grim reaper."

I looked around at the other contestants. They were ghostly pale. They'd likely had to endure the same "fat girl" speeches from doctors that I had. Luckily, Dr. Sloane seemed okay. Even if she did weigh us and make us change into the dreaded paper gowns.

She finished around 3:00 P.M. and turned us loose.

"Thanks, girls," she said. "I appreciate your patience."

* * *

As soon as I got back to my room I picked up the phone and dialed Donna's cell.

It was after 5 P.M. in Memphis, which meant my package had been delivered. The moment of truth had arrived! My fingers were shaking so badly I goofed up twice and had to start over. Finally, I managed to get the number right. I listened to it ring.

When she answered, I would ask her to open the package and tell me what was inside. I knew I should wait until I got home on Monday—that was what Nick would have preferred—but I couldn't. That was two whole days away. I needed to know NOW!

Donna picked up on the second ring.

"Is it platinum or gold?" I shouted into the phone.

"Is what platinum or gold?" Donna asked.

I hated it when she toyed with me like this. "My engagement ring!" I yelled.

"Oh, yeah, the package."

The tone of her voice was not promising.

"What happened?" I asked, my heart sinking.

"It's not so much *what* happened. It's who," she told me. "Your landlord wouldn't give it to me. He said it was a federal offense to read other people's mail."

All the energy drained out of my body and I toppled backward onto the bed. I felt like a deflated balloon. "You're kidding me."

" 'Fraid not. He said he couldn't release your mail to anyone but you."

"That bastard!"

"He isn't the friendliest man," she agreed. "But I do see his point. Anyone could say they're a friend of yours. He'd have no way of knowing. And like you said, this package is expensive. I'm sorry, Kat, I tried."

"I know you did. Thanks."

"I did see it sitting on the table, though," she said thoughtfully. "At least, I *think* I did. I couldn't get close enough to read the name. But it was a giant FedEx box, like the kind you'd use to ship a TV. Do you know if Nick sent it FedEx?"

I strained to remember. "I'm not sure, but I know he picked

the delivery time, so probably. But that can't have been my package," I said, shaking my head. "An engagement ring would come in a small box."

I heard Donna groan.

"Don't say it," I warned her. I hoped she'd listen, but she didn't.

"I hate to go here again, but I can't help myself. I'm your friend and this is disturbing on so many levels. First off, Kat, I had no idea you were so eager to get married."

I'm not. I'm eager to be engaged, to walk around flashing a diamond ring. Eager to have my life settled.

"And second off," Donna continued. "Do you really want an engagement ring from a *total stranger*?"

"Nick's not a total stranger!" I protested.

"Until you meet him, he's a total stranger," she argued. "And if he sends you an engagement ring—*in the mail*—he's a total stranger who's lost his mind."

"Let's change the subject."

"Okay," she obliged, her tone lightening. "How did it go today? I assume you're finished with your interviews if you're calling me."

I kicked off my shoes and rolled over to the far corner of the bed. "Not exactly," I said. "Or maybe a better way to put it would be, I'm not sure."

"Huh?"

I explained we were "on call" all day, uncertain of when—and if—we'd be summoned upstairs for another round of interrogations. I was about to launch into a tirade about Gigi and her attitude when I recalled what she'd said. *My lips are sealed.* I wasn't supposed to be talking about any of this! I surveyed the hotel room suspiciously, rifling through the nightstand and peering under the bed. I don't know what I expected to find. A hidden camera, a stashed tape recorder? If they really wanted to bug my room they'd have used something minuscule and undetectable. "I'd better not talk about this," I said. "My lips are sealed," I threw in for Gigi's benefit. If someone on the staff of *From Fat to Fabulous* was listening, I wanted to show I'd heeded their advice.

"Uh, okay," Donna said. "I didn't realize this subject was off-limits, too."

"No, it's not. I mean, it is!" I scrambled, struggling for the right words. "Legal reasons," I finally said, dropping my voice to a whisper.

"Why are you talking so low?" Donna asked, mimicking my tone.

"The room might be bugged!" I hissed. "I don't want anyone to overhear what I'm saying."

"Kat, you're too much. If there were bugs in your room, trust me, they'd be able to pick up whispering. And anyway, why in the hell are you worried about bugs?"

"We signed confidentiality agreements," I said, still keeping my voice low. You can never be too careful. "If we tell anyone from home what's going on out here, we could get disqualified . . ." I paused, dramatically. "Or even sued!"

"That doesn't surprise me. But I wouldn't worry too much about it."

"You don't know what these people are like," I insisted.

"Kat, will you please talk in your normal voice!" Donna said.

"Uh-uh," I whispered. "Bugs."

"If the producers were going to do anything, they'd tap your phone, not bug your room. They'd be concerned about your calling people at home and spilling secrets," Donna lectured. "Use your brain here."

I winced. Donna was being a tad harsh.

"And anyway," she added, "there are privacy laws protecting us from that kind of thing. We don't live in a police state."

There was a knock at the door.

"Kat," a voice called out. "You in there?"

"Donna, I gotta go," I hissed.

Slamming down the phone and leaping off the bed, I ran across the room. I prayed Gigi wasn't on the other side of the door, come to send me packing. I brought my eye up to the peephole. When I saw who it was, I breathed a tremendous sigh of relief.

"Hi Regan," I said, swinging the door open so she could step inside. I was surprised to find her standing there—she'd never asked my room number, or even what floor I was staying on. "What's up?"

"That Gigi woman has been trying to call you for half an hour but your line's been busy," she said. "She sent me down here to get you."

Uh-oh. My pulse quickened. "Do you know what she wants?" I asked, trying to sound casual. "Nothing bad, I hope," I added.

"No, it's good!" Regan beamed. "She wants to do an individual interview!"

"Today?" I asked, surprised. "I thought those weren't 'til Sunday?"

"Most of them aren't, but they're doing a couple this afternoon. I finished mine a few minutes ago." She bounced up and down on her heels. "It went fantastic. I really sensed a connection between me and Zaidee. I'm so excited, Kat! We must be their favorites if they asked to interview us again so soon!"

"I hope you're right," I told her, scrambling to the mirror and pulling a brush through my hair. "Just give me a minute to get ready." Secretly, I was worried. What if Regan was wrong?

What if the reason they wanted to see us so soon was because we were on the chopping block? The more I thought about it, the more concerned I got. I grabbed my makeup bag off the dresser and began fishing around for eyeliner and base. This might be my last chance to impress them. I owed it to myself to pull out all the stops.

"Hurry up," Regan said. "You don't want to keep them waiting any longer." She smiled broadly. "I'm one of the top finalists, I just know I am! I have to keep pinching myself to believe it's true."

"Regan," I began, pausing midstream to apply some pink lip gloss, "how can you be so certain?"

"Zaidee *herself* told me I did a spectacular job. She's the one who makes all the decisions."

On our way out the door, I asked her, "Have they scheduled your interview time for tomorrow?"

"No. They have to talk over some things first." Regan stopped, instantly looking worried. "I'm *positive* she'll call."

* * *

I squirmed around anxiously in a metallic folding chair that had been placed directly across from Zaidee. She was flanked by Gigi and three men who were assistant producers. I tapped my feet, waiting for them to start. They were flipping through notebooks and files, whispering among themselves.

"Jimmie, I want a tight close-up on Kat's face for the duration of the interview. Don't pan out unless I instruct you to."

A tall, dark-skinned man ambled over and started fooling around with a large camera that was fastened onto a tripod. "One sec," he called. "Give me a minute to frame the shot."

Once the camera was rolling, the producers took turns going down the line asking me questions.

"What is your primary reason for wanting to be on *From Fat to Fabulous?*" Zaidee began.

"To get a smaller body and a bigger wallet," I quipped.

"What is your secondary reason?"

"To change my life. I've lived the same dull existence for twenty-seven years. I'm ready for the next phase to begin," I blurted, surprising even myself.

"What do you see happening in that 'next phase'?" Gigi asked.

The truth of the matter was I saw myself getting skinny, becoming a world-famous novelist, and being Mrs. Nicholas J. Appleby. But I couldn't exactly tell them that. "Being thin has been a lifelong dream of mine," I said simply. "It's almost as though, once I become skinny, everything up until that point will no longer matter. My life will truly begin." Even as I said the words, I knew I didn't fully mean them. There were things I loved—my friends, my family, my sense of humor—but my weight always seemed to dampen them.

"How badly do you want to lose weight?" one of the men questioned. I thought it was kind of like asking, "How badly do you want to win the lottery?"

I decided to take a blunt approach. "I'd do anything on this earth to have a flat stomach." I wasn't lying. Given the choice between a flat stomach and, well pretty much anything else, I'd pick a flat stomach. Forget a first-class trip around the world, or a Porsche, or even a million bucks. None of them could compare.

"Other than meeting the physical requirements, why do you feel you'd make a good candidate for *From Fat to Fabulous?*" Zaidee asked. "What qualities will you bring to the show?"

I told her I was fun-loving, energetic, and ready for anything. "Good or bad, there'll never be a dull moment if I'm around!" I shouted. I hoped my voice oozed enthusiasm and self-confidence. They stared at me like I'd blown a fuse.

"What celebrity are you most like and why?"

I swallowed hard. "As much as I'd love to say Reese Witherspoon or someone else really gorgeous, I've gotta go with Roseanne Arnold."

You could have heard a pin drop.

"Roseanne?" Zaidee repeated. "That's not exactly a flattering comparison. Care to tell us why?"

No, not really, I thought. "Back in high school, kids used to make fun of me by saying I was her long-lost daughter." I cringed, sinking down into my chair. It wasn't one of my fondest memories.

"Were they referring to your physical appearance or your personality—or both?" Zaidee prodded.

"Physical appearance, definitely. On the inside I'm nothing like her at all. Of course, Roseanne and I look nothing alike, except for the fact that we're both big. But you know how people are. Fat is fat. They don't see much beyond that."

"Could you elaborate on what you mean?" Gigi asked, jotting something down in her notebook.

I let out an exasperated sigh. This wasn't rocket science. I didn't see why I had to spell out every little thing for them. "When most of the world looks at an overweight girl like me they don't see that I'm a kind person, or a loyal friend, or a good listener." I paused, feeling my throat clench up. "To them, I'm just a fat girl. Plain and simple. Everything about my identity is wrapped up in being overweight. It's like I'm stuck in this horrible shell of a body and try as I might, I can't get out from under it." Tears spilled over from my eyes and began their descent down my cheeks. In all honesty, I hadn't meant to cry. It wasn't a ploy for sympathy or even an attempt to make myself seem more "real." It just happened.

Zaidee snapped her fingers and one of the crew members came running over with a box of tissues. I wondered if that was his job, to sit there all day armed with Kleenex in case some contestant broke down.

I had hoped the tears would be temporary, but I felt myself reaching the point of no return. The stress I'd been feeling over the last few days, combined with my lack of sleep, caused the tears to come bubbling out of me with frightening speed. No matter what I did, I was powerless to stop them.

Laying my head down in my hands, I let loose.

Suddenly, I was eighteen years old again, attending my first and last session with a weight-loss counselor. I'd been told then, point-blank, that I was a bad candidate for a diet program. "You're too closed-minded," the counselor had said with more than a hint of irritation. "You use your weight to put distance between you and other people. As long as being large serves you, you won't slim down." I had wept then, too, and just like now, the counselor had plied me with Kleenex.

"I didn't mean . . ." I blubbered, losing my train of thought. "Sorry, I'm just upset." I hiccupped, pulling a wad of tissues from the box and wiping them across my face. If I hadn't done so already, I'd truly blown my chances now. There was no way Zaidee and company would want me after this pitiful display.

I was like a walking ad for Prozac.

"Don't apologize, Kat," Zaidee told me. She bit her lower lip and eyed me sympathetically. "You're not the first person to break down, and you won't be the last. These interviews have their tough moments."

Zaidee turned and shared a few whispered remarks with her fellow interviewers.

Here it comes. She's getting ready to let me down easy, I thought. Tell me thanks, but no thanks.

"I think we're pretty much finished for today," Zaidee said finally. She fixed me with a big smile. "We'll see you back here tomorrow morning at 10 A.M."

* * *

The following day, Sarah caught up with me outside the hospitality suite. I had just finished sailing through my midmorning interview—there were no tears this time around—when she came rushing up to me.

"You want to grab some lunch and then go to the Getty?" she asked, falling into step beside me. "There's a shuttle leaving every fifteen minutes or so that takes you right up to it. Or, if art's not your thing, we could check out the Beverly Center. I hear they've got some great shops out there—Dolce and Gabbana, DKNY, Armani. Not that I can afford any of that stuff, much less fit into it. But it's always fun to look."

I stared at her. "We can't leave."

"Yeah, I know they're about to serve lunch but, truthfully, I'd rather go out and eat somewhere. Even though that means spending my own money. It's our last day in Los Angeles. I'd like to see something of the city other than the inside of this hotel. You know I've been here three times, and all I've seen are hotels and airports?"

I opened my mouth to interject, but she kept going. "Maybe we could try Spago or the Cheesecake Factory? We could get a cab over. I know it's expensive, but I think it'd be worth it."

"There's not enough time," I finally managed to cut in. "Zaidee wants me back in the hospitality suite at one-thirty."

"Why would she want you back here? They've given us the afternoon off to go sight-seeing and relax . . ." Her voice trailed off. "Oh, I get it."

"Hey, I'm sure it's not what you think—" I put my hand on her shoulder.

"No, it's exactly what I think. I've been through this before, remember?" Her lower lip was quivering. I wondered where the Kleenex guy was when you really needed him.

"You can't read anything into it," I said, knowing full well that if the situation were reversed I'd be devastated. "Maybe they've already made up their mind to pick you?"

"That's not how it works," Sarah said.

I opened my mouth to protest but she cut me off.

"Well, I've gotta be going if I'm going to make the shuttle." Her shoulders slumped as she headed off toward the elevator.

* * *

I had just returned to my room and was preparing to pack my bag—the red-eye flight left at 1:40 A.M., but I had to be checked out of my room by midafternoon—when Gigi called me.

"Is this Kat?" she demanded as soon as I'd picked up.

"Yes." Who else would be answering my phone?

"Kat, how would you feel about taking the red-eye out on Tuesday instead of tonight?"

"Tuesday!" I exclaimed. She had thrown me for a total loop. "I have to be at work at eight o'clock tomorrow morning."

"The decision's yours, but I'd strongly advise you to stay the extra two days. There's a lot riding on this weekend. I'm giving it to you loud and clear—whether you stay or not will have a *big* impact on whether you're cast or not. Follow?"

With a comment like that, how could I refuse? I closed my eyes and took a deep breath. "Okay," I said. "Change my ticket. I'll stay."

Gigi hung up without saying good-bye. I unzipped my suitcase and began unpacking the items I'd put in it only moments ago. Since I hadn't planned on being in Los Angeles for this amount of time, I didn't have nearly enough clothes. Socks and underwear—two things that I refused to re-wear without washing—were at a premium. I was just about to call downstairs and see if the hotel had a laundry service when I remembered.

Richard Geddlefinger!

The big presentation with Mercer and Sons Funeral Home was on Wednesday. Even on down days, Richard frowned upon employees calling in sick. There was no way he'd let me skip work—right before the presentation, to boot—unless I had a doctor's note to back it up. On the other hand, if the circumstances were extenuating . . .

There's a saying I've heard Donna repeat many times over the years. "If you're going to lie, make it an *outrageous* lie." According to her logic, the bigger the whopper, the better. "No one will believe you'd have the nerve to make up such a ridiculous thing." Crossing my fingers for good luck, I dialed Richard's office line. After four rings, voice mail answered. I'd been counting on that. The Caller ID at Hood & Geddlefinger only shows the number while it's ringing, it doesn't store them once you've hung up.

"Richard," I began. "I've got to fly out to Denver right away to be with my parents. My father's been in a bizarre, freak accident."

9

"The Starbucks of the Funeral Home Industry!"

"We've gotta see how you respond in front of the cameras," Zaidee stated. "We have to know if you're able to relax and be yourself, or if you freeze up."

The last two days of the casting weekend started at seven in the morning and ended somewhere around midnight. Among other things, I had a three-hour psychological exam with an eating disorders specialist, then was given a list of "errands" to run. These ranged from browsing in a grocery store for an hour, to walking through the gardens of the Getty Center Museum, to eating at the McDonald's on Hollywood Boulevard. I was chauffeured from location to location in a minivan, trailed by a cameraman and an audio technician.

It was a bizarre experience.

Even more indescribable was the reaction I got from total strangers.

No matter where I went, I instantly became the center of attention. A group of Japanese tourists pointed and waved as I strolled through the stunning gardens of the Getty (Zaidee hadn't gotten clearance to film inside the museum, so I didn't see any of the artwork). They followed me around, snapping pictures and filming me with their camcorders.

Twice, I got asked for my autograph.

The first time, a young boy tentatively approached while I was eating at McDonald's. The second incident took place at the grocery store. A group of giggling teenage girls tailed me for a few minutes before finally cornering me in the dairy aisle. "Um, excuse me, but could I have your autograph?" With trembling fingers, one of them thrust a Chinese take-out menu into my hands, pointing to a small spot in the corner where there was a patch of white space.

"Sure," I said, fishing into my purse and retrieving a pen. I scribbled *Best wishes, Katrina Larson* across the bottom of the menu, and then passed it back to her.

"Thank you!" she gushed. "Thank you! Thank you!"

"Do you know who I am?"

They all stared at me blankly. "Kind of," said the girl who'd given me the menu.

"We've seen you in a bunch of stuff, but we can't remember your name," chimed in another one.

"You know," I said, deciding to come clean, "I'm actually not anybody important. I'm sorry to disappoint you."

They broke into nervous laughter. "Oh, whatever," the menu girl said, rolling her eyes heavenward. She cocked her head to the side, nodding toward the cameraman. "You're *famous*."

* * *

On Wednesday I dragged my exhausted body into work. I left directly from the airport and got there as quickly as humanly possible—I didn't even stop by my apartment to pick up Nick's surprise—yet I was almost forty-five minutes late. I half expected to find Richard waiting for me at my cubicle, but he wasn't. In fact, all was surprisingly calm in the workroom. This should have tipped me off, but it didn't.

I sat down at my desk and started checking my e-mails.

"Don't forget Kat, you've got a presentation meeting today," Cindy sang out, walking by my desk.

"Yes, I'm aware of that," I snapped.

"Sorry, from the way you're dressed I wasn't sure."

I looked down at my clothes. I was wearing the same light gray T-shirt and pair of black pants I'd worn on the plane. There was a dark spot near the bottom of the shirt where I'd spilled diet Coke during a bumpy portion of the flight. I'd tried my best to scrub it out with hand soap and water, but the stain had set.

I took a deep breath. "How nice of you to say so, Cindy."

"I'm only trying to do you a favor."

I looked up to see Donna sauntering in casually. She was midway to her cubicle when she spied Cindy. "How's life as a brownnoser treating you, Cynthia?"

"No complaints," she remarked, glaring daggers at the two of us. "Though, if I'm not mistaken, Kat is going to have a lot to complain about."

"What the hell is that supposed to mean?" I demanded.

"You'll find out," Cindy said, flashing me a wicked smile.

Just then, Richard popped his head out of his office. "Kat! When did you get here?" he called.

"I walked in the door five minutes ago."

"Well, you'd better get in the conference room. Our meeting

with Mercer and Sons Funeral Home starts in less than five minutes."

"What!" I exclaimed. "I thought we weren't seeing them until this afternoon?"

"It's been rescheduled."

I looked frantically at Donna. "I didn't know," she mouthed.

"Mr. G., I'd be more than happy to sub for Kat if she's not up to it," Cindy volunteered, not missing a beat. "She's been out of town for several days. She needs time to get back into the swing of things."

"I think Kat's more than capable of telling me what she needs," Richard said. I blinked in surprise. I had never heard him defend me before. "Kat, are you ready for today's presentation?"

"I'm ready," I told him, even though I wasn't. I felt nervous all over. "Let me grab a cup of coffee and I'll meet you in there."

* * *

"The toughest selling point about public relations is that we're not a brick and mortar field," Richard said, flipping through PowerPoint screens. "People often get us confused with advertising, but there's a notable difference. In advertising, you see the fruits of your labor in the form of a finished product: a television commercial, a radio ad, a poster. With public relations, we specialize in spreading word of mouth. We're like the proverbial man who isn't there. You can't see us, but you feel our presence."

"Mr. Gobbleberger," Gray Mercer began. His voice was crackly and his skin looked like old leather. He seemed ancient. I couldn't help wondering if he wouldn't need his own services in the very near future. "I don't understand what you're telling me. Please give me something I can relate to. Some kind of an example."

"Geddlefinger," Richard corrected. He smiled good-naturedly. "In my next life I'm coming back as a Smith."

"There's no such thing as a 'next life.' You either go to Heaven or you go below, but you don't come back to earth. The Bible tells us so," Mr. Mercer said. "What are you, some kind of Buddha worshipper?"

Uh-oh, I thought. The meeting had only started and already we were off to a bumpy start.

"Oh, no, I'm a Christian. Chalk it up to a poorly timed joke," Richard backpedaled.

"There's never a good time to joke about the Lord," Mr. Mercer said, scowling.

"You are absolutely right, sir."

As much as I hate to admit it, it was fun watching Richard squirm.

"At Hood and Geddlefinger we work very hard to ensure that all of our clients receive ample coverage in the press, and that the coverage is of a positive nature," Richard continued. "We accomplish this by crafting carefully worded press releases and spending countless hours devising marketing strategies. My associate Kat Larson is going to give you some examples of how public relations can help raise a company's profile. Kat?" He gestured toward me.

"An example?" I repeated in surprise. I hadn't expected him to throw the ball to me so early in the game.

"That's what we pay you for, kiddo."

Gray Mercer turned to face me.

"Okay, well, public relations firms do a lot of things for a lot of different companies," I began, stalling for time. My mind had gone completely blank. Not that I'd had time to prepare a speech in the first place, but I'd had a few things I planned to say. Now I was at a total loss. "We make a product or company known in a roundabout way, through word of mouth and product placements. For example, when you're watching a show like *ER* and you see someone wearing a Gap T-shirt, well, that's public relations."

"I don't watch *ER*," said Mr. Mercer, shaking his head.

"Oh, it's not just *ER*," I explained. "It's lots of shows. We—well not *we* as in H and G Public Relations specifically—but other firms get mentions of products in movies and on television, too. Viewers don't realize they've seen a product plug, but they have."

"Are we talking about subliminal advertising?" Mr. Mercer asked, alarmed. "Because that's what it sounds like to me and I firmly believe that to be illegal."

"No, nothing like that," I assured him. "I'm talking about product *placement*."

"Kat," Richard said sternly, "give this good gentleman an example of something *relevant,* please."

An idea occurred to me. It was so simple, so brilliant, and it was staring me right in the face. I pointed around the table at the paper coffee cups, and burst out, "Starbucks! That's a perfect example."

"Starbucks?" Mr. Mercer repeated. "The coffee store?"

"Yep, that's the one."

"Buzz?" He shook his head slowly. "You've lost me."

"Their advertising is very limited compared with most companies their size. Yet, everyone in the Western Hemisphere has heard of Starbucks. And you know why that is? Two words: word of mouth. Well, actually, that's three words," I fumbled. "But what I meant to say was *public relations*. Starbucks has an excellent public relations team that makes sure their name and product is out there. And that, Mr. Mercer, is what we would like to do for you." His face was the picture of confusion, so I added, "When people want a strong cup of coffee, the first place they think of is Starbucks. By the time Hood and Geddlefinger Public Relations is finished, Mercer and Sons will the Starbucks of the funeral home industry!"

* * *

"Give me one good reason why I shouldn't fire you?" Richard asked, pacing back and forth across the conference room.

He'd started in on me the second Gray Mercer left.

"Richard," I protested. "I did the best I could. How in the hell *do* you drum up good PR for a funeral home? Nobody has good connotations when it comes to funerals. It's a losing battle."

"You told Gray Mercer he needed product placement on *ER,* for God's sake!"

"Actually, those weren't my *exact* words," I pointed out. "But now that you mention it, *ER* would be a good place to promote a funeral home. Assuming we—"

"KAT!" he bellowed. "Will you stop babbling for one second and think about what you've done? You went into a client meeting and completely fouled up the pitch with bizarre, off-the-wall analogies. The Starbucks of funeral homes? What the hell were you thinking?"

He began massaging his forehead with his hand. "It's obvious you were grossly unprepared. Do you have anything at all to say for yourself?"

I grimaced. I had nothing to say for myself. And the worst part was, he was right. There was only one card left to play. "Richard, I have a confession to make. I wasn't in Denver this weekend," I said, drawing in a deep breath. "I was in Los Angeles auditioning for a new reality show. And while it is by no means certain that I will be cast, my chances are pretty good."

He stood there, his mouth agape. I waited for a few seconds to see if he would actually pull it together and say anything. When he didn't, I pressed on. "Before you fire me for lying to you, hear me out. If I get cast on this program, it may very well be the biggest thing to ever happen to Hood and Geddlefinger. It will be the ultimate product placement—*me*. By the time I'm through talking up your company, everyone this side of the Mississippi will want H and G representing them."

Richard's mouth closed, and then he smiled.

* * *

It had been five long, torturous days since the mystery package arrived.

The minute I got home I made a mad dash to my landlord's apartment. He grudgingly retrieved the FedEx box—the same large one Donna had described seeing Saturday—and advised me to have the post office hold my mail next time I was planning to be gone for so long.

His attitude didn't dampen my spirits. I was on cloud nine: not only had I managed to save my job, I'd even convinced Richard to give me a full four months of leave—unpaid, of course—if I made the cast. And now I had my present. That was all that mattered.

I didn't want to open it in public, so I ran the length of the apartment complex in about two seconds flat. Despite its large size, the box was light as a feather. How clever of Nick to disguise a small box with a big one! The instant I stepped into my apartment I ripped the box open.

Nick had sent me a dress.

Not an engagement ring.

A beautiful, stunning, red Gucci dress. Size four.

It was designed to fit a supermodel. Aside from being nearly see-through, the dress had a scoop-neck front that almost showed your belly button and the back was practically nonexistent. No matter how much weight I lost I'd never be able to wear it. It was cut to reveal a perfect body—there was no room for flaws. It looked like the kind of outfit a starlet would don for the Academy Awards.

I stared at that dumb Gucci dress for so long I was afraid I might go blind, my eyesight scarred by a sea of vibrant red. I felt like I'd been sucker punched.

Nick had also included the latest issue of *Status,* complete with the much-maligned Johnny Depp cover story, which had squeezed his section. Numbly, I flipped through it until I found Nick's articles. He didn't have much, but there was a short piece entitled "Gucci: The Favourite Comes Home Again."

The phone was ringing. I looked at the Caller ID. It was Donna. I let the machine get it. She'd only say "I told you so."

I wandered into the kitchen and twisted the cap off a bottle of whiskey. I got out my Snoopy shot glass—the only one I own—and filled it to the brim. Then I tilted my head back and downed it in one gulp. I felt like a bad Tennessee cliché. I had never much cared for hard liquor; the bottle had been a Christmas gift from Donna. Tonight, it was precisely what the doctor ordered. I needed all the (Southern) comfort I could get.

I had settled down on the couch with my bottle of whiskey and shot glass when Nick called.

And called.

He let it ring until the machine got it, then he hung up and tried again. Couldn't he take a hint? Besides, it was after midnight in England. What was he still doing up? It was a remarkable case of bad timing, but he seemed determined to get through to me.

On the fifth try, I finally succumbed.

"Hello," I mumbled.

"Kat!" he cried, sounding elated. "Where on earth have you been? I've ringing your place since Monday with no answer. I've been worried sick about you!"

"Sorry. I stayed out in . . . Denver," I said, catching myself right before I slipped, "for a few extra days."

"You could have sent me an e-mail or phoned to let me know. I've been going out of my mind!"

"I'm sorry," I said flatly. I couldn't muster up much energy. The whole thing was too depressing for words.

"Have you opened the surprise?" he asked excitedly.

I briefly debated telling him it had gotten lost in the mail or that my landlord had "misplaced it" but decided that was too cruel. "I haven't opened it, no," I lied.

"Well, what are you waiting for? Go on, open it!"

"Well, okay, if you insist . . ."

"I do," he said firmly.

I fumbled around on the ground for the box. Loudly, I ripped it in half and jostled it around. "Oh!" I feigned excitement. "It's so beautiful."

"Don't you like it?" he demanded.

"Gosh, Nick, I *love* it. I love it so much I'm speechless."

"Oh, Kat, I'm so pleased," Nick said. I could almost feel him beaming at me through the phone. "Did you get the magazine, too?"

"Yes, I did."

"So, have you tried it on yet?"

"The magazine?"

"No, the dress! Kat, what's going on with you tonight?"

"Jet lag," I said.

"From Denver? It's not that far, is it?"

"Uh, my weekend was tiring, sorry."

"So, about the dress . . . I bet you'll look stunning in it. Positively stunning. What do you think of the color?"

"Red? I love red."

"It's not *red*. It's watermelon pink. Red," he scoffed, "is for the working class."

I wasn't exactly sure what he meant, and I didn't want to ask. Considering both of us had jobs (even though Nick's family is so rich he has no need for one), weren't we a part of the working class?

"I wasn't sure on the sizing. Your clothes are cut differently in America than in Britain."

Without meaning to, he had given me the perfect opening. Right then and there I could have told him the truth—or at least some watered-down version of it. I could have said "the dress is gorgeous, but I think it's a few sizes too small" or "I've put on some weight lately so it won't fit. But by the time you meet me it will!" Not exactly honest, but not an outright lie. And there'd have been nothing shameful in admitting that. The dress was tiny, and the cut would be unflattering on 95 percent of the population. Even Donna—who *actually* wears a size four—would have had trouble squeezing into it.

Instead, I said: "It'll fit like a glove."

I dug my own grave.

"*Ahhh,*" Nick moaned. "Like a glove. My God, that's so erotic.

I've been picturing you in that dress for days now, imagining how your gorgeous little body would fill out every curve. I'd give anything to see you in it."

I imagined myself struggling into the dumb dress—which was just about the right size to fit one of my arms—and snapping a picture. He'd be in for a real shock then.

"Talking to you is such a turn-on," he whispered.

I knew where this was headed.

"I'm getting so excited imagining your soft little body filling out every inch of the material. . . ."

He had no idea how close he was to the truth.

"I'd give anything to kiss you right now," he said softly. "I'd run my mouth over your body, taste every inch of your skin."

I was becoming aroused despite myself. I loved it when he talked to me this way. On some level, phone sex with Nick was more satisfying than any real sex I'd ever had.

"Go on," I urged. "What would you do if you were here?"

"I'd do everything," he promised. "I'd spend hours pleasing you, Kat. I'd kiss you so passionately and gently. I'd run my hands over your entire body, run my tongue along your neck."

I could hear his breathing spike and I knew what he was doing.

"That would feel so amazing." I breathed. I had never been so free with anyone before, so open about my body and my desires. I hadn't even considered myself a sexual person until I met Nick. I let my body give in to the sensations.

I slid my hand down my stomach, moving it underneath my pants.

"I'm going to make love to you so softly and passionately," Nick whispered. "I'm a gentle lover. . . ."

10

Things Like This Never Happen to Me

I was sitting on my couch, feasting on reduced-fat Oreos and watching a B-rate chick flick when the phone rang. Caller ID said "out of area." Nervously I picked up the receiver.

"Hi Kat, Zaidee here," she said.

My heart started pounding. "Hello," I squeaked. I jumped up, frantically muting the volume on the TV.

"You doin' well these days, Kat?" Zaidee asked, sounding tired. "How's life treating you in the Bluff City?"

"I'm fine and it's fine," I said, wondering where she'd learned Memphis's nickname. "How about you?"

"I'm worn-out. Thanks for asking, doll."

Zaidee was not her usual breezy self. She was cautious, reserved almost.

This terrified me. I took it as a bad sign. In some ways it is easier to cope when you lose a race by a landslide, than when you come in second place. We sat in silence for what felt like hours, but was probably closer to ten seconds. I was aware of everything—the static of the cordless phone, the buzz of traffic outside my window, Zaidee's breathing. It all seemed to move in slow motion. I debated asking her right out if I'd made it, but I wanted to savor the last few seconds of hopefulness before she crushed my dream.

"Kat," Zaidee began, "are you sitting down?"

"No, I'm standing."

"Well, I think you'd better sit."

"I'm too keyed up to sit," I told her, my heart thumping in my throat. "I'll make you a compromise. I'll lean." True to my word, I propped my body against the living room wall. "Okay, I'm leaning against the wall. Hit me with it."

"You're in."

She spoke so fast, it almost sounded like she'd said "urine."

"OH MY GOD!" I screamed. "SHIT!" I spent the next minute alternating between spewing profanities and praising God. "I can't believe this is happening," I finally managed. "Things like this *never* happen to me! It's an absolute dream come true. Thank you so much, Zaidee!"

"No, thank *you*, Kat," she said. "You're going to make a wonderful addition to our show. So are you excited about coming on?"

I nodded yes for a few seconds before realizing she couldn't see me. "Yes, I can't wait!" I shouted. I hadn't meant to yell in her ear, but my heart was racing ninety miles an hour.

"Your life will never be the same after this," Zaidee promised. "Consider yourself warned." She let out a small laugh.

I stood there with my mouth gaping open. Then the dizziness started. It washed over my body like a tidal wave and I'm surprised I didn't keel over. It was a full minute before I realized Zaidee was still talking to me.

"Kat? You there?" Zaidee was asking.

I mumbled, "Hey," in a voice barely above a whisper.

"Thank God for that," she said, and then broke up laughing. "I was starting to think you'd collapsed. I was two steps away from dialing nine-one-one."

"No . . . I'm fine, I'm just . . ." My voice trailed off.

"Shocked?" Zaidee finished. "It happens. You'll be fine by the time you get on the plane. Speaking of which, I've got some pertinent information to go over with you. Gigi's in the process of making travel arrangements as we speak. Someone from the crew will meet you at the airport. I don't have the exact flight times yet, but it'll be sometime Sunday morning."

"Sunday!" I gasped. "You don't mean *this* Sunday, do you?"

"The one and only."

"That's two days from now! I can't possibly be ready by then. I haven't even told anyone I'm leaving town. I'll have to come up with some kind of an excuse!"

"It's got to be this Sunday, Kat. We've got a tight production schedule to stick to. Tell everyone you're going out of town to attend a cousin's wedding. I don't care what you say, just so long as you make absolutely no mention of the show. You're contractually bound to that, don't forget."

"Oh, I haven't forgotten," I promised her, thinking about Richard. And Donna. "But won't they find out when they see me on TV?"

"Of course," she said. "We're doing a huge media blitz the last week in May. We're getting wide coverage on you guys." She sounded pleased. "But until that point it absolutely must be kept under wraps."

"Maybe I'll tell everyone I'm going to England," I said finally. "I've got a close friend right outside London."

"Well there you go, then."

And while we were on the subject, I couldn't help but ask, "Zaidee, um, this might sound weird but is there any chance that *From Fat to Fabulous* is going to air in the UK?"

"It would be nice," she said. "I've got to tell you, though; the chances are slim-to-none. Reality show *concepts* are easy to sell overseas but the actual episodes are not. The ending has been spoiled by the time it airs, and the cultural clashes are frequently too big an obstacle. So, to answer your question, the world may one day see a British version of *From Fat to Fabulous* but no, my darling, it probably won't be starring you."

It was just the answer I wanted to hear.

* * *

"I'm counting on you, Donna. Work your magic."

"I'll do the best I can," she told me, folding a few Lane Bryant shirts and tucking them into my suitcase. "But I can't make any promises this will work."

"Just send these e-mails out twice a week, then skim through Nick's replies and add anything you think might be necessary. If he's complaining about *Status* tell him you're sorry to hear things aren't going well at work. That kind of stuff. So they don't seem pre-written," I said, handing her the disk.

"Kat, this is crazy." She shook her head. "For your sake I hope he falls for it."

"Me too. It's the only chance I've got."

I had spent the past day preparing thirty brief e-mails to Nick. Most of them contained short messages. *I'm sorry I can't be with you, I love you so much.* And stuff like *My dad is doing much better. The doctors think he might be getting out of the hospital any day now. Thinking of you lots. Love, Kat.*

It was pathetic and half-assed, but it was the only thing I could come up with on such short notice. I called him the night I talked to Zaidee, waking him up to say good-bye. "I have to go away to Denver for a few weeks, maybe more. My father's not well," I had lied, praying I wouldn't burn in hell for all my dishonesty. "I promise to e-mail you as often as possible. I know it's a lot to ask, but I hope you'll still be here for me when I get back to Memphis."

Nick's response had been one of complete sympathy.

"I'm so sorry to hear about this, Kat," he'd said. "Of course I'll still be there for you," he assured me. "I love you, Kat. Nothing's going to change that."

He'd even requested my parents' address so that he could send flowers. I could only imagine my mother's bewilderment when she received condolence flowers wishing my dad a swift recovery. It would be sure to freak her out, but with a little luck I could probably convince her they were from some nut. It was better than telling her the truth.

"And Donna, please don't forget to call my mom on the thirty-first when the announcement of the contestants goes out over the wire," I reminded her. "Not that Mom follows entertainment news, but I don't want her to hear it from someone else."

"I won't forget."

We continued packing for a while, being careful to make sure I wasn't bringing along any "contraband." In the packet Zaidee sent was a list with items that weren't allowed on the set. It included cell phones, pagers, audio and video recorders, CD players of any type, cameras, handheld computers, electronic organizers, and all other wireless devices.

I engulfed Donna in a hug. "I don't know what I'd do with-out you. Seriously, you are the best friend a person could ever ask for."

"I try," she said, then grew serious. "I honestly can't believe you're leaving tomorrow for *four* months." She hugged me back tightly. "I'm going to miss you so much, Kat. I don't know what I'm going to do while you're gone," she said, releasing me.

I gave her a half smile. "Pester Cindy Vander. Antagonize Richard. Send lots of e-mails to Nick," I said. "You'll have plenty of ways to keep busy."

I grabbed a piece of scrap paper off my nightstand and jotted down the password to my America Online account. "Here, you'll need it to access my e-mail," I said, handing it to her.

She folded it up and shoved it into her purse.

"Thanks again for helping me out with all of this. I'll pay you back someday, I swear," I said, dipping my head so she wouldn't see the tears in my eyes.

"Hey," Donna scolded playfully. "Don't get all sappy on me." She leaned forward and placed her hands on my face, tipping it upward. "Always remember, keep your chin up."

"Good advice," I said. "I don't want the cameras catching my double chin."

11

A Strange, Mismatched Group

"Empty your pockets and turn them inside out," Zaidee said. I obliged, tossing my wallet, keys, and some loose change onto a nearby table. I was standing with her inside a tiny rental house on the outskirts of L.A., along with two male crewmembers— one decked out with an expensive-looking camera, the other so beefy I made him for a bodyguard.

"I'll need to look inside your purse," Zaidee said, picking it up before I could object. She dumped the contents onto the table, and began poking through them. I blushed as she shoved aside a tampon and a package of birth control pills.

"Jimmie's going to do a quick check of your luggage," she informed me, motioning to the cameraman. He strutted over and unzipped the main compartment. Noticing my stricken expression, he quipped, "Don't be alarmed. Pretend I'm a U.S. Customs' Officer."

He was trying to be nice about it, but I couldn't help feeling exposed. Having a strange man rifle through your bras and underwear will do that to you. He quickly sorted through my bag, checking all the pockets and pressing his hand along the lining, presumably feeling for any hidden compartments. He looked like the DEA agents I'd seen in movies examining suitcases for narcotics. After a five-minute search, he zipped my bag back up and declared he was finished.

"All clear," he announced. He winked at me. "Relax. It'll all be okay."

Before I could respond Zaidee interrupted. "Time to go," she said, tugging on my arm. "Your limo's waiting."

* * *

We drove north on Sepulveda Boulevard, merging onto the freeway and blending in with the light Sunday afternoon traffic. Zaidee followed closely behind the limo, tailgating us in a shiny black Range Rover, as we headed away from the lights of Los Angeles and up into the narrow, twisting streets of the Hollywood Hills. The cameraman sat across from me in the limo, filming as I stared out the window, watching the scenery move past. The burly guy I'd assumed was a bodyguard turned out to be a sound technician, and he spent the trip perched next to the cameraman, propping a boom mic over my head. It was a thankless job; I didn't say two words during the entire ride.

We cruised along for nearly thirty minutes, driving up a maze of streets, some barely wide enough for the limo to squeeze through, before reaching our final destination, an enormous multitiered house on a street called Bryn Mawr Drive. It looked like the kind of place a hip young movie mogul would live; it was tacky in an understated way.

For the next fifteen weeks, it would be home.

Knees shaking, I stepped out of the limo and made my way up

the front steps. The cameraman and audio guy followed. Zaidee had instructed me to go inside as soon as we got there, so I gingerly pushed open the front door without bothering to knock.

"Hello?" I called, stepping into the massive front hall. "Anybody here?"

When no one answered, I continued forward, exploring the first few rooms. The downstairs was sparsely decorated, with beautiful hardwood floors and pristine white walls. The ceilings were high—at least twenty feet—and had been outfitted with gargantuan lighting fixtures. They were glaringly bright, and reminded me of the lights used to illuminate baseball games at night, though not that big.

Just off the front hall was a spacious living room, with a bright purple sectional couch, the kind that could easily seat ten or more people. A stationary camera similar to closed-circuit television cameras was mounted in the corner of the living room ceiling. It swung around noisily, following me as I paced the room. Unnerved, I continued on, exploring the front hall and ending up at the bottom of a large wooden staircase.

I was beginning to think I was the only one there, when a short-haired girl with a bright smile and olive-toned skin came dashing down the stairs.

"Hello!" she cried. She rushed toward me, her own cameraman trailing along behind her.

"Hi," I called back, feeling self-conscious. The size of the house—and the camera crew—was making me nervous. It was just now starting to sink in: *I am actually on a television show.*

"Another person! I've been sitting in this house for two hours with nothing to do." She had a light Spanish accent. "They have all the doors upstairs locked. I think there are three bedrooms, but we can't go in them. The note says so."

"Note?" I asked.

"Yeah, all the rooms upstairs are labeled—bedroom suite, bathroom, and so on." She stopped when she reached the bottom of the stairs and eyed me closely. "I know you," she said. "I remember you from the casting weekend."

"You do?" I asked, struggling to call up her face from my memory.

"We saw the doctor together. Kat, right?"

I blinked in surprise. "I can't believe you remember."

"I'm Luisa Olivares," she introduced herself, grinning broadly. Seeing my confused expression, she added, "It's okay, you don't have to remember me."

I liked her. She was open and friendly. But I didn't remember her at all.

"I am good with faces," she explained. "Not everyone has that gift."

One by one, the other contestants started arriving, and Luisa seemed to know them all.

"Her name is Maggie," she whispered to me, as a short middle-aged blonde woman walked in through the front door.

"Hello," the newcomer said, setting down her bags. "I'm Maggie Strickland. I turned forty years old last month. I am originally from Cleveland, Ohio, but I currently live in Jackson, Mississippi. I used to work as a chiropractor's assistant but now I'm a stay-at-home mom. I'm the wife of Thomas and the mother of a wonderful eleven-year-old son named Owen." Her voice was so even and her face so tight, I suspected she'd been practicing that speech for days. I also guessed that, with two already revealed, last names were no longer to be kept a secret.

Next in was Janelle, a fair-skinned girl who stood almost six feet tall. Her face was covered in freckles and she had long black hair that reached halfway down her back. "I'm twenty-nine years old and I have a master's degree in fine arts. I work as the curator of a museum in Indianapolis," she informed us. Janelle was unusual looking, in a good sense. She could have been a plus-sized model, if plus-sized models wore size twenty, instead of eight or ten.

Janelle mentioned she was thirsty, so we moved into the kitchen and began drinking diet Cokes and ice water. The refrigerator was otherwise completely bare, which was good, or I might have had a snack. I didn't want to be the first girl seen eating on television.

"What are you guys going to miss most while you're in here?" Janelle asked, sipping her water.

"Ooh, that is too easy." Luisa giggled. "Sex, sex, and more sex. My boyfriend, Jay, is fantastic in bed. He has got the biggest . . . *umph* you have ever seen!" She raised her eyebrows up and down suggestively. "We do it *every* single night. Don't know how I'm gonna make it fifteen weeks with no sex."

Fifteen *weeks*? I felt like telling her to try fifteen *months* and then come back and talk to me. Great. I was in here with the nympho queen.

Janelle was taken aback by Luisa's answer. Her face flushed bright pink and she quickly changed the subject. "That's nice. Uh, I'm going to miss my two cats the most. Frieda and Clarissa. What about you, Kat?"

I choked up. I knew who I'd miss: Nick and Donna. Just thinking about them made my chest ache. "I'll miss the comforts of home," I offered, deciding to keep it impersonal. Besides, I couldn't mention Nick, considering I'd hidden our relationship from Zaidee. "Just being around my friends and family, the people I love."

"Here, here," Janelle said, clinking her glass against my diet Coke can. "Maggie?"

Maggie had been strangely quiet this whole time and now I knew why. Her eyes were watery and her face was marred with anguish.

"You okay?" I asked her, concerned.

"My son," she said. "Owen. I didn't think it would be so hard to leave him."

"Poor thing," Luisa said. "That is rough."

"We had a long talk about it and I said, 'Mommy has to go, baby, but it's for your own good.' Owen knows I need to lose weight. I've got to improve my health so I can see my baby grow up." Her voice caught. "He's probably at home *crying* right now because Mommy isn't there to eat dinner with him."

"Isn't he twelve?" I asked, thinking Owen probably wouldn't appreciate "Mommy" talking about him like this on national television.

"Eleven," Maggie corrected.

"I'm sure he's okay."

"Daddy and him are gonna burn the house down by the time I get back. Neither one of them even knows how to cook."

"They'll be all right," I assured her. "They're probably playing Xbox and eating pizza as we speak."

This didn't seem to make Maggie feel much better, but at least she didn't cry.

For a long while, nobody else showed up. I was starting to wonder if it would just be the four of us, which would have made for a pretty weak show.

Then it happened.

"Kat!" I heard a familiar voice shriek. Startled, I whirled around and allowed myself to be embraced by Regan.

"I'm so glad you're here," she gushed, plopping down on one of the kitchen stools and stealing a sip of my diet Coke. "I was hoping you'd made it. I'm Regan Borrail," she said, beaming at the rest of the group. "Just think of me as the Irish President Vegan," she quipped, and then began launching into the County Mayo story.

I felt a pang of guilt as I realized how much I'd been hoping she *hadn't* made it. I picked up my soda can and wiped off the top with my sleeve. I thought about Sarah, and how desperately she'd wanted to get on. I prayed her face would be the next through the door.

It wasn't. The next contestant was a tall blonde with huge boobs and a surprisingly toned body for someone appearing on a show named *From Fat to Fabulous*. She looked like a porn star momentarily losing her battle with the bulge.

"Hey all, I'm Alicia Combs," she said, and then proceeded to hug and kiss each of us on the cheek. It felt awkward and artificial, but when she came around to me I leaned in and embraced her back. I didn't want to be labeled as an outsider right off the bat.

"How many more contestants do you think there are?" I said to no one in particular.

Alicia shook her head. "I'm it."

"No way," I said. "There's got to be more."

"Zaidee told me when I came in I was the final one," Alicia explained. "Sorry to disappoint."

"Six of us," Luisa remarked. "I was thinking more."

I glanced around. It seemed impossible that the cast was so tiny. I remembered my conversation with Sarah at the audition. *"They'll probably pick between ten and fifteen of us,"* she'd guessed then, and it had seemed a logical conclusion.

"How much weight do you kids want to lose?" Alicia asked. "Forty, fifty pounds?"

"I wish," I mumbled. My goal was closer to a hundred.

"Lordy, I hope I can lose eighty," Luisa said.

"Whoa . . . that's," I quickly did the math, "over five pounds a week. Kind of steep, don't you think?"

"It's not total weight that matters," Janelle said. "You just need to lose two pounds a week to get the money."

"Oh, it's not the money; it's my boyfriend, Jay. I weighed myself before I left for California and I'm 213 pounds. I never weighed this much in my life. He wants me to be 130 pounds and then he will propose."

"How tall are you, Luisa?" I asked.

She grimaced. "I am five-foot-four. So you see, it's no good."

"So, where is everyone from?" Regan asked, changing the subject. I suspected she wanted to move off the topic of weight. "And what do you guys do for, like, careers? I was born in Rhode Island but I grew up in Boulder, Colorado. I'm a first-year college student, majoring in sociology. I want to be a social worker or a high school counselor."

"Hey!" I exclaimed, catching what she'd said. "My parents recently moved to Denver. That's pretty close, huh?"

Regan nodded. "Like half an hour. Have they visited Boulder yet?"

I shook my head. "Not that I know of. They don't really travel much. The big move from Tennessee to Colorado will probably satisfy their wanderlust for the next decade."

"Boulder's so gorgeous, you have to tell them to go. I can show them around if you want," Regan offered shyly.

"I'm from Norwood, Massachusetts," Alicia cut in. "But I work in Boston. I'm a stringer for the *Boston Globe*."

I got the distinct feeling she expected us to be really impressed by this fact, but no one even acknowledged it.

"I was born in Cuba, but I've lived in Houston since I was nine," Luisa said. "I work in pharmaceutical sales."

"That's a big, big field right now," Alicia said knowingly. "Are you bilingual?"

"Bi . . . *sexual?*" Luisa repeated. "Sorry, girl, you're not my type."

"Ha ha," Alicia said, rolling her eyes.

Luisa began speaking to her rapidly in Spanish. "Answer your question?"

"I wasn't being offensive," Alicia protested. "I was just saying there's a big market for bilingual pharmaceutical sales reps. I wrote an article about it for the *Globe.*"

Luisa grunted.

I cut in, telling them that I worked in public relations.

"I almost went that route," Alicia said. "A lot of journalism majors do. The pay's way better than what you can make as a reporter."

"Not where I work," I scoffed. "Not only does my boss pay peanuts, but he micromanages the hell out of —" Immediately, I caught my mistake. I had promised to talk the company up, not bash it.

"Why don't you quit?" Maggie asked, giving me the perfect opening to correct my blunder.

"Hood and Geddlefinger Public Relations is one of the strongest PR firms in the country," I boasted. "When we take on a client, we do it right. The people we represent get amazing press. We're great at spinning articles."

Everybody stared at me in silence, and Alicia cocked an eyebrow.

"I'm from Memphis, by the way," I said quickly, immediately following it up with my standard line, "And no, I'm not an Elvis fan."

Only Maggie and Janelle laughed.

Regan looked puzzled, and said she thought Elvis was from California.

We were a strange, mismatched group.

For the life of me, I couldn't image how anyone—even the most skilled editor—could craft a show out of our lives. But here we were, smiling and grinning at each other. The cameras were rolling, capturing the minutest details of our existence. And very soon, millions of viewers would be sitting in their homes, watching this very conversation and hanging on to our every word.

12

In for a Penny, In for a Pound

A voice came over the house intercom system, summoning the six of us to the living room. Janelle winked at me. "Here goes nothing," she said.

We walked the short distance from the kitchen to the living room, and found Zaidee waiting. The coffee table was now covered with various pieces of videography equipment. She gestured for us to sit down. I noticed that a doctor's scale was positioned in the corner of the room. I didn't recall seeing it when I entered the house.

"Hello, my lovely little reality girls!" Zaidee enthused. "Welcome to *From Fat to Fabulous*. I know you're dying to get settled in, but before you do, I want to talk with you for a minute, go over some things about the show. This is a bit on the technical side, but I'd like you all to have a basic understanding."

She walked over and sat down on the edge of the coffee table.

"This is what's called a mic pack," she said, holding up a black-boxed microphone like the ones we'd worn at the auditions. "Each of you will be required to wear one of these at all times. I think you're all familiar with how they work, but I'll go over it briefly just in case. This part is called the belt pack transmitter," she said, pointing to the box. "In laymen's terms, it's what allows us to receive and record your every word. The wire, which should be concealed beneath your shirt, connects the transmitter to your lavalier mic, or lapel microphone, if you prefer." She quickly demonstrated how to fasten it onto our clothing.

"If you'll go ahead and put these on," she said, passing them out to us.

With shaking hands, I hooked up my mic pack. I looked around the room—the lights were glaring and the camera crew was scrambling, capturing every move we made. Zaidee's words kept playing over through my mind: *record your every word.* After so many years of feeling like a supporting player in a world full of leading ladies, suddenly *I* was the center of attention.

"You are required to wear your microphones every minute of the day. There are two exceptions—you can take them off to sleep and to shower. Nothing else. As soon as you wake up in the morning you'll need to put your mic pack on," Zaidee said. "Even if you're lying in bed staring at the ceiling, I want you miked."

It seemed a little extreme, but nobody objected.

"What about when we're, you know, *using the bathroom*," I asked.

A few of the other girls laughed.

"As uncomfortable as it may be, you'll need to keep the equipment on," she apologized. "It's awkward at first, but you'll get used to it. Before long this'll be second nature."

I couldn't imagine it would ever become second nature, but I didn't disagree.

"Another crucial rule," Zaidee went on. "During your stay in the mansion, there may be times when you'd rather not be filmed.

Unfortunately, that's something you gals are gonna have to learn to live with. Remember, above all else, *From Fat to Fabulous* is a television show. You can't ditch the cameras just because you're having a bad day."

She paused, letting what she'd said sink in. Then she continued, "In addition to our roving cameramen, there are twenty-five cameras stationed throughout the house. Some are obvious, like this one," she said, gesturing toward the swiveling camera mounted in the corner. "Others, not so." She pointed toward a small vase sitting atop the mantle that I could only guess housed a camera. "So please, keep in mind that at all times we'll have eyes and ears watching you. Okay?"

"When do we get to see where we'll be sleeping?" Luisa asked.

Zaidee grinned. "You won't have to wait much longer."

On that note, she left, promising that the host of *From Fat to Fabulous* would be in soon to take us on a tour of the house.

Luisa turned to me. "You want to be roomies, Kat?" she asked.

"Definitely," I said, feeling relieved. I had envisioned myself being the last one picked. "Maybe we can share the middle bedroom. If that's okay with everybody else, of course," I added.

"I wouldn't go making plans if I were you. I *highly* doubt they'll let us choose," Alicia interjected. "We're probably going to draw straws."

I hoped Alicia was wrong.

Knowing my luck I'd get stuck rooming with Regan.

A few minutes later, a tall, good-looking man with light blond hair and vivid blue eyes entered the room. I wondered where he'd come from; I hadn't heard the front door open. He smiled brightly at us as he stood in the center of the living room. He was wearing a pair of leather shoes, pressed black slacks, and an expensive-looking gray sweater. He had the fresh-faced good looks of a J. Crew model, with classic features and an all-American build. I stared down at my blue-jean skirt and red button-down top. It had seemed like a good choice earlier, but next to this Hollywood guy, I felt horribly underdressed.

For a long time, the host didn't say anything, he just stood there, watching us. The cameramen hovered, filming us from a variety of angles. There were three of them in all, plus a man holding a gigantic boom mic, much bigger than the ones I'd seen them use before.

This was obviously a very important moment on *From Fat to Fabulous*.

I had a fleeting temptation to break the ice with a joke, but decided against it.

"Hello, girls, and welcome to *From Fat to Fabulous*," he finally said. His voice was deep and smooth. "I'm Jagger Roth, your host for this magnificent, life-altering adventure. Over the next fifteen weeks you'll embark on the biggest weight-loss journey of your lives, a journey with some very high stakes involved. For some of you this experience will be exhilarating. For others, it will be devastating."

He was going overboard just a touch. *From Fat to Fabulous* wasn't a matter of life and death.

"All of America will watch your lives unfold. Some of you will crumble; others will rise above the rest. Who knows," he said, glancing around, "what type of stardom may await? I see breakout potential in all of you. Any one of you girls could become the next big thing."

"Yeah," Luisa snickered, "emphasis on the *big*."

"I see you've all spent some time getting acquainted, and that's good. The information you've gathered from your fellow housemates will be of great importance in the next few minutes. The more you know, the better chance you have of winning this next competition."

We all looked around the room suspiciously, trying to mentally catalogue everything that had been said during the course of the afternoon.

"But before we get started with our premiere competition, allow me to take you on a long-awaited tour of the mansion. Since you arrived in the house earlier today, the rooms upstairs have been locked." He paused, staring at us deviously. "No more." He produced an oversized key ring, the kind bailiffs carry in old black-and-white prison films. "Follow me, girls. Your destiny awaits."

First Jagger took us to a spacious home gym, located, ironically, off the kitchen. It had been outfitted with three treadmills, two exercise bikes, an elliptical runner, and a StairMaster.

"By working out in here, you can each earn up to a thousand dollars per day for your *Fat2Fab* Bank. All it takes is one hour. One hour a day and you can earn a grand," he said.

A handsome, muscular guy came strutting over.

"You've heard of Gold's Gym? Welcome to Greg's Gym!" he boomed, flexing one of his biceps. "I'm your all-in-one personal trainer, nutritionist, weight-loss guru. When you got a problem with weight, you come to *me*. I'm your go-to guy."

I didn't see how a Fabio wannabe could help me shed pounds. I made a mental note to stay as far away from steroid freak Greg as possible.

We trailed along behind Jagger as he walked quickly up the stairs. The camera crew followed in close pursuit. When we reached the top of the landing, Jagger stopped and spun around so that he was facing us.

"As you will soon find out, the mansion is equipped with

several bedrooms. Some are luxurious, and some are not so luxurious," he said. "Most of you will be sharing, but one lucky soul
will have her own *deluxe* suite equipped with a king-sized bed,
private sitting room, and a spacious bathroom with a Jacuzzi
tub. The rest of you will be bunking down in one of the two remaining bedrooms—each with its own pros and cons. The fate
of the game may rest on your sleeping arrangements."

Regan gasped. "What do you mean?"

"All in good time, all in good time," Jagger said mysteriously.

Using one of the keys from the gigantic loop, he unlocked the
middle of the three rooms, the one Luisa and I had discussed
sharing. He waited in the hall while we wandered inside. The
room was bare, but spacious, and had been outfitted with two
double beds and a small sofa.

"Not too shabby," Luisa commented. "I could sleep here.
What do you say, Kat?"

"You guys are so naïve." Alicia smirked. "Didn't you *listen* to
what Jagger said? We don't get to *pick* our rooms, we have to *compete* for them."

"Not necessarily. He hasn't told us how the rooms are going
to be divided up, only that our sleeping arrangements will impact the outcome of the game," I reminded her.

Jagger let us look around for a few minutes before calling us
into the master bedroom for a quick peek.

"Oh my God!" Regan stopped so quickly I nearly slammed
into her. "It's big!"

That was an understatement. Gigantic would have been more
on target. You could have crammed my entire apartment into that
bedroom—twice.

"Kat, what do you say you and I share *this* room?" Luisa joked.

"Over my dead body," Alicia said.

Jagger gave us a few minutes to look around before summoning us back to the tour. He gestured across the hall from the master suite to a room he dubbed the "Confession Chamber." "You'll have diary sessions in here every single day," he announced, rapping lightly on the door. "You may decide to go in of your own free will, or you may wait until the producers instruct you to enter. The choice is yours." He didn't open the door to show us the inside. "It is now time to go back downstairs. We have many other rooms to see," Jagger said, "and important things to discuss."

He led us on a lightning-fast tour through the rest of the house, listing the various amenities of different rooms. Every room in the house was the same in one way: None offered the Internet, a television, or a phone. The only perks we had were out back—a large swimming pool and a hot tub.

Well, I thought wryly as he showed us the pool, *I won't be using that.*

"Twice a week, you'll meet with me out by the pool to have a private one-on-one interview. Nothing formal, just a nice, casual chat about how things are going for you on the show," he informed us.

When we reached the kitchen things became markedly more interesting.

"While living in the *Fat to Fabulous* mansion, you'll be required to follow a routine," Jagger said. "Breakfast will be at nine o'clock each morning, lunch at noon, and dinner at seven P.M. As you can see, the refrigerator is stocked with healthy items." He opened the door to reveal a stash of fruits and vegetables that hadn't been there earlier. "But you will only be allowed to snack between the hours of two P.M. and four P.M. At all other times the refrigerator will remain locked."

"I thought you weren't going to starve us?" Janelle asked, looking concerned.

"Yeah, why shouldn't we be allowed to eat whenever we want?" Alicia chimed in. "It's not like the stuff in that fridge is going to make us any fatter."

"*Au contraire,*" Jagger said. "You won't starve. Should you become overwhelmed with hunger pangs or late-night cravings, there's one place in the mansion that's always serving."

He moved to the far end of the kitchen and began pulling open a thick, wooden door. There was no sign on the outside, nothing to indicate the virtual treasure-trove that waited inside.

"The Tomb of Temptation," Jagger announced, looking gleeful. "Go on, girls, take a peek."

I remembered it from the article. One giant sin-fest waiting to happen.

Gingerly, I walked in through the door and came face-to-face with the largest pantry I had ever seen in my life; it was almost as big as the entire kitchen. The Tomb of Temptation was filled with shelves lined with every type of junk food known to man. One wall was packed with sweets: cookies, cakes, candy bars, donuts, pudding. Even chewing gum. The opposite wall housed an assortment of Cheez-Its, nuts, crackers, breads, and every brand of chips I'd ever heard of.

"All right, back up slowly and nobody gets hurt," I joked, making my way out of The Tomb of Temptation and into the kitchen. I needed some breathing room. A place like that was diet suicide. I didn't know how I'd ever be able to lose my two pounds a week with all those goodies in the house.

When we were once again seated on the living room's purple sectional, Jagger hit us with a surprise. "There's something you all should know. The bedroom lights are hooked up to a timer system. At eight o'clock every morning the lights will come on and at eleven P.M. each night they'll shut off."

My jaw dropped and I noticed several other girls look at him in surprise. He had to be kidding.

He wasn't.

"This schedule has been designed with your best interests in mind," Jagger explained. "If you lie in bed all day you will never accomplish your goals. Without a strict regimen, many of you would be doomed to fail."

Jagger was starting to get on my last nerve. I, for one, have never been able to accomplish much in the morning. No matter which way you slice it, I am most alert and alive at night. I wanted to ask if someone had written him a script, or if he was making up the bullshit as he went along.

Unfortunately, the bullshit was only beginning.

"Each of you will have a bank, which I'll add money to as we progress. Every Sunday you will participate in a weigh-in. Those who have lost two pounds or more for the week will be rewarded with an addition of ten thousand dollars to your personal account. If there's a gain or loss of under two pounds, nothing will happen. However—"

Jagger paused, trying to drum up drama. It didn't work. We'd all read the publicity; we knew what was coming.

"—if you *gain* two or more pounds you will lose *twenty* thousand dollars! At the end of the game, whoever has accumulated the most money will take home her bank. The rest of you will leave empty-handed."

We knew all this already! I wanted to get on to the good stuff.

"During the course of your stay in the *From Fat to Fabulous* mansion, you will take part in a series of contests. Some of them will be individual competitions and some will be group competitions. Sometimes the rewards will be cash, sometimes there will be even greater things at stake. There is no pattern to the frequency with which these competitions will appear. So I advise you to do your best in all of them; you never know when another opportunity might come around."

Jagger paused, fixing us with a pointed gaze.

"Your very first individual competition will begin . . . now!" he boomed, startling me. "Tonight we're going to play a little game called In for a Penny, In for a Pound. If you can guess the pounds, it will be worth a lot of pennies."

I listened intently as Jagger outlined the competition's rules. It sounded unbelievably cheesy. We would be given a stack of five large yellow cards, each one bearing the name of one of our competitors. With a black Magic Marker, we were to write down the other players' weights.

"Some of you may know your housemates' weights, some of you may not. If you aren't sure, I'm afraid you'll have to guess," Jagger explained. "You'll have five minutes to write down your choices. Bear in mind, you cannot change your answers once the time is up. Whoever gets the most correct wins ten thousand dollars for her bank and the right to chose where she—as well as everyone else—will be sleeping."

"Wait a minute, wait a minute," Alicia cut in. "Let me get this straight. First place gets the first choice of bedrooms, right?"

Jagger nodded.

"But then shouldn't second place have second choice, third place third, and on down the line?"

"I'm afraid that isn't how things work on *From Fat to Fab-*

ulous," Jagger said. "If you want any say in where you'll be bunking these next fifteen weeks, you'd better win tonight's competition, Alicia."

"Whatever."

Jagger moved around the room quickly dispensing materials. Once he had finished, he announced, "Your five minutes starts . . . *now!*"

It was supposed to be a dramatic moment, but nobody reacted. We just sat there calmly, looking around at each other. Out of the corner of my eye, I could see Luisa sizing me up. She must have felt pretty dumb, having blurted out her weight the way she did. I picked up the card that read *Luisa,* flipped it over, and wrote *213.* I was secretly glad I hadn't told her anything about my size.

"Four minutes, girls," Jagger warned.

Thumbing through the stack, I pulled out Alicia's card and jotted down *185.* Maggie was pretty heavy, but she was also very short. I thought it over for a minute then put down *175.* By far, the hardest two to gauge were Janelle and Regan. Janelle was built like an Amazonian woman—toweringly tall with big bones. I had no clue what she clocked in at. I deduced *260* was a safe bet. And Regan, bless her heart, was enormous. Feeling a pang of guilt, I wrote *400 pounds* and prayed she wouldn't hate me for it. Under normal circumstances, I would have been nice and chopped fifty pounds off, but this was a competition. I wanted to win that master suite as badly as the next person.

"Okay, girls, time's up."

Alicia was still scribbling frantically and Jagger had to issue two warnings before she finally set down her marker. "This whole thing's rigged," she griped.

She was starting to agitate me.

"Kat, you're up first. Time to step on the scale!" Jagger boomed.

"What!?" I exclaimed. "Why me? Shouldn't we be going alphabetically?" My face was flaming with embarrassment.

"The order was predetermined earlier," Jagger responded.

I made my way slowly to the front of the room, kicked off my flip-flops, and hopped up.

"And the scale says . . . two-hundred and thirty-one pounds!" Jagger declared.

I felt sick. Either *From Fat to Fabulous*'s scale was wrong, or I'd packed on four pounds since leaving Memphis!

"Let's see what your housemates said. If you want to get the pennies, girls, you'd better guess the pounds!" He started on the left, with Luisa.

She held up her card, looking crestfallen. "I got 201," she said.

I felt a huge smile spread across my face.

Next, Maggie produced her response: *225*, which wasn't bad either. In fact, it was pretty close to the truth. So far, I liked what I was hearing. But it was Janelle's answer that excited me the most.

"Kat, I had you pegged at 183," she said, shaking her head. "Damn."

I wanted to hug her. Who cared if she was totally off-base? It was a huge compliment, no pun intended. All these years, I'd had no idea I looked much smaller than my actual weight! I was feeling pretty good, until Regan's turn came.

"I'm sorry, Kat." She stared down at the floor.

She held up her card and the sight of it nearly knocked me off my feet. "Three hundred pounds!" I exploded. "You think I weigh *three hundred pounds*?"

"It was only a guess!"

"A damn *awful* guess," I snapped. Regan had a lot of nerve.

And to think, I had actually felt *guilty* about putting down four hundred pounds on her card.

Alicia wasn't much better—she had me figured for 275 pounds. "Sorry, Kat," she said smugly. "I just call 'em like I see 'em."

I made my way back over to the couch, and plopped down. I was steamed. More than anything, I wished I could go back and change my guesses. I'd write down six hundred pounds for Regan and four hundred pounds for Alicia. That'd fix them good.

I was so caught up plotting revenge I didn't notice Maggie had climbed onto the scale until I heard Jagger call, "Two hundred and ten pounds!"

My guess had been off by thirty-five pounds—she carried her excess weight very well. As it turned out, most of us had screwed up, putting Maggie down for a much lower weight. The only person who came anywhere close was Regan who had, once again, overestimated with 230.

My luck went from bad to worse. Janelle, as it turned out, weighed only 219 making my guess of 260 seem ignorant and malicious. Most of us overestimated on Janelle, with the exception of Maggie, who nailed it with 220. I was nearly ten pounds too high on Alicia, who actually tipped the scales at 176. The only one I got right was Luisa but, then, so did everybody else.

The biggest shock of the evening came when Regan stepped onto the scale. She weighed in at 341 pounds—sixty pounds lower than my guess—but that wasn't what surprised me. When Alicia's turn came to hold up her card, she had written Regan's weight down at 250 pounds, twenty-five pounds *lower* than what she'd put for me!

"You think I weigh more than Regan?" I demanded, squaring off against her.

"You can't be serious," Luisa backed me up. "Look at them!"

Regan sniffed. "What's that supposed to mean?"

"No offense, but we're not exactly the same size," I told her, softening my tone a little.

"It's my opinion, Kat," Alicia said. "It's not scientific."

"You didn't answer my question."

"Fine then. If you really want to know, yes, I think you look bigger than Regan," Alicia huffed.

I glared daggers at her. I would get Alicia back if it killed me.

When all was said and done, Maggie prevailed. "I knew all those years working for Weight Watchers had to pay off someday." She beamed.

"Congratulations, Maggie!" Jagger enthused. "You're the winner of the premiere competition on *From Fat to Fabulous*. In addition to your ten-thousand-dollar cash prize, you are now the proud occupant of the coveted master suite. And what's more, you have the enviable task of selecting where the other housemates will sleep." He handed her the key to the room.

Maggie grinned. "Thank you, Jagger."

"Enjoy your new bedrooms, girls," he advised. "Remember, the fate of the game may rest in your sleeping arrangements." He hurriedly exited the room without so much as a good-bye.

"How would you girls like to do this?" Maggie asked. "The fairest thing might be to draw names out of a hat."

"No, the fairest thing would be if we went in order," Alicia interjected. "Luisa came in second, I was third, Kat's fourth, Regan's fifth, and Janelle's last. That's the way we ought to divide up the rooms."

I knew what she was doing. The next best bedroom after the master suite had two beds in it. If we did things her way, Alicia and Luisa would get to share it.

"No way," I argued. "I think Maggie should decide. If *she* wants to have a random drawing, that's what we'll do."

Maggie looked exasperated. "How about we take a vote? All those in favor of doing it Alicia's way, raise your hand."

I had expected the split to go in my favor, with three out of the five people voting for a random drawing, but Janelle screwed things up.

"I can't help it," she said, shrugging. "Alicia's idea is the fairest."

So there we were: me, Regan, and Janelle bunking together in the smallest of the three bedrooms.

* * *

"This sucks," I complained, as we dragged our suitcases upstairs and into our new quarters. I surveyed our surroundings. The room was tiny in comparison to the rest of the house, probably only measuring ten feet by fifteen. There were three small beds lined up parallel against the wall. "It's not much bigger than my bedroom back home. We're going to keep bumping into each other."

I wasn't exaggerating. Between the three single beds, two dressers, and the ever-present camera crew, there was scarcely enough room left over for our luggage. Here we were in a giant mansion full of sizeable rooms and they had stuffed us into a space not much bigger than a walk-in closet.

"Good going, Janelle," Regan scolded. "If you hadn't messed up the vote we'd have had a shot at getting the better room."

"True," she admitted. "But then you could have gotten stuck sharing with Alicia. This way, Luisa will have to put up with her. They may have the bigger room, but I prefer our situation."

That shut us up.

"Well, who wants which bed?" Janelle asked, looking around.

Regan snagged the spot by the window, while I settled down on the bed next to the door. That left only one option—the cramped space in the middle. Good intentions or not, Janelle was partly responsible for our situation. It seemed fitting that she get stuck with the worst sleeping arrangements.

We spent the next half hour unpacking and making small talk. I learned that Regan had an older sister whom she hated, and that her parents had been together since they were fourteen.

"Wow, I can't imagine," Janelle commented. "I'm only twenty-nine and I'm already twice divorced."

My eyes bulged. "Are you kidding?"

She shook her head. "I wish I could tell you I was, but no."

"What happened?" Regan pried. "Who divorced who? And why?"

As if on cue, a voice came over the house intercom. It sounded like Zaidee. "Janelle, please come to the Confession Chamber. Your daily diary session will commence in five minutes."

"Saved by the bell." Janelle sighed. "And, to think, I haven't even finished unpacking." She started out the door, then ducked back in and asked, "Have you guys noticed how biblical this place is? They talk to us over the house speaker like God. We've got the Tomb of Temptation and the Confession Chamber. They might as well rename the show *The Seven Deadly Sins*."

"I think that's already taken," I told her.

After she'd left, Regan turned to me. "Did Jagger ever say what the pros and cons are of the different rooms?"

"I assume this is it," I said, gesturing around. "Absolutely no space and a total lack of privacy."

"But Jagger was talking about the 'fate of the game.'"

"I think he was playing things up for the cameras. Maybe

they're going to give us different eating and exercise schedules based on where we're sleeping. Or maybe in all future competitions we'll be divided up into teams based on our room assignments. Either way, I'm sure it's nothing to get worked up over."

"I bet you're right."

I wasn't.

13

Earth-Toppling
Feminine Wiles

By the end of the first week, I felt on the verge of a nervous breakdown.

I woke at 8 A.M. every morning when the lights flickered on, showered, did my hair, makeup, and got fully dressed to make myself look presentable for the cameras. Then I staggered downstairs for the mandatory household breakfast.

It was excruciating.

From the moment I woke up I was in a horrible mood. I hated sharing a tiny room with two girls, hated being swarmed by cameras the second I moved, and hated pretending to have a normal, carefree meal with a group of virtual strangers. Eating was strictly limited to a diet of unexciting foods, and breakfast was especially miserable: wheat toast, a tiny serving of grape jelly, and some generic brand of low-calorie cereal. Sure, we could go into the Tomb of Temptation and snag a donut or a box of pancake mix, but as far as I could tell, none of us had ventured back into the forbidden pantry since our initial tour. No one wanted to be seen pigging out on national television.

Alicia griped nonstop about the menu. "We're dying out here," she complained, speaking directly into the camera one morning. "This isn't even a balanced meal. At least give us some bananas and raisins to put on the cereal."

"Here, here!" Janelle chimed in.

"Fruit is one of the healthiest things on the planet," Alicia continued. "It's absurd to keep it from us. We need something to get our blood sugar up in the morning."

She kept lobbying until one day she came out of the Confession Chamber grinning from ear to ear. "I threatened to sue them when I got out," she said boldly. "Told them our electrolytes are falling from exercising and they'd better reconsider their menu before one of us gets sick."

"She is a liar," Luisa whispered in my ear.

I thought so, too, but the very next morning there were apples, bananas, and oranges on the breakfast table.

After breakfast, we lapsed into days of nothingness, broken up only by lunch and dinner, and sessions in the Confession Chamber.

We had no books or magazines, couldn't watch TV, call anyone from home, or get online; all we could do was mill around the house and talk to each other. And after hearing about Regan's family history and Luisa's wild sexcapades for the umpteenth time, I was more than ready for a new hobby. I had to do something to distract myself, and fast. Then it hit me. I thought my stint on *From Fat to Fabulous* would provide me the opportunity to kill two birds with one stone: I'd get thin and rich in one go. But in actuality, I could achieve not two but *three* goals during my tenure on the show: beauty, riches, and *success*.

I was locked in a house with nothing to do. There would never be a better time to write the great American novel. We didn't have access to a computer, but I could write in longhand. The house was stocked with notepads and pencils—one of the few luxury items the producers had deemed us worthy of having. I hurried into the main hall and scooped up a stack of writing materials from the top drawer of the cabinet. With pad and pencils in hand, I encountered my first problem: where to set up shop.

My bedroom was no good. It was far too messy, plus there were no flat surfaces on which I could place the paper. I'd have to lie on my bed, balancing the pad on my lap. The kitchen had a massive island in the middle with tons of counter space, but it was far too heavily trafficked. Ditto for the living room.

I briefly debated going outside, but decided against it. It would have been the best place to write, but it was just past 2 P.M. Alicia was likely to be sunbathing on one of the lawn chairs by the pool, deep-frying her skin the way she did every day. I could just imagine her reaction when she found out I was writing a novel.

"Hey, Kat," she'd say with mock friendliness. "I'd be more than happy to read your first draft. Offer some revisions. Being that I'm a successful journalist for the *Boston Globe,* I have tons of expertise." Then she'd proceed to tell me how I sucked.

No, I needed somewhere quiet and secluded, with few distractions. I considered going into the Confession Chamber and asking for permission to set up camp in there, but opted against it. Zaidee was a writer herself and while she would certainly understand my need for privacy, revealing that I was drafting a book would make me privy to many unwanted questions. I wasn't very skilled at dodging her interrogations. Until I had the finished product, I wouldn't breathe a word about my book to anyone.

Eventually, I settled on the den by the fireplace. I sat on the floor, spreading my supplies out on the coffee table. My camera-man knelt down across from me. I had always envisioned my-self tucked away in some atmospheric study pounding out page after page on an old-fashioned typewriter. I certainly hadn't pic-tured myself being filmed while I wrote, but there was no way of avoiding it. Besides, I thought, this setup might have its advan-tages. Few novelists—if any—have a videotape documenting their creative process. I hunkered down and got to work, drumming up writing tips I'd heard. The only one that came to mind was the old adage, "write what you know." Well, that was out. My novel was going to be a romance and I wasn't about to have a fat girl as the lead character. No one would want to read a thing like *that*.

No, my main character had to be someone with pizzazz, sass, and charisma. She would be fun-loving yet glamorous. She had to be confident, without being arrogant. Just the way I would be once I got skinny. It would be a page-turner about a head-turner. I smiled. I liked that line. Maybe they would put it on the cover of the book.

My character's name had to be commanding, and it had to convey power as well as vulnerability. I picked up my pen and jotted down a list. *Lucinda. Julianne. Rosalind.* None of them were quite right. Then it came to me. *Cassandra.* Yes, I liked the sound of that. Dignified, yet accessible.

Once I had the lead character's name in mind, I moved on to the most crucial part of all. The opening line. It had to be strik-ingly brilliant, something that would hook readers from page one. I thought this over for a while, rolling my pencil around in my hands. Then I wrote:

Cassandra's lips are the color of roses.

I stared at it, and then scratched it out. It seemed a tad clichéd.

Besides, roses come in several different colors. I didn't want anyone to get confused and think Cassandra's lips were yellow from
jaundice. Furthermore, there was always the possibility, however rare, that a dirty-minded individual might assume I was referring to Cassandra's *other* lips, the ones located in her nether
regions.

I cursed myself for hanging out with Luisa so much.

Then I hastily scrawled *nether regions* across the bottom of
the page. It was a keen reflection, one I might have use for later
in the story.

Flipping to a clean sheet of paper, I tried again for my opening:

*Cassandra is a modern-day Aphrodite, a woman so beau-
teous many a fine-looking stud has become enraptured with her
elegant charms, falling under the spell of her astounding and
earth-toppling feminine wiles.*

I read it over, and much as it pained me to admit it, the line
was garbage. When I'd composed the passage in my head, it had
sounded so polished, so fresh. But between my brain and my
hand, something had gotten lost in the translation.

The line needed fixing, but I had no clue where to start. How
could I turn what I had written into something on par with a
Janet Evanovich novel?

I examined the passage, struggling to analyze its contents.
There was a lot of imagery and possibly I'd used too many ad-
jectives. I reread the sentence again, this time wincing at how
wordy it was. I didn't want to overwhelm readers right off the
bat. Also, I wasn't entirely certain where I'd gotten the phrase
earth-toppling, or if it was even a phrase at all. It seemed like a
bit of a mixed-metaphor.

Forcefully, I stabbed the pencil into the page, scribbling out the offensive text. Forget the first line. What I needed was a guidepost, something to steer me through the rough parts and keep me on track.

I needed a title.

Once I had that, the story would definitely follow suit.

But coming up with a title proved to be equally challenging. I considered, and rejected, several options: *The Beauteous Lover, The Able-Bodied Vixen, Coworkers of the Heart,* and *For the Love of a Woman, Cassandra.*

I frowned. I couldn't remember ever having such a difficult time getting the right words on paper before. I'd written many things—press releases, for instance—and I'd never had this kind of trouble before.

It was frustrating, but there was a consolation. I might not be able to craft a successful romance novel, but in some ways I was *living* one. I already had Nick, my perfect romantic hero. Now all I needed was a sleek, sophisticated body like all the heroines on the romance covers. Then I'd be all set.

"Hey, girly, what's up?"

I leapt nearly a foot in the air, throwing my arms across the coffee table in a quick effort to shield my writing. *Nice job, Kat,* I scolded myself. *Way to be inconspicuous.*

"Hi Regan," I said, glancing up over my shoulder to see her hovering behind me. For such a heavyset person, she had a real knack for sneaking up on people.

"Whatcha working on?"

"Nothing, really. Just some letters to home."

Her eyes got huge. "Kat, you can't send those! You know we're not allowed to mail stuff, right?"

"Yes, Regan, I'm well aware of that fact. Just because I write some letters doesn't mean I have to send them. I'm going to save them until I get home. Did you need something?"

"Uh-uh."

I wanted to ask her why the hell she'd come over to bug me if she had nothing to say, but thought better of it. There was no sense in being deliberately rude.

"So what's everybody else doing? Anything interesting?"

"Um, let me think. Alicia is sunbathing, Maggie's taking a nap, and Janelle and Luisa are in Greg's Gym."

"They're working out?" I asked in surprise. All six of us had put in an hour that morning. When there's a thousand dollars at stake, exercise becomes a lot more enticing. Luisa seemed especially taken with Greg—she frequently blew him air kisses and made countless jokes about how she'd give him "a real workout" if he was interested.

Regan's cameraman leaned around so he could capture both of us in his shot.

"I think they're more hanging out with Greg than anything else."

"Ah, that's right. Luisa's got a thing for him." I gave an exaggerated wink, which, naturally, was lost on Regan.

"What's with your eye?"

"Nothing, I was winking at you." I did it again, for emphasis. "You know, just my way of saying Luisa's into Greg. . . ."

"Oh yes, he's dope!"

I stood up and stretched my legs. My cameraman followed suit, rising then immediately ducking so as not to block Regan's cameraman. I wondered if they felt stupid, standing there filming us like that. Surely one camera would suffice.

"Let's go in the kitchen. I'm starved," I said, retrieving my notepad and pencils.

"God, me too. The food here is not so good."

We padded down the hallway and into the kitchen. I yanked open the refrigerator door and began scrounging around for something to eat. "What are you in the mood for?"

"Surprise me with something extra tasty!"

She had requested the impossible. "Well, let's see. We've got your baby carrots, your celery, your broccoli, and your cauliflower. That about does it for vegetables. Fruits include pears and peaches. We have fat-free peanut butter substitute and some fat-free, cholesterol-free Swiss cheese, both of which we could enjoy on some fat-free, dairy-free crackers. Pick your poison."

"Kat, that's not funny."

"It wasn't meant to be."

She sighed. "Can you pass me a peach?"

I took two out of the fruit drawer then shut the refrigerator door. We munched quietly on our peaches for several minutes, trying hard to ignore the whirring noise of the cameras. I had just swallowed my last bite when Regan said, "This isn't helping."

"I know, they make me nervous, too," I confessed, sneaking a peek at the cameraman out of the corner of my eye. "Try and ignore them."

She shook her head miserably. "No, not that. *This.*" She held up her peach pit. "If anything, I'm even hungrier than I was before I ate it!"

I felt her pain. "I've been hungry since the moment I got in this stupid house. The least they could do is give us something edible. I mean, there are low-calorie foods that have *flavor.* Barbecue rice cakes, for example. Or baked chips. I figured we'd at least have stuff like that. But, no. We get one extreme," I gestured toward the fridge, "or another."

We turned in unison to face the Tomb of Temptation.

"Hey, Kat, you think they've got some baked chips in there?"
I shook my head. "No way. I'm not going in to find out."

"Oh, come on. It's just a pantry," Regan said. "It only seems
sinful because they gave it that name."

"Regan, you can't be serious."

"Think about it! We have this great gym but we can barely
exercise because we're hungry all the time! How can we be expected to lose weight if we don't exercise?"

Deep down, I knew better. I knew I hadn't exercised any more
than was required to get paid because I hadn't wanted to, but at
the moment, under those circumstances, Regan's logic seemed
infallible.

"Okay, you win. Let's check it out," I said, rising from the stool.

I had said the magic words. I felt like Ali Baba, unlocking the
cave with his command of "Open Sesame." With my simple decision, the kitchen had begun buzzing with activity. Out of
nowhere, a girl from the crew appeared, holding a boom mic.
Regan's cameraman had positioned himself in front of us and
was now walking backward, filming us as we came toward him.
We were flanked on both sides by my cameraman and the girl
holding the boom mic.

We were about to make big news in the *From Fat to Fabulous*
household.

"Here goes nothing," I said, leaning past the cameraman to
open the door.

It swung forward noisily, creaking like the entrance to a haunted
house. I stepped inside and flipped on the light switch. It smelled
wonderfully of fresh baked cakes and pies. "Let's make this
quick," I ordered, scanning the shelves.

"So many choices!" Regan bounced on her heels. "How am I
going to pick just one?"

I heard some muffled talking, and then one of the cameramen spoke up, "You can pick more than one thing."

My jaw dropped. In all the days I'd been here—seven in total—I hadn't heard so much as a peep out of the crew. Initially, their silence had troubled me. I wished one of them would open up, crack a few jokes. Now that it had happened, it was making me uncomfortable. I hastily fetched a small bag of Fritos from the shelf. "I'm finished," I said, backing out of the room, cameraman in tow.

"Hang on, Kat. This is the highlight of my week!" Regan said. She sucked in a deep breath, savoring the aroma. "Growing up, I was never allowed to eat fatty foods. My parents always wanted me to be thin like my sister, Briana." She groaned. "The perfect goddess. They compared me to her every single day. And Briana got to eat cookies, while I ate cottage cheese. She could eat whatever she wanted and still weigh 102 pounds."

"Metabolisms are evil," I agreed. "Wicked, vile things."

"I want to enjoy this moment for as long as I can."

"Well, then, enjoy it alone," I snapped, hurrying back into the kitchen. Didn't Regan see she was playing right into their hands? She was embodying the worst of the fat-girl stereotypes—the compulsive foodaholic.

As quickly as possible, I took a seat at the counter. Ripping open my bag of Fritos I began eating them at breakneck speed, popping several into my mouth at a time. I was dreading the moment Regan came out to join me. I'd be damned if I was going to let those bastards get any footage of two fat girls having a pig-out party. I had nearly finished the entire bag by the time Regan emerged, her arms loaded down with high-calorie foods. She made her way over to me, setting her bounty down on the counter.

"Look, Kat!" she beamed. "I got butterscotch cookies, brownies, pizza-flavored Pringles, which aren't as good as real pizza but they'll do. And I also—"

"Uh, I think I'm going to be sick," I said, rising from my seat. It was a bold-faced lie, but I needed an excuse to get out of there fast. Another second, and I'd have been a goner.

"Are you okay? Do you want me to come with you?"

"No, no, I'm fine," I said. "You enjoy your snacks."

I darted out of the kitchen and went running up the stairs. I had to get as far away from the scene of the crime as possible. My cameraman followed close behind, overtaking me at one point and racing into the hall bathroom. He seemed utterly perplexed that I turned left, and went into my bedroom instead.

And then I realized. Of course. They thought I was going to make myself throw up.

Janelle wandered into the bedroom. "What was all that commotion about?"

"A little mass pandemonium in the kitchen. I had to make a quick escape."

She raised an eyebrow.

"Regan and I ventured into the Tomb of Temptation," I explained.

"Got it."

"The camera crew was going berserk," I said, feeling slightly self-conscious. I hated talking about people when they were in the room. "They were filming it like one of us was about to give an Academy Award–worthy performance. They even brought out that boom mic thing. It was kind of upsetting."

"Where's the mic now?" She glanced around.

"Probably still on Regan. She's downstairs having a small feast."

"There's a lesson here," Janelle said, smiling wryly. "If you want more screen time, eat."

I blinked in confusion. "They've never cared so much before."

"That's because before, you were eating carrot sticks, which they can't use. They need to get you eating cheesecake. On a show like this one, that's what makes great TV."

14

From Fat to Fabulous

From Fat to Fabulous's crew outnumbered the contestants three-fold. And those were just the ones we came into contact with in our daily lives—the cameramen and sound technicians. There was no telling how many others lurked behind the house's walls, silently observing from the mysterious place Janelle referred to as "master control."

In addition to the wall cameras that had been stationed throughout the house, each of us had been assigned two personal cameramen. From what I could tell, they worked rotating shifts, twelve hours on, twelve hours off.

The cameramen followed us around faithfully, nipping at our heels day and night. There were only two exceptions. They left us alone when we were *incapacitated* in one of the bathrooms (though, if you were merely blow-drying your hair or applying makeup in front of the mirror, they'd squeeze in). And whenever we were participating in some kind of a group event—a challenge or even a friendly chat—only three cameramen were present. If all six of us wound up in the same room at the same time, three of the cameramen would drop out of sight.

"It'd be overkill," Janelle explained. "When you've got that many cameramen, they start getting in each other's way."

My daytime cameraman—a young, extremely skinny guy with blond hair—showed up around two o'clock each afternoon. On the rare occasions that I stayed downstairs late chatting with Janelle or Luisa in the kitchen, I saw "blond boy," as I referred to him, leave around 2 A.M. In the mornings, an older, dark-haired man with a beard was there, shoving a camera into my face the second I crawled out of bed.

From Fat to Fabulous also employed six sound technicians outfitted with boom mics, and at any given time there were three in the house. They rotated among the contestants, taking their orders from headsets and often appearing when a fight, or some other interesting turn of events, was brewing. I never understood the necessity for this, considering we wore our mic packs virtually 24-7.

At first, I found it difficult to tell the crew apart, particularly the cameramen. They all dressed similarly, in jeans and black T-shirts, and their faces were almost entirely obstructed by the equipment they carried. There were a few exceptions. Both of Regan's cameramen were black, and in the daytime Maggie was followed around by a camera*woman*. I wondered how the producers had decided to divide up the crews, if there was any rhyme or reason behind it. I wondered, also, if the cameramen had any say in who they were assigned to. I often found myself wanting to talk to them, to ask them, but stopped myself. It would have been useless—they never cracked.

Luisa tried on many occasions to get her daytime cameraman

to break his reserve. She thought he was cute, "in a scrawny white-boy kind of way," and enjoyed toying with him. "You want a drink of water?" she'd taunt. "Need to take a piss break?" He stood stoic and rigid the entire time, never so much as cracking a smile. It reminded me of the queen's guards at Buckingham Palace—the ones so famous for their rigorous discipline. I've seen them so often on TV that, whenever I try to picture England, the image of them immediately springs to mind. Nick hates that.

"It's as if the American networks have no footage of England aside from The Houses of Parliament and Buckingham Palace. You see a story about York on CNN, and they throw up a clip of the Thames," he told me once. "Never mind that York is more than two hundred miles from London."

We were contractually bound to spend a minimum of thirty minutes a day in the Confession Chamber. There was no schedule for who had to go when; as long as the room was free, it was fine to go in. We could break up our diary sessions into fifteen-minute increments if we wanted, so long as we logged the full half hour before midnight. We were welcome to go over our allotted time if we wanted and, conversely, the producers could force us to stay in there longer. Whenever they came over the intercom and summoned one of us to the Confession Chamber—which usually happened right after a heated argument or right before one started—we had to go, no objections.

Some of the contestants hated it. Luisa, in particular, found the process loathsome. "I got nothing to say for half an hour," she griped. "I sit in there like a dummy staring at the camera." Maggie wasn't particularly interested, either. She preferred to spend her days sleeping. As for me, I thrived on it.

The Confession Chamber was the one place I could speak my mind freely and honestly. I could say anything I wanted without

fear of being ridiculed, or even interrupted. We were always interviewed, and the number of questions varied depending on how
talkative you were. They usually started out by asking, "What's
on your mind today, Kat?" which opened up the door to a whole
host of possibilities.

It was a bit like *The Wizard of Oz*. The interviewer sat on the
other side of the wall, posing questions and watching me through
a two-way mirror. Usually I could place the voice—often Zaidee
herself did the interviews—but occasionally there was a new
person, a strange man or woman whom I didn't recognize.

A typical session would go something like this:

"How do you feel about your housemates?"

"Some of them are good . . . some not so good."

"Is there anyone in particular who has been annoying you
lately?"

"Alicia," I'd say. It was always Alicia.

"What does she do that bothers you?"

"She's started calling me Kit Kat, which I find insulting."

"Have you told her how you feel?"

"I tell her all the time. She says that nicknames are a form of
endearment."

"How are your weight-loss efforts going?"

"You guys are all-knowing, all-powerful. You tell me."

I liked to play it coy with them at first, but pretty soon I'd suc-
cumb to their prodding. It didn't take much to get me to speak
my mind. Day after day I sat there in that big cushiony chair,
mouthing off about whatever came to mind. The Confession
Chamber was an open forum. I felt like a politician giving an important speech; all ears were on me. I started using it as a plat-
form to spout my ideas about weight loss and fatphobia.

"We understand that human beings have different colored eyes and skin, that certain people go bald while others have a full head of hair, that some of us are short, some tall. Noses, mouths, feet, and ears all come in different shapes and sizes. So why not bodies?" I asked. "Why does most of society behave as though all of us—no matter who we are, no matter what our lineage— have been born with *identical* metabolisms? And that those of us who are heavier than 'the norm' got this way out of sheer gluttony? Is it so impossible to believe that our bodies are different by force of nature?"

"Do you feel the world treats you unfairly because you're overweight?" Zaidee responded.

"There's a definite bias, yeah. I mean, I know I overeat sometimes, but people act like that's all I do. And think of how different the reaction would be if I forced myself to throw up every time I pigged out, instead of keeping it down? People would feel sympathy toward me, not revulsion."

I thought of Cara Magley, and the promise I'd made to her that day we went shopping for plus-sized clothes. I had told her that if I got on television, I would challenge America's stereotypes about the overweight. No matter how personal the topics became, I honored my vow.

"My bra size is a 38C, which is by no means gargantuan," I said in one particularly heated session. "Yet, whenever I go to Victoria's Secret I can't find anything that fits me. I search and search and turn up *maybe* one or two 38C's. But they've got lots of 32C's, and lots of 36DD's. How often do you find a non-surgically-enhanced skinny girl with a rack that big? Does Victoria's Secret own stock in silicone implants or something? Because I am seriously starting to wonder."

On some levels it was embarrassing, but I knew all across America millions of big women were watching, cheering me on for speaking the truth. For all I knew, I might be the voice of a new generation.

The Gloria Steinem of fat girls.

* * *

"I can't believe you're really letting me do this," I said, staring at the tiny portable phone. "I thought phone calls were strictly off-limits."

Jagger nodded. "They are. But this is a special case. Tomorrow's the big announcement. Zaidee's giving you guys one phone call each. You get five minutes. And, it goes without saying, it's going to be taped." He smiled. "But then, you probably could have guessed that, right?"

He leaned forward and handed me the phone. His hand grazed mine.

It was May thirtieth, the day before the press release was slated to go out informing the world that Luisa, Regan, Alicia, Janelle, Maggie, and I were the contestants for *From Fat to Fabulous*. I had gone out to the pool for my interview session with Jagger and learned Zaidee was blessing us with a brief phone call home. It was bittersweet. I couldn't pass up the opportunity, but I knew I'd be left homesick and heartbroken when it was over.

"It's kind of like how they give prisoners one phone call," he said.

I shuddered. "Bad image."

"Maybe. But I do kind of feel like a warden sometimes." Jagger raised his eyebrows up and down in rapid succession. "Go on and make your call. Your five minutes starts as soon as you dial."

I stared anxiously at the phone, turning it over in my hands. For days I had been craving contact with the outside world. The obvious choice was to call Donna and beg her for information about Nick. Trouble was, I had no real way of asking without being obvious. I'd kept Nick a secret and didn't want to let the cat out of the bag now. I could get kicked off the show for lying on my application.

The most logical choice, therefore, was to call my parents. My mother and father didn't have the slightest clue I was going to be appearing on a reality show. My dad I wasn't worried about. He took most things in stride. But my mom was another story. My mom is not the hippest person when it comes to popular culture. She gave up entertainment television when *The Cosby Show* went off the air. But somehow, someway—whether through a commercial, an article in the paper, or even a well-meaning friend— she'd find out. She'd turn on the television, and there I'd be, in all my debauched glory.

I didn't want her to keel over from the shock.

Crossing my fingers for good luck, I punched in my parents' number in Denver. Predictably, Mom answered before the phone had finished its first ring. My mother's paranoid like that; she's convinced every call is a matter of life and death. When I was a child, her logic, though bizarre, made the tiniest bit of sense. "What if you were kidnapped and had managed to escape from your captors long enough to call me?" she said once. "I'd never forgive myself for not answering in time."

My entire upbringing was fueled by her strange beliefs, which rotated from hopeless apathy to extreme paranoia. One minute she was terrified I'd contract the bubonic plague from playing in the park sandbox; the next she'd given up caring altogether. "Why bother? The world's nothing but a giant deathtrap," she'd say, sighing. "No matter what you do, death finds you in the end."

Her reactions were, at best, unpredictable. There was no telling what she'd say about *From Fat to Fabulous*.

"Hi, Mom," I said. I didn't waste time asking how she was doing. That was an open-ended question that would invite a twenty-minute answer. I had to cut to the chase. "I need to tell you something."

"Oh my God!" I heard her draw in a breath. "You're pregnant!"

"Mom, no! Good God, that's not even possible," I said, feeling my face flame up.

"What do you mean by that?" she asked, suspiciously.

"Nothing," I assured her. "Don't worry about it." It had been many long agonizing months since I'd had sex. The last thing I wanted to do was admit that to all of America.

"Kat, you're not gay, are you?" she demanded.

"Mom!" I exclaimed, horrified. "Believe me, I'm straight. Now, I've only got five minutes here, less than that by now, and I've got to get this out." Before she could butt in, I blurted out: "I'm in Los Angeles. I got cast on a reality television show."

"Pat!" she screamed, summoning my father to pick up the extension. "Oh dear," she said. Then, "Oh, no!" She alternated between the two for a few seconds until my father picked up the line.

"What's going on here?"

"I'm on a reality TV show," I said.

"What channel?" he asked.

"Huh?"

"I'm going to go put it on."

I groaned. "Dad, I'm not on right *now*. We're filming. And I've only got a minute or two before the producers cut me off. I just wanted to say that I love you guys and I'll be thinking about you lots. And I'm sorry I didn't tell you before now, but I couldn't."

For the first time in what seemed like forever, both of my parents were speechless. Finally, as the last few seconds of the phone conversation dwindled away, Mom asked, "You're not on that island show, are you? Because, if you are, don't drink the water! Those people come home infected with parasites and all kinds of deadly tropical diseases."

I rolled my eyes. "No Mom, I'm in L.A. The water's perfectly fine."

"Hey, what's this show called?" my dad asked. "I wanna be sure and watch it."

"Uh, it's called *From Fat to Fabulous*," I whispered, as though lowering my voice would somehow make the title less humiliating. "It's a weight-loss show."

"Hmph," my mother said.

My father let out a small cheer. "Good for you, then. I'm glad to see you're finally doing something about your . . . problem. Such a shame to suffer with that for so many years. You've always had such a pretty face," he said.

Mercifully, our conversation was cut off before I could respond.

* * *

From Fat to Fabulous premiered on Saturday, June first at 8 P.M. Eastern Time—almost two weeks after we'd first entered the house.

Zaidee announced the news over the loudspeaker that morning.

"As of tonight, all of America will be watching *From Fat to Fabulous*," she said simply, then clicked off.

Nobody was happy with the time slot.

"Saturday night is the graveyard of TV," Alicia began ranting as soon as we found out. "We'll be lucky to get five million viewers."

"Think lower," Janelle said. "We're a summer show, remember. It'll probably be closer to three million."

"We're going to wind up one of those flash-in-the-pan shows," Alicia griped. "This isn't what I signed up for at all."

The whole thing was too depressing for words. Nobody wanted *From Fat to Fabulous* to fail—we were hoping it would become a pop culture icon like *Survivor* or *American Idol*. Even Maggie and I—the two contestants who professed to have the least interest in becoming celebrities—were visibly disappointed.

"I kind of always pictured *From Fat to Fabulous* being a hit," I admitted. At that moment, I realized how desperately I wanted fame. I vowed to do my part to spice things up. So when a reporter named Dean Abrams-Kreegley came to the house later that day to interview us for *Entertainment Weekly*'s online edition, I was ecstatic.

My first meeting with the press.

My first chance to radiate star potential. Me. In a feature on *Entertainment Weekly*'s website, one of my favorite magazines since I was a teenager. I thought, *This must be how Julia Roberts felt on the eve of* Pretty Woman's *release*. One minute I was a nobody, the next I'd be a household name.

I had to pinch myself to believe it was true.

Dean Abrams-Kreegley was a short, unremarkable-looking man with a small potbelly and a receding hairline. He wasn't unattractive, nor was he the slick celebrity reporter I'd been expecting. He looked like somebody's middle-aged dad. He interviewed us one at a time in the living room, writing frantically in a notebook. I wanted to ask him why, considering he had placed not one, but two, tape recorders down on the table in front of me. But I thought it might be a stupid question, the kind of thing they taught you in Journalism 101. And the last thing I wanted was to be known as the Girl Who Asked Stupid Questions.

Gigi Rucker sat in during all our interviews, carefully monitoring what was said. It was a bit nerve-wracking, but before long I was able to put her out of my mind, ignoring her the way I'd ignored the cameramen since day one.

Dean's visit was a much-needed breath of fresh air: I was so tired of staring at Janelle, Alicia, Maggie, Luisa, and Regan, I'd have welcomed anyone—my mother and father notwithstanding—into the house. He asked a lot of general questions: how I'd found out about *From Fat to Fabulous,* what motivated me to apply. At every turn I attempted to insert something poignant and heartfelt. "I'm here as an ambassador for big girls everywhere," I said, treating him to a sincere smile. "Through this show, I'm going to make sure the world knows how truly kind and wonderful most overweight people are. You shouldn't fear us. We're not monsters, contrary to popular belief."

"Interesting," he mumbled, jotting something down.

I beamed. I hoped they'd use that for a pull quote.

"Kat," Dean said, flipping through a stack of notes. "It says here your favorite book is *The Great Gatsby.* I find it very striking that you'd pick that, given how many of the themes in the novel—set in the excess of the Jazz Age—could be applied to today's reality television craze. Do you care to comment?"

Did I care to comment? What was this, Freshman Lit? *The Great Gatsby* has nothing to do with reality television! I bit my lip.

Dean added, "Consider Gatsby's incessant posturing, as well as his desire to become well-known and well-respected. It wasn't enough to gain wealth; he needed to have the fame to feel satisfied. Much as many otherwise ordinary people so desperately crave the short-lived fame that comes along with a television appearance."

I glared at him. He had a lot of balls, calling my shot at fame "short-lived."

"There's a whole host of ways you could connect it to America's fascination with reality shows. When we watch these programs we're seeing normal citizens portrayed as larger-than-life, Gatsbylike characters. And consider, also, how Gatsby achieved the Great American Dream, much like a modern-day reality star. Because the American Dream is no longer rags-to-riches. The new American Dream is fame," he said. "Everybody wants to be the next big thing."

When Dean still didn't get an answer, he tossed me an easy one, "Who's your favorite character in the book?" He eyed me suspiciously.

It was obvious Dean thought I hadn't read the novel.

Well, I'd show him. I *had* read *The Great Gatsby*. Unfortunately, I'd read it nearly ten years ago. The only character popping into my mind was Gatsby. I couldn't say him, for obvious reasons. *Think,* Kat, *think!* I scolded myself. I looked to Gigi for help, but she just shrugged. I squinted my eyes, struggling to remember. But no matter how hard I concentrated, the names that came to mind were Redford and Mia. As in Robert Redford and Mia Farrow, the actors who'd starred in the movie version of the book. I knew Redford had played Gatsby, and Mia his love interest. But, for the life of me, I couldn't recall her name. Then it came to me. Like light illuminating a darkened room, my mind filled with knowledge.

"Nick," I said at last. "My favorite character in *The Great Gatsby* was Nick."

I had never been so grateful to Nick Appleby in my entire life. He didn't know it, but he'd jogged my memory.

Dean raised an eyebrow in surprise. Clearly, he'd expected me to bomb.

"I like Nick because he's a silent observer and as the narrator he offers all these really great insights to the reader." It was a vague answer, and probably something that would never make the article. But I was relieved, nonetheless. If I'd failed to come up with anything, he'd have surely written about how foolish I was, not even recalling the simplest of details from my all-time favorite book.

"So you work in PR. What's that like?"

I brightened. Finally, a bona fide chance to talk the firm up to the media. "I work for a top-notch firm named Hood and Geddle-finger. We're talking the best of the best. Make sure you get it right," I instructed. "It's spelled G-e-d-d-l-e-f-i-n-g-e-r."

"Okay," Dean said, not writing it down.

"I love it there, but it's not my dream career."

"That's interesting. What do you want to do?"

"Write romance novels. I love happy endings," I told him, wondering what he'd say if I requested his business card. After all, he might be a good contact person for the future. Maybe he could get a review of my book in *Entertainment Weekly*. I decided against it. I wasn't sure about the protocol, and didn't want to appear inappropriate, or naïve.

"I have it in my notes that you'd like your autobiography to be called *Height/Weight Disportionate*," he said. "Now, is that a misprint?"

I shook my head. "It's a play on words. Like taking that saying 'height/weight proportionate' and altering it to fit me."

"Right," Dean remarked, scribbling in his notebook. "And you want your title to be *Height/Weight* Dis*portionate*?"

I stared at him, realizing what he'd said. "Dis*pro*portionate," I corrected.

"That's not what it says here." He thumbed through his stack of papers, retrieving a Xeroxed copy of my application form. I stared down at the page and saw, much to my horror, in my late-night dash to finish the application I'd misspelled the word.

"It's an honest mistake," I fumbled. "I was tired."

"We're pretty much done here," Dean said, rising from his seat and shaking my hand. "It's been nice talking with you, Kat. Good luck in the competition. Would you mind sending Maggie Strickland in?"

* * *

"Okay, guys, worst fat-girl moment."

"Oh, God," I groaned. "Do we really have to do this?"

"Yep. It's on the card," Alicia said.

The following Tuesday, Zaidee came on over the house inter-com and ordered us into the living room. When we got there, we found a stack of index cards containing various "discussion questions."

"Sit in a circle and go through the list," Zaidee's voice com-manded, drifting down from the ceiling.

I hated all the games she made us play. I often found myself wishing we did something useful, like learning how to cope with stress eating, or discussing tips to get the most out of our exer-cise sessions. But, no. We played games.

The first question on the list was simple: *Describe your worst fat-girl moment. What makes it stand out above the rest?* Alicia was playing emcee, prompting us to play along.

"I don't think I can pick only one," Regan said. "There are too many."

We all nodded. It was true. How could we roll a lifetime of in-sults and demoralization into one pat answer?

"Okay, I'll go first," Maggie volunteered. "A few weeks ago

Thomas, Owen, and I go out for a steak dinner. Thomas and Owen place their orders, no problem. But when I ask for the twelve-ounce sirloin, the waiter tells me, and I quote, 'Ma'am, I suggest you have the grilled chicken salad. I don't feel comfortable serving you a steak.' So I say, 'What I eat is my choice.' Then he says 'Ma'am, when a patron is too drunk, a bartender cuts him off—he brings him a club soda instead of a beer. When I see someone so obviously obese I cut them off from fattening food.'"

My jaw dropped. I made a mental note to never visit Jackson, Mississippi, again so long as I lived.

"Whoa," Janelle said. "What the hell was his problem?"

"You should have told him you were on Atkins," I volunteered. "That would've shut him up."

"I'd have squirted ketchup in his face," Luisa chimed in.

"I've had that happen to me," Regan said sadly.

Maggie looked alarmed. "Someone's squirted ketchup in your face?"

"No, I'm talking about nasty servers. Lots of times when I go out to eat, waiters tell me about the dieter's special, or offer to show me the low-calorie menu items."

"Guys, I don't think that's the kind of thing they're looking for," Alicia jumped in. "It says, '*worst* fat girl moment.' Those are pretty trivial things you're talking about."

"That *was* my worst moment," Maggie said indignantly. "Unless I go back twenty years, before I was married."

"Alicia, has a waiter ever been mean to you like that?" I asked.

"No," she admitted.

"Well, then, don't call it trivial."

"Whatever." Alicia rolled her eyes. "I'll go next. Show you girls how it's *done*. Two years ago, I was dancing in this club—"

"Pole dancing?" I asked innocently.

Regan burst out laughing so hard diet Coke spewed out her nose. "Sorry, Alicia," she said, running into the kitchen to get a napkin. "Kat, you are so mean."

"Fuck her. She's jealous," Alicia said. She waited until Regan had returned, and then continued talking. "As I was saying before Kat *rudely* interrupted, I was in this club dancing and this man came up to me. Really nicely dressed—designer suit, the whole nine yards. He introduced himself and said he was a talent scout for ICM, and he was looking for some hot new acts to represent."

"Ooh," Luisa said. "Let me guess, he wanted to 'represent you' in his bed?"

Alicia glared at her. "Hardly. The guy was legit. He wanted to sign me as a dancer, take me on the road for backup gigs with people like Janet Jackson."

I narrowed my eyes suspiciously. I couldn't imagine any legitimate talent scout approaching a random girl at a dance club and inviting her to come on the road with Janet Jackson.

Janelle and I exchanged pointed looks. "So, what happened next?" she asked.

"Okay, so they flew me from Boston to New York and I met with all these record label execs and danced for them at their offices."

"What does this have to do with being big?" I asked. "Remember, they want your worst big-girl moment."

"Wait for it," she snapped. "It's coming. So, after I dance they were totally going to offer me a contract to go on the road but then this one exec guy goes, 'Nope, she's too fat. All our dancers have to wear a four.'" Alicia sat back, folding her arms against her chest triumphantly. "So there you have it. Because I wasn't a size four or smaller I couldn't go."

Never in my life had I heard a story that reeked of so much bullshit, on so many different levels.

"Alicia, girl, you are a *liar*," Luisa said. "They don't do it like that. The musicians pick their dancers. It's got nothing to do with some record label guys. If you get to dance with Janet Jackson, it's 'cause Janet picked you from a casting call herself."

"Have you ever been a backup dancer for a major act?"

"Nope. But I hear things."

"Apparently you hear things wrong." Alicia shook her head. "That's how it happened."

"Lordy, here we go again. All night, she talks like this," Luisa griped.

"What's the point of this?" I asked, trying to head off a fight. "I don't see why we have to waste our time answering a bunch of dumb questions."

"My guess is, they need some more footage for this week's show," Janelle suggested. "They'll probably edit it so it looks like we just happened to be sitting around talking about these things."

"Really?" Regan asked in surprise.

"You wouldn't believe the things they can do with editing." Janelle laughed.

15

Weight of the World

At the end of our fourth week in the house we were given a small treat: pasta with meat sauce and garlic bread for lunch. It was a welcome surprise; until that point our lunches had consisted of either grilled chicken salads with fat-free dressing, or turkey sandwiches with a side of carrot sticks. It got old, quick.

"Eat up. You're going to need your strength," Zaidee warned mysteriously, then clicked off of the intercom.

"What was *that* all about?" Regan asked.

"I guess Greg's going to work us really hard or something," I said. "Teach us how to bench-press the cameramen."

We laughed. Greg had become an inside joke. Our visits to the gym were turning out to be largely unhelpful, as Greg seemed more concerned with getting screen time than teaching us proper form. While most of us were sticking to a daily exercise schedule to fatten up our bank accounts, Greg had little impact on us. He was too busy preening for the cameras.

When lunch was finished it was Jagger, not Greg, who came for us. "Hi, girls," he said, breezing into the dining room. "Did you have a good meal?"

"Excellent," Janelle supplied. "Thanks."

"Glad to hear it," he said, motioning for us to follow him. "The next contest is unique in many ways. It's called Weight of the World on Your Shoulders. You'll be competing as individuals, but whether you succeed depends on how the group does as a whole," Jagger explained, when we'd settled into the living room. "In order to receive your reward, each of you must perform a separate task. All of the tasks have an embarrassment factor. Some higher than others."

I rolled my eyes. Here he went again with the dramatics.

"But before I divvy up the challenges, how would you all like to get a look at your reward?" Jagger asked, producing a briefcase. Without waiting for an answer, he laid it on the table in front of us and flipped open the top.

"Oh my God," I said. The others had similar reactions.

"We get to keep all that?" Regan squeaked.

"How much is it?" Alicia demanded.

Jagger pulled a wad of bills out and ran his fingers over the edge. "This briefcase contains seventy-five thousand dollars in one-hundred-dollar bills. Finish today's challenge successfully, and this will be added to your bank. Fail, and your bank accounts will be twenty thousand dollars lighter."

"Hold on," Alicia said. "So, if we don't complete our assignments we'll each lose twenty grand. But if we win, we'll only get . . ." She thought for a minute. "Twelve thousand five hundred dollars. That doesn't sound fair."

Jagger grinned. "You've underestimated us, Alicia. If you

win, you'll be given seventy-five thousand dollars *apiece*. Still wanna call the competition unfair?"

"Uh, no," Alicia said, "I think I'll keep my mouth shut."

"Finally," I quipped, "my prayers have been answered."

She scowled at me. "You might want to try shoving a cork in it sometimes, too, Kat. God knows nobody around here wants to listen to you ramble all day."

I was about to zing her with a comeback, when Jagger held up his hand for silence. "I wouldn't advise you girls to start arguing. Like I said before, teamwork is a vital part of Weight of the World on Your Shoulders."

I folded my arms across my chest and sank back against the couch. As much as it burned me up, I knew he was right. From the sound of it, we were going to be required to accomplish some pretty tough feats. I didn't need to waste any more energy on Alicia than I already had.

"Let the games begin," Jagger said, pulling out an opaque black box, with *Fat2Fab* written on it in huge pink letters. "In this box are six envelopes, each containing the instructions needed to complete one of the challenges." He fished out a small gold envelope and held it up for emphasis, then dropped it back in with the others. "You'll each take turns drawing. Unseal the envelope . . . and seal your fate."

I groaned inwardly at the bad pun.

"Whatever task you get *you* must complete. No exchanging."

Once again, the order had been predetermined. Alicia was up first. She made a big production of digging around in the box for several minutes before finally selecting an envelope.

"If you would be so kind as to read it to the group," Jagger instructed.

"Okay," she said, ripping it open. "'Get out those dancing shoes and sharpen up your vocals,'" she began, "'because tonight you will perform in front of a crowd of hundreds at Club Mango in West Hollywood.'"

I watched her eyes grow large as they scanned over the second half of the page.

"Read it out loud, Alicia," Jagger prompted.

"Oh, sorry," she said, startled. It took a lot to shock Alicia. I couldn't imagine what was next. "Okay, where was I? 'Club Mango in West Hollywood,'" she repeated, finding her place. "'*From Fat to Fabulous* has taken the liberty of entering you into Club Mango's monthly Britney Spears look-alike contest. Pull out all the stops singing and dancing to two of Britney's biggest hits. Make sure you put a little heart and a lot of soul into your routine. Because in order to successfully complete the assignment, you've got to get the crowd behind you.'"

She stared at Jagger. "This is bullshit. I could try my best and there's no guarantee I'll win."

"You don't have to win," Jagger said. "All you have to do is get cheered, not jeered."

"It should really be enough that I enter." She stormed back to the couch and plopped down. "I can't control what other people do."

Maggie went next, drawing a challenge that was easier than Alicia's, though still humiliating. She had to walk up and down the Santa Monica Pier collecting one thousand signatures for "National Fat Acceptance Day."

"Is there such a thing?" she asked, confused.

Jagger shook his head. "You'll be attempting to establish it."

"I don't understand why you want me to do this, but I won't say no," Maggie remarked, shaking her head.

When Luisa's turn came, she bounded up to the front of the room. "I cannot wait. A chance to get out of this house!" she said, rubbing her hands together in anticipation.

Her tone changed as soon as she opened the envelope. "Oh, no . . . It says, 'Laughter is the best medicine and tonight you will be playing doctor. Crack up the crowd at The Laugh Lizard on the Sunset Strip with your fifteen-minute comedy act. The joke's on you—literally. Your comedy routine will consist of nothing but fat jokes, supplied for you by *From Fat to Fabulous*'s talented writing staff.'"

Luisa stood there for a minute, speaking rapidly to herself in Spanish.

"In English, *por favor*," Jagger instructed.

"Yeah, I will do it," she said, and then calmly sat down.

"What were you saying?" I asked her.

"Cussin'," she said. "Trying to slip past the censors." She grinned. "Maybe they don't know Spanish."

I doubted that, but I admired her gusto.

Janelle went next, drawing the most horrible challenge of all: posing nude for a group of art students at UCLA.

Her face went white as a ghost when she saw it, but she quickly recovered. "Piece of cake," she said, looking sick to her stomach.

"I'm so sorry," I told her when she'd rejoined us on the couch. "That sucks." But what I really thought was, *Thank God it's not me.*

"No, no. Don't be sorry," Janelle insisted. "I can do this. Really, I can do this."

If Janelle handled it the best, then Regan certainly handled it the worst.

"I have to dance with the Laker Girls!" she wailed, after ripping open her envelope. "During the halftime show at tonight's play-off game!"

"Regan, please read the clue out loud in its entirety," Jagger said firmly.

She ignored him. "I have to put on that tiny uniform and dance in front of all those people!" She burst into tears.

Janelle and Luisa rushed forward to console her.

"It's going to be okay," Janelle said, stroking her long hair. "It'll be over so quickly you won't have time to think about it."

Luisa agreed. "And you get to go out into the *world* tonight." She sighed. "Think how good it will be to leave this house. Maybe you will get to see some of La La Land."

"I don't wanna see Los Angeles!" she cried. "I want to stay right here where I am, safe in this house."

Jagger let Regan bawl for a little bit, then he summoned me. I had gotten so caught up in the commotion that I'd forgotten to take my turn.

"Kat, by process of elimination this last golden envelope belongs to you." He held out the box, making me reach inside to claim my fate.

"All right," I said, "here goes nothing."

I tore into the envelope and began to read. It was a poem. "'Love is in the air tonight/ Beneath the flickering candlelight/ Will you dine with your soul mate?/ Or suffer through a painful blind date?/ At six-thirty your chariot will arrive/ Steal a kiss and win the prize.'" I stopped to consider this for a minute. Bad poetry aside, the clue hadn't made a whole lot of sense. "So let me get this straight—I have to make out with some strange guy in order to win? What is this? Porn TV?"

Jagger flashed me a quick sympathetic smile, then focused his attention on Regan. "A car will pick you up in two hours," he told her. "Make sure you're ready."

Regan had temporarily calmed down but at Jagger's words, she started crying all over again.

"Now that you're all aware of your roles in the Weight of the World on Your Shoulders, I'd advise you to start preparing. Kat, your date will arrive at six-thirty tonight, and Janelle, your posing session will take place Monday afternoon. As for the rest of you . . . it'll be a waiting game. You won't know when your time will come."

Regan sniffled loudly, and Janelle leaned over to give her a hug.

"As you've already seen, the hardest part of this competition will be mental," Jagger said. "Remember, all six of you must successfully complete your individual challenges. If one of you fails, all of you lose. Additionally, the outcome of the game won't be revealed until all the tasks have been completed. In other words." He stopped and looked around at us. "You cannot breathe a word to anyone. When the time is right, I'll announce the results."

With that, he made his way down the hall and into the production room.

Despite Jagger's suggestion to keep the in-fighting to a minimum, we started arguing the second he'd left.

"I think we should forget this whole thing," Regan said. "Since we're all competing together, it doesn't matter if we win or lose."

Luisa disagreed. "Seventy-five thousand dollars is a lot of money. It matters very much."

"No, it doesn't," Regan insisted. "Only one of us can win the *From Fat to Fabulous* bank—the one with the most money in it at the end. I think we should forget about it."

"Are you nuts?" Alicia demanded. "That's seventy-five thousand dollars extra one of us could walk out of here with."

Luisa nodded vehemently. "Exactly what I'm trying to say."

"There's no guarantee that I'll win it," Regan said. "I could humiliate myself tonight and for what? If I don't win the show, I won't see a penny of that seventy-five grand I helped earn. Plus, I have to do my task tonight. What's to stop the rest of you from changing your minds and backing out later?"

She had a point.

"Let me get this straight. You're afraid you'll humiliate yourself at the Lakers game and then we'll all decide to blow off our challenges?" I asked.

She stuck out her lower lip. "Yep."

"We won't do that," I assured her, hoping I was right. "We're in this together. You do your part, and we'll do ours."

Secretly, I was glad I'd drawn the easiest task. Sure, I had to go out on a blind date with some guy who, in all likelihood, would turn out to be a giant oaf. I even had to kiss him on national television. But as far as I could tell, my challenge had nothing to do with weight and it wasn't even all that embarrassing. Besides, I'd never been out on a blind date before and I had no idea what to expect—tonight would serve as a practice run for when I met Nick.

"Girls," Maggie, ever the mother-figure, interjected. "We have to consider the bottom line. Stop thinking about the money. Stop thinking about your pride. Think about why you came on *From Fat to Fabulous* in the first place—to prove something to the world. To prove that overweight people are just as good as anyone else. What kind of a message will we send out if we quit? I have my son to think about. What kind of example will it set for him if Mommy gives up in the face of adversity?"

I didn't know about Maggie, but proving something to the world hadn't been my primary motivation for being on the show. It was in the mix, all right, but it was shoved beneath the more pressing reasons: weight loss, Nick Appleby, and money. In that order.

"Maggie's right," Janelle chimed in. She'd remained uncharacteristically quiet during our conversation. I noticed, now, that some of the color was starting to return to her face. "The last thing I want to do is pose nude in front of a group of art students. But you know what? I'm going to do it if it kills me. And"—she gave us a crooked smile—"it very well may."

Alicia looked thoughtful. "I have a suggestion. Let's take a vow. We'll all swear right here and now *not* to throw these competitions. Win or lose, we'll all give it our best shot. Deal?"

"I'm in," I told her.

Janelle, Luisa, and Maggie quickly agreed. It all came down to Regan.

"Okay," she said reluctantly. "I'll do it. But don't expect me to be happy about it."

"It doesn't have to make you happy. You just have to do it," Luisa said.

Janelle snickered. "My ex-husband Matt used to say those very words to me, every single night."

* * *

It wasn't until an hour later that I realized what Regan was up to. I overheard her in the kitchen, pleading with Alicia.

"It's fixed," Regan griped. "Why else would Janelle—the only artist in the whole house—be the one who gets to pose nude?"

She had to be joking. "What do you mean, 'gets to pose nude'? You say that like it's some kind of a prize," I said, walking into the room.

Regan jumped in surprise. Alicia shot me a foul glare.

"Compared to cheering at the Lakers game, it *is* a prize!" Regan wailed. "I have to put on a teeny uniform and dance around in front of a crowd of twenty thousand people! I'm going to be sandwiched out there between all those beautiful girls."

"Would you honestly rather trade places with Janelle?" I asked, in disbelief. Crowd or no crowd, getting naked in public sounded horrifying to me. The sort of thing I had recurring nightmares about.

"I'd rather trade places with *you*," Regan snapped.

"No shit," Alicia agreed. "But Regan, I think you're wrong. There's no way the competition is fixed. Otherwise, I'd be the one going out with the hot young stud, not Kat. That would make for much better TV."

"Get over yourself," I said, rolling my eyes.

"Kat's task is the only one that doesn't have anything to do with weight," Regan continued. "It isn't fair."

"It's a game," I reminded her. "Of course it's not fair."

"Don't stress about it, Regan," said Alicia, patting her on the head. "Kit Kat's 'hot date' will probably be so dull they won't even air it. My guess is it ends up on the cutting room floor." She ran her fingers across her throat in a slashing motion.

"I've got a great idea!" Regan burst out. "Maybe you could switch with Kat and I could switch with Maggie," she said, going on as though I wasn't even in the room. "Wouldn't that be exciting?"

"We're not allowed to trade," I reminded her.

"I know that's what Jagger said, but if anyone can talk Zaidee into it, you can," she prodded Alicia.

"It might be worth a shot," Alicia mused.

"You have this way with Zaidee," she continued, gaining enthusiasm. "Remember when you complained about the breakfast food and the next morning she put out fruit? Come on, Alicia, she *listens* to you."

"She does, doesn't she?"

It was all I could do to keep from screaming. "You two are so full of it," I burst out. "A game's a game! You can't change the rules just because you don't like them!"

"Easy for you to say," Alicia criticized, at long last acknowledging me. "You'd be crying your eyes out if you had to cheer at the Lakers game. I think Regan's handling it remarkably well, all things considered."

"Thank you." Regan beamed.

Alicia tousled her hair. "Don't worry, Regan. We're going to tough it out together."

"Oh puh-*leeze*," I groaned. "You've got an awful lot of nerve, acting like your task is sooo hard. All you have to do is enter a glorified karaoke contest. Big whoop."

Alicia glared at me. "I never said it was *hard*. I just said I didn't want to do it."

"Yeah, well I don't want to go on this 'blind date' either," I confessed. "So what's the difference?"

"There's a big difference," Regan argued. "While the rest of us have to suffer, you get to do something fun. Who knows, you might even meet a wonderful guy and fall in love." She sighed.

"You may think it's fun, but I'm a nervous wreck."

Alicia eyed me curiously. "Kit Kat, don't take this the wrong way, but have you been out on very many dates before? Because I get the distinct feeling that you haven't."

Regan cracked up.

"No," Alicia said, holding up a hand to silence her. "Jokes aside. I'm being absolutely serious."

I was stung. I wanted to shout into her face, to tell her all about Nick Appleby, my sexy, wealthy, European boyfriend. But I wasn't stupid. "Boy, you'd love that wouldn't you. Big old Fat Kat going on her first date on national television," I snarled. "To answer your question, yes, I've been on many, many dates."

Luisa chose that exact moment to come sauntering in. It was a good thing, too, because Alicia and I were gearing up to have a major fight.

"They gave me the script," she said, waving around some papers in the air. "The jokes I have to tell." She made a face.

"Oh, God, how bad is it?" I asked.

"Not good," she said. "I have to talk about being a BBW, or Big Beautiful Woman. I have to give them our 'battle cry.' What that is supposed to mean, I don't know."

"What do you have to say?" Regan asked, momentarily distracted from her own impending doom.

"Ahem," Luisa cleared her throat and began reading. "'It's not the size of the ocean, it's the motion of the ocean.'"

"Yuck!" Alicia cried. "That's absurd. And everybody knows it isn't even a valid point."

"No," Luisa agreed. "It's not. I also have to say, 'It's good to be large and in charge.' Then I have to say, 'Once you go fat, you never go back.'"

"That's the truth," Regan said solemnly. "Ever since I gained weight in the third grade I haven't been able to take it off."

"I think they mean the guy," I told her. "Like, once a guy gets with a fat girl he'll never want another thin girl again, which is complete crap. Most guys hate dating bigger women and, on the rare occasion they do it, it's a onetime thing."

Luisa nodded. "Damn straight. Oh, I also have to go, 'Fat girls are better because we serve up meat with our gravy.'"

"That's enough!" Alicia burst out. "They can't make you stand up and spurt this trash. It's not even funny, it's just plain dumb. Nobody's going to laugh; they're going to stare at you like you're some kind of a moron."

"You're totally right," I said, turning to Alicia, our fight momentarily forgotten. "There's got to be some way Luisa can get out of this."

"My comedy act is called FAT: It's Not a Four-Letter Word," Luisa offered, looking miserable. "The title is so bad."

"This show's writers are hacks," Alicia said. "They wouldn't know a joke if it hit them in the face."

"Well, why are there writers on a *reality* show, anyway?" I demanded.

"They script the competitions," she said. "And somebody has to compile Jagger's script. Though, as dumb as it is, you'd think that bozo came up with it off the top of his head."

"Jagger's not so bad," Luisa said.

I groaned. "What are you, his cheerleader?"

She shrugged it off. "After he interviewed me yesterday we got to talking. He's a smart cookie. He's got a business degree from Penn State."

Zaidee's voice clicked on over the loudspeaker. "Luisa, please come to the Confession Chamber."

"No, not again! I've already been in there an hour today!" She stomped out of the room.

"You know, Regan, I'd talk to Zaidee about letting me go on that date, if it weren't for one thing," Alicia said.

Great, we were back to this again.

"What's that?" I asked, heaving my shoulders in a sigh.

"If I went, it would drive the censors wild. My date would

probably be too hot for network television." She snickered. "Some of the affiliates might even pull the show because of it."

"Give me a break!" I exploded. "What are you planning to do, blow some guy on national television?"

She stared at me in mock horror. "Of course not. I'm not a *slut*. But things might get kind of hot and heavy, that's all."

"What makes you so sure of that?" I challenged.

Alicia smiled. "I have that kind of impact on guys. Always have."

"You have that kind of impact on *everybody*. You're very persuasive," Regan said. "That's why you've gotta go talk to Zaidee for me. Get her to switch up the assignments. Please, Alicia! You can take the date and I'll go out getting signatures. Maggie can dance with the Laker Girls. I'm sure she won't mind."

I glared at them. Who the hell did they think they were? They couldn't just rearrange the game however they felt like it.

"Shouldn't you be getting ready for your big night out, Regan?" I reminded her. "You've only got half an hour until the car gets here."

"Alicia," she said, looking hopefully at her. "If you're going to talk to Zaidee, can you do it now?"

Alicia shrugged. "I'm sorry, babe, but I'm going to take a pass. The more I think about it, the more I kinda want to play Britney Spears."

Regan went stalking out of the room, her eyes, once again, filled with tears. This time no one tried to stop her.

16

Technical Difficulties

Six-thirty came and went and my mystery date never showed.

Over the course of my dating life, I've been stood up more times than I care to remember. Usually, I take it personally. In this instance I was relieved.

I waited in the living room for what seemed like hours, drinking Perrier and gabbing with Janelle. Before long, we'd started feasting on Hershey's Kisses and potato chips, which we'd snagged from the Tomb of Temptation. I hadn't eaten dinner with the group since I was expecting to go out with this mystery man, so I was starving. Our cameramen hovered as we chowed down.

"Have you ever been on a blind date?" I asked Janelle.

"Are you kidding me?" She scrunched up her face. "I've been on nearly two dozen. And that's just in the last year." Catching my stricken expression, she added, "Okay, I'm exaggerating— but only a little. All my life people have been trying to set me up. Everyone seems to think they know the 'perfect guy' for me."

"Tell me about it," I groaned. "Over the years I've come to realize that when someone says, 'I have the perfect guy for you,' what they really mean is, 'I have the perfect *fat* guy for you.' People fix big men up with skinny cheerleader types all the time. Yet, nobody would ever *dream* of setting up a big girl with a thin guy."

Janelle nodded solemnly. "You know why that is, don't you?"

I shook my head.

"In our society, overweight men are considered sweet and cuddly. Teddy bears, if you will. But overweight women? We're whales." Janelle smoothed a wrinkle from her shirt, knocking her lapel mic off in the process. Before she even had time to re-place it, a voice came on over the intercom. "Janelle, please put on your microphone immediately."

She jumped. "Sorry," she mumbled, hastily refastening it.

We stared at each other in surprise, the realization of the cameras seeping in once again.

"You know what they're going to do with your blind date," Janelle, ever the reality-TV theorist, remarked.

"I have no clue," I said, unwrapping a piece of chocolate and popping it in my mouth.

"Come on, Kat, you're hipper than that. They'll slice and dice the footage to make it look like you were so nervous on your date you ate a mountain of food."

I laughed. I was so hungry I could have eaten a mountain. "It figures I'd do this the night before weigh-in," I groaned. "I'm probably going to be up ten pounds tomorrow," I said, folding up the empty bag of chips and placing it on the floor.

Despite the circumstances, we were having a pretty good time. If it weren't for the boom mic, the cameras, and the blar-ing lights, it could have been a typical girls' night. On some level, I was able to fool myself into thinking that Janelle was

Donna. Despite their physical differences, they reminded me a lot of each other.

"Maybe this means you don't have to go," Janelle offered, munching on chocolates. "It's not your fault if the guy canceled."

"We don't know for sure that he canceled," I said.

I had gone into the Confession Chamber twice to ask what was going on, and both times Zaidee had stonewalled me.

"As soon as I know something definite, I'll pass that on to you. Sit tight," she'd instructed.

"Maybe this is a part of their master plan," I said, taking a gulp of Perrier. "This mystery guy's probably going to show up two hours late and have 'forgotten' his wallet at home."

Janelle giggled. "I get it. A day late and a dollar short."

"Right. And he'll be dressed in dirty jeans and a wife-beater's shirt. In the car ride over, he'll keep picking his nose and wiping it on his pants."

"Gross!" she shrieked. "Person trying to eat here."

"Then we'll get to some fancy-schmancy restaurant with a name like Chez Philippe, and dumb butt will order snails, and then proceed to throw them up all over the table."

Janelle set down her chocolates. "I think this is a lost cause."

I ignored her protests. I was having too much fun. "And after we have some extraordinarily expensive meal, he'll ask me to pay."

"Of course."

"And since the show has my wallet, I won't be able to."

Janelle smiled, getting into it. "You'll have to go in the back and wash dishes for two hours to work off your escargot."

"Then he'll try and grope me in the car ride back, and I'll have to fight him off with a stick. And finally, at long last, I'll go in for a quick peck on the cheek and he'll try and shove his tongue in my ear."

"Yep," she said, cracking up. "I bet you're right."

"I know I am."

"This guy's going to be a total jackass. All you have to do is kiss him by the night's end. That's it, right?"

"Uh-huh."

"So, obviously, the producers want to make that as hard as possible," Janelle said thoughtfully. "If the guy they send over is beyond gross, you're not going to want to lay a hand on him."

"Exactly," I agreed. "It's probably going to be the date from hell and it'll take all the strength I have not to get up and leave midway through."

I was so sure we'd nailed it. So when Zaidee came over the loudspeaker and called me into the Confession Chamber forty-five minutes later I figured it was to tell me my date was running behind. It wasn't.

In fact, Zaidee's news totally threw me for a loop.

As soon as she'd told me, I hurried back downstairs to run it by Janelle.

"This is really weird," I muttered, shaking my head.

"What's up?"

"Technical difficulties," I said, looking at her in bewilderment.

"Technical difficulties?" Janelle repeated. "What, was this guy's face so ugly he broke the camera?"

I laughed. "I don't know. Zaidee wouldn't tell me anything. She just said 'technical difficulties' and left it at that."

"So when's your mystery man going to be here?"

"That's the weirdest part," I told her. "He isn't. The date's been postponed indefinitely. They're going to reschedule it at a later time."

* * *

The next morning Regan was missing.

"She never returned from the Lakers game," Janelle said, waking me just before 8 A.M. The overhead lights had not yet switched on, though sunlight had been creeping in through the windows for hours.

"Who?" I asked, still half-asleep.

"Regan!" Janelle said, shaking my arm. "She never came back from cheering at the Lakers game last night!"

"Oh," I said, the realization dawning on me. I rolled over and rubbed the sleep out of my eyes. Sure enough, Regan's bed was empty and, more telling, still made up from the day before. "That's weird. Maybe the Lakers won and she went out with Shaq to celebrate," I quipped.

"Very funny. I was thinking more along the lines of she hurt herself trying to do a complicated move. Kat, what if she's in the hospital or something awful? Or what if she got so fed up she quit the show?"

As if on cue, the overhead lights sprang to life. "Ugh," I groaned, yanking the covers up over my head. "I can't deal with this at the crack of dawn." As long as we made it downstairs in time for breakfast, the producers didn't seem to mind if we slept in from time to time.

Janelle sighed. "You go back to sleep. I'm going to go find out what I can about Regan."

"Mmm hmm," I mumbled, dozing off.

A few minutes later Janelle was back. "I went into the Confession Chamber," she said, ripping the covers off of my head.

"Ahh," I grumbled, as light flooded my eyes. "You're not going to let me miss this, are you?"

"Nope." She plopped down on the foot of my bed. "It's too good."

"All right," I said, hoisting myself up on my elbows. "You've got my undivided attention. What happened?"

"From the sound of it, your guess wasn't so far off."

"My guess?" I repeated, confused.

"You said she was probably out celebrating."

"Oh yeah, with Shaq. You're kidding, right?"

Janelle pursed her lips and shook her head. "Get this—Zaidee told me that Regan was a total smash last night, and the show gave her a special reward for going first. Zaidee wouldn't dish on whether Regan succeeded or not. But I think it's pretty obvious, don't you?"

"Damn!" I cried, instantly pissed-off I hadn't drawn the Laker Girls challenge. "Did she say what it was?"

"No, she said we'll find out later, when Regan gets back. But Zaidee refused to tell me when that will be."

As it turned out, Regan didn't come back until late in the afternoon, just before our first weekly weigh-in. Her face was flushed, her eyes bright. I had never seen her so happy.

"Kat," she said when she saw me. "They love us out there!"

"So, it wasn't that bad?" I asked tentatively.

"It was *amazing*!" she enthused. "Everyone was clapping and cheering for me. They all knew my name!"

Since I wasn't allowed to ask her whether she'd succeeded or not, I changed the subject. "What were you *doing* last night? We've been worried sick."

"Interviews," she squealed. "Then Zaidee took me out for this really expensive Italian meal." Regan twirled around happily for a minute. Then her face fell. "There's only one bad thing."

She paused. "I think *Fat2Fab* tanked in the ratings Saturday night."

"Why would you think that?" I asked. "I mean, if everybody knew your name then it must have done well."

Regan looked skeptical. "When I talked with the guy from *Us Weekly* this morning he kept asking if I was disappointed with how the show was doing."

Janelle's eyes grew large. "Where was Zaidee when he said that?"

"I don't know. But that other producer woman, Gigi Rucker, was sitting right next to me the whole time."

"And she let him talk to you about the ratings?" Janelle asked, incredulously.

Regan shrugged. "She said I had a right to know."

* * *

The weekly weigh-ins were held every Sunday, just before dinnertime.

In my first four weeks, I'd managed to drop seventeen pounds, a monumental accomplishment. Surprisingly, they turned out to be one of the least embarrassing things *From Fat to Fabulous* forced us to do. I had fully expected Jagger to march us out in a big group, then force us to step up on the living room scale.

Instead, we got weighed in Greg's Gym, quietly, and in total privacy. It was the one place where Zaidee allowed us to hang on to a shred of dignity. The decision of whether to reveal our weekly weight to the other contestants was left totally up to us. Our progress wasn't posted on a chart, and Jagger didn't announce it in his usual dramatic fashion.

To be perfectly honest, this shocked the hell out of me.

"How come they're not making our weigh-ins into a huge ceremony?" I asked Greg one morning, while chugging along on the treadmill.

"Some things are personal. So says Zaidee. Me? I think they should do it in Dodger Stadium."

Despite his crudeness, I was hit with a rush of exhilaration. "Does that mean they're not broadcasting it on the show?" I asked hopefully.

He shook his head, then dropped to the ground and began doing push-ups. "Nothing doing," Greg grunted. "The viewers see everything. Zaidee just doesn't want to embarrass you while you're in the mansion."

"Oh." I upped the pace on my treadmill, struggling to push myself past three and a half miles an hour. So far this week, I'd managed to bag four thousand dollars in exercise points. Despite my initial resistance, boredom had motivated me to seek out a regular routine. Every morning after breakfast, Janelle and I worked out for an hour on the treadmills. We did it religiously, pushing each other even when we'd rather have been perusing the Tomb of Temptation, eating brownies. I felt filled with hope. As if maybe, after so many years of trying, I'd finally found the secret to losing weight. The magic bullet.

"You could figure it out if you really wanted," Janelle commented, mopping the sweat off of her face. "The banks."

"Huh?" I asked, confused.

"Jagger reveals everybody's banks on Monday. Just do the math. Then you'll know who lost and who gained."

"Still ought to be a ceremony," Greg said, hopping onto the elliptical trainer and flying into motion. "They gotta do something to get some excitement on this show. This is supposed to be my big break. Yeah, right," he scoffed.

Janelle turned and looked at me. I knew what she was thinking. First the *Us Weekly* reporter, now Greg. There was only one thing it could mean.

The ratings.

From Fat to Fabulous was a flop.

But why did Zaidee want us to know?

* * *

"Zaidee tells me you want to be a writer?" Jagger asked, leaning back in his chair. The spacious pool glistened behind him. He smiled. "Everybody's got a story to tell. Or, at least, that's what my creative writing professor in college used to say."

I stared at him in surprise. "You took creative writing?" I asked. "I thought you were a business major?"

"It's a vicious rumor," he said, laughing. "No, seriously, how did you know that?"

I blushed. I didn't want him to think I'd been fixating on him. "Luisa told me," I supplied.

Jagger nodded. "Blame my father for that one. I wanted to be a writer, or even a journalist like Alicia, but my dad was dead set against it. So I swallowed my creative jones and slugged through an accounting degree." He stopped talking, and leaned forward in his chair, studying my face. "You're funny, Kat," he said. "Here I am supposed to be interviewing you and you wind up interviewing *me*."

I gave him a grin.

"So, anyway, tell me more about this novel you're writing."

"There's nothing to tell."

"I bet it wasn't that bad," he said gently.

"Jagger . . ." I said, letting the word roll off my tongue. I was eager to change the subject. "Where'd you come up with a name like that?"

"I didn't." He smiled. "It was my parents' doing. Honest."

"Come on!" I eyed him suspiciously. "There's no way you were christened *Jagger*. It's a stage name, right?"

"You would think so, but nope. Jagger Thomas Roth, that's what's on my birth certificate. My parents were big—we're talking *huge*—Stones fans," he explained. "It was either this or Mick. In some ways, I prefer Jagger."

"Yeah, I do, too," I said, surprising myself. Up until that very moment, I'd always thought it seemed silly, over the top.

"Jagger," I said again, drawing it out. It sounded kind of nice.

* * *

By the end of the sixth week, Janelle, Luisa, Alicia, Regan, and Maggie had all completed their challenges for Weight of the World on Your Shoulders. I had no idea whether they'd succeeded or not, but it didn't matter. We couldn't get the money unless all six of us did it, and my blind date was still MIA.

"When do I have my challenge?" I asked Zaidee over and over in the Confession Chamber.

She'd never answer, not outright. All she'd say was, "Soon."

17

The Weighting Game

"Tonight's competition holds two rewards," Jagger said the following evening. "Triumph and you will not only be awarded twenty-five thousand dollars for your *Fat2Fab* Bank, but you'll get something that, in many ways, is equally valuable. A phone call from home."

I stared at him in disbelief. "Are you serious?" I asked.

He told us he was. "Whoever wins tonight's competition will get a five-minute phone call from home."

"Girls." Maggie turned to face us. "I think you're all aware of how desperately I miss my son. I would give anything on this earth to talk to him. And since none of you have kids, I'd also like to say that a mother's love is the kind of thing that can't be paralleled by boyfriends or husbands. I just wanted to let y'all know that," she said, slipping into a slight twang.

Alicia shrugged. "What are you hinting at? That we should let you win?"

Maggie looked down at her hands. "I'm merely *suggesting* it would be fairest to let me have that phone call. I have an eleven-year-old at home."

"No!" Luisa burst out. "I don't agree."

"You've got that right," Alicia seconded.

Maggie's eyes narrowed. "If the situation were reversed, I'd do it for any one of you." She looked around at us accusingly.

"Maggie," Janelle began gently. "We all feel bad that you miss Owen so much. And if it were merely a competition to win a phone call home, we'd feel differently. But there's twenty-five thousand dollars at stake. And since you won In for a Penny, In for a Pound, you've already got a ten-thousand-dollar lead on the rest of us. None of us can afford to throw this. You're going to have to compete fair and square."

"If tonight's event is physical, then the odds are stacked against me!" Maggie yelled. "I won't win. I'm twice your age."

"Be logical," Janelle said. "You really think they're gonna test our endurance? None of us are in that great of shape. It'll probably be trivia."

Maggie ignored her. "Regan? Kat?" she asked. "You two are being awfully quiet over there. Are you going to be money-grubbers too, or do you actually have hearts?"

I chewed on the inside of my lip. Maggie was a grown woman. Nobody held a gun to her head and forced her to leave her son at home to come on *From Fat to Fabulous*. As much as I sympathized with her, this was a game and twenty-five thousand dollars was a lot of money. "I'm sorry," I said, apologetically. "But, I don't think it's fair of you to ask us to throw the game. When you signed up you made a *choice* to leave your family."

"Uh-huh," Regan said, piggybacking off my answer.

"This is ridiculous," Maggie huffed. "You girls are being selfish."

Jagger, who had been standing back observing our argument, took command of the situation. "Tonight's competition is called Find the Fat."

I was struck by a horrible image: the six of us, lined up behind a curtain while Jagger lifted up our shirts and measured our body fat with one of those horrible clamp devices. Whoever had the lowest body fat ratio would win. Or maybe he'd have us guess each other's body fat percentages, the way we'd guessed each other's weights?

"Before you all get too upset, let me explain how this works . . ."

Jagger started talking about the importance of eating a balanced diet and finding the hidden fat in foods. *Foods.* Not people. Phew. I breathed a sigh of relief.

As it turned out, Janelle was right; we were competing in a trivia contest.

"In this box, I have a sampling of ten foods." He picked up a large black crate that had *Fat2Fab* painted across the side in hot-pink letters. "I'll ask you questions about the fat or calories in each of these items. Whoever guesses the closest on each food gets one point. At the end of the game, the player with the most points wins."

Jagger handed us each a stack of yellow cards and markers. The cards were identical to the ones used during In for a Penny, In for a Pound, except there were no names written on them.

"After I read each question, you'll have sixty seconds to answer. If you're ready, ladies, we'll begin," he said.

The first question was a gimmie: Which has more calories, a plain bagel or a glazed donut? Or so I'd thought. When the time came to produce our answers, only Janelle and I said bagel; everyone else put donut.

I couldn't believe they'd gotten it wrong. I had read many, many times that—despite popular belief—bagels generally have more calories than donuts. And even if I hadn't already known the answer, I could have easily deduced it. After all, they weren't going to give us something painfully easy, like which has more fat, cake or grapes? True to the competition's title, we were supposed to "find the fat" in unsuspected places.

"Your standard bagel packs a bigger caloric punch than a donut," Jagger said.

"Shut up!" Regan objected. "That *can't* be true."

"A deli-variety bagel contains between three hundred fifty and four hundred calories, while a glazed donut has two hundred and fifty calories," Jagger informed her. "One point Kat, one point Janelle."

Maggie shot us a look of death.

The second question was slightly harder. "How many grams of fat are in a McDonald's Big Mac?" Jagger asked, waving the forbidden treat in front of us. It smelled heavenly.

I wrote down forty-five, but it turned out to be thirty-three. Janelle got it with a guess of thirty. However, once again, Alicia, Maggie, Luisa, and Regan had all guessed way beneath the mark. Alicia's answer was the worst: seven grams.

"I thought we were talking about saturated fat," she complained. "You didn't make that clear."

"I'd advise you to listen more closely next time."

I got the next question, correctly guessing that a piece of angel food cake was lower than a reduced-fat frozen yogurt.

The game continued, with Janelle and I staying neck and neck, and Regan trailing by two points.

"Okay, ladies, we're down to the final question. It's currently a tie game between Janelle and Kat. This next question will determine the winner. Since the rest of you have no chance of winning, you'll sit this one out. How many calories are there in a Burger King original Whopper sandwich?"

I blinked in surprise. I knew what a Burger King Whopper was, but was that the same thing as a Burger King *original* Whopper *sandwich*? Those two words threw me for a loop. I couldn't figure out why Jagger put them in, unless there was some kind of significance. I glanced to my left, where Janelle was busily writing on her card. During my college stint on Weight Watchers, I'd spent countless hours dissecting the menus at various fast food restaurants but, for the life of me, I couldn't recall how many calories a Whopper had.

"Kat, I need an answer."

"Uh, hang on one sec," I said, scrambling to come up with something. Finally, I wrote down eight hundred calories, praying I hadn't gone too far over.

We revealed our cards. Janelle had said six hundred calories, which sounded like an excellent guess. I cursed myself for not having thought of it.

"This is incredibly close—the winner has prevailed by a mere ten calories. A Burger King original Whopper sandwich contains seven hundred and ten calories. The winner of Find the Fat is . . . Kat!" Jagger announced.

"Oh my God!" I cried, jumping up and down.

Maggie muttered something under her breath and stalked out of the room.

Janelle reached out and hugged me. "Congratulations."

"Kat, your bank has now received twenty-five thousand dollars. And as the winner of this competition you will also receive a five-minute phone call from home. Please go immediately to the Confession Chamber to claim your prize."

* * *

"You have three choices," Zaidee said, when I'd sat down on the soft red chair in the Confession Chamber.

I stared at the cordless phone sitting on the floor in front of me, a luxury that had been temporarily brought in for my reward.

"Yes?" I asked. "What do you mean, choices?"

"On line one we have your friend Donna Bartosch from Memphis. On line two, we have your mother, Lynne Larson, from Denver. And on line three we have Cara Magley, also of Memphis. You may only talk to one of them. I'll give you thirty seconds to decide."

I felt a brief surge of disappointment. Part of me had hoped they'd have Nick Appleby from England on line four, but I knew that wasn't possible. And, truth be told, I was glad.

There was only one problem.

Who to choose?

I picked up the phone and turned it over in my hands.

There were really only two considerations—Donna or Mom. Nothing against Cara, but if I picked a friend at all, I'd have to pick Donna. Not only was she my *best* friend, but she was my closest link to Nick while I was in this house. If I wanted to find out any information about him, she was the one to talk to.

But then there was the problem of Mom . . . If I didn't choose her, I'd hear about it every day for the next thirty years. She would never understand why I, her one and only beloved daughter, had opted to speak with "some girl" instead of "my own mother."

"All right, Kat, have you made your selection?" Zaidee asked.

I took a deep breath and let it out. I knew what I had to do. "Yes, put Donna Bartosch on," I said, silently begging Mom to understand.

Zaidee coached me briefly, going over a list of topics that were off-limits. I wasn't allowed to ask Donna what kind of press *From Fat to Fabulous* had been receiving, and I wasn't allowed to tell her anything about the competitions.

"In a minute the phone will ring," Zaidee informed me. "Your five minutes begins as soon as you answer."

"Thanks," I said, sinking back against the chair.

It seemed like a million years passed before the phone finally rang. I was so panicked, I fumbled it in my hands, nearly dropping it. "Hello?" I screamed, when I finally managed to answer it.

"Kat? Oh my God, it's really you, I can't believe it!"

"It's me," I yelled back. I was hollering so loudly I felt like my dad.

"How are you?" Donna asked. "Are you okay?"

"I'm holding up. It's crazy out here. I still can't believe I'm on television," I said. "Are you taping it?"

"Yeah, they keep showing commercials for it," Donna began. "And there was a huge article in the Appeal section of today's paper—"

"You're not allowed to discuss media coverage of the show," a man's voice came over the phone line, causing me to jump nearly a mile. They were listening in on my conversation. In all likelihood they were also tape-recording it to use on the show. And to think, they hadn't even asked me. I thought it was illegal to tape record a phone conversation without getting prior permission? Well, now Donna would see firsthand what kind of people I was dealing with here. Maybe she'd understand why I'd been so paranoid that my room was bugged that casting weekend.

"Sorry," I told the man. "Hey, Donna, how are things at work?"

"You still have your job," she said. "Cindy's been trying to get Richard to let you go, but he's beside himself. Ever since it went out in the news today— Oops," she said, catching herself. "Better not talk about that."

We gabbed on for another minute, with Donna informing me she'd talked to my parents the day before.

"Your mom was totally freaking out," she said, laughing. "She can't even bring herself to watch the show, it upsets her too much. But I talked to her for a while, and she's cool with it."

I was starting to panic. Time was running out and I hadn't yet found a way to work Nick into the conversation. I couldn't come right out and ask about him, for obvious reasons. And I was afraid if I brought him up, Donna might blurt out his name. The last thing I needed to do was tip off the producers to my secret.

As it turned out, there was no need to worry.

"Kat, there's something else." Donna paused for a long moment, and I thought our conversation had been cut off. "There's a problem with . . . Charles Dickens."

"No!" I shrieked, then composed myself. "What kind of problem? Is it . . . over?" I asked, feeling my throat tighten in fear.

"Uh-uh, it's nothing like that. It's just. Well, you see, Charles Dickens called H and G the other day."

"What!" I cried. "What did he say?"

"It's complicated. I don't know if—"

And then the line went dead.

I sat there, hoping against hope that Donna would come back on, finish what she'd started to say. But the only voice I heard was Zaidee's, speaking to me through the intercom.

"Time's up," she said.

* * *

There are lots of things fat people aren't supposed to do.

Visit the beach. Wear revealing clothing. Pig out in public.

From Fat to Fabulous was determined to make us do all of them. After Regan danced at the Lakers game and Janelle posed nude, I didn't think the competitions could get much worse.

Then they hit us with the volleyball game.

The stakes in this contest were the highest yet. In addition to a monetary prize of seventy-five thousand dollars, we'd be given a copy of the trade magazine *Hollywood Heat*—which, not coincidentally, had a cover story on *From Fat to Fabulous*.

"Find out, once and for all, what's being said about you in the press," Jagger taunted, waving the magazine in front of us.

I sucked in a breath. Seeing my face on the cover of a glossy magazine felt alien, surreal.

"We can't beat a team of pro volleyball players," Regan complained. "We shouldn't even try."

"You don't have to win the match, you just have to win one game out of three," Jagger informed us, smoothing an imaginary wrinkle from his shirt. He was decked out like a surfer boy, in a white T-shirt and brightly patterned shorts that hung down to his knees. Brown flip-flops housed his feet. A pair of expensive-looking sunglasses sat perched atop his head, and a coconut shell necklace adorned his neck. He looked prepped to film an episode of *Baywatch*.

The seven of us stood on the crowded Venice Beach boardwalk, surrounded by a plethora of cameramen and sound technicians. Zaidee had even commanded a large camera on a crane. It sat in the sand, hanging over the volleyball court. A small crowd was starting to gather, pushing in past the hotdog vendors and the T-shirt sellers to catch a glimpse of us.

"We can totally do this," Janelle said excitedly. Ever since Jagger had announced the competition, Janelle had been ecstatic. "I played competitive volleyball in college," she enthused. "This is right up my alley!"

The rest of us were more skeptical. "Regan's right. We can't beat some professional team," I argued. "Why bother trying?"

"It ain't meant for us to win," Luisa agreed. "They want us to go out in bathing suits and look stupid. They're not gonna let us read about ourselves in a magazine. And Zaidee doesn't want us to get another seventy-five grand. Our bank accounts are getting too big."

Janelle shook her head. "Maybe they're doing this to make up for Weight of the World on Your Shoulders."

"Hey," I cut in, defensively. "We haven't officially lost that yet."

Five pairs of eyes turned to glare at me.

"It's not my fault," I griped. "How can I be expected to win a competition if I can't even compete?"

"So compete now," Janelle said. "The worst part is the bathing suits."

Regan was beyond mortified. "I am *not* wearing a bathing suit in public. I already had to wear a cheerleader's uniform."

Maggie didn't seem to care one way or another. "I'll do whatever's best for the group," she said self-righteously. "Even if I'm the only one who feels that way."

Only Alicia shared Janelle's eagerness. And, given her fondness for lying, there was no way of knowing if what she said was the truth. "Listen to Janelle," Alicia insisted. "I played on my high school's volleyball team."

"I don't think it's the game that we're worried about," I said. "We're worried about the bathing suits."

"Alicia and I will keep you guys covered as best we can," Janelle said, as if I hadn't spoken. "You guys just try and keep the ball off the sand. If you can get it up in the air, I can spike it back."

There wasn't much use arguing, so Regan, Luisa, and I gave in.

"Jagger!" Janelle called. "We're going to do it. Where do we go to get changed?"

"Follow me, ladies," he said, leading us over to trailer turned makeshift dressing room out in the parking lot. "Your uniforms are inside."

"Uniforms?" I asked, following Luisa up the stairs and into the trailer.

She opened the door and then stopped dead in her tracks. "I knew it! I knew Zaidee was gonna do this to us. What did I say?" Luisa demanded, stalking into the trailer and grabbing one of the hangers.

"Oh no!" I wailed, with a sinking feeling. Deep down, I'd known it, too.

"Bikinis, right?" Janelle called from behind us.

"Hell, yeah, it's bikinis," Luisa grumbled.

She was still blocking the door, so I pushed past her, clearing a path for the others. One by one, we filed into the dressing room, followed by two cameramen and a sound tech.

"Look at these!" I cried, picking up one of the pink, two-piece monstrosities, with *F2F* written across the butt in black letters. I held it out at arm's length, as though it were someone else's dirty laundry.

Janelle ran her hands through her hair in exasperation. "Oh, well," she said eventually. "At least they aren't thongs."

"These are pretty flattering, actually," Alicia commented. "Very conservative." She picked up the bikini top and held it by its string.

She was right, but it didn't matter. A bikini was a bikini. Any way you sliced it, they were a big girl's worst nightmare.

"I don't wanna do this," Regan moaned.

"I don't either. But I will, for the good of the team," Maggie said dryly. "And I'm the oldest one out here. My body sags worse than any of yours."

"You mind stepping outside so we can get changed?" Janelle asked the camera crew.

They obliged. "Leave these on the table," the sound tech said, gesturing toward our mic packs. "Not using them today. Boom mics," he murmured, heading outside after the cameramen.

It should have been a simple thing, changing into the bathing suits and going back outside. But other than Alicia and Janelle, everybody was too self-conscious to get undressed with other people watching. Even other fat girls. So we trudged back outside, using the dressing room one at time. Then, wrapped in large white beach towels, we made our way down to the sand, where the court had been set up.

The crowd—sizeable to begin with—had now swelled to encompass what looked like hundreds.

"Christ, there's a lot of people here," I murmured.

"Saturday," Luisa reminded me. "Everybody goes to the beach."

"Great, just what we need. An audience."

"Don't worry about them," Janelle said. "Once we start playing, you'll forget they're even there."

We took our positions on the court. Our team had first serve, and Janelle managed to hit a clean shot over the net, though our opponents returned it sharply. Janelle dove forward but her hands didn't even come close to connecting with the ball.

"What they just did, that's called a kill," she said, sheepishly. "It means there's no possible way to return it."

It was an unfair match from the get-go. The other team was made up of strong, athletic women, some of whom had been playing competitively since they were kids. We lost the first game easily, bagging only seven points against the other team's fifteen.

Worse still, we were exhausted.

"I always thought volleyball looked easy," I grunted, wiping sweat off my brow. "Who knew bopping a ball around in the sand was so *hard*."

"Everything's easy until you've actually tried it," Janelle pointed out.

"No kidding," I said.

I had to admit that, despite my initial reservations, I was actually having *fun*. Janelle had been right; as soon as we'd started playing, I'd managed to lose myself in the game, tuning out the noise of the crowd. I even forgot, temporarily at least, that I was a fat girl wearing a bikini on a crowded beach.

Until we took a break, that is.

"Go ahead, take twenty. Get something to drink, stretch your legs," Zaidee said, after we'd blown the second game, losing by four points. She brushed past us to confer with the primary cameraman.

Luisa and I grabbed our towels and then trotted up toward the boardwalk to browse through the various vendors. We felt awkward in our bathing suits, but this was a rare chance for freedom and we had to grab it. We had just started examining some woven jewelry when it happened.

"I know who you are," a voice called from the crowd. A woman was pointing a boney finger at me. She was in her mid-fifties with short blonde hair that was streaked with gray. "Katherine," she said.

"Kat," I told her, pulling my towel tightly around my bathing suit. "It's short for Katrina."

"You're the girl from that *Fat* show."

I grimaced. "Yeah."

Luisa began backing off, slipping down to the sand and out of the limelight.

"My son has been watching you on television," the woman said, and for a moment I thought she was going to ask me to autograph something for him. I couldn't have been further off-base. "Yes, you're the one my son has been talking about." Her expression changed to disdain. "The way you fire off your mouth is a disgrace!" she exploded. "You think the whole world should take pity on you because you have a weight problem? Well, I'm here to tell you there's not a person alive who feels sorry for you. You're lazy," she snarled. "And you know something? Not only are you lazy, but you're stupid and mean."

Her words hit me like a punch in the gut.

Lazy. Stupid. *Mean?*

How could she say I was mean? She was the one insulting a total stranger!

Out of nowhere, a man approached, his face lit up with rage. "You're a pathetic excuse for a human being," he said, frowning. "I saw you complaining about how much you hate exercising. I tell you, exercise is a *privilege,* not a punishment. God gave you a perfectly fine body and look at what you've done to it! My wife lost her leg to cancer nine years ago. Before she got sick she was a triathlete. She'd give anything to have her leg back, so she could compete again. And here you are, all the blessings in the world, and all you do is complain."

This had to be some kind of joke.

Certainly, the producers had paid these people to come along and stir up drama?

Before I could respond, Zaidee was at my side, shooing them away. "Get back on the court," she instructed.

I was grateful that she'd intervened.

"Break's over," Zaidee announced.

I resumed my position, but it was a lost cause. My game was totally thrown off. First I screwed up serving, then I got in Maggie's way and wound up knocking her down.

"Ow!" she screeched, rubbing her backside as she stood up. "Be careful, Kat."

"Yeah, last time I checked, volleyball wasn't a contact sport," Alicia said.

By the end of the third game—which we miraculously won fifteen to thirteen—I was so upset I couldn't see straight. I didn't even care about the prize.

"Congratulations, girls, on a job well done," Jagger boomed, joining us on the court. He walked around shaking each of our hands and smiling. "Tonight marks an important turning point in the game. Within the next few weeks, several twists will take place, shocking the house to its core."

"Wh-? . . . what?" Regan sputtered.

"All in good time," Jagger said, smiling. "You'll find out on the first ever *From Fat to Fabulous* live show, coming up within the next few weeks." And with that, he was gone.

Live show? This was the first I'd heard of it.

"Hey, cheer up, Kit Kat," Alicia said. "We won. Twenty-five G's! And, even better, *Hollywood Heat*!" She threw her arms around me in a sisterly hug.

I shoved her off. "How can I cheer up? They're turning us into a freak show!"

"Well, I've got something that'll cheer you up," she said, looping her arm through mine. "Look over there."

I turned to see a small film crew coming over.

"MTV," she hissed. "Here it is—my big break!"

Zaidee rushed over and spoke briefly with the crew. Then she came trotting across the sand toward me and Alicia. "Why don't you gals sit down on the sand for just a minute, and let them get a shot of you sunbathing."

A lanky assistant came over and set down several beach towels and accessories. "Just try and act natural," he instructed before turning to go.

"No thanks," I grumbled. The last thing I wanted was for MTV to film me lounging in a bikini.

"That wasn't a question," Zaidee snapped. "They're broadcasting live from the beach today and you girls are going on in ten minutes." She stalked off before I had the chance to object.

Alicia sat down on the sand, watching patiently as Zaidee pushed back the sea of onlookers. "It's cool, Kit Kat," she said. Her eyes traveled the length of my torso. "I understand why you don't want to be on MTV. The camera adds ten pounds."

I glared at her, not saying a word.

"Here." She picked up a bottle of sunscreen and tossed it in my direction. "Just get behind me and pretend to rub this on my shoulders. I can hide most of your body that way."

I'd about had it with her. There was only so much pestering and belittling one person could take before they cracked. "And just why, exactly, does my body need hiding?" I demanded, fully aware of how she'd answer.

"Seriously, Kat, do you even need to ask that? You have a major weight problem, isn't that obvious? Even with the few pounds you've lost, you're still a heifer."

I was so stung I said nothing. But a few minutes later, when MTV came over, the opportunity for payback arose.

As I sat behind Alicia, rubbing sunscreen on her narrow shoulders, and as she babbled on, telling the MTV host all about her career aspirations, I gently slid my fingers up to the bow of her string bikini. Swiftly, purposefully, I yanked it.

"Ahhh!" she shrieked, as her bikini top came tumbling forward. Her arms flew up, shielding her chest. She was quick, but not quick enough. For a split second, they'd caught her topless.

"What the hell are you doing?" she demanded, whirling around.

I shrugged. "Sorry."

* * *

"There they are!" Janelle cried, racing over to the coffee table.

Spread out in a fan formation, were six copies of *Hollywood Heat.* The cover had a collage of our faces, with the title "The Weighting Game: An Insider's Guide to *From Fat to Fabulous.*" We sprang forward, nearly trampling each other in our hurry to reach the magazines. Regan scooped up the stack, quickly passing them out to us.

I cracked mine open, discovering that the cover story was actually a five-page spread with lots of photos and very little text. I had planned to pore over the article for days, reading and rereading it until I'd memorized every detail. "There's barely anything here to read."

"It's enough," Regan said sadly, her eyes scanning the page. "Wait until you see what it says."

I plopped down on the couch and started to read:

The ratings are in, and over fourteen million viewers agree: *From Fat to Fabulous* has become America's spiciest summer show! Fat girls with sex appeal? Who knew! Here's your guide to the six contestants who make up this addictive reality smash:

Regan Borrail: The Kid Sister

Perhaps fellow *Fat2Fab* contestant Alicia put it best: "She's like your little sister who isn't so little." With a starting weight of 341 pounds, Regan is by far the heaviest of the girls. At nineteen, she's also the youngest—and the sweetest, with an endless supply of hugs and kind words for her competitors. While the other contestants trade insults, this Boulder, Colorado, native adheres to the old adage, "If you don't have something nice to say, don't say anything at all." "I believe in karma, and I believe in following your heart," Regan says. "And I treat everyone with respect, no matter what."

Alicia Combs: The Flirt

Boston babe Alicia Combs proves day in and day out that when it comes to sex appeal, size DOES matter! A 176-pound stunner who flaunts her more-than-ample assets (oh, those low-cut shirts!), Alicia has attracted a loyal fan base of male admirers. "Simply put, she's hot," says Zaidee Panola, *Fat2Fab*'s executive producer. "She's got meat on her bones. It's been a long time since America had a sex symbol who could fill out a dress the way she does." No kidding! This budding journalist can shake her stuff at *Hollywood Heat* anytime she wants.

Janelle Kerwin: The Strong Silent Type

Nicknamed "No-Tell Janelle" by her first ex-husband, Matt, this 6'0" tall cynic is as tight-lipped as they come. Prone to spending long hours sitting quietly in the Confession Chamber, Janelle leaves you wondering what lurks behind her cool exterior. Either there's a lot going on upstairs, or twice-divorced Janelle's a few cookies short of a dozen. Our guess would be the former.

Kat Larson: The Brat

A lot of words have been used to describe Kat, most of them beginning with the letter *B*: We chose the nicest one for our heading. Never one to hold her tongue, Kat enjoys blaming others for her weight problem. She demands sympathy for her so-called eating disorder, even going so far as to claim she deserves more pity than bulimics. Her constant skinny-bashing and rants about her unfair lot in life have spawned hate mail, and anti-Kat websites. Yet, *Fat2Fab*'s host, Jagger Roth, defends her character. "Kat comes across as bitter, but in person she's very warm and funny. I think as the show progresses, viewers will see her in a more sympathetic light." A more sympathetic side to Kat the Brat? We'll believe it when we see it. . . .

Luisa Olivares: The Gossip

Busybody Luisa is *Fat2Fab*'s resident blabbermouth. Prone to eavesdropping and snooping through the other contestant's rooms, Luisa is the go-to girl when you're looking for a little dirt. Her diary sessions often result in major revelations about her fellow housemates. Not that we mind. So far, Luisa has spilled the beans on a number of the behind-the-scenes highlights, including juicy details on Janelle's failed marriages (she's a commitmentphobe who can't stop cheating), Alicia's beauty secrets (girlfriend has an aversion to panties), and Kat's poor luck with men (she can't seem to keep a guy satisfied, if you catch our drift). With friends like this Cuban spitfire, who needs enemies?

Maggie Strickland: The Southern Belle

This Jackson, Mississippi, import has fought hard to adapt to big-city life. An old-fashioned Southerner who is used to good manners and clean livin', Maggie has struggled to stick to the show's weight-loss program. In her few weeks on the series, she's only shed a pound and a half. A homemaker at heart, Maggie has pined end-lessly for her eleven-year-old son, Owen, drowning her sorrows with late-night trips to the Tomb of Temptation. Despite her lack of weight loss, Maggie wins us over every time with her gentle heart and strong family values. And, shucks y'all, we just love her accent!

I felt as if our whole situation—everything I'd known while I was in this house—had grown wings and mutated, turning into something horrid and unrecognizable.

I was The Brat.

Or, they might as well have come right out and said it: The Bitch.

It all made sense now. The way those people had shouted at me on the beach. The hatred in their eyes. Maggie was The Southern Belle? Maggie, who was from *Cleveland* and had only lived in Jackson, Mississippi, a short time, was *The Southern Belle*? What about *me*? I was born and raised in Memphis, Ten-nessee! Home of the Blues, the Birthplace of Rock'n'Roll, and a bona fide Southern city if there ever was one!

But, no. They couldn't call me The Southern Belle.

I was The Brat.

And Luisa! Luisa, whom I'd trusted every day since I'd entered this house, had turned on me. All this time, she'd been buttering me up, tricking me into spilling secrets. Regan had the same re-alization. "How *could* you?" she demanded, squaring off against Luisa. "I thought you were my friend and you're a big fat motor-mouth!"

"Yeah," I agreed, shaking my head in disbelief.

Luisa shrugged. She was about to respond when Janelle cut in, "Hey, guys, did you catch this? We have *fourteen million* viewers! Those are unbelievable numbers! Low ratings, my ass! I bet you anything Zaidee lied about the low ratings to get us to kick it up a notch!"

"America thinks I'm sexy!" Alicia enthused, prancing around. "Not that I'm surprised. But it's flattering. You know what, Kit Kat?" she said, rolling up the magazine and whacking me on the head. "I was so mad at you earlier for exposing my glorious breasts on television. But now that I think about it, you've done me a favor. What do you wanna bet Hugh Hefner's going to offer me a half million to pose in *Playboy*?"

Oh, God, there'd be no stopping her now. Her ego would be gargantuan by the time she left the house.

"Fucking morons!" I blurted out.

"Kat," Janelle cautioned. "Be careful."

"I am not going to be careful! Those *Hollywood Heat* bastards have written lies about me. I'm going to sue them for libel," I fumed.

"You can't," Alicia responded smugly. "You don't have a case. I'm a journalist. I know about these things."

I opened my mouth to let her have it when I felt an arm grip hold of me tightly. It was Janelle.

"Kat, I really think you should go upstairs and lie down. Cool off for a while."

I started to object but something in her face stopped me.

"This," she said, nodding at the cameramen. "This is where they're getting it. You've got to control your outbursts. You're only giving them more stuff to use."

"Whatever," I said, rolling my eyes.

But I kept my mouth shut.

* * *

"Hey, Kit Kat, I just had my weigh-in and I'm down again this week," Alicia sang out Sunday afternoon. She waltzed into the kitchen, cameraman in tow. It was an unnecessary announcement. Everyone could see she was slimmer. "Go, me!" She punched her fist into the air, cheerleaderstyle.

"Congratulations," I grumbled, staring down at my bowl of baby carrots. I'd been prodding at them with a fork for ten minutes, trying to force myself to eat one. They tasted like dirty water.

Alicia opened the refrigerator and retrieved an apple. "I knew I'd be lower, that wasn't a surprise. But look at this." She lifted up her shirt, exposing the area from her bra down. "My stomach is a million times smaller than it was when I came on this show."

As if on cue, my cameraman swung around and zoomed in on Alicia. I guess the sight of me eating carrots couldn't compare with bare flesh.

I had to admit, she did look good. A little *too* good. What she said next confirmed my suspicions.

"I've lost fifty pounds since I got here."

"Fifty!" I gasped, dropping my fork. It landed on the counter with a clank. Suddenly, both cameras were on me. "We've been here less than two months!"

"I know." She grinned. "Isn't it fab?" She took a knife out of the drawer and started cutting up her apple on the chopping board.

"Isn't what fab?" Regan asked, wandering into the room.

"Alicia just got back from weigh-in. She lost again," I said, beating her to the punch.

"Hey, no fair! I wanted to tell Regan my good news. You always blurt stuff out," Alicia complained. "You're a bigger gossip than Luisa."

"Oops . . . I did it again," I sang. It was a lame comeback, but it was the best I could come up with on the spot. Out of the corner of my eye, I saw one of the sound guys come in with the boom mic. *Uh-oh.* That was never a good sign.

"Are you under a hundred and fifty pounds yet?" Regan enthused. " 'Cause that's a really big milestone."

"Girl, I've *been* under a hundred and fifty." Alicia had finished slicing her apple and was now sucking on the pieces seductively. "As of today, I'm one-hundred-twenty-six pounds and counting."

"I'm so happy for you," Regan screeched, dashing around the table and engulfing her in a hug. "You should be so proud of that."

She glowed. "I am." The two of them continued embracing for a few minutes.

Something fishy was going on. Alicia had never been huge to begin with, and now she was downright slim. "Alicia, how tall are you?" I asked, staring at her pointedly.

"I'm five-ten."

"And you've lost fifty pounds since you got here, which means you weighed one-seventy-six before. Right?"

She nodded. "Duh, Kit Kat, you were there for our initial weigh-in, remember?"

It didn't add up. "I thought you had to be a size sixteen to come on this show?"

"You do," Alicia said, "and I was."

Regan nodded vigorously. "Me, too."

I wasn't sure who the more reproachable liar was: Regan, who was obviously downsizing, or Alicia who had, quite possibly, upsized to get on TV.

"How do they judge it?" I asked. "You know, did they ask you for a sample of your clothes when you auditioned?"

Alicia burst into laughter. "Don't be absurd, Kat."

"No, I'm serious. How did they know you were telling the truth about what size you wore?"

Her eyes narrowed. "Are you calling me a liar?"

"I probably wouldn't be the first person."

We glared at each other for a long moment, then she said, "In case you've forgotten, Kit Kat, envy is one of the seven deadly sins."

My mind flashed back to a campaign H&G had done last fall to help promote a new Memphis club, Seven Sins. I decided to throw in a quick plug. "Well," I scoffed, "you seem so bent on announcing your weight to the world, Alicia, you ought to hire your own PR firm. You know, like the talented and prolific Hood and Geddlefinger Public Relations. Not that we'd take you as a client. We're too classy for that."

"Cool it, you guys," Regan said, shooting me a puzzled look.

It was too late. Neither of us was going to back off now.

"It's not my fault that I've lost more weight than you have," Alicia continued. "What have you lost? Ten pounds?"

"Twenty," I corrected. It was the truth. I felt my face growing hot. At first I thought it was from embarrassment, but then I realized it was the overhead lights. I couldn't be sure, but I suspected they'd gotten brighter. My cameraman had certainly gotten closer. His lens was now only half a dozen inches away from my left cheek. "Since you've lost so much weight, what size do you wear now? How the hell do your clothes even fit?" I asked.

"I'm a ten now and Zaidee brought in some new clothes."

Alicia let out an exasperated sigh. "What's with you? As soon as you lose some weight, you'll get new clothes, too."

"Show me your tag." I didn't believe her. A five-foot-ten-inch woman would not be a ten at one-hundred twenty-six pounds. Judging by Alicia's frame, I'd have pegged her as a six, or even a four. "Let me see," I demanded.

"No," she told me. "It's none of your business what size I wear. I lost fifty pounds and that's that." She whirled around and stomped over to the Tomb of Temptation. "I think I deserve a little treat for my efforts."

This time, both Regan and the cameraman followed.

I was fuming, but I didn't want to give her the satisfaction. Without another word, I charged up the stairs, stomping my feet as I went. When I reached my room, I flung myself down face first on the bed. I wanted to turn the lights out, but it was only 3 P.M. I knew what was about to happen, but I fought it for as long as humanly possible. Hot tears were stinging my eyes, threatening to pour out at any minute, yet I didn't want that side of myself shown on TV.

I started crying, trying to keep my face muffled by the pillow so it wouldn't be picked up on camera. I knew he was there. I could hear him moving around behind me, adjusting positions to get the best shot possible. *Let him stand there,* I thought smugly, *and film the back of my head.* I wasn't about to let him get a shot of my tears.

I don't know how long I lay there. It must have been awhile. I had just started to doze off when I heard the door creak open.

"You okay, Kat?"

Slowly, I rolled over, rubbing my eyes.

It was Janelle.

"I've been better," I admitted.

"You can't let Alicia get to you."

I struggled to keep my voice from wavering. "It's not so much Alicia as it's just the show in general. You heard the way those people on the beach spoke to me. All of America thinks I'm a stupid, fat bitch!" I began sobbing louder. I couldn't help myself; it was a hard pill to swallow.

She walked over and sat down on the edge of my bed.

"Editing or not, they can't show things you haven't done. If you give them five minutes of anger, that's the five minutes they're going to use. Over ninety-nine percent of what goes on in here will wind up on the cutting-room floor."

It was a scary thought, but I knew she was right.

I may not have lost much weight, but I had never felt so small in my life.

18

An Enormous Twist

We waited for the thirty-minute live show with a sense of morbid curiosity.

Everybody had a different opinion on what to expect.

"They're going to make us vote somebody off," Luisa guessed, as we all sat in the deluxe master bedroom, waiting to be called downstairs. "Like on *Survivor.*"

"They can't," Janelle argued. "They don't have enough contestants."

"Then maybe Zaidee's gonna bring in a replacement?" Luisa snapped her fingers. "She's probably gonna offer one of us twenty-five thousand dollars to walk out the door!"

"You think Zaidee regrets choosing us?" I asked.

"I know she's happy with *me*," Alicia said. "She tells me all the time."

"Right." I rolled my eyes. "And just how often do you talk to her?"

"Every single day. When I go in the Confession Chamber she raves about how fun I am," Alicia said. "Fun and spicy."

"Maybe the girl who's lost the most weight gets a special reward?" Janelle surmised, still pondering the twist. "Like a visit from a family member, or a brand-new sports car?"

"I was thinking more along the lines of an endorsement deal," Alicia said.

"Like a commercial?" Regan asked, twirling a strand of hair around her fingers.

"That's where the *real* money is," Alicia continued. "TV appearances, book deals, commercials, the whole nine yards. God knows I deserve to get all that. I've got more breakout potential than any reality TV star I've ever seen."

I felt my body tense up. How dare she lay claim to those things? *I'm* the one with the breakout potential, I fumed silently. *I'm* the one who should land a six-figure book deal and a guest appearance on *Will & Grace*! Alicia has a lot of nerve, trying to steal all my glory. "I'm going to get dressed," I said, stalking out and heading to my own bedroom.

Janelle followed me. "What are you going to wear?" she asked.

"I don't know." I shrugged. "I want to fix myself up, we're going to be on TV."

She laughed. "Kat, we're always on TV."

"I know, I know. But like you always say, they edit most of it out. Tonight we're guaranteed they're not going to chop us."

"True," she reneged, reaching into the closet and pulling out a long black dress. "What about this?" she asked. "Too fancy?"

"It's nice but it's the kind of thing you'd wear to a formal ball."

Janelle ducked back in and retrieved a brown skirt and a cream-colored scoop-neck top. "How about this? Better?"

I nodded. "Much."

She set the clothes down on her bed and then brushed her hair into a high ponytail. "Know what you're wearing yet, Kat?"

"Black pants and a pink button-down. I think it's the only thing I've got that won't totally wash me out on camera."

"The lighting in this house *is* the pits. We're both pale; we probably come off like ghosts." She turned to the cameramen saying, "We're changing, guys," before shooing them out the door. As soon as we were alone, she lowered her voice. "I'm nervous—what if Luisa's right? You think we'll have to vote somebody out?"

"Nah," I said, with more confidence than I felt. "It's like you said, there are only six of us. They can't afford to drop any lower."

"Want me to help you get ready, Kat?" Janelle asked. "Do your hair and stuff?"

I bit my lip and glanced at her school-girl ponytail. It looked juvenile and didn't match her sophisticated outfit. "No thanks," I said simply. "I think I'll just wear it tucked behind my ears."

* * *

At 4 P.M. Zaidee summoned us to the living room. The show was going live at 5 P.M. Pacific Time—eight o'clock on the East Coast—and they needed to get us prepared. The downstairs had been blocked off all day, so I expected to find it slightly rearranged. But when we got down there I was shocked; our living room looked like a tornado had plowed through it, lifting up our possessions and dropping new ones in its wake.

The purple sectional couch was gone, replaced by a row of tall, orange director's chairs. Three enormous cameras had been set up on dollies in the living room—one dead in front of us, and two angled at us from the side. Thick black, gray, and orange wires covered every inch of the floor behind the cameras. Extra lights had been brought in, and there were boom mics hanging from the ceiling.

Zaidee and a man I didn't recognize were frantically barking orders to the crew. Twice, they changed the setup, moving the director's chairs into a semicircle, then putting them back in a row. My stomach churned with nervous anticipation as I watched. Every little move and sound made me jump. I really felt like I was *on TV*. Ten minutes before the show was due to start, Zaidee disappeared and Jagger came out. He stood silently in the center of the room, eyes half-closed, head bent toward the ground. I couldn't tell if he was lost in concentration, or if he was nervous to go live, too.

Finally, it was time to start.

"Stand by!" yelled one of the cameramen. "Intro's rolling!" After what seemed like forever, the cameraman said, "And we're coming in . . . in five . . . four . . . three . . ."

He didn't say the last two numbers, just mimed them with his hand. When he reached one, he pointed his finger toward Jagger.

"Good evening, and welcome to the first live edition of *From Fat to Fabulous*! I'm your host, Jagger Roth. We're coming to you live from inside the Hollywood Hills hideaway, where our six *Fat2Fab* contestants are nervously awaiting tonight's revelations."

He turned to face us. "How are you feeling, girls?"

"Pretty good!" Alicia called out.

"I've been better," Luisa admitted.

"Well, brace yourselves, because you're in for a wild ride!"

Jagger began a lengthy recap of the week's events, starting with the volleyball game and moving into the results of the most recent weigh-in. "Currently, Kat and Janelle are tied for the lead, with banks of $120,000. Alicia is a close second, with $117,000. Both Luisa and Regan rank in at under $100,000. And Maggie, you're bringing up the rear with $48,000. Since coming on *From Fat to Fabulous*, you have gained fourteen pounds."

I gasped. I don't think any of us realized how far behind Maggie was.

Jagger strolled over until he was standing directly in front of her. "I'd like to get your opinion, Maggie," he said. "You've made several comments about the role age has played in this game. Do you feel being the oldest contestant puts you at a disadvantage?"

Maggie nodded vehemently. "Absolutely!"

"How so?" Jagger prompted.

"I'm a forty-year-old woman. I don't have as much energy as these young girls. I can't be expected to go jogging every day. And my body burns fat slower," she said.

"Ah, yes, I was coming to that. Do you feel having a child has made it harder for you to lose weight?"

Again, Maggie was adamant. "Absolutely. Don't get me wrong. I love my son, Owen Strickland, dearly, but he is partly responsible for my weight problem."

Jagger pressed on. "Yesterday, you said something in the Confession Chamber that I'd like to explore."

I stared at him in horror. *Is Jagger planning to reveal all the private things we've discussed in the Confession Chamber?*

"You said, and I quote, 'It's Owen's fault that I'm fat.' Is that correct?"

Maggie squared her shoulders. "Yes, I said that. The truth is, and none of you girls will understand this, because you don't have kids," she said, looking around at us apologetically, "but after you have a child your life is never the same. I gained weight in my pregnancy and that weight won't come off. As much as I love Owen and hate to blame him for it, it's his fault."

"Does Owen know you feel this way?" Jagger asked.

I snorted. We were live on television. If he hadn't known before, he certainly would now.

Maggie gulped. "Yes, he does."

"And how does that make him feel?"

"It hurts him very much that it made Mommy fat to have him. That *he* made Mommy fat. But he knows it's his fault and he accepts that."

"Is Owen watching right now?" Jagger asked.

"Oh, yes, I'm sure he is."

"Is there anything you'd like to tell him?"

"Owen," Maggie spoke directly to the cameras, "Mommy loves you and she misses you. And even though it's your fault that Mommy has to be here, she doesn't hate you for it."

I wanted to lean over and smack her. She has got to be kidding! Every woman gains weight during a pregnancy, and many of them lose it. If she hasn't managed to slim down after giving birth, it isn't anyone's fault but her own! I can't believe she would blame Owen.

"Kat, you look like you're dying to comment," Jagger smiled encouragingly.

Uh-oh. It probably would've been wise for "Kat the Brat" *not* to comment. But I couldn't help myself.

"As a matter of fact, I do have something to say."

I saw Janelle cringe. I knew what she thinking. *Don't do it, Kat. Just shut your mouth. You're only going to regret it later.* But I wouldn't regret it. This was a live show! Zaidee couldn't twist and edit what I said. "I don't think it's fair of Maggie to blame her son. She had a weight problem long before she ever got pregnant."

"No, I didn't!"

"Yes, you did! When we were discussing our worst fat-girl moments you said you'd been overweight for *twenty* years."

"I—"

Jagger announced it was time to break for a commercial.

It figured. Just when Kat the Brat was standing up for a child they shut me down. I sighed, and Maggie and I waited out the commercials glaring at each other. When we came back from the break, Jagger proclaimed, "At the end of last week's episode, we promised an enormous twist was in the works . . . a twist to shake the foundation of *From Fat to Fabulous* to its very core."

I jerked upright in my chair and Regan shifted nervously.

"Our contestants have no idea what's in store, but I can promise you there are about to be some monumental changes in the *Fat2Fab* house. Our first night in the mansion, you'll remember that the girls competed for room assignments. I hinted then that the fate of the game might rest in that one competition. And tonight, we're going to find out why."

Here it comes, I thought. I looked nervously at Regan and Janelle. Out of the corner of my eye, I saw Luisa and Alicia exchanging glances.

"I'd like to welcome a young lady who defines the word *fabulous*. While you have never met this next guest, you're more than familiar with her. Over the past few months she's been a hot topic of conversation in the *Fat2Fab* house. So now, I am proud to introduce," Jagger paused, "Briana Borrail!"

I heard someone scream—Regan, probably—and the front door popped open to reveal one of the most gorgeous women I've ever seen.

"Regan," Jagger said. "Say hello to your new roommate! As of tonight, you will be sharing a bedroom on the main floor with your sister, Briana."

Predictably, Regan threw her head in her hands and started weeping. It was an awful moment, and you couldn't help but feel sorry for her. All her life, Regan lived under her sister's shadow.

Until now, *From Fat to Fabulous* was the only thing she'd ever done fully on her own.

I stared at Briana. She was wearing a pair of tight gray pants, black high heels, and a black strapless top. She had a full, perky bosom that easily supported her shirt. In all honesty, she was built like a *Playboy* Playmate, and I could see no similarity between her and Regan. Their faces were totally different, and Regan easily outweighed Briana by more than two hundred pounds. It seemed a cruel joke of nature that they were sisters.

"Wassup!" Briana cried, raising her arms in the air.

"Our next guest—who will also be joining the cast as of tonight—is the epitome of class and style," Jagger said. "He comes to us all the way from Merry Olde England. I love this guy's name, it sounds like something straight out of a Charles Dickens novel."

I watched the door swing open, and I heard Jagger speak, his voice drawn out as though in slow-motion in that final moment before the guillotine dropped.

"America, say hello to Nicholas Appleby!"

19

Nothing Bad Is Going to Happen

I ran.

Out of my seat, through the living room, up the stairs, and into my bedroom. I could hear the cameraman thundering along behind me. I didn't look back—not even to sneak a glimpse of Nick. I kept right on running until I'd reached the closet—the only sanctuary available. I flew inside and slammed the door. I dropped onto my stomach, pulling dresses and shirts off the racks and burying myself beneath them. It wasn't much of a hiding place, and I knew it wouldn't last for long.

"Kat!" I heard a voice scream.

It was a woman's voice. Zaidee.

"Go away," I hollered, my sound muffled underneath the pile of clothes.

"Kat, I need to talk to you."

"I can't talk," I sobbed. I wiped my face off with the sleeve of one of Regan's shirts. *How? How? HOW? How had the show found out about Nick? Who told them?*

"Kat, we're in the middle of a *live show* right now," Zaidee lectured. "Remember what I said on your first day in the mansion? You can't ditch the camera crews because you're having a bad day."

"This is a little more than a BAD DAY." I hiccupped. "This is my WORST FUCKING NIGHTMARE COME TO LIFE!" I gasped, realizing what I'd just said.

"Watch your language," Zaidee scolded.

Charles Dickens. Jagger said Nick's name reminded him of a Charles Dickens character. . . .

"We're *live*, Kat. You've got to come back downstairs *immediately!*"

That's too big a coincidence . . . they must have put two and two together from my phone conversation with Donna!

"It's written into your *contract*, Kat. You're required to participate in the filming of all live shows!"

"Zaidee," I begged. "Please don't make me go back. I can't do it. I can't. *I can't!*"

"What are you so afraid of, Kat?"

I had no choice. I had to tell her the truth. "Nick Appleby, who is now downstairs, has no idea I'm overweight," I confessed, blurting it out all in one breath.

Zaidee was quiet for a minute. Then she said, "I know, Kat. I know all about your situation."

"Oh my God." I gasped. "He's told you everything?"

"We know, yes."

"So you see why I can't come out of here until he's gone!"

"Listen, Kat." Her tone grew firm. "I do not come in here and interfere with the filming process unless a breach of policy has been made. Unless a contestant crosses a line. Kat, tonight you've crossed that line."

I began crying harder, producing great big sobs that wracked my entire body.

Zaidee softened her tone. "I'm sorry you're so upset. But nothing bad is going to happen if you come out. Nick's downstairs waiting to meet you for the first time, waiting to talk to you."

"I can't let him see me," I bawled. "He'll hate me."

"Kat." She sighed. "Nick has *already* seen you."

"What!" I gasped, mortified.

"He knows," she told me. "Believe me, he *knows*. Nick's seen tapes of the show. He knows why you're here. And he wants to talk to you. He wants to straighten things out. You've got to give him that chance."

I didn't have a whole hell of a lot of choice.

"All right," I said flatly. "You win."

Slowly, I pushed open the door.

Zaidee saw me, and her eyes bulged. "Tate," she barked to the cameraman, running her fingers along her neck in a slashing motion. "Cut the shot. Tell Roger to go to cam three." He dipped the lens down toward the floor.

Tate. I never thought of my cameraman as having a name before.

"Honey, I am going to do you the biggest favor of your life." She grabbed ahold of Tate's headset and started talking into it. "Roger, hold on cam three for about two minutes, get the full back-story. Yeah, I know what I'm doing. Uh-huh, try and make it interesting. Yeah, I'm aware that you're the director, you dick." She laughed. "No hard feelings. I owe ya, okay? Oh, and get Stevie up here *immediately* for a quick touchup on Kat. Tell her to haul ass."

I stared at her in surprise. It was all unfolding at about a million miles per hour. I couldn't figure out which way was up.

"Kat, doll," Zaidee said, fixing me with a look of tenderness. "Don't take this the wrong way, but you look like a train wreck. That pretty little mug of yours is caked in snot, tearstains, and mascara."

I drew in a breath.

"Don't sweat it, hon. I'm getting our makeup artist up here to do an emergency procedure. Think of this as CPR for your face," she said, cracking up at her own joke. "Boy, you don't know how good you've got it, kiddo," she said.

I was instantly reminded of Richard Geddlefinger. He always called me that. Suddenly, I longed desperately to be back in Memphis, back in my boring life, attending one of Richard Geddlefinger's marathon Monday meetings.

"I'm playing God here, much to our director's chagrin," Zaidee said. "Enjoy your miracle, hon. I'm letting you clean up before we get the shot of you meeting your English boyfriend. And you're not going to give me any trouble anymore, are you? No more running away from the cameras, eh?" She put her arm around my shoulders and gave me a tight squeeze.

I nodded miserably, staring at the floor.

"Tate, go ahead and film this, we're gonna cut between cam three and cam four," she said.

Tate swung the camera back onto his shoulder and aimed it at me.

"Here, get your lavalier back on straight, Kat," she ordered, pointing toward my microphone. I looked down at my shirt. The lapel mic had slipped off and was now hanging at my side. I pulled it to the top of my collar, and clipped it back into place.

A moment later, a mousy-haired woman with glasses appeared, carrying a big metallic box that resembled a tool kit. I could only assume she was Stevie, the makeup artist.

"Sit," Stevie ordered, practically shoving me onto the bed. She wiped my face down with makeup remover and then set to work. She whipped out an array of beauty products, and began applying concealer, base, and powder. Then she touched up my eyes with some eye shadow and a fresh coat of mascara.

"Don't ruin this, okay?" she said. She left as quickly as she came.

Zaidee gave me a thumbs-up sign. "Go get him," she mouthed.

Slowly, I rose from the bed. I had stalled Nick for nearly five months, using every excuse I could think of to avoid meeting him, so I could lose weight. And now here he was, waiting for me downstairs. Nick Appleby, in the flesh.

Waiting in the *Fat2Fab* house.

I started down the stairs. It was time to face the music.

* * *

Janelle was standing at the bottom of the stairs waiting for me.

"Oh my God, Kat, are you okay?" she asked. Her cameraman had followed her over, and he and Tate scrambled to stay out of each other's shot.

"No, I'm terrible," I told Janelle. "This is the worst thing that's ever happened to me." My voice broke and I couldn't continue. I couldn't stop thinking about Stevie and her stupid orders not to mess up my makeup. "Janelle, this is so awful."

"I know," she said, her bottom lip quivering. "Matt's here."

"What!" I gasped. "As in your bastard ex-husband Matt?"

She grimaced. "Yes. That'd be the one."

"What the hell is he doing here?" I cried. "What is this, blast from the past night?"

"The show tracked him down in Indiana."

"Holy shit!" I said, once again catching myself a second too late. I felt a brief pang of guilt for making the censors work over-time, but quickly dismissed it. If Zaidee and her crew were going to shock me by bringing on my secret lover, then they deserved whatever they got.

"Ladies," Jagger called, appearing in the hall, "I need for you to come back and take your seats with the rest of the cast."

I felt like a convicted killer, heading to my execution.

I was a dead woman walking.

"We've gotta make it through tonight," Janelle said, grabbing my hand and holding it for support. "After tonight, it will all be over and things can go back to normal. Or, as normal as can be expected in this crazy place."

When I got to the living room, I saw they had added more chairs so the new arrivals could sit. Janelle perched next to a fair-haired man with a buzz cut. He had to be her ex-husband Matt. But my eyes traveled over him with only a passing interest.

All I saw was Nick.

Tall, dark, and handsome Nick.

He looked exactly like he'd described himself to me over the phone. Exactly like his pictures. On some level, I'd expected a horrible flaw in his appearance. Some reason to explain why he'd spent so much time on a long-distance relationship. When people go online to meet lovers it's so they can lie, right? Make themselves into who they've always wanted to be. Just like I had. But there was nothing wrong with Nick. He wasn't four feet tall. He didn't have a receding hairline. He wasn't an eighty-year-old man with no teeth and a flask of Viagra. He was exactly who he'd said he was.

And that only made it worse. I had no way to redeem myself. At least if we had both been fakes, our lies would have canceled each other out. But, no, I was the lone fraud. This was without a doubt, one hundred percent my fault.

I took my seat next to Nick.

"As you may remember," Jagger began, "in the very beginning I mentioned the 'fate of the game' could hinge on your room assignments. Everyone assumed I meant the sleeping arrangements chosen the first night. But you underestimate us," he said, raising an eyebrow. "I was actually referring to one of our biggest twists. From this night on, some contestants will have to share rooms with people from their pasts . . . people who will make playing the game very difficult."

You could have heard a pin drop.

"Regan," Jagger said, turning to face her, "as soon as the live show is over you'll pack your bags and head out."

"I'm being kicked off!" Regan shrieked.

"Ah, on the contrary. We're giving you and Briana some quality family time. You'll now be bunking together in a tiny bedroom downstairs. Janelle and Kat, you'll stay where you are . . . for now. But who knows when the room genie may reappear and shuffle around your fate?"

I groaned at his cheesy joke.

Beside me, Nick laughed.

"This is so awkward," I said, looking down.

For a long moment, Nick didn't say a single word.

Then he leaned across the chair and kissed me, square on the lips. It was fast and awkward. Certainly not how I'd pictured it happening. But then, this wasn't how I'd pictured our first meeting, either. He leaned back, folding his arms across his chest. From head to toe, he was dressed in black. Black pants, black sweater, black leather shoes.

"Hi, I'm Nick," he said in his soft British accent. He extended his palm to me.

I slapped my big, sweaty hand into his. His skin was dry and smooth.

"Do you want to go somewhere after this is over, so we can talk?" he asked.

"I can't leave the house," I said lamely. "It's not allowed."

"I know that." He ran a hand through his hair. "I can't leave either. I'm moving in here. Didn't they tell you?"

What? "No, they didn't tell me anything," I said numbly, aware that the entire room—not to mention millions of viewers—was listening to our conversation. "Until I heard them announce you, I had no idea you were coming. Seeing you has put me in a state of total shock."

"Well then, that makes two of us."

20

Trying to Keep Us on Our Toes

"Your best bet is to play it safe," Janelle said. "Wait until Nick approaches you."

"Yeah, let him make the first move," Regan chimed in.

"Because if you start chasing him around, pleading with him to talk to you, it's going to make you look desperate," Janelle continued, "which you definitely are not!"

"Definitely," Regan nodded emphatically.

I was beginning to wonder if Regan had a thought of her own. All she ever did was second other people's opinions. And anyway, as much as I appreciated their confidence, I didn't buy it. How could they say I wasn't desperate when I so obviously personified the term? It had been eight days since Nick arrived in the house and, thus far, he'd barely spoken three sentences to me. Three sentences in *eight* days.

As soon as the live show had ended Nick was whisked away by the producers, to do who-knows-what. Then he was given "some private off-camera time" (four days to be exact) to adjust to being on the show.

I was dying to find out what was going through his head.

And why he'd kissed me during the live show.

But once his "private off-camera time" ended, Nick moved into the downstairs bedroom suite (previously closed off) with Matt. I'd tried numerous times to approach him and start a conversation, but he was doing his damn best to avoid me. He kept a completely different schedule from the rest of us—eating, sleeping, and exercising (as it turned out, he was an avid runner prone to spending ninety-minute stretches on the treadmill) when he pleased. I *could* have cornered him in Greg's Gym, but it was too embarrassing. Even though I was getting the hang of not feeling self-conscious while I worked out, I didn't want to have my big showdown with Nick surrounded by treadmills and elliptical runners.

My only link to him was via Matt, Janelle's ex-husband. He kept me informed by passing along little tidbits of information through Janelle. According to Matt, Nick was "having an especially hard time adjusting" to living in a reality TV fishbowl. It wasn't anything personal against me, and once he got acclimated, he wanted us to sit down and "have a long talk about our feelings."

It was slightly encouraging, but given the way the info had been passed down—from Nick to Matt to Janelle to me—there was no telling how accurate any of it was. For the life of me, I couldn't imagine Nick telling Matt he wanted to discuss his feelings. Did men even talk to each other that way? I suspected Janelle had thrown that part in to make me feel better.

"But what if Nick keeps ignoring me?" I asked Janelle. "We've got five weeks left in this nightmare. I can't possibly avoid him for over a month!"

"Oh, there's no way Nick will be here for the duration," Janelle said. "He doesn't fit with the dynamic of the show."

"Don't be so sure." Regan shuddered, jutting out her lower lip. "Briana's talking like she's here to *stay*."

For once I couldn't blame Regan for pouting. She was under a tremendous amount of stress. Her life had been thrown into huge turmoil by the arrival of the unexpected guests. Living in the cramped downstairs bedroom with Briana was turning into a nightmare. Making matters worse, they were sharing a queen-sized bed.

"Zaidee wants them crammed in like sardines. That way Regan and Briana are forced to hash out their differences," Jagger had disclosed to me privately, looking decidedly uncomfortable. I wasn't sure if he was uneasy with their sleeping situation, or if he felt strange for confiding in me. I wondered how the producers felt about Jagger sharing these secrets with me.

I didn't tell Jagger, but I secretly wished Zaidee had forced me to move into a room (and a bed) with Nick. At least then he'd have no choice but to acknowledge me. Given a few minutes of time to plead my case, maybe I could make him realize I was the same girl he'd fallen in love with—just seventy pounds heavier. And I was working on that, chipping away at my weight problem. Didn't that count for *something*?

As it was, Nick and Matt's bedroom door remained closed and—incredibly—they had a lock. Whenever Nick was out and about, he went around wearing a CD Walkman, humming. It seemed grossly unfair that Nick, Matt, and Briana were allowed extra amenities (like access to Nintendo Gameboys and CD players) while the rest of us suffered in total isolation.

"Don't stress about it," Janelle said. "Just focus on your game plan for losing weight and winning challenges, that's the only way—"

"Kat, please come outside by the pool. Your interview session with Jagger will begin in five minutes," a voice called over the house intercom.

"Sorry, kiddies," I said, standing up. "Looks like it's that time again."

"How come they never let us know anything beforehand?" Regan complained. "Yesterday I was about to hop in the shower when Jagger ordered me to go to the Confession Chamber. I was sweaty and gross and looked like a beached whale."

"They're trying to keep us on our toes, keep things spontaneous. If we knew what was going to happen in advance we'd be too prepared. They want us to slip and say something stupid."

Janelle's reality TV savvy never ceased to amaze me. I often wondered how she'd gotten cast in the first place, considering she always seemed to be one step ahead of the producers. "Well, whatever. I've got too much on my mind right now to worry about prepping for some dumb interview."

Janelle eyed me sympathetically. "Want me to pump Matt for more information?"

"Nah," I said. "I'm going to talk to Nick myself."

"Really?" Regan asked incredulously. "How are you going to get him to talk to you?"

"Who knows? I'll bludgeon him over the head if I have to," I joked. "Wish me luck, gals."

I headed downstairs and into the backyard. I had come to a decision. No matter what it took I was going to confront Nick. I was sick and tired of dancing around things. Good or bad, I needed to know where we stood.

If I had any chance with him at all.

* * *

"So tell me about this boyfriend of yours," Jagger said, settling into the chair across from me.

I shifted uncomfortably in my seat and stared down at my hands. "You want to hear about my *boyfriend,* do you?" I asked, unable to keep the sarcasm out of my voice.

My boyfriend. It sounded strange, foreign. Was that what Nick was?

"Yeah, I'm very interested to hear more about your relationship." He smiled at me. "Any guy worthy of your attention has gotta be pretty special."

I knew it was a line. A cheesy line, probably prewritten for him by Zaidee or one of her cronies. After all, it was Jagger's *job* to pry stuff out of us; and flattery, as they say, will get you everywhere. I clung to it anyway. I was feeling low as pond scum, and his flirtation was oddly comforting. "There's really nothing to tell," I said lamely. "We were sort of seeing each other, but now it's kind of up in the air."

"Uh-huh. What do you mean by 'up in the air'?"

Wasn't it obvious? Did I have to spell it out for him? "Well, it's been over a week since Nick came into the house. How often have you seen him around me?"

Jagger nodded. "You guys have been pretty distant. What's the story there?"

"What's the story?" I repeated. "I'm fat. That's the beginning, middle, and ending—the story of my life. Never mind that I'm smart, or loyal, or funny. At least I *hope* I'm all those things."

Jagger fixed me with a small grin. "You are."

"Well, thanks. Anyway, that doesn't matter. I'm fat, and that's all Nick cares about. Hell, that's all anybody cares about.

My whole life, that's the only thing that's mattered." My self-doubt had reached a fever pitch, and I struggled to keep it in check.

Jagger looked alarmed. "You can't honestly think that."

"I don't think it; I *know* it."

"Kat, you're overreacting."

Overreacting? My mind flashed back to our volleyball game. I remembered the man and woman who'd chastised me on the boardwalk. Total strangers who had *hated* me. I was a whiner, they'd said. I was lazy. Stupid. Mean. Before I could say anything, Jagger spoke again.

"Honestly, Kat, do you really believe one so-called 'bad' quality cancels out all of the good ones you have?"

"I don't know. I guess."

"Because it doesn't. People aren't *that* shallow. Well, maybe out here in L.A. you might find a *few* people who are that shallow." He laughed good-naturedly. "But what do you care what shallow people think anyway?"

I sighed. If only it were that simple. "I wouldn't care . . . but it's just, I don't know, I always measure myself up to other people and I come up short. Sometimes it's like the world is this exclusive club and I'm not a member."

"Come on, isn't that paranoid?" Jagger frowned. "The first step is to stop being so negative. It's self-destructive."

"Yeah, I know." Truth be told, I wasn't normally so self-indulgent. But I'd been publicly humiliated in front of all of America. I was entitled to wallow a little.

"If you feel this bad about yourself, you're never going to be happy, no matter how much weight you lose."

What was he, an armchair shrink? "Once I'm thin enough, self-esteem will no longer be an issue."

"But who classifies when someone is 'thin' enough?" Jagger countered. "When you can wear a bikini? When a doctor gives you the seal of approval? When Hugh Hefner calls and invites you to do a *Playboy* spread?"

"No, it's nothing like that," I said. "It's simple, really. I want to be thin enough so I don't turn beet red when someone tells a fat joke. I want to be thin enough so that I never get embarrassed when shopping for clothes. Thin enough that no one ever calls me lazy, or dumb, or ugly, or worthless. I want to be thin enough so that no one would ever even *dream* of calling me fat."

Jagger nodded. "It seems like you're placing a lot of emphasis on what other people think and say."

I shrugged. "Maybe."

"Okay, then, what if I tell you you're thin enough? Does that count?"

I blushed. "If you meant it, it might. But we both know that's not true." I patted my protruding belly, wishing I could push it down, flatten it out.

"Say I do mean it. Say I prefer women who aren't skin and bones. Say I prefer women like you, Kat."

"But you don't," I argued, my mind whirling at the prospect.

"I might."

"There's not a man alive who does. Guys want a Cameron Diaz, not a Camryn Manheim."

Jagger laughed. "And you know what every guy on earth wants, huh?"

"Sorry, I'm being a pain in the ass. I'm in a foul mood. I'll admit it." I couldn't help smiling in spite of myself. Despite the fact that Jagger knew all the sordid details of my life—including my real weight—I was comfortable around him. And the feeling was obviously mutual. Jagger was *definitely* flirting with me big-time.

It was an unexpected—and highly welcome—experience. Then he burst the bubble.

"Full disclosure: I don't actually prefer larger women."

I felt like I'd been run over by a truck. He'd lured me into believing him, and then slapped me in the face with reality. "Oh, right. See, I told you so," I said, dejected. How much rejection did I have to endure in the name of this damn show?

"I don't prefer any type of woman," he said, still smiling. "Big, small, it doesn't matter to me. I honestly don't think about that kind of stuff. When you like somebody, they become more attractive to you—no matter how they started out looking. And if you don't like them, they're the ugliest person in the world."

"Right." I wasn't falling for his cornball shtick twice.

"So, back to what we were talking about," Jagger said. "Tell me about this boyfriend of yours."

"Oh God, haven't we already been through this?" I groaned. "Nick won't talk to me. End of story."

"Yes, but I've got an answer to offer you."

"Sure, fire away. I'll try anything. Well, just about." I wouldn't eat a bowl of live roaches. This wasn't *Fear Factor*.

"What if I arrange a romantic dinner for the two of you? Candlelight, wine, the works! That way you could have some private, uninterrupted time together."

I was stunned. "That would be amazing," I said. "You could *do* that?"

"Of course," Jagger said, winking. "Anything for one of my leading ladies."

I groaned inwardly. Right when I was lured into thinking Jagger was a decent guy, he'd start up with the smarmy attitude. "When could we do it?" I asked, trying to steady my pulse.

"How about seven o'clock?"

"Seven?" I repeated. "As in, seven o'clock *tonight*?"

"Yep, tónight's the night." He rose from his chair, signaling that our interview was over. "Be downstairs in the living room at six forty-five sharp. I'll arrange everything."

I stared at him in shock. That was less than an hour away. Janelle was right; they did like to keep us on our toes!

"Wow," I said. "Thanks, Jagger! I can't believe it—a private dinner for just the two of us!"

"Yep. Just you, Nick, a couple of cameramen, and the sound guy!" he quipped.

*   *   *

"Whatever you do, don't throw yourself at him," Janelle warned, as she applied eyeliner to my left lid. "Don't lay all your cards on the table. Let Nick show you his hand first."

Luisa burst out laughing. "I got a better idea. How 'bout you let him show you his *dick*?"

"Oh, God, this is going to be a disaster," I wailed. I was upstairs preparing for my "private, uninterrupted time" with Nick. Janelle, who was much better with cosmetics than hair, had graciously offered to do my makeup. Luisa was curling my hair.

"Hey, chill out," Luisa advised. "What are you afraid of?"

"A whole *bunch* of stuff," I said. "What if I laugh so hard I spray wine out of my nose?"

"At least you'd be laughing," Janelle said with a shrug. "If you're laughing that's a good sign."

"What if I choke on a piece of food and Nick has to give me the Heimlich maneuver? He'll have to put his arms around my body and then he'll feel how fat my stomach still is! Oh my God, I will *die* of embarrassment if that happens!"

"Girlie, you need to calm the fuck down!" Luisa said. "You keep this up, you'll be so nervous you'll puke on his shoes."

Great. One more thing to worry about.

"Everything'll be fine," Janelle said soothingly. "Just relax and be yourself. You guys had a great thing going over the phone and online, so build on that. Don't focus on all the stuff that can go wrong."

Which was pretty much everything. "Okay," I agreed, taking a few deep breaths.

Janelle gently applied eyeliner and shadow to my right lid. She finished up with some mascara, then topped it off with blush and lip gloss. I got dressed (in all black—I wanted every ounce of its slimming power), and it was six forty-five on the nose.

"Wish me luck," I said, starting out the door.

Luisa gave me a tight hug, and Janelle patted me softly on the back. "Not that you need it, but good luck," she said. "You're going to have a *wonderful* time tonight."

For the life of me, I hoped she was right.

21

Of Course It Wasn't My Plan!

When I first started chatting online with Nick I never would have predicted our first date would take place in front of all of America. Even though I was a few minutes late, Nick still hadn't arrived. I darted into the downstairs bathroom for one final appearance check in the mirror, and was surprisingly satisfied with the reflection.

My hair was curled into tiny ringlets and piled elegantly on top of my head; my face was delicately made up to show off my best features, and my body? Not so bad! The outfit was decidedly slimming, true. But my weight had dipped to 199 pounds, making me nearly thirty pounds lighter than when I'd first joined the show. To some people, 199 pounds might sound pretty hefty, but for me it was thrilling. I was in the hundreds! I was only one pound away from the big two-double-0, but *still*. That one pound gap felt as wide as the Grand Canyon.

I was ready to knock Nick dead!

My nighttime cameraman Tate stood dutifully by my side, filming my every move. I returned from the bathroom, and still no Nick. According to my watch, it was two minutes till seven o'clock. I remembered Jagger's instructions to be here at six forty-five sharp. Obviously, it wasn't being strictly enforced.

After what seemed an eternity, the double doors to the living room swung open.

Like me, Nick was dressed in all black—but he was wearing an expensive-looking suit with a black shirt and a shiny black tie. His dark hair had been cut shorter since the last time I'd seen him, and it was slightly spiked.

"Lovely to see you, Kat," he said, smiling slightly.

He extended his hand and I shook it.

I felt a massive blush creeping along my skin. "Nice to see you, too," I managed, removing my sweaty palm from his and wiping it casually against my pants. I felt in desperate need of a syringe of Botox—Alicia said a few shots in your palm is enough to paralyze your sweat glands for six months.

We stood awkwardly for a couple of minutes; then Jagger came sauntering in. He was dressed in a white tuxedo and his hair was slicked back. He gestured toward me with a little bow.

"Greetings, Mademoiselle Katrina," he said in a French accent. "Monsieur Nicholas. I will be your Maitre D' for the evening. Follow me please," he instructed. "Your adventure awaits."

I was hoping our "adventure" would take place at a fancy restaurant somewhere in downtown Los Angeles, but we weren't venturing outside the mansion's backyard.

Literally.

Jagger led us outside where an elegant table for two had been erected. We would be dining in full view of the *From Fat to Fabulous* household. And, as Jagger had promised, two cameramen and a woman holding a boom mic were present. I wasn't fazed; I had given up on privacy a long time ago.

"Tonight we've prepared two separate menus for you," Jagger explained once we were seated. "One menu contains a decadent four-course meal prepared by one of California's most celebrated chefs. The other contains a two-course, macrobiotic dinner intended to help keep you, Kat, on track with your diet. Which one you choose from is entirely up to you." He handed us each a menu.

"I'm not trying to slim," Nick said, without even flipping his open. "I'll take the gourmet meal."

I peeked inside the menu at the two-course macrobiotic fare. *Rutabaga Delight followed by Fish Fillet with Organic Mustard Sauce.* They had some nerve using a word like *delight* in the same sentence as *rutabaga*. I couldn't think of anything that sounded *less* delightful. Then again, seeing how I was far too nervous to eat, what difference did it make?

"I'll have the second option—the macrobiotic health-food dinner."

Nick nodded his approval.

"Ah-ha! Not so fast," Jagger said gleefully. "I said you could choose *one* of the menus—I didn't say you could choose *both*. I'm afraid you'll have to come to an agreement on which one you want. You're both going to be dining from the same menu."

Nick flipped open his menu, then wrinkled his nose. "We're staying with the four-course gourmet meal," he announced.

I hate it when someone speaks for me. "Actually, Jagger, we need a moment to decide."

"What on earth for?" Nick demanded. "Rutabaga Delight sounds positively unpalatable."

"I'm trying to be *healthy.*" I wasn't sure what offended me more, that he'd insulted my decision, or used the word *unpalatable* with a straight face.

"One night won't make much difference," he said.

"Actually, it will. Everything adds up!" We were off to a terrible start.

Nick shot me a stony glare, and I decided it wasn't worth the argument. *Pick your battles,* I scolded myself silently. *He's right, one night won't matter.* "You know what, let's take the gourmet dinner. What the hell."

With that decision out of the way, I wondered what we should talk about first. Then he started the ball rolling. "Has it been difficult for you?" he asked. "Being in the public eye twenty-four/seven?"

"I don't really think about it," I said. "I guess it hasn't sunk in."

"You can't *pay* for this kind of exposure."

Exposure? Before I could ask him what he meant, Jagger returned with a bottle of Merlot and began pouring it into two glasses.

"I'll taste," Nick held up his hand, causing Jagger to stop midstream. He made a face. "Perhaps you ought to fetch me a fresh glass and we can start over? Don't you know how to properly serve wine?"

Jagger looked bemused, but he quickly removed the offending glass and summoned a new one from the kitchen, and poured a small amount. He handed the glass to Nick.

Nick sloshed the liquid around, then brought it to his nose and took a deep whiff, before at long last taking a sip. He closed his eyes momentarily, then opened them again and pronounced, "Excellent. You may pour."

Good grief! What was with his holier-than thou attitude?

Jagger left, and Nick and I resumed our conversation.

"So what did you mean, 'You can't pay for this kind of exposure'?"

"Celebrity. No one sells celebrity like America," Nick explained. "Being on this program will open doors for me."

"So that's why you're here?" I asked. "Because you want to be famous?"

He softened. "No, Kat, it's not like that." He took a sip of wine. "But I had to take a considerable amount of time off to be here. I had to make sure there was some identifiable payoff."

A considerable amount of time? I took a huge gulp of wine. "Why would you jeopardize your job after you found out that I was, uh, big?" I blurted it out before I lost my nerve. "I thought you didn't like big girls?" I felt humiliated, begging for his approval. But I was so glad we were having an *actual conversation.*

"It's a bit complex," he said. "I don't *dis*like you merely because you're fat."

I winced. I'd rather be called anything but the *F*-word.

"To be totally honest, Kat, I'm not quite certain of how I feel."

"Right."

"It's all been very confusing. But I'm having a good time in California." Nick raised his glass in the air. "Cheers."

I raised my glass to his. "What are we toasting?"

"Shoes," Nick said. "Brilliant, magnificently crafted shoes."

"What?" I asked, not following.

He swung his feet around the side of the table revealing a pair of black leather loafers. "Prada," he announced, beaming.

I was completely baffled. Shoes were worth a celebratory drink?

"The square toe is the best part," he continued, pointing toward the front of the loafers. "I'm amazed you haven't commented on them." He seemed genuinely offended that I hadn't noticed his decadent footwear.

"Your shoes are great. I like your suit, too," I offered. "It's really nice."

"Nice?" He laughed. "For sixteen hundred pounds it had better be nice."

I quickly did the math in my head. I wasn't sure of the exact exchange rate, but I thought the British pound was worth close to twice the dollar. Which meant his suit had cost over three thousand bucks! That was four months' rent! I couldn't think of anything to say. I shopped at Wal-Mart, Target, Old Navy, and Lane Bryant.

"I'm a clothes snob," Nick said, smiling. "Who are you wearing?"

I tried to think of a way to deflect the question. My black heels were from Sears, and my pants and shirt had been supplied by the show (and came, I knew, from Lane Bryant). As we'd begun to lose significant amounts of weight, Zaidee had brought in outfits for us to select from. Incentive, I guess. "I'm not really sure. This outfit was a gift."

"Are those Marc?" Nick asked, catching sight of my feet.

"Marc?" I repeated, confused.

"Marc Jacobs," he said. "What other Marc *is* there?"

"No, they're not. Marc Jacobs is a little out of my price range." He was starting to grate on my nerves. I took a big gulp of wine.

Nick ran his fingers along his brow line, smoothing the hairs into place. "I can't believe I was foolish enough to post you that stunning gown." Nick laughed. "There's no chance you'll be wearing *that* anytime soon."

The last thing I wanted was to delve into a heated discussion about the size-four Gucci dress on national television. Fortunately, Jagger picked that precise moment to resurface with our first course of the evening. I breathed a huge sigh of relief as I saw him heading toward the table, a waiter's tray in hand.

"Roasted red pepper and goat cheese tartlets," he pronounced, setting two plates in front of us. "*Bon appétit!*"

Given the circumstances my *appétit* wasn't so good, but I was loopy from the wine and thought it best to get some food into my stomach. I picked up the tiny fork and began cutting the tartlet into squares.

We lapsed into an uncomfortable silence, engaging in strained small talk through both our first and second courses. All the while, I gulped glass after glass of wine, polishing off one bottle of Merlot and then starting in on another. My tongue felt raw and parched from so much alcohol and I should have had the sense to slow the pace a little.

The main dish arrived—steak tips with pumpkin-seed pesto. As soon as Jagger set down our plates, Nick whipped out a pack of Marlboro Lights.

"You didn't tell me you smoke!" I exclaimed, startled.

"Well, you didn't tell me you were overweight, so I guess we're even," Nick retorted, putting the cigarette between his lips and striking a match. "I have one before and after every meal. It helps me digest food better."

I snorted.

"Was it always your plan to find a man online and mislead him?" Nick asked, pushing his plate aside and concentrating on his cigarette. "Or was that something you came up with on the spur of the moment?"

I nearly choked on a bite of steak. "Of course it wasn't my plan!" I couldn't believe he'd said that. "I only told you I was skinny because it seemed so damn important to you that I look like a supermodel." *Simmer down,* I cautioned myself.

"A girl doesn't have to look like a supermodel to catch my

interest," he argued. "I do prefer women to be exceptionally slim, but only for health reasons. I want the woman I love to live a long, fulfilling life."

Health reasons? I stared at Nick as he continued to nurse his cancer stick. "You know," I said, "some women develop eating disorders so they can be 'exceptionally slim.'"

"Yes, but *fat* people are *never* healthy," he countered. He took a long, slow drag off his cigarette and blew the smoke out into a perfect O. "There's quite a difference between being of normal weight and being obese," he began.

"This is fucking hopeless," I said, putting down my fork and standing up. I took a few steps and then stopped. "Even if I lost a hundred pounds, you'd never like me, would you?" He started to say something, but I continued on. "Let's call this off before I make an even bigger fool out of myself." I was primed to make a dramatic exit when Jagger came rushing to the table.

"Calm down, Kat!" he whispered, putting his hand on my forearm.

I felt a strange, exciting sensation when he touched me, even though I knew he was only egging me on for the good of the show.

"Don't give in. It's not like you to quit." His expression was earnest and reassuring. "Can you make it thirty more minutes?"

"Thirty minutes!" I exclaimed. "This is going way too badly for that." I was starting to feel like I might burst into tears.

"Don't do me any favors," Nick said, stubbing out his cigarette. "I'll be quite fine sitting here alone. Or, Jagger, you can send out Briana Borrail if you'd like."

"Yeah, I guess she's more your type," I sputtered, grabbing ahold of Jagger to steady myself. The bottle of Merlot I'd downed was taking its toll.

"Briana's an utter knockout," Nick agreed. "But she's a bit thick."

"Thick?" I repeated, clinging tightly to Jagger. The girl probably weighed a hundred pounds soaking wet. "You're joking, right?"

"Thick up here," he clarified, tapping his head. "The other day she told me they were building a bridge so you could drive between America and Britain. She said this new bridge was going to stretch between California and London."

"But California's on the wrong side of the country!" I said, swaying. I looked at Jagger—he'd been strangely quiet, silently observing our exchange.

"Yes, I know." Nick smirked. "She also wondered how I spoke such brilliant English, seeing how I'm not from America and all."

"No!" I exclaimed.

"Yes! Briana thinks everyone abroad speaks French."

I wasn't sure how to respond. Part of me wanted to laugh; the other part felt bad he was making fun of her.

"Hey, don't look so down, Kat. I was only messing about with you earlier," Nick said suddenly, tilting his head and looking into my eyes. "Sit back down; let's finish out our meal."

"Well, I guess I could."

"I won't bite. Promise." He winked.

Jagger steered me back to the table and deposited me in my seat. "I'll have dessert out as soon as you guys finish the steak tips. Enjoy yourselves," he said, slowly backing away.

"Why have you been avoiding me?" I blurted out.

Nick sighed and set down his fork. "You really want to know?"

"It's a logical question."

"Yes, I suppose it is. I'm not in the mood to answer it, that's all." He paused for a moment. "Although now's as good a time as any to do this."

"Do what?" I asked nervously. *Please don't let this be what I think it is.*

"It's been very difficult these past few weeks, ever since I found out you weren't who you'd claimed to be," he explained. "I needed some time to sort through my feelings and decide how I wanted to proceed." He gave me a halfhearted smile.

I drew in a breath. "And have you figured anything out?"

"You have to understand something, Kat. I've spent my life looking for the right woman. With you I thought I'd finally found the perfect mix of all the qualities I wanted. But I was naïve and you were dishonest." Nick sighed. "And so I blame us both for this."

I had a sick feeling in my gut.

"You're a lovely girl, Kat, and you'll likely make some other man very happy one day."

Some other man. Focusing on the ground, I asked, "Are you saying what I think you're saying?"

"I'm afraid so."

He laid his hand on top of mine. I jerked it away.

"Please don't be upset. This isn't easy for me, either. I've invested a considerable amount of time in this as well."

I couldn't speak. Nothing I could say would sound right or appropriate. I fingered my lapel mic and averted my eyes from his gaze. "But you said you loved me," I finally whispered.

"I loved a person who doesn't exist." He paused. "You were never who I thought you were, Kat. I look in your eyes and I see a stranger. Not one I'm interested in getting to know better." I sucked in a breath, stunned by the sharpness of his words.

"It was a silly thing to do, getting involved over the Internet," he continued. "What can I say? I was bored, and you offered the rare promise of something different."

"I never meant to lie." Tears welled up in my eyes, threatening to spill over. "It was stupid and I got carried away. I just wanted you to like me. We had so much in common . . ."

As I spoke, my mind starting sifting through the evidence. Nick and I didn't like the same music or food. I knew virtually nothing about his family. We'd never discussed our goals or dreams, our feelings about life. He was obsessed with brand names; I'd happily shop at the Gap if their stuff fit. Where were all these traits we'd supposedly shared?

"If your body matched your personality you'd have men queuing up for miles," he said softly. Seeing my stricken expression, he added, "I mean that as a compliment."

"So we're breaking up." Sour traces of stomach acid rose to my mouth. I swallowed hard, forcing it back down.

"I hope we can be friends," he offered, sounding less than genuine.

"Sure, we could do that," I said. "It might be fun." *Fun like PMS. Fun like a hangover.*

"I'd like to remain on favorable terms, considering we're going to be living together for the next month or so."

"Yes, considering," I repeated, my voice flat. So Regan had been right—Nick and the other guests would be staying with us until the end of the show.

"There's something I want to ask you," I said flatly. "Why did you kiss me the night of the live show?"

"It's a bit unusual, really," he began. "Firstly, I did it because I needed to know how I felt. I wanted to kiss you, Kat. Don't doubt that."

I smiled. "And how did it feel?"

"Awkward. Strange."

Strange? That didn't sound promising.

"And I did it for the game."

"Game?"

"'Weight of the World' or something. I can't remember the exact title."

He'd lost me. "What did *that* have to do with anything?"

"Zaidee showed me the previous episodes and I knew if we kissed you'd win seventy-five thousand dollars. Nobody asked me to do it; I wanted to help."

Nick was my blind date? It was too stupid, too ironic to be true. But the timing didn't add up. "How could you have been my blind date? That was supposed to happen weeks ago."

Nick ran his fingers through his hair. "What does it matter?"

"It matters." I strained to collect my thoughts. "Because, it doesn't add up."

"I'm not entirely certain, but I believe the plan was for some ex-boyfriend of yours to come on the show. Then when Zaidee found out about me she switched things at the last minute."

It didn't make sense. "But . . . when were you supposed to be here?"

"I was slated to come back in June, but I wasn't able to take off work until now. Deadlines."

"Have you been watching me all this time?" I wailed, beating my hands against my face. "Zaidee swore *From Fat to Fabulous* wouldn't air in England!"

"It doesn't. Kat, what are you going on about?"

And then I asked it. The one question I should have asked him right from the start. "How did you find out I was on a reality show?"

Nick stabbed a piece of steak with his fork, swirled it around in pesto sauce, and then placed it in his mouth. He chewed for a minute, then swallowed. "Your chum Donna told me."

"What the hell are you talking about?" I asked unsteadily.

Nick took another bite of steak and slowly savored it. "You really want to hear this?"

"Yes," I said, quivering. I felt sober, awake.

"You had that girl sending me those ridiculous e-mails, pretending to be you. Which wasn't very convincing, by the way. Then one day she wrote the truth, confessing that you weighed fourteen stone." He paused, then clarified, "Two hundred pounds."

"You're lying," I said indignantly. "Donna wouldn't to that."

"Apparently she would." He turned to face the cameras, and announced dramatically, "Ask Zaidee if you don't believe me. She'll tell you the exact same thing."

I shook my head in disbelief. "Why would Donna do that? For God's sake, she *wouldn't*! We've been best friends for almost five years. She has a key to my apartment! We trust each other with everything!"

Nick looked visibly annoyed. "Who knows, but she did what she did. I'm not lying."

I felt the weight of it sinking down around me.

In all our years of friendship, I'd never once done anything to intentionally hurt Donna. And here she'd plunged a knife into my back! All those years of me being in the background and Donna being the beautiful, stunning star . . . maybe that was the way she wanted it? I had never one-upped Donna, not with anything. Now here it was, my chance to be in the limelight, and Donna couldn't stand it.

I remembered our conversation that night at On the Border, the way she'd chided me, insisting Nick was a major catch. *Insisting—in a roundabout way—that he was too good for me.* And now, given the chance, she'd blown my cover, plunging me into the worst experience I could imagine.

Waves of nausea washed over me. "I can't deal with this now," I said, rising.

My stomach surged and I dashed into the house, bumping past the cameramen. The scenery spun and the ground seemed to tilt beneath my feet. I barely made it to the living room before I bent forward and pitched the contents of my gourmet dinner onto the floor. The thick yellow liquid gathered in a pool, seeping down into the carpet. Without making a move to wipe up the mess, I stumbled past, seeking solace in the nearest bathroom.

Nightmarish events aside, there was one bright spot.

At least I hadn't puked all over his Prada loafers.

22

Define Crap

I was a mess. My hair had fallen in a tangle around my shoulders. My face was red and puffy, stained with streaks of mascara. I sat sprawled out on the cool tile of the bathroom floor, wailing.

"You okay?" Jagger called, knocking lightly on the door.

"I'm fine," I sobbed. Which, of course, I wasn't.

"Do you want to talk about it, or do you need some time alone?" he asked.

I didn't really want to talk, but I didn't want to be alone, either. "You can stay," I gulped, sniffling. I leaned forward and opened the door.

He walked inside and sat down on the edge of the bathtub. "Anything I can do?"

"No." I started crying again.

Jagger produced a small packet of Kleenex from an inside pocket of his jacket and handed it to me. I noisily blew my nose.

"It'll get better," he said. "Hey, I've got some good news for you. Because of your kiss with Nick, you guys won Weight of the World on Your Shoulders. I'm making the official announcement tomorrow morning after breakfast. But Zaidee said I could tell you tonight. She thought it might cheer you up."

I was beyond cheering up at this point. "You know what's so ironic?" I said, laughing bitterly. "I never even figured out if we were officially dating. I feel like I fabricated the whole thing in my mind. Is it possible I wasted almost six months of my life on a relationship that didn't truly exist?"

"Of course it existed. Nick's a living, breathing human being."

"Yeah, maybe that's the problem."

Jagger raised an eyebrow. "What, you usually prefer guys without a pulse?"

In spite of my foul mood I smiled. "Not exactly. What I meant was, while Nick was in England everything was easy and safe. He could be my dream guy."

"And you could be his dream girl?"

"Exactly," I said. "How fucked-up is that? Am I so much of a freak that I can't handle a real relationship?" I wiped my nose on the back of my hand, disgusted. "What's next, a pen pal affair with a prisoner?"

"You're not a freak," Jagger said.

"At least Nick had the guts to be himself online. I'm the insecure, miserable mess of a person who faked everything. I'm the one who said I had a flat stomach." I cringed at the memory.

Jagger shrugged. "It wasn't *all* fake, was it? From what I understand, you lied about your weight, but you more or less told the truth about yourself otherwise. So Nick got to know the *real* you, he just didn't have the right overall picture. "

"That doesn't make it any better. I'm still a liar. He has every right to hate me."

Jagger paused, then took off his mic. "Your boy Nick's not as—how should I put this? He's not as *pure* as he seems."

I stared at him in confusion. He was allowed to take his mic off?

"Nick agreed to this dinner because it served his purposes; he didn't give a damn about talking to you. He was all set to snub you for the rest of the show. He acts like he's some kind of martyr, but he's got an agenda."

An agenda? "What kind of agenda?" I asked, swallowing.

"He told you himself during dinner," Jagger said, giving me a pointed look.

"He's doing this to get Briana's attention?"

"Think bigger."

"Regan?"

Jagger laughed, then said, "I'm serious. Just replay tonight's conversation in your head. You'll figure it out." He put his mic back on and left before I could drill him for more information.

* * *

In the morning, Nick's claims about Donna seemed downright ridiculous.

There was no way she'd sell me out like that, no way at all. I'd let my paranoia, an unfavorable trait—which had taken center stage since I'd come on *From Fat to Fabulous*—completely take over. As soon as I felt stable enough to stand up and walk without falling down, I'd head into the Confession Chamber and demand Zaidee tell me the truth. The real truth.

As it stood I had a big day ahead of me.

The producers were giving us an exciting and rare privilege: a phone call to our parents. They'd been hinting for a few days that the "infrastructure of the game" was changing. Lo and behold, we were now going to be allowed "routine, but limited" contact with the outside world via weekly five-minute phone calls. I didn't care how brief or monitored they were—I was dying to talk to anyone. This week we were allowed to speak with our immediate family.

A few hours later I made my way downstairs and devoured a handful of saltine crackers and a ginger ale before heading into the Confession Chamber. I was eager for things to return to normal.

Or as normal as they could be on a reality show.

Nick was back to avoiding me. Regan told me he hadn't come out of his room all morning. For the life of me, I couldn't figure out what had happened to the sweet, impeccably mannered, intelligent man I'd known online and over the phone. Was I really so vile that I brought out the worst in him?

"How are you today, Kat?" Zaidee asked, as I sat down in the Confession Chamber's plush red chair.

"Well, I got dumped last night. How do you think I am?"

"Elaborate, please," Zaidee said.

"I feel like crap."

"Define crap."

"I don't think it needs a definition," I snapped.

"It might be helpful. There are degrees of crappiness, you know."

I rolled my eyes. "There's something else I'd rather address. Nick told me a story last night that pretty much amounts to a bold-faced lie." I let out a low, harsh laugh. "Not that I put any stock in what he says, but just to be extra sure, can you clear something up for me?"

"I'll try."

"He swears my friend Donna told him about *From Fat to*

Fabulous, but I know that's not the case. I know you guys are the ones who tracked him down and brought him here. I just wanted you to know that he's a liar." I announced this as though it were some great discovery.

"Kat, doll, I hate to tell you, but Nick's right. *He* called *us,* not the other way around."

"Okay. But he didn't find out from *Donna.*"

"Donna did in fact give him the news. I spoke with her myself not too long afterward."

"No," I said, shaking my head. "She's not like that. She wouldn't have told him. I mean, why *would* she tell him? *Why?*" I asked, looking where I knew the camera was, as though I were speaking to her directly. "Why would you do that to me? Was it some kind of a stupid joke?" I was crying now. "Didn't I mean anything to you? Didn't you value even *one thing* about our friendship? One thing at all?"

"Go on, Kat; it helps to talk."

"No," I said, rising from the chair. "I have nothing to say to anybody. You people can go to hell!" I announced, storming out the door, without even waiting to get the phone call to my parents.

I was turning into a first-rate drama queen.

No wonder I had been nicknamed Kat the Brat.

* * *

Later that day, after a long nap, and a longer time just lying on my bed thinking, I decided it was time to make a change. Throwing out sarcastic comments was a part of my personality, and I couldn't turn that off. But I could sure as hell do something about my slide into immaturity. And I'd better do it quickly.

I started with Jagger. He was outside by the pool, interviewing Maggie about her lack of progress. I waited patiently by the back door until they'd finished. When the interview ended, I waved. Jagger smiled, unclipped his mic, and came strolling over.

"Feeling better today?"

"I'm good, yeah," I said, making a deliberate effort to be positive. I was determined to put last night's embarrassing dinner behind me and start clean. Maggie came pushing past us, stalking into the house. "She okay?" I asked.

"This is about a lifestyle change," Jagger said, "and Maggie's trying to come to terms with that. She wants a quick fix."

"Nobody calls it a diet anymore, they call it a lifestyle change. Like that somehow makes it easier, more exciting, less likely to fail."

He laughed good-naturedly. "You may have a point there."

"So, I was wondering if I could talk to you for a few minutes?" I asked.

He looked at his watch. "I've got a production meeting in five."

"Oh, I can go quickly."

Jagger cocked an eyebrow. "Can you now?"

"Yes! Well, no. I mean, sometimes." We were off to a weird start. His coy comment had thrown me.

"What'd you need to talk about, Kat?" He steered me back on topic.

"I wanted to apologize for the way I've been acting lately. I've been a real pain to be around. Very moody and argumentative. I'm sorry."

"No, you're fine," Jagger said.

"This whole Nick situation is really messing with me. Earlier today I blew off the phone call with my parents."

"I heard about that. Any particular reason?"

"I got dumped and stabbed in the back," I said. I squinted against the bright sun. "My mother probably thinks I hate her now, though."

"Given the circumstances she'll understand."

"You don't know my mother," I said. "She takes everything personally."

"So call her now."

"You say that like I can just pick up a phone and dial."

"No, of course you can't. But go up to the Confession Chamber and ask Zaidee if she'll let you," Jagger suggested.

I shook my head. "She'd never agree; I'm not that lucky."

"Just ask her. Zaidee can be abrupt, but she's not evil."

"I don't know, maybe."

Jagger tilted his head and looked in my eyes. "Look, don't let Nick Appleby ruin this experience for you. There'll be plenty of time to sort through your personal relationships once the show wraps. But you can't do anything about them now, so why stress yourself out? This is your fifteen minutes; have fun with it."

Maybe he was right. It was worth a shot. "Thanks for that. I needed it."

"Anytime," he said, heading into the house.

True to Jagger's prediction, Zaidee allowed me to phone home.

"We've got your mother, Lynne Larson, on the phone. Go ahead and pick up, Kat."

I grabbed the receiver.

"Kat!" my mom shrieked. "Thank God! We've been worried sick about you. Your father's gone to the doctor's, so he can't talk," she rushed on. "But, rest assured, he's not on his death-bed. Much as that must disappoint you."

"*What?*"

"It's very disrespectful," she told me sternly, "going around saying your father's dying of a rare disease. Do you hate us that much, Kat? Is that what you're wishing for?"

Oh, *God*. My mind flashed back to the conversation I'd had with Nick, "I have to go away to Denver for a few weeks . . . maybe more. My father's not well," I'd told him.

"Your father was devastated when he found out," she said.

"How *did* he find out?" I asked, envisioning the headline: KAT THE BRAT FAKES TERMINAL ILLNESS. Maybe Donna had blabbed about that, too?

"Nicholas called," she said. "He tracked down our number and called to offer his condolences. Poor boy was worried to death. And you," she scolded, "you care so little about your parents that you go around telling people we're dying."

"Mom, I swear I didn't mean it that way!"

"Do we embarrass you, Kat?"

"No, it's nothing like that—"

"Because I'd say you've done a pretty fine job of embarrassing the family. The things you've been talking about on national television! Sexual matters and whatnot!"

"Mom, I'm sorry," I said. "What can I say? Sex sells."

"Yes, but does it have to be *your* sex?"

She continued to chastise me for my "upsetting" behavior. When Zaidee finally came on the line to inform us that the call was over, I breathed a tremendous sigh of relief. I'd never been so glad to see five minutes end.

* * *

I was unable to focus on anything but Nick. I weighed in at only 197 pounds, but he was all I talked about, thought about, dreamed about. And I was driving everybody mad.

"What the hell is so appealing about him, anyway?" Janelle asked me as we folded laundry in our room. "Because I don't see it. Although yesterday Regan and Luisa were saying how hot he was."

"I think with those two it's partly to do with his money." It had never been about that for me. "Although, in actuality, he's not rich, his parents are."

"I'm not rich, my parents are," Alicia mimicked as she came into the room. "Hello! If your parents are rich then, ipso facto, *you're* rich."

"What do you want?" I asked. I was in no mood to put up with her.

"Nothing much, just thought I'd come see what you two losers are doing," she said, brushing aside Janelle's laundry and taking a seat on her bed.

I ignored her dig. She opened her mouth wide, giving an exaggerated yawn.

"So, what does your boy toy Nick do that makes him so much money?"

I bristled. He wasn't my boy *toy*. He'd barely even been my boy*friend*. "Nick's the fashion editor for *Status*. It's a swank British men's magazine, kind of like *Esquire*."

"I know what it is," Alicia said nonchalantly. "What I meant was, how does Nick have the money for a designer wardrobe? 'Cause magazine pay is barely above slave wages."

"It's not Nick, remember?" I said. "His *parents* are rich."

"How much do you think they have?" I could see the wheels turning.

"I have no idea," I told her. "I know they have a couple of vacation homes. Or, holiday estates, I think he called them."

"It might be interesting to know. Maybe you could ask him for me sometime? If you guys happen to talk in the near future," she added.

"No problem at all," I told her in my best sugary sweet voice.

"That girl is such a royal pain," I said, as soon as Alicia had skipped out the door in search of someone else to torment.

"You realize she's going to make a play for Nick," said Janelle, who had been listening quietly the entire time.

"Let her." I shrugged. "She won't get very far. Alicia's pretty, but she doesn't measure up to his impossible standards. No one does."

23

Match Made in Heaven

"For today's competition we've decided to mix things up," Jagger began. It was the following morning and all nine of us—the original *From Fat to Fabulous* contestants plus Nick, Matt, and Briana—were milling around in the backyard. Three heart-shaped booths had been set up in a row. An enormous flat-screen TV sat beside them.

"Since we now have three additional guests in the house, we thought it was only fair they be allowed to compete," Jagger continued. "So I present you with today's challenge, Match Made in Heaven. This revealing competition will test your compatibility. You're going to be paired up into three teams of two: Janelle and Matt, Regan and Briana, and Kat and Nick. Your success—or failure—is directly linked to how well you know your partner."

Jagger quickly outlined the rules for Match Made in Heaven, which sounded like a slightly altered version of *The Newlywed Game*. "You'll begin by filling out surveys on a variety of unusual and enticing topics. Then we'll meet back here for a quick quiz. The goal is to guess your partner's answers. Every time you get one correct, you earn five points. At the end of the game, the couple with the most points wins!"

"Why, you don't say!" I jumped in sarcastically.

Jagger gave me a small laugh. "Today's prize is going to be a little different, a little outrageous . . . but more on that in a minute."

Briana threw her hands up in the air and let out a squeal. She turned and stuck her tongue out at Luisa. "Suckers! Betcha wish you had someone to partner with!"

Jagger held up his hand. "Not so fast. You didn't *really* think we'd leave three of our finest ladies out, now did you? Who do you think wrote the questions for Match Made in Heaven?"

Regan gasped. "No!"

Jagger gave her a sideways glance. "Oh, yes. Earlier this morning we summoned Alicia, Maggie, and Luisa into the Confession Chamber where, with the help of our producers, they crafted twenty entertaining questions for Match Made in Heaven. Their goal was to stump you guys. Because every time you get an answer wrong, Alicia, Luisa, and Maggie will earn five points. At the end of the game, if they've earned more than you guys, they'll be taking home the ultimate prizes."

He gave us a minute to digest this information. Then Janelle, Regan, and I were led back into the house to complete our questionnaires while the rest of the group remained outside. "Act fast," Jagger cautioned. "We're going to get started in just a few minutes."

I had no idea what kind of answers Nick would give, or how well he'd be able to deduce mine. I was eager to find out.

I sat down on the living room couch and quickly answered the questions, which ranged from humorous to bizarre. *Do you believe in ghosts? How old were you when you got your first* kiss? *What is your favorite candy bar? What's the bravest thing you've ever done? Who is the bossiest person you know? What's the juiciest piece of gossip you've ever spread?*

About ten minutes later, Jagger resurfaced and collected our surveys.

"All right, gals, it's show time!" he announced, escorting us out into the backyard.

"Please have a seat in the love booth next to your partner," he instructed. *Love booth?* I groaned inwardly as I made my way over to Nick.

"Hi," I said shyly, squeezing in beside him.

"Nice to see you," he mumbled, without turning to face me.

"Quiet on the set!" Jagger ordered. "I need everyone to sit tight until I give the command."

I rolled my eyes. A few production assistants I'd never seen before scurried about, frantically adjusting the lighting equipment and microphones. Gigi Rucker came over, bringing Alicia, Luisa, and Maggie with her. They sat down in folding chairs facing us.

"Gotta love the scenery," Alicia said, eyeing Nick. Jagger quickly shushed her.

After what seemed like an eternity Jagger began speaking. "Up until this point all of our challenges have had a cash reward. Today we're getting a little bit crazy. This time we're offering you something sweeter!" He dramatically swung around, pointing his finger at the flat-screen TV. On cue, the television sprang to life. A slick, black tire rolled into view, then the camera cut back to reveal a silver Subaru Impreza cruising down the highway. It swung effortlessly around the sharp curves while a voiceover informed us about the car's mighty horsepower and turbo-charged engine.

"And this gorgeous car could be yours—"

"If the price is right!" I jumped in, unable to resist.

Jagger snickered. "Try if the *points* are right. Earn the highest score today and not only will you each win a sleek new Subaru Impreza, but you'll also get this!" Jagger announced, as the TV suddenly switched to a gorgeous shot of soft sandy beaches and palm trees. "An all-expenses paid, seven-night stay in Maui!"

There's an enticing idea. Reward a group of overweight girls with a trip to the beach.

"And if that wasn't good enough," Jagger continued, "you'll also win a pair of Schwinn mountain bikes!" he announced, as the image of a man and woman cycling along a dirt trail came onto the screen. *Ah, yes. Exercise equipment.* For the life of me, I couldn't understand why they were being so game-showy.

As soon as the video montage ended, a production assistant came running over with a stack of large red cards. "We've put your survey answers on here," she informed me. "Hold these up when Jagger cues you. Until then, keep them down here." She leaned around and gestured toward a pocket that had been built into the side of the seat. They're numbered on the back so *make sure* you don't screw up the order." She turned and gave a stack to Nick. "Same deal," she said, and then hurried off to distribute cards to the rest of the players.

Once everyone had been accommodated, the game commenced. "We're going to run through the survey responses," Jagger said. "The goal is to read their minds, if you will. Predict how they've answered. Remember, every correct answer brings you five points closer to winning that cool new ride and Hawaiian adventure. Janelle, I'll start with you." He strolled over to her. "If Matt could take a dream vacation anywhere in the world, where would he go?"

Janelle smiled. "That's easy. Thailand," she said. "Matt's obsessed. He has a shelf of travel books about Southeast Asia."

Jagger cued Matt, and he held up one of his red cards. It read *Thailand*.

"Five points for the ex-lovebirds!" Jagger announced and a bell began dinging.

"And Regan? Where would Briana go on a dream vacation?"

"The beach," she said automatically.

"Be more specific."

"I don't know . . . the Bahamas."

Briana produced her card, which said *Bahamas*.

Jagger turned to face me.

My mind went blank. As far as I knew Nick had already visited some of the world's greatest cities—Madrid, Rome, New York. Plus, I had no clue whether his ideal holiday would be lounging on a beach, traipsing through a museum, or skiing in the Alps.

"Paris," I finally said, figuring it was as good a guess as any.

Nick let out a huge sigh, and pulled out his card. "South Africa," he snarled. "What were you thinking? I can't stand the French."

Jagger cleared his throat. "Moving right along. If your partner could use a voodoo doll on anyone who would it be and why?"

"Sammy, because he screwed Matt over in a business deal," Janelle answered correctly.

"Darlene, who stole Briana's fiancé last March," Regan said, bagging another five points.

I had no idea who Nick wanted to prick with a voodoo doll. I scrambled for a minute. "Can I say myself?" I joked. Jagger shook his head. "Uh, okay then, Johnny Depp?"

Jagger raised his eyebrows. "That's an unusual choice, Kat. Elaborate please."

I knew it was lame but I couldn't think of anything else. "Nick's section in the magazine got cut because his coworker landed a last-minute interview with Johnny Depp."

Nick laughed. "She's right, you know." He held up his card.

I was dumbstruck. Of all the questions I expected to ace, that wasn't one of them.

"Good job, guys! You're successfully holding the single gals at bay. So far they've only earned five points. Next question . . . what's your partner's most unusual talent?"

"I'd have to go with knitting," Janelle said. "It sounds weird, but Matt's amazingly good at it. He makes the best sweaters." Matt held up his card, once again matching her.

"Dancing," Regan said, glossing over the fact that she was supposed to name something unusual.

"Freak," Briana said, "you know my most unusual talent is being able to tie a cherry stem into a knot with my tongue."

Jagger posed the question to me and I was stumped. "His knowledge about shoes," I said sheepishly.

"Wrong!" Nick told me, holding up a card that read *surfing*. Surfing? When had Nick learned to surf? Last time I checked, it wasn't a big sport in the UK.

We continued on for a few minutes, with the questions growing more personal. "When was the last time your partner cried?" Jagger began.

Janelle bit her lip. "When his mother died last Easter," she said, and Matt confirmed it.

Regan goofed the question, wrongly guessing Briana had last cried over a bad breakup with some guy named Gibbo.

When my turn came I tensed. In my entire life I had never seen a man cry. My father was hardly the type to let loose his emotions—unless, of course, the emotions were anger or agitation—and none of my guy friends had so much as shed a tear in front of me. Did tears come easily to Nick, or was he one of those macho types who cried once a decade? "Nick cried when his grandmother died," I fudged. I had no idea if this was true; in all our phone conversations we had never discussed grandparents.

Nick groaned. "I cried when someone scratched my Jaguar in Boots's car park."

Jaguar? Boots? He'd lost me. "You drive a Jag?" I asked, stunned.

"It belongs to Daddy," he explained briskly. "I borrow it from time to time."

"The boot's the front of the car, right?"

"No, the boot is what you Americans call the trunk. And that's not what I meant. I'm referring to an accident I had in the *parking lot* of Boots, the chemist. It's quite a famous chain throughout Europe," he said, exasperated.

"All right, Janelle," Jagger said, cutting off our conversation, "name the last time in Matt's life that he was truly afraid."

"Poor Mattie. He had a panic attack while trapped in an elevator in downtown Indianapolis," she said, patting him on the arm.

Matt nodded. "I can't believe you remember that," he said, looking truly impressed.

Regan went next, correctly guessing that Briana had been terrified when she rolled her SUV on the highway.

When it came my turn, I used the only thing I could think of. "Nick was afraid of meeting me face-to-face."

Nick pulled out his card and held it up. "On the flight from London to Los Angeles," he said. "I'm terrified of flying."

"Damn it," I cursed under my breath.

I watched as Alicia and Luisa gave each other high-fives.

Jagger moved on to the next question. "Who in Nick's life is most critical of him?"

I paused. It was a tough call. "His father," I guessed.

Nick sighed in exasperation. "Not even close," he said, holding up his card. It read *My sister, Sophie.*

Nick had a *sister*? In all our phone conversations and e-mails he had never once mentioned her. How could a major thing like that never have come up? From across the yard I could see Alicia smiling, likely thrilled that I had just given her another five points.

I sank down in my seat to brood.

Janelle and Matt continued to rule the competition and even Regan and Briana—who for all practical purposes seemed to be mortal enemies—scored surprisingly well. Meanwhile, I flubbed my way through the remaining questions, wrongly guessing on such topics as whether Nick had ever cheated on a test (*no*) and whether he'd had a one-night stand (*yes*). I did get a few right— like if Nick could be stranded on a deserted island with any celebrity, he'd pick Jennifer Garner. But I couldn't ignore the fact that I'd missed some of the biggest questions. My God, he has a sister and I didn't even know!

Once we'd finished going through our partners' answers, Jagger began questioning Matt, Briana, and Nick.

"What is the juiciest piece of gossip Janelle's ever spread?" he asked.

"Janelle doesn't gossip. Period," Matt insisted.

She nodded. "Good job, honey."

Honey? Uh-oh . . .

"Regan told the world that I got a nipple piercing," Briana said, and Regan frowned.

"I didn't tell anyone about that," she pouted, pulling out her card, which read, *Affair with professor.*

Briana burst out laughing. "Oh, yeah, you're right. Me sleeping with my prof *is* juicier." The two of them began giggling.

"Nick?" Jagger prodded.

Nick blinked in surprise. He looked a million miles away. "Oh, right. Let's see . . . the juiciest piece of gossip Kat has spread would probably have to do with that boss of hers, Richard. She's always going on about his long-winded meetings. . . ."

My face flamed red. Just what I needed. My grievances about Richard Geddlefinger aired on national television! And, worse still, it wasn't even the right answer. I pulled out my card, which said *Donna dumping Chip.*

Jagger moved on. "Matt, who is the bossiest person Janelle knows?"

He gave a shy shrug. "My mother. Janelle and my mother never saw eye to eye."

Janelle gasped. "No way, Mattie! I adored your mom."

He brightened. "Really? I thought you loathed her."

"No, trust me, she was precious." Janelle laughed, and held up her card, which read *Alicia Combs.* "This was worth losing five points over."

"Laugh all you want. Just remember who you're giving those points to," Alicia sang out.

Regan and Briana missed the question as well.

Then it was Nick's turn. "The bossiest person in Kat's life is herself."

"I'm afraid I can't accept that answer," Jagger said. "It's against the rules."

"Make whatever rules you want," Nick said. "I'm giving you

the absolute truth on this one; it's your decision whether or not you accept it."

"I'm not bossy." I bristled at the insult.

"You tell everyone what to do," he argued. "All the time."

Jagger raised his eyebrows. "Getting back on track, let's add a little romance into the equation. Matt, tell me, what age was Janelle when she had her first kiss?"

"I know it was with Troy Coltrone, and I think she was fifteen," he said. "Am I right?"

Janelle grinned from ear to ear. "God, it's so cool that you know this stuff," she said, confirming his answer.

"Briana?"

"Um, Regan was sixteen? No, eighteen," she decided.

Regan shook her head. "I was fourteen, Briana! You don't pay attention to me at all," she wailed, squeezing shut her eyes as tears began to form. At first I thought she was overreacting; a second later I was ready to join her.

"Nick, how old was Kat when she got her first kiss?"

He took a deep breath and let it out slowly. It seemed like he was thinking his answer over, but in actuality he was gathering up his nerve.

"Twenty-seven," Nick announced.

Alicia laughed out loud.

"What the hell?" I asked, holding up my card that read *Sixteen*. He was obviously joking.

"I think Kat was twenty-seven when she got her first real kiss," Nick said smugly. "From the way it felt the night I kissed her you could tell it was the first time."

I stared at him in horror. What kind of a low blow was that, dissing me on national television? Did he care *nothing* about my feelings or, at the very least, the integrity of the game?

Before we could get to another question, a production assistant came rushing over and handed Jagger an envelope. He didn't open it. "What I have here in my hands is both an invitation and a test," he said, strolling along in front of us. "It's a test of how compatible you are . . . and an invitation to take things to the next level."

Oh, God. Knowing my luck, now they'd force Nick and me to make out and let Alicia, Luisa, and Maggie critique our moves.

"Ever since the live show, Regan has been sharing a room with her sister. It's been a fun experience for both, providing ample opportunity to bond."

I snickered. I didn't think *fun* was the term Regan would use to describe it.

"As promised, your room assignments are about to get a little more interesting." Jagger held up the envelope. "I have here the keys to two cozy, romantic bedrooms, previously closed off to our houseguests. Janelle and Matt; Kat and Nick—the choice is yours. You can stay in your original living quarters or move into a new romantic hideaway. Saying yes reflects how much faith you have in your relationship. Saying no reflects doubt. I need your answers now."

Janelle turned pink. "What do you want to do, Mattie?"

Matt's voice grew soft. "I don't know . . . I kind of think we should go for it."

Janelle swallowed hard. "What the hell," she said, breaking into a smile. "It might be interesting."

"Yeah," Matt said, grinning, "it might be."

It was amazing, seeing how, despite time and circumstance, the two of them were still so connected.

"Nick and Kat?" Jagger asked, gesturing toward us. "I need your decision?"

I drew in a breath. "Oh, boy . . ." It was a tough choice.

"I'm not at all interested," Nick said simply. Apparently, it was only a tough choice for one of us.

"That's pretty abrupt. Want to give your reasons?" Jagger asked.

"I think it's quite obvious," Nick said. "Why would I want to live with *Kat*?"

He said my name as though it were a dirty word.

A funny thing happened at that moment. My body was baking under the hot lights but inside I felt frozen solid.

My mind faded from the game. I went through the motions, dutifully holding up my cards when cued, but I felt lifeless. I didn't care when Janelle and Matt won the cars, the trip, and the mountain bikes. I didn't care when Alicia and Maggie began chastising Jagger over the "unfairness" of the scoring system. I wasn't even interested that Nick had actually gotten a few answers correct (wagering that I believed in ghosts and that my favorite candy bar was Snickers).

All I cared about was how mean he'd been, and how terrible I felt when I was around him. And there were the things I didn't know. In all the time we'd talked, he'd never mentioned his fear of flying, or his knack for surfing, or his own *sister,* Sophie.

Maybe it was my fault for not asking the right questions, or maybe Nick had deliberately kept parts of himself a secret.

Either way, I couldn't shake the feeling that I'd never known him at all.

24

I Was Seeing Stars

"You weigh 193," Greg pronounced, as I stepped off the scale the following Sunday. Since being dumped by Nick and stabbed in the back by Donna, I had thrown myself into an exercising frenzy.

Alicia, on the other hand, had thrown herself at Nick.

She'd flirted, flashed her cleavage, and hung around in Greg's Gym, pestering Nick while he ran on the treadmill. She'd even stooped to a new low—lounging around in a bikini to catch his attention. It was excruciating to watch. Not only was Alicia blessed with perfect blond hair, perfect clear skin, and perfect perky boobs, but she'd effortlessly shed her excess pounds, revealing a gorgeous new physique. Sure, she still had a tiny pooch around her stomach and a small amount of cellulite on her thighs, but overall she looked amazing.

It didn't seem to be paying off. Aside from a few friendly greetings, Nick hadn't given her much of a response. But at least he was talking to Alicia.

"I thought we were going to be friends?" I told Luisa later

that day as we chopped pineapple for a snack. "I don't understand why he's such a wall of silence."

"He's probably mad that you guys bombed on that last challenge," she said.

I groaned. "How was I supposed to know Nick has a fear of airplanes or that he loves surfing? He never told me any of that. All he talked about was fashion."

"Nick's loco," Luisa said. "Messed-up big-time."

"He needs to be on medication," Regan agreed. "He's obviously polar," she said, and I laughed.

"You mean bipolar, right?"

"Polar," she insisted. "One minute he's up, the next he's down. It's a disease."

"Sure, okay," I obliged. I didn't want to get into the semantics of it with her, and besides, I'd wanted to name my autobiography *Height/Weight Disportionate*. I had no room to talk.

"Howdy, Kit Kat," Alicia said, coming into the kitchen. "Others." She gestured toward Luisa and Regan. "Thought you all might like to know I'm making some real headway with Nick. Considering how little you and Nick have in common . . ." Seeing my stricken look, she added, "No offense, honey, but you didn't even know Nick had a sister. Even *I* knew that!"

I gulped. Had Alicia really known about Sophie? If so, I felt like a world-class fool.

"So Zaidee's arranging a romantic dinner for me and Nick tomorrow night. Isn't that great?"

"What?" Luisa gasped.

I fought hard to keep from reacting. *She's only doing it to get to me.* "That *is* great." I decided it was time for a different tactic. "I'm glad to see Nick's moving on with his life," I said, with enthusiasm.

"You are?"

"Yes, I am," I said, thinking *keep your friends close, your enemies closer.* I put down the pineapple I'd been chopping and turned to face her. "I wish only the best for you two." *You're both snobs. You deserve each other.*

"The only bad thing is *Jagger's* going to be our server. I used to think he was cute, but now I realize he's just so," she paused, as if searching for the right word, "simple."

"Simple?"

"And he'll probably try and flirt with me during dinner."

"I highly doubt that." *Puh-leese.*

"I'm a guy magnet, so you never know," she said. "And if all goes well, Nick might wind up inviting me back to his room."

"Good luck with that," I said cheerily. And then, as though nothing would make me happier in the world, I leaned over and gave her a quick hug. "Just make sure to go barefoot," I advised her sweetly. "Nick's got a real foot fetish."

* * *

The evening of Alicia and Nick's romantic dinner, I killed time by playing drunken charades with the other houseguests. Even Maggie, who now spent the majority of her time napping in her private suite, came downstairs and joined us. Luisa fetched a few cartons of light beer from the Tomb of Temptation, and we spent a solid two hours drinking and goofing off.

It was a wonderful distraction, and I forgot about Nick.

Until around eleven o'clock.

We had finished our game, and the alcohol had worn off by that point. I wasn't the least bit tired so I ventured outside to lay by the pool and stare up at the stars. Gazing up and out, seeing the night sky that stretched on for countless miles beyond the house I felt free. I'd been out there for God knows how long when it happened.

"Hey Kit Kat, what's shaking?" Alicia said, sneaking up behind me.

I jumped. "I didn't hear you come out. How was your dinner?"

"Mmm. My head's spinning."

"Too much to drink, eh?"

She smiled, and put a *wouldn't-you-like-to-know* expression on her smug face.

I tried to fight it, but my curiosity got the best of me, and I played right into her hands. "What, did you guys hook up or something?" I scoffed.

She plopped down on the lawn chair next to me and stretched out her long, slender legs. "Nick was *in-cred-ible* in bed. I was seeing stars."

I felt nauseous. "You're such a liar," I spat out. "Do you honestly expect me to believe you slept with Nick? 'Cause that's so fucking ridiculous it's not even funny."

"There was no sleeping involved." She turned to stare directly into the camera. "It was forty-five minutes of nonstop action. It's a miracle I can walk. I'm gonna be sore tomorrow." She laughed and then massaged her legs for emphasis.

My mouth was gaping open. This was obviously a joke.

"You have no idea what you're missing," Alicia continued. "You should have gotten him while you had the chance."

"You are such a liar!" I shrieked. "You're just saying this to get attention!"

"Stop being bitter, Kit Kat. You lost him, I found him. And you know what they say—finders keepers."

She was unbelievable. I couldn't listen to another minute of this; I had to get out of there. "You guys deserve each other," I told her, jumping up from the lawn chair. I stormed into the house. I needed some time alone, to make sense of it all.

And, well, who doesn't think better on a full stomach?

I'd never gone back into the Tomb of Temptation, not since that first time with Regan. Sure, I'd tasted some of the goodies that others had taken out, but I'd managed to keep myself from succumbing to its lure. No more. I stumbled into the kitchen, nearly tripping over Regan, who was slumped across the floor. "They're doing it," I burst out, shaking. "They're having sex!"

She looked at me slowly and shrugged.

"Don't you even want to know who I'm talking about?"

She didn't say anything.

"ALICIA AND NICK! I figured he had a thing for your sister—and I could accept that because she's gorgeous. But no, he's sleeping with Alicia! Fucking. Screwing. Making love," I said, trying out all the words I could think of to describe it. None fit.

"Huh."

I had reached my boiling point. I wanted some kind of a response—a simple "that sucks" would have sufficed. Something, anything! As it was, Regan was barely even listening. "And later tonight you, Janelle, and I are going to run around the backyard naked!" I shrieked, trying to elicit a reaction.

"Yeah, we could do that."

"Regan!" I exclaimed, sinking down on the floor next to her. "What's wrong with you? Why aren't you saying anything?"

"I just spent forty-five thousand dollars." She closed her eyes, then rephrased it. "I *lost* forty-five thousand dollars from my *Fat2Fab* bank."

My jaw dropped. I momentarily forgot about Alicia and Nick. "How?"

"I ate it."

"What?!"

She gestured toward the Tomb of Temptation. "It costs money now."

I stared at her in disbelief. "What do you mean 'it costs money'?"

"We can't just go in and get what we want. We have to buy it." She pointed up again and I saw it. Fastened onto the Tomb of Temptation door was a small touch screen, the kind used at ATMs. "You type in what you want on there, and it dispenses it. Like a big vending machine."

"But we had beer from there earlier tonight . . . that was free."

"They changed it." She sniffed. "I just bought a box of cookies and a bag of chips."

"And that was forty-five thousand dollars?"

"I also bought a medium pizza," she said, hiccupping. "Pepperoni and onions."

She wasn't lying about that last part. I could smell the onions on her breath. "But, that shouldn't have been more than twenty bucks!"

"It's expensive," she said, sighing. "Like ten thousand for a donut."

"Oh, Regan," I said putting my arms around her for a hug. "*Why* did you eat that stuff?"

"I was upset. I had to."

"Whatever was bothering you, you should have talked to someone about it. You can't run to the Tomb of Temptation whenever something bad happens. You can't eat away your problems," I said. As soon as the words left my mouth, I realized what a hypocrite I was. I'd been totally primed for a binge-fest of donuts, candy, and chips myself. I was no better than her.

"It's Briana," Regan whispered. "I can't live in this house with her. She's driving me crazy."

"She's not that bad," I said, even though I hadn't spent enough time around her to make that call. "You guys did pretty well on Match Made in Heaven, which proves you're somewhat compatible."

"Who cares if we're compatible? Briana tells me I'm a disgusting pig. She says even if I lose weight I'll have all this excess skin and still be a gross fattie."

Ouch. "Briana also said they're building a bridge to connect California and Great Britain," I offered.

"Yeah." Regan nodded. "I've heard about that, too. It's supposed to be ready by 2007."

Apparently being thick ran in the family. "Well, I wouldn't put much stock in anything Briana says." Borrowing a line from Jagger, I added, "Besides, she's shallow. What do you care what shallow people think?"

"Nick's shallow, and you care what he thinks."

She had me there. At the mention of Nick's name, devastation washed over me again. "Have you got any leftover pizza?" I asked.

She shook her head. "But there's plenty more where that came from."

I stood up and began punching up food items on the menu. "Jesus. I can't believe they're charging fifteen thousand dollars for a piece of cake!"

Regan nodded sadly.

I thought it over for a minute, then said, "What the hell, every girl deserves a splurge now and again." I ordered up a bottle of vodka for thirty thousand dollars.

"Beer before liquor, never been sicker," she cautioned.

"Trust me, there's no way I could feel any sicker than I already do."

Regan's eyes met mine and we started to laugh, big gut-busting wails. I bent forward, holding on to my stomach with my hands and I laughed so long and so hard I thought I might throw up.

* * *

Jagger tugged gently on my shirt sleeve. "Kat?"

Somewhere between my fifth and sixth vodka and diet Coke I'd passed out; my body slumped sideways on the kitchen floor. I blinked my eyes, trying to come to grips with my surroundings. I looked around the kitchen and noticed Regan was gone. "What are you doing?" I mumbled. "You're never here this late."

"It's six in the morning," he said. "I get here at this time every day."

"Holy FUCK!" I said, wide awake. I could see tiny slivers of sunlight streaming in through the kitchen window. "Where's Regan?"

"She passed out on the couch. I took her back to her room. Here," he said, helping me up. "Put your arm over my shoulder and I'll take you upstairs."

"No, I can make it," I said, struggling to stand. My head was spinning.

"I heard what happened with Alicia," he said.

The memory came rushing back, and my body buckled. "They had a big night. . . ." I said bitterly.

Jagger nodded. "I heard the audio." He pulled me up, wrapping his arms around my waist. "Just put your weight on me."

"I'm fine," I insisted. I was too embarrassed to put my weight on him. I didn't want Jagger to feel all 193 pounds of me. The house was dark, but the camera crew was there nonetheless, capturing everything.

"It's okay," Jagger said, as I started to slump into him. He steadied me in his arms. "It's turning into a pattern . . . every time we arrange a dinner for Nick, you wind up getting plastered."

"God, you're right. I'm normally not a drinker. What the hell's wrong with me?"

"Nothing, you're human," Jagger said. "Anybody would be upset." He held me tighter, pulling me into an awkward hug. "I'm sorry," he said. And then his lips moved up slightly, just beneath my ear. "Nick's sleeping with her because it puts him in the spotlight," he whispered. "Zaidee suggested he'd get more screen time if he had a 'story line.' They planned it all out. She told me herself. I don't know if that makes any difference."

I moved back, staring at him for a long moment.

I was so grateful for what he'd said, so shocked by it. Jagger's face swam before me and, buoyed by alcohol and gratitude, I gave him a brisk, unexpected kiss. On the lips. "Thank you," I slurred. "For helping me out."

He looked taken aback. "You're welcome," he said, guiding me up the stairs and depositing me into my bedroom.

He was just setting me on the bed when Janelle stuck her head in the door. "What are you guys doing?" she asked suspiciously.

Jagger laughed. "I should ask you the same thing. Shouldn't you be cuddled up with Matt right about now?"

"Things between us aren't like that," she said. "We're getting to know each other again. Anyway, I couldn't sleep. Matt snores, you know." She looked at me. "Kat, are you hurt or something?"

"She's had too much to drink," Jagger explained. "She needs to sleep it off."

Janelle was there in a heartbeat, pulling off my shoes and helping me under the sheets. She propped a pillow behind my head and covered me with a blanket.

"What in the world is going on with you?" Janelle asked, crouching down beside me and stroking my hair. "I've never seen you look so out of it."

I started to answer, but my eyelids were drooping and I knew I wouldn't be able to stay awake long enough to do the story justice. "Tomorrow," I mumbled, snuggling under the covers. Right before I dropped off, I turned my head in search of Jagger, but he was gone.

* * *

There are a lot of things a good night's sleep will fix, but Alicia and Nick wasn't one of them. In the light of day the situation with them was even more disturbing to me. Worse still, I was horrified that I'd planted a big, wet, drunken kiss on Jagger's mouth.

I'd probably gone and ruined our budding friendship.

"I can't believe they slept together," I said, my voice barely above a whisper. Janelle was seated at the edge of my bed, so she patted my feet. "All this time I thought I couldn't be with Nick because I wasn't a size four. He'll make an exception for *her,* but I don't even get a *chance?*"

Janelle sighed. "Kat, why are you still worrying about what Nick does?"

"I can't just shut my feelings on and off like a switch."

"But the guy has no personality! He's a carbon-copy of a human being."

I thought for a minute. "You honestly don't find him charming?"

"Yes, it's really charming how he ignores you all the time."

I sighed. Over the phone, and in our e-mails, Nick had seemed brilliant, full of life. I felt he could show me a part of the world I'd never seen, teach me about things. I had spent so much of my life waiting; when I met Nick, it seemed that *finally*, my life had begun. But in person he was nothing but an ass. "On the phone he seemed so different, so passionate—"

"Passion's not always a good thing," Janelle pointed out. "Hitler was passionate."

I grimaced. "Nick's handsome."

"I've always thought the way a person looks is the least interesting thing about them," Janelle mused. "Take Matt. He studied sign language in high school and now he volunteers as an interpreter for the deaf. I find that so intriguing. And those are the kinds of things you'd never know merely by looking at a person."

"It's the same way with Jagger," I agreed. "When I first met him I thought he was good-looking, but in a cocky and arrogant way. But he's become way more attractive as I've gotten to know him."

"I knew something was going on between you two!" Janelle winked at me.

"Not even." I sighed. "But we're friends." *Or were until we shared a drunken kiss.*

"You're blushing."

"It's hot in here," I argued.

"*Sure,*" she said.

I considered telling Janelle about the kiss, then decided against it. If it had just been the two of us, hanging out at a bar or sitting alone in my apartment, I'd have easily spilled. But seeing how everything we talked about was privy to the viewing audience . . . there was no need to add more dirty laundry to what was already an enormous pile.

25

Kill Me Now

The final three weeks of *From Fat to Fabulous* went by in a blur.

Alicia and Nick were in full-blown couple mode, prancing around the house holding hands, flirting, and kissing. I did my best to avoid them, but it wasn't easy. Nick was going out of his way to spend time around me.

"Good morning, Kat," he'd say every day, as he and Alicia strolled out of his bedroom together, coming into the kitchen to eat breakfast in their bathrobes. "Lovely to see you," he'd say as he sat down next to me. He'd be looking at me out of the corner of his eye while he embraced her. And then they'd spend the next few minutes trading noisy kisses.

I focused on losing weight, but I'd already lost the game.

After blowing sixty-five grand in the Tomb of Temptation that night with Regan, I'd slipped into third place, trailing Janelle and Alicia. In one fell swoop, my little indiscretion had taken me out of the running for first place. Unless Janelle and Alicia both screwed up big-time, I was destined for third. And Janelle was doing so well she'd likely have beaten me anyway, even if I hadn't blown it. The funny thing is, I'd lose the game even though I'd managed to shed over forty pounds. And Regan, who had lost the most weight of any of us (nearly sixty pounds!), was in dead last. Eating snacks in the Tomb of Temptation had taken her bank balance all the way down to zero.

I was coming to realize *From Fat to Fabulous* had little to do with weight loss.

We were going out with a bang, in a special live finale. According to Zaidee, the introduction of Nick, Briana, and Matt had provided a "tremendous boost in the Nielsen's." I was dying to know what the ratings were, but would have to wait until I got out of the house.

I counted down to the live finale with trepidation.

I couldn't forget how things had gone during the *last* live episode.

"Never thought I'd say this, but I'm going to miss this place," Janelle said on the final day, as we packed our suitcases in preparation for the grand exit from the house. Despite having moved in with Matt, Janelle still had two drawers full of clothes in my room. Janelle glanced around at the bare walls and blinked. She had a hint of tears in her eyes.

"What are your plans?" I asked, thinking that I wouldn't miss this house at all.

"I'll probably visit my parents in New York and then go back to the gallery. What about you?"

"I'm going to Denver for a few days. My parents arranged it last time we spoke on the phone," I said. They were finally convinced that I did *not* want them dead, which was a relief. "After that . . . who knows?"

"Thirty minutes till show time," my nighttime cameraman, Tate, informed us.

It was only the third time I'd ever heard him speak. "It's been nice knowing you, Tate." I halfway expected a response, but he remained stiff, pretending as though I hadn't said a word.

"You think you'll keep in touch with Jagger?" Janelle asked.

"That would be nice, but I highly doubt it." Jagger was no longer friendly and flirtatious with me.

She cocked her head to the side. "You guys got kind of close toward the end."

Until I went and blew everything by kissing him while I was wasted. "We'll see what happens," I said vaguely.

"I'm going to get changed," Janelle said, picking up a pair of pants and darting into the bathroom. "Back in a sec."

My eyes wandered around the room, taking in everything for the last time, committing it to memory. It seemed unfathomable that I'd no longer be sleeping here, or eating breakfast down-stairs, or talking with Janelle every day. She'd meant the world to me, and who knew if I'd ever see her again?

Even if I did, it wouldn't be the same.

I was overwhelmed with uncertainty and apprehension. There was no telling what was waiting for me on the outside. Zaidee had mentioned that we would be required to give a series of exit interviews (satellite TV and radio) as soon as the show ended. Beyond that, it all became fuzzy. Somehow, I would have to slip back into normal life. Only I'd be going back to Memphis with-out Nick, and without a best friend. My dreams of stardom and a writing career hadn't panned out. I was still battling the bulge. I *had* shed weight, and was now a size fourteen. Hardly skinny, but I was proud of myself.

When all was said and done, I was happy I'd taken the risk of coming on the show. My falling-out with Donna, my failed relationship with Nick—they were bound to happen one day. Maybe *From Fat to Fabulous* hadn't really changed my life, just sped it up.

"You ready?" Janelle sang out.

"Ready as I'll ever be."

"Let's get this show on the road," she enthused, emerging from the bathroom. She was decked out in a stunning red top and flared blue jeans, capped off with a gorgeous pair of black high-heeled boots. Her long dark hair had been pulled into a classy ponytail at the back of her neck, and she'd applied a fresh dusting of makeup.

"You look fabulous," I told her, and I meant it.

She smiled and curtseyed. "But the question remains, have I gone from *fat* to *fabulous*?"

I slung one arm around her, and grabbed my duffel bag in the other. "Absolutely," I said. "No contest."

* * *

"Keep it clean tonight!" the floor director announced as we took our seats. "We're on a five-second delay, but watch your language!"

I looked around the room, memorizing everything: the blinding overhead lights, the enormous cameras on dollies, the frantic motion of stagehands and producers and sound techs. The glamour of it all had escaped me until now.

"Stand by," the floor director called. "We're coming in live in five . . . four . . ." I listened to him count down and my eyes went misty.

This was it.

After tonight I would fade into obscurity, my life no longer in the limelight.

"Well, America, it's been one long and wild ride," Jagger began, walking along in front of us, hitting his marks. He looked amazing in a pair of faded jeans and a light-gray button-down shirt. "Our contestants have been through fifteen weeks of hell, tinged with drama, heartache, and triumph. Now it's time to find out just who has gone FROM FAT TO FABULOUS!"

The scene was surreal. I watched Jagger recap the last few days' events, and then segue into the "ultimate revelation: which girl has *conquered* her battle of the bulge to become America's most FABULOUS NEW REALITY ICON?"

There *were* two surprises that came out during the finale.

The first was when Jagger announced the order in which we'd placed. As I (and probably everyone watching) predicted, Janelle took home the whole pot. She'd lost weight fourteen out of the fifteen weeks we were on the show, and succeeded in every single challenge. But *I* came in second, Luisa third, Maggie fourth, and then Regan was next. Alicia was dead *last*!

"What happened, Alicia?" Jagger asked. "It looked like you were primed to win the whole thing. How'd you wind up losing?"

"Well, Jagger, when Nick came into the house, my priorities changed," she said. "I realized there were more important things in life than money and weight loss."

"Yes, but you frequently commented in your diary sessions that your motto is 'you can never be too rich or too thin,'" he countered. "Has that changed?"

"It hasn't," she said smugly. "But I knew I had no shot at winning. Let's face it—Janelle was an Amazon warrior when it came to diet, exercise, and challenges. I couldn't beat her. So I decided to let go and have a little fun."

"And how, exactly, did you let go?" he asked.

"I spent my *Fat2Fab* Bank buying treats from the TOT. Bottles of wine, imported chocolates—romantic things Nick and I could enjoy together," she explained.

"Will the two of you be staying together?" Jagger asked, addressing the question to Nick.

"Alicia means the world to me," Nick gushed. "When I started this I never guessed I would meet such a beautiful, amazing lover."

"Kill me now," I muttered, turning my head away from my lapel mic.

"What about Kat?" Jagger asked, causing me to jump at the sound of my name. He briefly made eye contact with me, then looked away. "You came into the house to meet her. What went wrong there?"

I inched down lower into my seat, willing myself to disappear.

"Kat and I were online lovers," Nick said, and I winced at the term. "As I've found out, those sorts of things don't translate well into actual relationships. If time permits, I would like to be her friend."

If time permits? What the hell was that supposed to mean? I shot him a poisonous glare.

Mercifully, Jagger changed the subject, opting instead to grill Regan and Briana about what it was like sharing a tiny bed for nearly two months.

"It's impossible to get a good night's sleep when you're bunking with a human whale," Briana complained, and I gasped.

Poor Regan looked near tears. "I tried to stay on my side of the bed, but it was a *really* little bed!" she wailed.

Fortunately, Jagger changed the subject. "Now, I'm sure all of America is dying to know how you girls have changed over the last three months. Regan, I'll start with you. Briefly, summarize your before and after stats and what you've learned from your time on the show."

"I started out weighing around 340, and now I weigh 283! I've learned to be tough and to fight for what I believe in. So my body's thinner, but my skin's thicker," she announced proudly. *This* was a thicker skin? I couldn't imagine how sensitive Regan must have been before.

"I've found love," Alicia said, squeezing Nick's hand. "And I've perfected my body. I've gained and lost weight all my life. This time I'm thin for good. I know how to put myself out there and be in the limelight, and how to play up my best features. I know how to get attention when I need it. How to be a star, that's what I've learned."

"And your stats?" Jagger prompted.

"Oh yeah. I've gone from 176 to 133."

Jagger zeroed in on Luisa, who said, "I was 213 before, now I'm 197. Not so bad. But not so good either." She shrugged. "What do I care? I'm a great woman; any man would be lucky to have me."

Maggie was less enthusiastic. "This show *made* me fat. It should be called *From Fabulous to Fat!*" she groused. "I was in the low 200s when I came in here; now I weigh almost 230! You guys ought to be sued for false advertising."

Janelle was a bit more diplomatic. "Some of us have changed, some of us haven't. I've dropped around fifty pounds, and now weigh 169. But inside is where the biggest changes have taken place. I see things differently now."

Jagger nodded and then turned toward me. "Kat, I've saved the best for last."

I blushed, wondering if it was just another line or if he meant it.

"What have you learned from your stint on *From Fat to Fabulous?*"

"What have I learned?" I repeated. It was a deceptively complex question. "I've always thought I was a bad candidate for weight loss. But, as you can see, I've shed over forty pounds, so that can't be true. You know, I used to look at skinny people and wonder why they ever had problems. I thought being thin equaled being happy. I've learned that my life isn't going to magically become perfect one day, and no matter how much weight I lose there are certain things I'll never have control over. Once I accepted that, losing weight wasn't so daunting. I don't worry so much anymore about whether I'm fat or thin, because in the end it doesn't matter. I've stopped judging myself so harshly. "

My eyes focused on Jagger intently, willing him to give me some sort of a sign that he would miss me, that we had been friends. He remained detached and focused, dramatically presenting Janelle with her check—which was the second shocking event of the night. Over the course of the show, Janelle had wracked up $220,000 in her Bank. But the producers, "out of the kindness of their hearts," as Jagger put it, had cut her a check for $250,000.

"Because you worked so hard we thought we'd round that figure up," he explained, handing her an enormous check. "Does anybody have any final thoughts?" Jagger asked, opening up the floor.

"Watch for me, America!" Alicia said. "I'm going to be huge."

"So long," Maggie said, "and hello to everyone in Jackson, especially my wonderful son, Owen."

Seizing the moment, I quickly threw in, "If you need a PR firm, call Hood and Geddlefinger." A few people snickered and Jagger quickly cut me off.

"Thank you, America," he said. "And until next time, I'm Jagger signing off for *From Fat to Fabulous*."

And then it was over.

"All clear," I heard the set director call.

As if on cue, Zaidee came strolling into the living room, sporting one of her glamorous designer pantsuits and waving her hands around animatedly and everyone stopped and stared. It was a strange moment, because it took me back to the grand entrance she'd made at the casting weekend so many months ago.

"Dolls!" she shrieked. "You have all been killer tonight, simply killer! I can't thank you enough for your hard work these past few months. But we did it! You guys are fucking awesome! We've got a wrap party going next door, so feel free to head over and enjoy the eats. I'll catch you all later. It's been real."

And with that she was gone, breezing out the door as quickly as she came.

26

I Ain't Getting Any Younger Here

The night of the finale I was far too dazed to make any rational decisions. I just bopped from one interview to another, fielding a series of inane and often invasive questions.

What's your favorite McDonald's meal?

"Chicken McNuggets."

What size bra do you wear?

"Why? Are you planning on buying me lingerie?"

What's your favorite reality TV show?

"If I said *From Fat to Fabulous,* would you call me a narcissist?"

How did it feel to lose the $250,000?

"I'm really, really happy for Janelle."

How do you feel about Nick and Alicia?

"How do you THINK I feel?"

Are you dating anyone right now?

"I just reentered civilization. I haven't had time to meet anybody yet." (Mercifully, no one on the outside seemed to know anything about my pseudo-kiss with Jagger. It must have been edited out.)

When the interviews wrapped, I'd said tearful good-byes to Janelle, Luisa, and Regan. We exchanged phone numbers, e-mail addresses, and promises to see each other. "I love Tennessee," Luisa had said. "I go to Nashville all the time for business. We should meet up." Janelle was headed to New York for a few days to visit her mother, and Regan was staying out in California to "look for acting work." Maggie had skipped out on half the exit interviews, citing "extreme fatigue," and Alicia and Nick were making the rounds together.

As a couple.

"We're the hottest thing going right now," Alicia taunted. Nick trotted along to all the interviews, hanging all over Alicia, throwing me the occasional wayward glance.

When the media circus ended, I was numb and disoriented. I boarded the flight to Denver in a mild daze, blissfully unconcerned with the fact that nearly everyone on board—from the fellow passengers to the flight attendants—knew me by name. I knew it was fleeting. Soon I would fade back into oblivion, slipping quietly into the Reality TV Has-Been Hall of Shame.

Staying with my parents served as a decompression chamber of sorts. After four months of being monitored round-the-clock by a fleet of cameramen, my mother's prying eyes seemed like a natural fit.

I spent most of my first four days of freedom lounging around my parents' house in my pajamas, surfing the Internet, and watching TV. I craved CNN *Headline News* the way I used to crave potato chips. So much had happened in the outside world while I was away and I was hungry to catch up.

After four months living under constant duress, it was surreal to sleep and eat whenever I wanted; to talk on the phone; to take a bath without listening to the overhead whir of a CCTV camera. At the end of my first week out, I got two follow-up calls from the staff of *From Fat to Fabulous*. The first was a nasal-voiced production assistant who fired off a barrage of questions.

"This is a courtesy call," she began.

I nearly hung up, assuming it was a telemarketer.

"I wanted to follow up and see how you're adjusting?"

"Oh—fine, fine. I'm getting into the swing of things."

"Sleeping well? Eating? Are you having any physical or psychological problems?"

I got the feeling that she was going down a checklist.

"Other than the fact that all of America thinks I'm a brat? I'm fine."

She didn't acknowledge my joke.

"The show keeps a psychologist on retainer if you feel the need to talk. But please be advised these services will only be made available through December of this year," she said, seemingly eager to end our conversation. "After that, you're on your own."

I concluded it was less of a courtesy call, and more of a let's-cover-our-butts-in-case-of-a-lawsuit call.

The second "follow-up call" was infinitely better. I was just getting out of the shower one night when my mom pounded on the bathroom door.

"Here," she said, thrusting the cordless phone at me. "Some man for you." She stood there expectantly, waiting to listen to my end of the conversation.

"Mom, how about a little privacy?" I teased. "Seeing how I've barely had any over the last couple of months, it might be nice for a change."

She was visibly irritated, but she granted my request. "Don't know what you have to say to *some man* that you can't say in front of me," she snipped.

"Hello?" I said, padding down the hall to the guest bedroom. In all honesty, I had no idea who to expect. My list of male friends was virtually nonexistent, and I knew hell would freeze over before Nick would contact me again.

"Kat?" a familiar voice asked. It took me a second to place it.

"Jagger?" I replied. I was stunned—and incredibly pleased.

"I got your number from Zaidee. Is this a good time to talk?"

"Yeah, you have perfect timing." I wrapped the towel tighter around my body. "Five minutes earlier and you would have caught me in the shower."

He laughed. "I'll have to remember to call earlier next time."

I blushed. "What's up?" I asked, trying to sound casual.

"Not much. I was working on my novel when I thought I'd take a break and call you."

His novel. I couldn't help picturing him, all rugged and poetic, filling up page after page with his prose. "Wanna read me a passage?" I asked.

"Let me polish it up a little. I think it's better if you read it all at once."

I climbed into my pajamas and discarded the towel in the hamper. "I'd love to. Any idea when you'll be finished?"

"A month or two. I'm a little stumped at the moment, so I thought I'd call you for some inspiration."

My heart started racing. Jagger found me inspiring!

"When I'm blocked I often find talking to someone will help," he went on. "I've actually struck up conversations with the garbage man, just to get my mind recharged. You'd be amazed how inspiring that can be."

Oh, great. I was in the same category as the garbage man.

"What's new with you?" I asked, for lack of anything else to say. Suddenly I felt stumped. It was one thing talking to him when the cameras were rolling. I'd done that before, I was comfortable with it. But this was different.

"I've got an audition next week for some voice work," he said. "My agent's trying to get me on a new Disney film."

"Wow." I breathed. "That's really cool. I keep forgetting how famous you are."

He burst out laughing. "Not even."

"Oh, come on," I said. "You're Mister Television and Feature Film Star."

"I've done one television show, a handful of commercials, and I might—*might*—get some vocal work on a Disney film. It's a really *small* part. Literally. I'm auditioning to play a talking snail."

I laughed. "You're *still* pretty famous."

"You're as famous as I am. We were on the same show, remember?"

I plopped down on the bed. "I guess you're right. I never thought of it that way."

"Speaking of *From Fat to Fabulous,* are you in touch with any of the other girls? Regan? Janelle? I know you guys were tight."

"I haven't spoken to them, no. But we traded contact info so I'm sure we'll be in touch."

"That's great," Jagger said. "I feel kind of weird saying this, but I really miss those girls. I felt like I got to know you all so well."

"You could call them," I suggested.

"I don't think it's my place."

"You called me," I pointed out.

"That's . . . different. You and I are different."

"Are we?" I asked, my breath quickening. "How do you figure?"

"Now you're embarrassing me." He cleared his throat. "I'm going to get all shy."

"You? Shy? Be serious! You're one of the most outgoing people I've ever met!"

"I *am* serious, Kat." Jagger lowered his voice. "You probably think I lead this crazy party lifestyle, when in fact I'm a total homebody."

"It's true. You know everything about me, and I know virtually nothing about you," I said. "I don't even know your vital stats."

"My vital stats?" he repeated, laughing. "Like what? Age, rank, and serial number?"

"You know what I mean. Your age, your favorite color, your favorite sport, favorite actors. Simple things like that I have no idea about."

"Ah, I see. Okay, then. I'm twenty-eight; I'll be twenty-nine in March. Which makes me a Pisces, if you're into that. My favorite color is blue, and my favorite sport is basketball. My favorite actor is Kevin Spacey, my favorite actress Nicole Kidman. Anything else?"

"I think that about covers it."

"That reminds me. You know the network's planning a sequel, don't you?"

I tensed up. "To *From Fat to Fabulous*?"

"It's a definite possibility, but don't say anything to anybody. I'm two steps away from losing this gig as is."

I blinked in surprise. "You're kidding! They wouldn't do *From Fat to Fabulous 2* without you as a host?"

Jagger paused. I was afraid I'd touched off a nerve. "It's complicated," he finally said. "Let's just say Zaidee wasn't a hundred percent thrilled with my performance."

"Really?" I grimaced at the memory of his many cornball antics.

"She thought I wasn't dramatic enough, among other things. There's also a strong possibility they'll want to go with a female host next time. Someone who's very, ah, how do I put this? The phrase Zaidee used was '*Baywatch bombshell*.' She thinks it will create all kinds of drama in the house to have a bikini model hosting the show. Personally, I don't see it."

Apparently, he didn't realize how jealous women could get. "I'm sorry to hear that."

"Don't be. I'm at least partly to blame for the situation. On some levels I overstepped my role."

I couldn't help but ask, "How?"

"You really wanna know?"

"Of course," I said. "But you don't have to tell me if you don't want to."

"No, it's okay. I want to." He paused for a long moment. "It was because I kissed you," he said, his voice dipping down into a whisper.

I could actually *hear* my heart pounding.

"I wasn't supposed to get involved with any of the contestants— it's actually in my contract. That's why I was so cold toward the end. Zaidee threatened to fire me if I didn't stop fraternizing with you."

So he wasn't mad at me . . .

"Now she's worried I'll try and hit on the contestants in the sequel. Which is stupid, because I'm nothing like that."

I felt my voice catch in my throat. "Blame it all on me," I said quickly. "I'm the one who kissed you, not the other way around. And I was drunk."

"Does that mean you regret it?"

I gulped. "Honestly?"

"Yes."

I took a deep breath. It was so hard to say the words. I had to practically force them out, kicking and screaming. "I don't regret it, no."

"Kat, this might be hard for you to believe, but around women I get so shy and nervous that everything I say comes out wrong." He paused. "But with you it was different right from the start. You were so feisty, and not afraid to speak your mind. Win or lose, you just put yourself out there. You took risks. And for some reason I felt comfortable around you. It takes me so long to be comfortable around people, but with you it happened right away."

Hearing him say that felt incredible. I struggled to maintain my composure. "Thanks," I managed.

"And at first I just thought of us as good friends, but then when you kissed me—"

"Katrina!" my dad boomed, picking up the extension. My father has classically bad timing. "Are you still on the phone?"

"Uh, yeah, I'm talking to a friend of mine."

"I need to call my buddy about our football pool. Can you wrap it up in five minutes?" He clicked off the line before I could respond.

"Oh my God," I groaned. I was dying to hear the rest of Jagger's sentence.

"Talk about a mood killer."

Holy shit. It was like being in high school, all over again. "I'm so humiliated," I told him.

"Don't be. Maybe we can talk again soon."

"Okay. That would be great—"

"I ain't getting any younger here." My father was on the extension again.

"Dad! It hasn't even been *one* minute! You said I could have *five*!"

"When you pay the phone bill you can have as much time as you want."

He hung up again and I let out a sigh.

"When exactly are you going home to Memphis?" Jagger asked, laughing.

"Five more days," I groaned. "Five more days."

27

Don't You Know?

The final week at my parents' condo flew by. I had expected it to drag, but before I knew it, I was hopping a Northwest jet back to Memphis. Jagger and I had exchanged several e-mails, since I didn't dare attempt to talk to him on the phone again until I was in my own apartment. He was intriguing and complicated—two qualities I love in a guy—and we continued our flirtation.

But we never discussed the kiss.

I was dying to learn what his intentions toward me were.

* * *

I arrived home to find things in an unexpectedly pristine condition.

My apartment had never looked so good. It was spotless.

No, make that impeccable.

Someone had cleaned the place within an inch of its life. The kitchen floor had been mopped and waxed. The refrigerator— barren, except for a few canned soft drinks and light beers—had been scrubbed. My bathroom was immaculate. My living room and bedroom had been dusted and vacuumed, and my bed was freshly made with clean sheets. My fish were alive and well-fed.

Donna was the only person who'd had access to my place while I was away.

Why would she do something like this? A peace offering? A guilty conscience?

On the middle of the coffee table was an envelope with my name scrawled across the front in Donna's loopy handwriting. I ignored it, instead opting to take a shower and unpack my suitcases. Then, since there was no food in the house, I called the nearest Chinese take-out and ordered a carton of vegetable lo mein and garlic broccoli. When the food arrived, I devoured my meal in silence, not even bothering to switch on the television. It was an intense, dizzying feeling being alone again.

I had just finished eating when the phone rang. The sound was so deafening in the quiet apartment that I nearly leapt out of my skin. The Caller ID showed a Los Angeles area code, which caused my heart to flutter in my chest. There was only one person it could be. Jagger.

"Hi, Kat," he said. "Is this a good time to talk?"

"Of course," I said, *it's always a good time to talk to you.*

He was awkward at first. "Did you make it back okay?"

"Safe and sound," I quipped. "God, it feels good to be home."

"I'll bet. What's it been, four months?"

"Something like that."

"Do you have a roommate?" Jagger asked.

"Nope, just me, myself, and I."

"How'd you keep your place up while you were in L.A.?"

It was a logical question, though it sent my mind reeling back to Donna, and the letter she had left. "Uh, my friend kept tabs on it."

"Nice friend," he said, not questioning the issue.

"So, what's been going on?"

"I found out yesterday I didn't get the Disney part. There will be no talking snail in my future."

"Oh, no! I'm sorry. For what it's worth, I'm sure that other guy will do a horrendous job. They'll rue the day they didn't hire you."

"Woman," he corrected. "They went with a woman."

"Well, they should have gone with you." I paused, gathering up my nerve. "There's something I've been meaning to ask you. The other night when we were talking on the phone and my dad picked up, you were about to say something. What was that?"

"Ahhh," he said, chuckling. "I was wondering when we'd come back to this. You can't see me, but my ears are turning pink right now."

"Don't be nervous," I said, but secretly I found it adorable.

"So, uh, yeah, what I was saying the other night . . . I kind of thought of us as friends. I really liked being around you and having fun together. And I thought maybe we could keep in touch after the show wrapped."

"Uh-huh. Was that all?" I prompted him.

He laughed. "But then when you kissed me it was strange."

"Strange?" Oh God, I was a *strange* kisser?

"Unexpected is probably a better way to describe it. I felt so awful, knowing what Nick did to you. You played it off like you were strong, but I could see you were upset. And so I wasn't thinking in terms of anything happening with us. But then you kissed me, and it felt *amazing*. And I hadn't expected that. But I worried that maybe you had done it because you were vulnerable, and on the rebound."

My body tingled. "No, it was nothing like that at all. I did it because I wanted to. But I was so drunk I honestly don't remember it very well." As soon as the words had left my mouth I wanted to take them back. "That probably didn't come out right."

"I know what you meant. That gives me an excuse to refresh your memory," he teased.

"I'd like that," I said. I couldn't believe this was happening. I pinched myself to make sure I wasn't asleep.

"I had an idea the other day," he began slowly. "I hope this isn't too forward, but would you like to come out and visit me in L.A.?"

I wasn't sure if he was joking or not, but I decided to run with it. "I'd love to. Just say the word and I'm there."

"How about the week after next?"

I gasped. Apparently he *was* serious. "Really?"

"Sure, why not? I'd love to see you again."

"I'm supposed to go back to work at Hood and Geddlefinger soon. I mean, I've gotta call my boss and set up a start date. Besides, I'm totally strapped for cash."

"I could buy your ticket," he offered. "My dad's a pilot for Delta, so I can get plane tickets dirt cheap. It would be like a hundred dollars, tops."

"That's really sweet of you to offer," I said. "Where would I stay?"

"My house. I've got a guest bedroom that I never use. I could take you out, show you around L.A. How does that sound?"

It sounded amazing, magical, enticing . . . scary. "Can I have a few days to think it over?"

He laughed. "Of course you can. But there's something else I should probably tell you. I do have an ulterior motive for inviting you here."

I braced myself.

"A good friend of mine named Ronnie Mendhelson is working on a project for MTV," he said. "She's developing a morning show, *Wake-Up Call,* that's being billed as *The View* for the eighteen-to-twenty-five set."

"Okay," I said, not seeing where he was headed.

"Anyway, I mentioned to Ronnie how you and I were close and she got *very* excited. They've still got two hosting slots open and they're looking to fill them with a soap-opera vixen and a reality star."

My pulse quickened. "Meaning what?" I asked, not wanting to jump the gun.

"I was supposed to keep this on the down-low, but I can't resist telling you. Ronnie said you were on their shortlist, along with a girl from *Big Brother* and an *American Idol* runner-up," Jagger told me. "So I talked you up, told her you're really funny and charming, and that there's never a dull moment when you're around. By the time I was finished, she was practically salivating!"

I wasn't sure which was more exciting—that Jagger had called me "funny and charming" or that *I was on the shortlist for an MTV show*! "You're kidding, right?"

"Nope, I'm totally serious. Now I don't know if you'd be interested in doing another TV show. That's something you'd have to decide. But Ronnie's dying to talk with you. My gut tells me you're a shoo-in for this, Kat. If you flew out here week after next you could kill two birds with one stone—hang out with me and meet with Ronnie and the MTV team in person."

"Why on earth would she be interested in me? Why not get some twenty something hard body?" *Good move, Kat. Talk yourself out of a job.* But I couldn't help it, I had to be honest. "I have no track record. I'm a reality TV has-been. I'm 'Kat the Brat!' What good am I to them?"

Jagger laughed. "Don't you get it? Yes, you were 'The Brat' but everybody knew your name. A lot of people loved you and a lot of people hated you, but either way, they all tuned in to *watch* you. Kat, don't you know? You were the breakout star!"

* * *

I'd been putting it off for long enough and I knew it was time. With a pit the size of a boulder in my stomach, I retrieved Donna's letter from the coffee table and tore into it:

Dear Kat,

I owe you an explanation. I don't know if what I have to say will change anything or not. But I have to try.

Yes, I told Nick about the show. Not that it matters any-more, but I'll tell you my reasons. When you went out to Los Angeles, I sent out the e-mails just like you'd asked me to and things were going smoothly.

At first, Nick was worried about your dad. But then he called your parents' house and found out your father wasn't sick, and he was livid. He wanted to know why you'd lied. He was threatening to end things—to never speak to you again. He said that, no matter how bad the truth was, it was better than lies.

So I told him. I told him about From Fat to Fabulous. *I thought that maybe if he knew the great lengths you were go-ing to—that you were willing to lose weight just to be with him—he'd finally be convinced that you cared. How many women would embarrass themselves on national TV to win a guy's heart? I thought he'd understand, and that everything would work out for you two.*

Never in a million years did I dream it could backfire the way it did. When I found out Nick had contacted Zaidee and was being brought onto the show I didn't know how to react. I wanted to protect you, to warn you. But there was nothing I could do. I had created this monster, and now I had to watch you live through it on national television.

When you first got out, I couldn't face you. I was too ashamed. I saw the way you'd been talking about me, and I knew how angry you were. I had nothing to say for myself. I didn't think I could make the situation any better.

I wasn't trying to be malicious. I really thought I was do-. ing the right thing. That doesn't make it better, but at least now you know why.

There's something else you need to know. If you never listen to another word I say, hear me now: I love you, Kat. You're the best friend I've ever had. On the show, you wondered out loud if I could name even one thing about our relationship that I valued. I can't name one thing. I value everything.

Love,
Donna

I folded the letter up and placed it back in the envelope, letting her words sink in.

For the first time, I understood the position I'd put her in. She'd been backed up against a wall, sucked into a stupid web of lies that I'd created. She'd only been trying to help.

I looked around my immaculate apartment. My plants had all been watered, my fish had been fed. Without Donna's relentless care, my place would have fallen into total disarray. But she'd been over here, meticulously tending to the details of *my* life while I was away. I didn't know another person in the world who would have done that for me. With trembling hands, I reached for the cordless and dialed her cell. She answered on the fourth ring.

"Hi," I said timidly.

"I was going to let the voice mail pick up, because I was afraid you might yell at me. But then I figured it was better to go on and face it."

"I'm not going to yell."

"You have every right to."

I shook my head vehemently even though I knew she couldn't see me. "Donna—"

"I'm sorry."

"No," I said. "Please don't. I'm the one who screwed up. I never should have dragged you into this."

She paused. "He's an asshole, Kat. You're better off without him."

"I know that," I said, my throat tightening. I was on the verge of tears. "I love the apartment. It looks amazing over here. I can't thank you enough for keeping up with it."

"Hey, what are friends for?"

I couldn't think of anything to say for a long moment, and then I threw out, "You want to go do something tomorrow? Get a cup of coffee, or go see a movie?" It seemed best to meet on neutral ground.

"You know me. I drink like ten cups of coffee a day. What's one more?"

"Starbucks?"

"I've got a better idea," she said. "A little coffee shop I discovered. It's pretty unusual and I guarantee you'll like it. And you won't even have to go incognito. I doubt anyone there has even heard of *From Fat to Fabulous*."

"Sure, sounds great," I said. A root canal would have sounded great. I was dying to see her.

"Grab a pencil; I'll give you directions," she said.

I rummaged through my desk for something to write with. "You've organized this place so well I can't find anything," I told her, laughing.

* * *

We met at Otherlands, a funky little coffee shop on South Cooper in Midtown. I had driven by it a million times, but never thought of stopping in.

"I discovered it!" Donna said, even though the place had been there for at least ten years. "They make the ultimate coffee drinks," she promised. "And like I said, I seriously doubt you'll be recognized here."

She was right on both counts. Not only was their coffee divine, but the tattooed, multi-pierced barista seemed completely oblivious to my reality-star status. Either that, or he was kind enough not to make a scene.

"For here or to go?" he asked, barely giving me a second glance. The place—which catered to an eclectic crowd of artists and wayward poets—provided a refreshing escape from the Starbucks scene.

I sat on a futon by the front window, stirring my skim cappuccino and basking in the glow of anonymity while Donna waited for the barista to warm up a blueberry scone. A minute later she plopped down beside me, flashing a friendly smile.

"It's good to see you again."

"It's good to see you, too," I replied stiffly.

"You look great, by the way. I can tell you've lost a lot of weight."

"Thanks," I said, smoothing my button-down shirt against my noticeably smaller body. I wasn't skinny, not by a long shot, but it felt great to wear a size fourteen.

"Looks like the show left you pretty fabulous after all."

We sat in silence for a moment, sipping our coffee and staring awkwardly at each other.

"These things are incredible," Donna said, spreading lemon butter on her scone. "Seriously! It's awesome."

"It smells nice."

"I love scones. They're the perfect mix of savory and sweet."

I wasn't sure how to respond, so I concentrated on my cappuccino. It was strange to watch someone eat and not feel jealous that I wasn't having any. My cravings for junk food hadn't gone away, not completely, but they were less urgent. Living under the microscope of *From Fat to Fabulous* had forced me to scrutinize my eating. It had become painfully obvious that I often took in more than I realized, eating to soothe anger, boredom, and pain. It wasn't an easy thing to overcome. But knowing, as they say, is half the battle.

"You know, I used to love donuts, but they're too rich for me now," she said between bites. "Scones hit the spot."

Was this what our relationship had been reduced to? Pathetic conversations about pastries?

"Kevin and I come here all the time," she said, and I blinked. Two minutes into the conversation and already I was lost.

"Who's Kevin?"

"Oh, sorry. My boyfriend. I keep forgetting how long you've been gone."

Apparently. "You have a boyfriend now?"

She giggled self-consciously. "Yeah, his name's Kevin Arp. He's a lawyer from St. Louis. He moved to Memphis last month to be with me."

"Sounds serious." I felt so left out of her life.

"It is," Donna admitted. "I think this might be it for me. I think"—she paused—"that Kevin might be the man I'm going to marry."

"You sound embarrassed about it," I blurted out. It was the truth; she looked ashamed.

"It's because I know how messed-up things are right now," she said sadly. "I don't want to make the situation any worse."

"What situation?" I asked, even though I already knew.

"Our friendship," Donna said, tearing off a small piece of scone. "I just want us to be normal again."

I squeezed her hand, my eyes welling up with tears. "I want that, too," I said, feeling like a sap. "But everything's so different now. You'll be out with this new guy all the time . . . I don't know where I fit in anymore."

She turned to face me. "How can you ask that? Didn't you read my letter?"

"Of course I did."

"You mean the world to me, Kat. I've never had a friend like you before. It's cheesy, I know, but I've kinda pictured us growing old together. . . ."

I laughed.

"Me and you, guzzling coffee and gossiping about men—I never want to lose that." She squeezed my hand back.

I smiled. "We won't."

I gave her a quick hug, and then pulled away. I hadn't realized how much I'd missed this. It felt so good to be back in Memphis again, to be normal. We started chatting after that, dishing on all the latest news. We caught up on our love lives, and I even spilled the story about Jagger. "So tell me about this Kevin Arp guy. He must be pretty amazing if you're thinking of marrying him."

"I can't wait to introduce you. I think you'll really like him. He's smart and funny—great-looking, too. But tell me more about Jagger. He's a catch. And *famous*!"

"Don't jump the gun. I haven't caught him yet." I blushed, glancing around the room self-consciously. I didn't feel right discussing our relationship in public. Luckily, no one in Otherlands was paying the slightest bit of attention.

"So, you'll catch him soon enough," Donna assured me. "From what you've told me, the guy's crazy about you."

"Maybe," I said, polishing off the last few drops of my drink. "But it's still too early to tell."

"When will you see him again?"

"Funny you should mention it," I said. I filled her in on Jagger's invitation to visit him and audition for *Wake-Up Call*.

Donna's jaw dropped. "What in the world are you waiting for? If I were you I'd have hopped the first plane outta here!"

"It's not that simple."

She rolled her eyes in mock exasperation. "Honey, it is simple! You book a ticket and you *go*, end of story. Kat, this is incredible!"

"But I just got back," I sputtered. "I've only been in Memphis for twenty-four hours. And what will I tell Geddlefinger? I'm supposed to start work again soon."

"Memphis can wait; it's not like the city's going anywhere. And as for Richard? What do you want with that job anyway? Here you've got the chance to land a high-paying TV gig and you're worried about H and G?"

"Yeah, but H and G's a sure thing; *Wake-Up Call*'s a maybe."

"So what if you don't get it? It's worth chancing. *Jagger*'s worth chancing. You can find another PR job if you have to."

"In this economy?"

She looked me straight in the eyes. "I know you, Kat. If you don't do this you're always going to regret it." Donna reached into her purse and handed me her Nokia. "Give Jagger a call right now and let him know you're coming. If you get out there and it sucks, you can always fly right back. What are you so afraid of?"

"I don't know . . . the unknown, maybe? Right now my relationship with Jagger is perfect. It can only go downhill from here."

"Kat, you've kissed the guy once. Believe me, things can only get better. Imagine how incredible it will be, getting to know him without the cameras. All the longs talks you'll have. The drives up the coast. The nights alone in his bed . . ."

"You're proving my point exactly. What if I get out there and he turns into some kind of a monster or something?"

"Do you honestly think that will happen?"

"No." Jagger wasn't that type of guy. Not by a long shot.

"But if you're really that uncomfortable with it, pay for your own ticket."

"With what money? In case you've forgotten, I've been out of work for four months."

Donna mulled this over for a few seconds, then proclaimed, "Let me buy it."

"No way! I can't."

"It's the least I can do," she said. "I ruined one of your relationships; let me build you another one."

"You didn't ruin it," I said.

"Either way, I'm buying this ticket."

I took a deep breath. "You really think I should fly out to Los Angeles and do this?"

She wrapped her arms around me in a tight hug. "I'll help you pack!"

"Um, excuse me, I'm sorry to bother you."

Donna and I jumped, then quickly moved apart.

"Oh, hi," Donna said.

"I just couldn't help noticing you." The guy was cute, early thirties with chin-length blond hair. He would have looked more at home on a California beach than in a Memphis coffee shop. "I'm Blake." He turned to face me, his eyes locking on mine.

"I'm Kat," I offered, "and this is Donna." His expression was so warm and friendly that I found myself smiling.

"I was thinking—and I hope this isn't too forward—but maybe you'd like to go out with me sometime?" Blake was staring directly at me as he said it.

I thought it over for a minute, the realization dawning. "You know me from the show, right?"

His brow wrinkled in confusion. Then he snapped his fingers. "That's it! I knew you looked familiar. You were at the Coldplay show last month, right?"

I laughed. "Not likely."

"Ah, then, maybe I've seen you around somewhere else." He paused. "I'd love to take you to dinner."

It felt so strange, alien. But I loved it. "Thanks!" I beamed. "But I'm kind of seeing someone right now."

Blake nodded. "Can't blame a guy for trying." He gave us a quick wave and turned to go.

As soon as he was out of earshot, Donna nudged me. "Look at you!" she said, sounding genuinely pleased. "I think being on TV has worked wonders for your confidence."

I smiled. She was right.

Donna turned and winked at me. "You know something, Kat? Right about now I'd say you're the definition of fabulous!"

28

A Breath I Hadn't Realized I Was Holding

"You look terrific," Jagger said, beaming as he set my bags down in the LAX parking lot two weeks later.

I was wearing a knee-length black skirt and a light pink shirt, purchased the week before at the Gap. It was the first outfit I'd ever bought there. Shopping—once the bane of my existence—was now thrilling, though in some ways bittersweet. Although Cara and I were still friends, she had declined my offer to go shopping together. The dynamic between us had changed.

"Uh, thanks." I blushed, meeting Jagger's gaze. "You look great, too."

Whenever someone compliments me, my first instinct is still to argue, to prove them wrong. If they say I'm pretty, I immediately want to point out all my body's flaws. That was the old Kat; I bit my tongue.

"You know, I never pictured you with a car like this," I said. It was a Mercedes SLK Roadster convertible.

Jagger held the passenger's side door open for me. "It's a little extravagant," he admitted.

I climbed inside and snuggled down into the cushy leather seat. "I never thought of you as the convertible type, either."

Jagger hoisted my bags into the trunk. "Well, nothing beats driving along the coast with the top down." He climbed into the driver's seat and started the engine. "And considering this car was free, I wasn't about to turn it down."

"Free?"

"Zaidee gave it to me," he offered, steering the car out of the LAX parking lot.

My jaw dropped. "You're kidding, right?" I blurted out.

Jagger laughed. "Nope. It was a gift from the show. Zaidee's the one who okayed it." He pulled the Mercedes up to the on-ramp, waited for the light to turn green, then merged onto the freeway. "It's actually a loaner, sort of like a company car."

Before long, we were cruising along the freeway, the wind whipping our hair. "I can put the top up," Jagger offered.

"No, leave it down," I said, tilting my face up to the wind. I liked the feel of the warm air on my skin.

"Before I forget," Jagger said, shouting over the noise of the road, "I heard some news about Nick Appleby."

My heart quickened. Here I was, cruising along in a gorgeous Mercedes, next to an amazing guy, and Nick Appleby had found his way back into my life. I didn't even like him anymore, but some part of me was still, inexplicably, attached. He'd faded out of my life so swiftly and completely. I wanted the chance to wrap it up, once and for all.

"What news?" I asked.

"He landed a commercial."

I couldn't believe it. Just as Nick had predicted, his dreams of stardom were coming true.

Jagger changed lanes to pass a dilapidated pickup truck. "Alicia's going to be in it, too."

"I guess they really were meant for each other," I said, accepting it for the first time. I watched the scenery as we sped past for a bit. "So what's the ad for?" I asked at last, the wind whipping strands of hair against my face.

Jagger laughed, shifting into high gear and speeding up. "That's the best part. I was going to wait and tell you when we got home, but this is too good. The commercial is for Lucky Flushes Toilet Bowl Cleaner."

"What?" I guffawed. *I had expected Armani, or fine wine, or, at the very least, something like deodorant. But toilet bowl cleaner?* "Where did you hear about this?" I asked, as Jagger took the next exit, guiding the car onto Hollywood Boulevard.

"Gigi Rucker," he said, downshifting and stopping at a light. "She spoke with Alicia. Lucky Flushes wants Nick to wear an apron and complain that cleaning will mess up his fancy designer outfit. Then Alicia comes in and scrubs the toilet."

I was dumbstruck.

Jagger reached over and squeezed my hand. "It's so great that you're here," he said, letting go to change gears.

"I'm glad I came," I said.

* * *

We spent the morning sightseeing in Los Angeles and driving along the coast, capping it off with lunch at a small Mexican restaurant in West Hollywood. By two o'clock I was exhausted, so we headed back to his place for a little R&R.

I was antsy on the car ride over, wound up from the day's events and becoming tense about spending so much time alone with Jagger. I was going to be staying with him for five days. What if we ran out of things to talk about?

Jagger lived in a split-level house in Beverly Hills, with a Spanish-style décor—it was painted beautiful vibrant colors, with open, airy rooms, and high ceilings.

"This is great!" I enthused, as I walked inside.

Jagger followed behind me. "I'll show you around," he said, setting my bags by the front door and leading me down the hall. "This is the guest room," he said, stepping inside a cozy bedroom. The walls were painted in a rich peach color and there was a comfortable-looking double bed with a fluffy white comforter. "There's a bathroom around this corner," he said, leading the way. He continued the tour, showing me the beautifully tiled kitchen, the living room, office, and his spacious master suite.

"Your place is fantastic," I said.

He smiled. "I love it, but it gets lonely sometimes."

I wasn't sure what to say, so I looked down. "You have gorgeous floors."

"Thanks. They came with the walls and ceiling," he joked.

My mind went blank. "Well, that's good. Because it would have been awful if they hadn't." *Jagger's nervous, too,* I reminded myself.

"So I have a surprise for you tomorrow," he said, clearing his throat.

"A meeting with MTV?" I was having serious second thoughts about auditioning. It was on my mind the entire time I was on the plane.

"No, I'm still waiting on Ronnie to call me back with a definite time. But that reminds me, you probably ought to have representation. I can call my agent at ICM and ask if he'd be willing to rep you. If not, I'm sure he'd give me a referral."

"Oh, wow. I don't know. It's all happening so fast." Talk of agents and auditions unnerved me. I was taking so many risks, already, visiting him. Who knew if any of them would pay off?

He eyed me quizzically. "Are you okay?"

"I'm just tired, that's all," I lied.

"Why don't you take a nap," he suggested. "We can talk about this later. Meanwhile, I'll call Ronnie and let her know you're in town. I'm sure she'll want to meet with you as soon as possible."

"Okay," I said, heading into the guest room. I changed into my pajamas, climbed into bed, and waited impatiently for sleep to engulf me. Five minutes ago I'd been so tired, but now my body refused to unwind. I lay there, silently cursing myself for holding back my feelings. As I tossed and turned, my mind drifted, returning over and over again to the same worrisome thought. Maybe this had all been one giant mistake and I should have just stayed in Memphis, in my little apartment, where everything was comfortable, and boring, and safe.

* * *

I awoke to the smell of something cooking, a light delicious aroma that floated throughout the house. Disoriented, I staggered out of bed and put on a fresh change of clothes. Then, rubbing the sleep out of my eyes, I wandered down the hall in search of Jagger.

I found him bent over the kitchen counter, chopping cucumbers and carrots while he chatted on his cordless phone. A pot of water boiled on the stove.

"Uh-huh," he said, balancing the phone between his shoulder

blade and ear. I wasn't sure whether I should interrupt him or not, so I stood there listening quietly. "That's amazing. Yeah, I'll keep that in mind. Well, she's staying through Sunday, so anytime between now and then. We've got plans tomorrow. I'm taking her for a picnic on Catalina Island."

A picnic! A wide smile spread across my face. So that's what the surprise was! I backed out of the kitchen, not wanting him to realize I'd overheard.

"Friday at ten sounds perfect. I'll double-check with Kat and let you know if there are any problems. *Ciao.*"

I waited a few minutes and then strolled into the kitchen.

"Hey!" he said, looking pleased to see me. "I didn't realize you were up. How are you feeling?"

"Refreshed," I said. "What are you up to?"

"Just doing a little cooking. Believe it or not, I'm not so bad in the kitchen. Even if I don't know how to 'properly serve wine,'" he said, winking. "I was going to whip up some penne and a salad. But if you're not in the mood for Italian or you'd rather go out tonight, this will keep."

He cooks, too? This is getting dangerously close to perfection.

"No, Italian sounds great," I said, sitting down on a kitchen stool.

"Are you thirsty?" Jagger asked. I nodded, and he retrieved a mineral water from the fridge and handed it to me. "So I just got off the phone with Ronnie. She wants to know if you're up for meeting this Friday at ten A.M.?"

"How do you know her?" I asked, attempting to change the subject.

"She directed a few commercials I did and we've kept in touch," he explained, dumping the carrots into a large salad bowl. "Does Friday work?"

"Uh, maybe," I stalled.

"Is everything okay?" he asked, eyeing me with concern.

I bit my lip. "Mostly."

He seemed taken aback. "Is it something I did?"

"God, no. It's just . . . I don't know how to explain this."

Jagger set down the vegetables and turned to face me. "Try me."

I decided to come clean. "It's this MTV business. It's freaking me out," I said, letting out a breath I hadn't realized I was holding.

He looked confused. "Really? Why? It's not a big deal," he assured me. "Well, of course it's a *big* deal, but it's nothing to get stressed over."

"That's just it. The stakes are too high. I don't know if I can handle it." There, I'd said it. I'd admitted I wasn't cut out for this business, that I was too much of a coward to try my hand at the Hollywood fame machine.

Jagger gave me a lopsided grin. "The stakes of *From Fat to Fabulous* were high and you did that."

"That was different. That wasn't real show business."

"So? With *Fat2Fab* you were risking a lot more. You were being filmed *constantly*." Jagger took a few more steps, until he was right in front of me. "What are you afraid of, Kat?" He placed his hand gently on my forearm and I drew in a breath. It was tough to concentrate when he was this close.

"You think I'm so fearless, but you're wrong. I'm scared all the time," I admitted.

"I never said you were fearless. I said you put yourself out there. There's a difference. That's what I admire about you. You risk things. You're a lot braver than you give yourself credit for." He put his hands on my waist and gently guided me off the stool.

I leaned forward, hugging him. He had a wonderful, rugged smell of cologne mixed with aftershave. "So are you," I said, resting my chin on his shoulder. It was electrifying to touch him again after so long. My heart felt like it was going to beat right out of my chest and float away. "I'm scared of the 'what ifs.' What if I audition and they hate me? What if I make the show and it bombs?" I said in a voice barely above a whisper. "What if I move out here and then a month later have to pack my bags and head back to Memphis?"

Jagger squeezed me tightly. "Hollywood's a tough town, but you'll manage. And if you have to move back it won't be the end of the world. Either way, I don't want to lose this," he said, nuzzling the side of my face. "Us." He gently trailed kisses down my neck. "Besides," he murmured, his breath tickling my ear. "I've always wanted to visit Graceland."

He kissed my neck for a moment longer, his lips soft and tantalizing. Then he pulled away abruptly, leaving me virtually panting for more.

"I'd better put the pasta on if we're going to eat at a decent hour," he said, looking slightly flustered. "I could do garlic bread, if you'd like."

"That sounds good." I struggled to regain my composure. "On second thought, maybe we'd better skip the garlic?"

Jagger gave me a shy smile. "Good call."

We stood there in a comfortable silence for a few minutes. He was such a calming person. I remembered how soothing he had been that night of my disastrous dinner with Nick. "Hey," I said, making a decision. "You can go ahead and call Ronnie and confirm with her."

He raised his eyebrows. "So you're going for it then?"

I smiled. "Yeah."

"There's no way of predicting what will happen, how far things will go."

He had a valid point. "A few months ago I *never* would have imagined I'd be here, sitting in this kitchen, watching you cook me dinner."

Jagger picked up a bottle of olive oil and began dribbling it over the lettuce. "Yet, here you are." He smiled.

"Here I am."

Epilogue

Right after the news went out that I'd landed a hosting gig on *Wake-Up Call,* Nick phoned and asked if I'd given any thought to reconciliation.

At first, I thought he was joking.

He feigned ignorance, pretending not to have read the latest gossip rags. Jagger and I were a couple. A very happy couple.

"That's brilliant that you're going to be on MTV, Kat!" Nick had said. "And it makes what I have to say even harder. I behaved so foolishly when we met. I didn't recognize your potential. I was thinking only of what would best serve my needs at the moment."

He went on to say he hadn't been in love, but was merely "helping" Alicia, and that she was "helping" him. In other words, they'd been mutually using each other. "Zaidee pressured me into it, saying a love affair would boost ratings. I should never have listened to her," he'd said. "It was you I really wanted to be with, not Alicia."

"That's too bad."

"Next time I'm in town let's get together for a coffee," he'd said. "I go to L.A. quite frequently now. So often I'm thinking of leasing a flat there."

"I'm really busy and, you know, I've got a serious boyfriend and a new job to deal with."

"I see."

"I'm sorry," I'd said, then stopped myself. I had no reason to apologize.

"Well, then, if you wouldn't mind putting in a good word for me with MTV?"

"Yeah, if time permits," I'd told him, and then hung up the phone.

So Alic   Nick were breaking up. It seemed everyone else was gettin   her: Donna and Kevin Arp were engaged and Janelle w   ing reconciliation with her ex-husband Matt (oddly en   eing on the show had brought back their feelings for   her). Even Regan had a new boyfriend—and would be   part in *From Fat to Fabulous 2* as a special consultant.   -mail back and forth on a regular basis, and we're planning to meet up soon.

These days my AOL inbox is always full. Despite being nicknamed The Brat, I've won my fair share of fans. Heavy women all over America e-mail to thank me for speaking out on their behalf. Sometimes they stop me on the street or in restaurants and say hi.

I have no illusions. I know that fame is fickle, and that remaining in the limelight for longer than fifteen minutes is an admirable feat. But I'm optimistic. And I'm risking things. I'm not waiting for life to start anymore.